SIX AFTER MIDNIGHT

BY

WILSON MARSH

1

Copyright © 2007 by Wilson Marsh

Cover design and photograph Copyright © 2007
Fast Track Text and Imagery

Visit us at www.SteelMoonPublishing.us

ISBN: 978-0-6151-5192-2

Printed in U.S.A./Steel Moon Publishing

10 9 8 7 6 5 4 3 2 1   1 2 3 4 5 6 7 8 9 10

NOVELLAS

OUIJI

DEATH CLOUD

THE ATTORNEY AND THE WEREWOLF

SHORT STORIES

Dedicated to:

Megan and Al Marsh
Two bright stars in a dark universe.

OUIJI

By
W.G. Marsh

OUIJI NOTES:

Ouiji was originally written as a NANOWRIMO novel. That stands for National Novel Writing Month. It is an exercise where the writer is challenged to write fifty thousand words in one month. That was where the first half of the book was written.

The second half was written two years later; from January, 2007 to June 2007. While the first half was written in one month's time, its rewrite took two months.

Ouiji is one of two stories dealing with the concept of supernatural justice. This one is treated a bit more seriously than the other.

Some might note that the spelling of the title does not match the way that they spell it, or perhaps the way that they have seen it spelled elsewhere. Trust me. This is an accepted spelling, although not always the most common spelling, it seems.

D-41 - the "clone" in the story. This is a bit of trivia that is now - sadly - irrelevant. However its explanation should be included. During NANOWRIMO there was another author - Jonathon Michaels - who was writing his own book. In the course of conversation we decided to have a "tie-in" contained in our stories. Nothing major, just an idea or concept to where, if someone read both, they would say, "Hey! That was mentioned in such and such." In this case D-41 was a military project in his book that was used here. I do not believe his story was ever finished.

With all the meandering I've done, all that remains is to wish you happy reading…and pleasant dreams.

- WGM
  Tucson, Arizona

CHAPTER I
The Party Crasher

The evening began as a social gathering, not a party. Purely a group of friends congregating for an evening of fun after a day of work. With the addition of alcohol, however, there had been many evolutions. Evolutions that had not taken centuries, but a scant three hours.

"Bill, get your ass over here. Now, William, if you please." A regal, if tipsy, command from the editor and owner of *Spectral Images*, the tabloid for which Bill worked as reporter and photographer.

"Yeah, boss. What's the buzz?" Bill asked; drink in hand and craving a cigarette. The cigarette would have been a creature comfort not related to stress, for tension had taken a hike three drinks ago. He slowly and with caution worked his way towards the host.

The circle of onlookers parted, their eyes not looking to Bill's, but lingering on an object resting on the table. He looked, blinked, and took another swallow of his drink. "It's a Weggie board. You guys are playing with flippin' Weggie board?"

Stafford grimaced. "It's Ouiji board, not weggie. Pronounced 'wee-gee.' Weggie is when you stain your shorts," he paused, "but this board could make you do that too." He looked up at Billy. "This isn't just *any* Ouiji board. This is *the* Ouiji board."

"What makes this one...," Billy stopped short, "...holy shit! It isn't ...this isn't the one from the Thompson murders is it?"

Stafford removed his glasses and wiped them on the Irish linen tablecloth. "We have been referring to it in print as the Thompson Blood Bath. Yes, this is one and the same." He replaced his glasses and peered through them at the board. Only his eyes touched it, his hands went to his lap and stayed there.

"Beautiful isn't it? We borrowed the board and planchette from the surviving relatives...for a hefty fee of course. It will make a splendid backdrop against which to set our next article on the debacle. You will note the blood splatters, both gravitational and velocity, have not been removed from the board's surface."

All heads dipped closer to view the brown smudges on the surface. The planchette appeared far older than the board.

"That in itself is worth an additional five thousand readers."

"So, this was the game," Billy said quietly, "they were playing just before they died."

"If we are to believe the forensics report," replied Stafford. "Three of the bodies were still slumped in chairs around the table. The other four were running from the table area when they were struck down." He shook his head. "One managed to get out of the house. His body was found almost two miles away. I managed to get a look at the coroner's photos and some of the crime scene pics. Ripped to shreds. All the vics."

"That bad?" asked Billy.

Stafford glanced up. "Worst I ever saw. Like someone with a chain saw playing cat and mouse. It was bad enough that the photos made me pucker so bad I forgot to bribe the coroner out of copies." He shrugged. "Too vivid for us to print, anyway."

"Now that's a first," came a voice from the back. A small chorus of chuckles traveled around the room.

Billy reached forward and laid his hand flat on the surface of the board then picked up the planchette. Chair legs scraped on the costly tile, screeching as Stafford pushed back his chair in alarm.

"Dammit, don't be doing that," hissed Stafford.

"Why? It's just a Ouiji board. A little gory, but just a toy."

"I beg to differ," came a quiet voice from the doorway. "What you so foolishly hold in your hand is anything but a toy. An instrument...yes, but a toy? Perhaps the plaything of Satan's child, but not something to be brandished as an amusement by mortal man." Leaning on a cane of diamond willow, an old man waited in silence.

Stafford stood and walked halfway across the room. "Karen," he instructed his aide, "please get Mr. Spetzer a brandy. In a snifter if you please."

Gray eyebrows raised, and some confidence fled the eyes of the unsolicited guest. "Well...it seems you know my name and more. I am honored I am of interest to men such as yourself." He pointed to a chair with his cane. "Would it be an imposition to ask...?"

"No, by all means. Forgive my lack of manners. I should have offered," apologized Stafford. Intercepting his aide, he relieved her of the glass, and with a slight bow presented it to the seated man before continuing.

"Spetzer. Yes, I know that name. It wasn't known to me yesterday, but,..." he shrugged, "...I have my sources." Stafford sat on the arm of a couch near his guest.

"I have a staff of 500 people. Mostly reporters, photographers, communication operators and such." He smiled. "In their midst are about a dozen private investigators. Cretins so greedy they would take candid photos of their naked mothers to make a buck off me, but that's okay. So long as that lure is before them, they are moderately competent and loyal. It wasn't much of a contest. You drive an old Buick. You don't lock it when you go shopping. My people followed you, pulled the registration from the visor and wrote the name down. A receipt on the floorboard from K-Mart and another from Louie's Spirit Shop. Fifteen bucks for brandy." He shrugged once more. "That isn't the question you really want to ask though, is it?"

Spetzer laid his cane across his knees and gratefully accepted the brandy. "No. No, it is not." The brandy disappeared in a sip and two gulps; a short cough then he spoke. "Of primary importance...have you attempted to use the Ouiji board?"

"No."

Shoulders slumping in relief, Spetzer gave a weary smile. "Thank God. Although I suspected you hadn't." He gestured with his hand. "No dead bodies strewn around. A few passed out, but still breathing. Young man, if you would please, return that damnable object to the table."

Billy did so, and Spetzer's shoulders relaxed further.

"Then the next question. Why would you go to the trouble to check out an old man?"

"Ah. Now we home in on the subject." Stafford stood and paced. "Your existence was revealed to me. More by accident than anything.

You undoubtedly read about the Thompson Blood Bath..." The old man cringed. Stafford hesitated, and then apologized. "I'm sorry. Didn't mean to be crude. You heard through the media about the deaths that occurred. Your curiosity was aroused, for reasons I can only speculate about - though I retain hopes of being enlightened - and you went to the scene of … of the incident." He waved in dismissal, "You were discrete about it, don't get me wrong. However, you *were* observed. When I was dealing with the grandchildren for temporary possession of the board and slider, one of them noticed you at the edge of the police cordon. He mentioned - in passing only- that you looked quite similar…older…more stooped…but similar to the man who gave the board to Thompson for safekeeping. He was present as a child when the board changed hands."

The old man sighed. "Yes, he was there. A precocious child, but well mannered I suppose."

Stafford returned to his perch on the arm of the couch. "It was a helluva long shot, but I make a living checking out long-shots."

Spetzer nodded. "Then why didn't you approach me at the time? Verify who I was and if I was?"

The editor waved magnanimously. "No need. I know people. I know how they react. There was no way you could keep from coming to me when you realized I had the board. If it wasn't you, then no harm no foul. You wouldn't hunt me down, and all I would be out is a couple hundred dollars for the private dicks." He stopped. "What I don't know is the significance of the board. Just a hunch on my part, once more."

The two men sat and stared at each other. No one in the room spoke and time stretched into minutes before the old man prodded. "Now you must ask me. The question is on the tip of your tongue. You cannot help but ask."

Stafford closed his eyes in defeat. "What the hell *is* this thing?"

Spetzer smiled in victory, and began.

"Many think that Ouiji started in 1848, in a small town called Hydesville. In New York state. They are wrong. Wrong by thousands of years and miles. You have heard of Druids?" he asked.

All in the room nodded.

"When you think of Druids, you probably think of the Celtic Druids who appeared around 600 B.C. Most do. Before them were the others. Known as the Beaker folk, a very mysterious people for any age.

The Beaker folk are believed to have put up the massive monuments, Stonehenge and such, at about 2000 years B.C., if memory serves me. Their followers, the Celtic druids, reverted to natural shrines," he hesitated, "and perhaps unnatural beliefs."

They…the Celtic druids, that is…had a very sophisticated method of government and education. They were farmers, for the most part. Their farms still exist today, as many of the surviving farmsteads in Britain are on old Druid sites.

Education was top-notch, and it would normally take up to twenty years of teaching for a druid to be accepted into an order.

In 55 B.C., Julius Caesar raided the sites in Britain. More importantly, he wrote of the druids.

'...know much about the stars and celestial motions and about the size of the earth and universe and about the essential nature of things, and about the powers and authority of the immortal gods; and these things they teach to their pupils...'"

He stopped and looked upon the people hanging on his words. "We don't have twenty years, but twenty minutes should suffice for your education."

CHAPTER II
Master, Apprentice and Grave

A hard land with hard ground. The young man, barely old enough to claim that title, toiled hard. His hands had worn the bark from the pole he was using to loosen the hard packed earth, with its hidden rocks, and in turn, the bark had worn the flesh from his palms. Sharpened, then tempered in the flames of a campfire, the once pointed tip was blunted, forcing him to drive the stake ever harder into the ground.

"Aye lad, the rod is bigger than you, but you are making progress," the old man leaning against a nearby rock encouraged.

Waist deep in a hole as wide as he could reach with both arms and as long as his body, the man-child stared at his work. It seemed a hopeless chore.

"Master, I have been digging since moon rise, is it not...?"

"Nay, lad. You must toil until the rising edge of the sun burns on the horizon. The depth matters not, but you must dig as best you can during the darkness."

Concern darkened the elder's eyes. "Lad, you know I cannot lift a hand to help you. Only those born on the same day as he who died was born can perform this task. Only those can place him in his grave and make the magic work. One dead to rest, one live to toil."

"Aye, Master. I understand." The youth knelt and once again started scooping the loosened dirt and rocks up with his hands, tossing it from the hole.

"Tis good then, lad. Now, while you work, recite to me what you have learned of this. You are ten circles into your education, and I do expect you to remember the body of your lessons."

Grunting with effort the youth repeats his lessons in short bursts, dictated by his heavy breathing.

"Born on the same, yet living beyond, he must burrow into the bosom of the earth, a resting place for the dead to make...when the eye of day is gone...and toil he shall until the eye of day returns to look upon his labor...then with the new day's birth and blessing...the dead shall be laid in the comfort of the earth."

He looked from his bleeding hands to the ground.

"Master, this does not strike me as much comfort, a bed of frozen dirt and rock."

The Master laughed. "For us perhaps not. Now do not attempt to purchase yourself respite in idle talk. Or perhaps you have forgotten the rest?"

"Nay, Master, I forget naught," he replied, wiping dirt from his face. "Upon the chest, above once beating heart, the seed of the oak shall be placed. As man feeds from the breast of nature shall nature feed from the breast of man." The glance from his Master bid him return to work. "But Master, one thing I understand not. Many die and many live who were born on the same day, if not year. Why must it be I and why must it be this man?"

The Master pulled a coarse blanket around him tighter, chilled from the subject if not the night air. This matter was not one to concern the student - yet...but this apprentice had worked without question to date. Knowledge was not something to withhold and while the youngster's hands must work in the dark, his mind should be rewarded with the light of understanding. The Master fell into the voice he always used when lecturing.

"Man lives, man dies, tis a part of nature. In death, one might think each man is the same. Not so. Not so if one is calling upon Nature's magic." He pulled a flap of the blanket over his head and let it dangle across his face, so only his mouth was visible.

"This man you are burying. In death, he looks like all other bodies, but there is a difference. To understand this difference, you must reflect on the differences between man and beast. What separates us from the animals of our world? I know you think that speech and thinking are traits above the beasts. Nay, you are mistaken.

The difference is that man has two traits not found by any other species. The want and desire for justice, and by that desire the ability to commit offenses against his own kind. Without the desire for justice there could be no offenses for we would not perceive them as such…and lad…do not place a noble cloth upon the word 'justice.' The word is simply vengeance wearing a regal gown."

The Master pointed to the cadaver lying down-wind of them. "For this man, death was an injustice. He died by the hand of another. For what reason we know not. The person who took his life, we know not.

You see, lad, it is easy for us to chart the stars and predict their movement. You look into the heavens and study. With time the mystery is clear. However, one cannot look into the hearts of our fellow men and predict their movements. Only the eyes of the gods can peer into our hearts and determine the truth. Only their ears can listen to their dead tongues. So we must summon them and enlist their assistance."

The young man looked around in alarm, causing the Master to laugh, ending in a spasm of coughing. When he had regained his composure he reassured the youngster.

"Be at peace. None shall appear to help you in your labor or pilfer the tongue from your mouth." He chuckled once more. "When we elders clap, students run for our beck and call. When we summon the gods, they do not respond so quickly. In your lifetime, yes, in my lifetime, no. When fifty circles of the sun around the God Rocks have passed, then, perhaps, you will see a god."

"Then it is true," said the pupil sullenly.

"Then what is true?" asked the Master.

"I must live my life here in the village, never leaving its realm. I must never take a woman for my side, or know one in pleasure. I must eat only the simplest of foods and never partake of the mead…."

The Master raised his hand, silencing the student. "Where have you learned this lesson?"

"From the other students. They told me what would be expected of me."

The old man shook his head. "And their words you took for truth….aye. Lay aside your pole and sit next to me for a moment. These words you need give close attention."

Jumping from the hole he squatted before his mentor. Reaching out a hand the Master grasped him under his chin and raised his face so their eyes met. "Now, heed what I am about to say. Were that which you were told true, they you may as well lay down in the hole you dig and I would cover you with dirt. If a wise man knows not the truth, he keeps his peace.

The foolish will talk for days, spouting words in hopes they will be believed.

You may leave this area, after your lessons are ended of course, and travel. It is not only allowed, but encouraged. In the course of you life you will eat what you please, and probably too much of it. You will drink of the mead, and assuredly too much of it. Moreover, of the womenfolk, you will steal their hearts and they yours. Your heart will be broken and mended time and time again. You will discover the meaning of life. Many times. Each time it will be true, if only for the moment."

"These words be true, Master?"

"These words are true."

"Then Master, what be the purpose of that I do?"

"Ah, the purpose..." The Master released the student's chin. "The purpose of your actions are both singular and multifold. In performing this deed you are giving your oath to finish the matter at a later day. When fifty more circles of the sun have passed, you shall return to this site. I admonish you not to die before then, it is rather important. At that time you will find a tree growing here. A tree birthed from the seed we plant today. You will stand next to the tree and raise your hand to the level of *your* heart. It is at that height you will cut the tree in half. By whatever means available to you, a section of tree the thickness of your thumb, and in size the circumference of the tree shall be removed. This you shall...."

CHAPTER III
Master and Planchette

Fifty years, he thought. *Long years, but not all harsh.* The old man sat before his table as the sun slowly dipped below the horizon. Silver light to gold. Gold to copper. Copper giving up the last of its glory to the darkness. The flickering of his tallow lamp slowly became noticeable against the stonewalls inside his home.

He supposed the house was a bit stark and barren, having only table, chair, blackened pot hanging above a dead fire, and the smallest handful of personal effects.

Far cry from twenty years earlier, when his life-mate had festooned the house with wildflowers of every color. Bits of rock and crystal had sparkled from shelves and crannies giving all a life of its own.

All dark now, both life and day. Still and all the memory of her brought comfort. Not as much comfort as her warm body tucked against his during the night, but enough to bring a smile to his lips.

"Now I have you for company," he said aloud, addressing the disk of wood lying before him on the table. "If I had intelligence, you would go immediately into the fire while there is both time and option. The plan was well formed, but the thoughts behind it flawed." He picked the wood up and studied it.

"You are to represent justice; whatever that may be. Does man ask for justice in error? Does he even understand that for which he asks?" he inquired of the silent oak slab. Placing it back on the table he rose. Moving to the door, it opened silently on its greased leather hinges. Outside, his eyes searched the blue-gray gloom for the items he had finished preparing that half-day.

Earlier, before the tree had been hewn, hooves and bones were methodically crushed and powdered between mortar and pestle. This fine powder was then mixed with water in the cooking pot now hanging over the ashes.

For a day and a half the mixture had boiled and simmered, rendering it into a thick, viscid mass. When it dropped to a temperature that allowed it to be handled the glue was smeared across the surfaces of a dozen squares of tanned leather. Each treated piece was carried to the beach, and laid face down on the sand. Thus coated, they were returned to the front of the stone hut to dry and harden.

As he bent, stacking the stiff slabs into one pile, a voice called out from the darkness. "Aye, you be here. I come with that for which you asked."

From the darkness a small figure appeared. The visitor was old, and age had stooped the man to where one could imagine him able to reach downward and touch the ground without additional bending. In left hand was a staff, in right a leather bag.

He waved the bag, banging it against the staff so the contents clicked together softly. "There be a dozen of them. Take care when ye open the bag. Dump them out; do not dreg its depths with yer hands." He laid the bag at the feet of the hut's owner. "Not my best work, but my best was years ago. Sharp they be," he cautioned. "Sharp enough for that which you fabricate, Targus."

Not waiting for thanks or payment, the visitor turned and disappeared into the night.

And Targus the old man, Targus the Druid Master, tucked the bundle under one arm, the slabs under the other, and reentered his home.

Setting all on the table, he returned his attention to the wooden disk. The work was tedious, but not hard. It would give him long hours to contemplate that which he was building. His eyes turned to the stone wall, where the flickering lamp revealed a parchment with runes. A name. A name that could not - would not - be spoken until completion of the task. The final act before his part in this play was completed.

Targus shivered. The night was not cold, but his soul was. Walking to the fireplace, he built a small fire to melt the frost that gathered around his heart. He stared into the dark recess he had built so many years ago, above the firebox and beneath the mantel.

Soon.

The added light would help him see what he was carving, but it was not yet time. When he had been outside, the moon had not risen. This particular deed must take place far from the eye of the sun, performed in the darkest shadows of the night, under the watchful guidance of the moon. Lamps and fire mattered not. They were tools of man and nature, but the fire of sun, nay. The only light that purified was luna.

He dumped the bag his visitor had brought upon the table and they spilled forth in random shapes and sizes. Thumb to hand-sized bits of knapped flint. Gray, caramel colored and black. The only thing they shared in common was their sharpness. Picking one up, Targus peeled a paper thin slice of callus off the palm of his hand. Sharp enough for this monstrous carving.

The pattern was neither intricate nor artistic. Targus set out to carve the circle into a symbolic heart shape. With the flint knives the shape gradually took shape in his hands as the wood shavings built up.

When it was completed, he knew not. He awoke to the sun shining against the greased paper of his windows.

His hands ached from grasping and clenching both tools and wood. His back hurt from sitting slouched over the table while sitting on a stool. His chest felt heavy and painful, while sometime during his few minutes sleep, his arm had brushed against the chert blades, nicking flesh in a dozen places. The blood had seeped forth to harden in a blackened crust.

Rising, Targus hobbled to the fireplace once more. His hands searched the gray ashes until he found the orange sparks which lay hidden under their powdery blanket. Laying dry grass atop the burning jewels, he blew upon them until flames danced once more. Atop the smoky blaze, he stacked kindling and topped that with wrist thick logs. Smiling at his success, he brought the carved wood from the table and gently set it inside the small recess. Here was its oven; its incubator. Here it would dry over the next two days. Not hot enough to char or burn, but steady warmth radiated from the heated stonework of the fireplace, drying whatever moisture was left. Exhaustion, mental and physical, washed over him in waves of dizziness. He staggered to the corner where sweet grass and straw covered the floor and collapsed into a dreamless sleep.

CHAPTER IV
The Twins, the Master and Death

The figure gently nudged Targus with a bare foot. Eyes blinking against the light of the day, Targus sat with a start, his eyes jumping to the fire-place. The fire was now new and needed more for heat, than light.

"Aye, Targus. I fed yer fire for you and take heart," he said with a cold smile. "I did not feed it your precious project." The man turned and walked to the door. "Although I will tell you. I thought upon it. I thought upon it hard."

"As have I," said Targus.

Rolling to his side, belly, then knees, Targus forced himself erect. As erect as his years would allow. "I thank you for your kindness, brother Timmathy."

Timmathy laughed. "If indeed it be kindness. I see that Maerlyn did pay a visit." He nodded towards the flints on the table. "Those be his doing."

He looked closely at Targus's eyes. They were sunk in his head, dark shadows beneath them. The skin hung from his face in folds. "Targus. You will come with me this day. You must eat. If you deprive yourself of sustenance much longer, the scythe shall strike you down and then your masterpiece will go to the grave with you. While that I would not mind, I should enjoy neither digging a hole for you, nor chopping the wood for a pyre."

"Aye, Timmathy," Targus spoke softly. "You are right, but you need not fret. Turn yer eyes to the pathway. I believe my needs are about to be cared for."

Half walking, half running, two pupils were climbing the gentle path to his home from the beach. One carried a wicker basket while the other juggled a stoppered gourd.

"So young," said Timmathy.

Targus smiled. "As were we once, but still they have seen 18 cycles."

"Tis hard to remember that far back. All that remains of my childhood are the cursed teachings."

The two pupils stopped before them, panting from exertion. "Good morn to you, elders," they spoke in unison.

In mock anger, Targus proclaimed, "It be you two! What mischief are ye about? Tis far too easy to blame the trickery on each other, when we old men cannot tell you apart."

The two girls turned and grinned at each other. One spoke, "That be what our parents say. That be why they have never given us proper names." She laughed. The two yellow haired waifs were twins. "So we answer to anything."

Targus laughed. "Or nothing, as you see fit. What is it this old man can do for you this morning?" He asked in feigned ignorance.

Taking Targus by the hand, they led him back into his home. At the door, both turned and waved cheerfully to Timmathy, who nodded back with stone face and turned to start his journey home.

Inside, they cleared his table and set forth their simple feast. A loaf of bread, wild berries picked that morning, a small chunk of goat's cheese covered with herbs, and a dried and salted fish.

"Aye lassies. Long has it been since I have seen the likes of this breakfast."

The girls giggled, one going to the wall where a drinking horn hung from its leather strap. As she reached for it, the other's eyes flashed warning, before she spoke.

"Nay, sister. The mead is special and will make a fine end to this meal."

The other stopped, shoulders tensing, and spoke without turning.

"But of course, sister." Turning, a frozen smile was on her lips.

Ravenous, Targus consumed the food set before him. At his side, a girl appeared with horn of mead.

"We could have let him drink of the mead first, then eaten the food ourselves," snipped the girl standing over the sleeping man. "Then we would not be standing here with empty bellies."

"An empty belly will not hurt you, my sister," the other said cheerfully. "On the other hand, it might have pushed him over death's door."

"Then we would have completed the task ourselves."

"That could not be. This you know. Were we to complete it, all we would have is a pretty bauble," she turned away once more, "and all the years of learning - the pain of fire - would have been for naught."

The impatient sister shuddered, her hands going to her belly, as the memory washed over her.

ॐ•ॐ

It was an evening with dark mood and bright moon. Twelve people gathered inside the stone monument, dedicated to the seasons and celestial bodies. In its center, one stone slab lay, its dedication had been to the gods.

Five hooded women. Master Elders. Five hooded men. Master Elders also. All traveling far for this night and ceremony.

Two girls, both having seen sixteen cycles of the sun, and neither having known the touch of man.

Twelve pitch torches, one in each stone archway of the monument. The flames writhed in the gentle night wind, and spit tiny beads of molten sap, a warning for people not to venture close to them.

Near the center stone a brazier cast a dull red glow from the embers inside; blue flames still rose from their surfaces.

One hooded figure looked skyward, and a woman's voice issued from beneath the cowl.

"The time draws near."

From beneath her robes she removed an object and placed it in the brazier, nestled with the red hot coals.

Yet another dark figure moved to stand before the two girls and extended his hands, offering small flagons of drink.

"Drink this now. It will ease that which is about to happen."

With trembling hands, the girls followed the quiet instructions.

Taking the empty flagons, he pocketed them inside his robes before he spoke again. "The ceremony is for both of you, for we know not who will be chosen." Raising his arms, the sleeves of his robe fell back and exposed hands more skeletal than human.

"The tasks before you are many and will last the length of your lives. Perhaps longer for one of you. You will care for the Creator, and when *his* task is complete, you will care for the Creation. This you know.

The knowledge being given you now is this.

The Creation is but the gateway for a god. A god with no name at this time, just as the both of you have never had names bestowed. When he is called, he shall choose one of you. To that person he shall give a name, and in turn, tell you the name given him by the creator."

Another approached the speaker, and their hoods drew close. One nodded in agreement, then pointed to the heavens. "The time draws near. Look to the moon."

In the heavens, the full moon still shone, but on its lower edge a shadow lay. A dark crescent stain that slowly covered its surface.

One figure had left unnoticed, then returned. Over his shoulder he carried a goat, which struggled feebly. It had eaten of grain mixed with powder that stole its will.

"Tis not right!" boomed a voice from the darkness of his hood.

"All were in agreement, " chastised the Master of this Ceremony.

"Two sacrifices are required. This we all know." Responded the voice.

"Two sacrifices are required," agreed the Master. "And two shall be performed. One on this night, of the sacrifice you bear. Another in the future," his shape seemed to swell.

"If we chose tonight...and chose wrongly...all the years would be for nothing. We are agreed and bound. The choices will be marked, and the decision left for the creation."

"Then we should..."

"No!" The Master cried. "If were performed this eve, a say in the matter would not be given to the sacrifice. Any more than the matter discussed with the goat you bear. A say on future eve shall not be granted either."

Burly under robes, yet another assisted the bearer of the goat. It did not struggle as the two placed it on the waist high stone table. Two more figures come forward and all four legs of the goat were imprisoned and held immobile. From the hands that grasped each leg, the girls could tell the captors were men. These were not skeletal hands, but the hands of strong men who worked the fields.

The set of skeletal hands appeared at the head of the table. In their grasp was an obsidian blade the color of the night sky. Reflections of the torches sparkled from its glassy surface.

"An offering...the first..."

In a blur, the knife descended, penetrating the sacrifice's throat on one side and erupting out the other. In the shocked moment the goat froze and the blade was ripped upward, followed by a fountain of blood that appeared as dark as the blade.

A bubbly foam of blood followed, capturing the bleat of terror that never reached the animal's mouth.

In three minutes time, all struggles had ended.

The robes of the Master were covered with sacrificial blood, and its blackness dripped down the sides of the stone.

Cold air upon her legs cut through the mental fog. The death of the goat had a dream-like quality, and even the spray of blood had only made her heart race a bit faster.

The tang of cold now washed around her hips and between her legs. Hands from behind pulled the robe off her body and over her head. Its coarseness scraped her neck and face. Thoughts lagged seconds behind the actions of the world.

In her ears she could hear voices, but they were as waves crashing on the beach, blurred and liquid sounding. Vision left, but returned before she could respond to it. The robes were now gone.

In the tight circle of hooded clan, the girl stood naked. The Master observed her eyes; she was ready.

In turn her eyes roamed the circle, but did not focus on any one thing. When asked questions, she gave no indication of hearing. Pale hair shimmered as she moved her head, lips parted slightly and saliva edged its way down from the corners of her mouth. Her lips felt numb and dead.

Her skin responded to the cold night air, its surface pebbled from the cold. The cold caused her nipples to harden, standing out in color as well, for the skin was now devoid of all blush, pale and waxen in the moonlight.

The Master wiped the goat's blood from the handle of the knife and gripped it firmly again. Raising the jagged blade he laid its tip between her breasts. With only the slightest pressure, the skin parted beneath its touch and the cut, though shallow, released a rivulet of crimson that flowed down her chest and stomach.

With knife, he motioned to the table.

Her mind rushed upward like a swimmer reaching for the surface of the sea, having dived too deep. Too many things were happening and their combined sensory input had pushed the stupor aside. Her chest stung and she could feel the warmth of the blood that flowed across frigid flesh.

Her feet lost contact with ground and the world spun, a flash of moon, a flash of torches; then all stabilized and stars, ringed with dark faces in hoods, filled her vision.

As she rocked side to side, the surface on which she lay felt wet and sticky. Her arms and legs were restrained, pulled apart and she realized she was held as the goat had been.

Bending downward the Master inspected the tool inside the brazier. Iridescent waves washed up its handle where the heat radiated throughout its length. Picking the girl's plain tunic robe from the ground, he wrapped it around the handle to protect his hands. Wisps of smoke drifted from the cloth and told of intense heat, even far up its shaft.

The end that previously resided in the coals was bent and spiraled, forming a circle the size of a man's palm, cutting the circle into fourths, one for each season, was a cross.

"Before you are two, unnamed and unmarked by man," he spoke to the moon, now engulfed by eclipse. Its body showed a ghostly red. "With this ceremony we mark our words, deeds, and bodies of the chosen two, as our promise for your favors."

Mesmerized by the glowing brand, the girl lay silent and still.

Approaching yet closer, he inspected her belly. There he found the required site. Below navel and above maiden-hood, the ribbon of drying blood bisected it. Without word, the brand lowered. Flesh sizzled and blackened beneath its kiss, the acrid smoke rose in the night air. Pulled away as fast as it was applied, blackened skin adhered to it, revealing cooked red flesh bordered by the charred.

A cheer sprang from the onlookers, but it could not drown out the scream from the girl.

Laying the brand back to bed in coals, the Master motioned for the other girl.

❧◦❦

The girl's hands drifted from the scar concealed beneath her tunic to her face. "Sister first born," she said softy, using the only name that was permissible. "Do you think our parents agreed to that which be-falls us?"

"I know not, second born. Were they yet alive, I would ask. In my heart, I pray that they knew nothing of what is to become, but so many things point to the opposite."

"Then does it not bother you that soon…one of us…" The first born silenced her with a gentle kiss on the lips.

"Talk not of the future, when this day stretches before us."

Together they tidied the house. It took but a short time, as the old man has such few belongings.

The second born stopped, placing her hands on her hips. "Tis so drab in here. While you check the wood, perhaps I shall gather some sprigs and blossoms to please both eye and nose."

The first born frowned. The offer was nice, and this disturbed her. Sister was not known for her compassion or caring. She found herself saying, "Would be pleasant. Take care to return before dark."

"I shall."

Shaking off her unease, the first born walked to the fireplace and extracted the heart shaped wooden platter. The fire itself had burned low, but the small oven held comfortable warmth.

"Ah, so plain in appearance to hold such power." To her eyes, and the eyes of her sister, the wood was surrounded by a pale blue luminescence, just as the tree had before it was cut down. Her teachers - not the old man, but her "other" instructors - had told her it was brand-fire. A vision given to both sisters after the painful magic under a blood moon eclipse.

First and second born had been present when the tree was hewn. It was horror to them. Their eyes had seen blood flow from the tree when the bits had cut into it. Their ears had heard the high-pitched screams. As it fell, the brand-fire had swelled in intensity, until they had to squint their eyes. When it hit the ground, the screams had stopped and the light died down, but had not disappeared.

All the years and pain for this wafer of wood. At least it dries properly, displaying no cracks, she thought.

Replacing it in its cubby, she tossed several hand's full of wood on the dying fire, then sat in the front door, back against one side and feet propped against the other, watching the sea. The blue of the sea blended with the blue of the sky; leaving an indistinct horizon.

High on the hillside beyond the house, the second born's feet were propped also, ankles atop the shoulders of her lover.

Hips high in the air, the muscles of her thighs tensed with the fierce thrusts. In this position, the skin and muscle of her belly folded together, and the scar gave small pangs of agony to accent the pleasure.

Moans grew to full throated screams, until drawing back, his seed splashed against the scar standing guard above the golden red hair where legs flowed into body.

Arms and legs entwined, they slept the sleep of the satiated, far from the eyes of man, under the god-eye of the sun.

Targus awoke at the same time second born stepped foot inside the door. The first born frowned. Only four fingers could be set at arm's length between sun and horizon. Late for the second to return and late for Targus to awaken. The sleeping potion had been stronger than it should have been.

"Aye and you lassies let this old man sleep the day away." He yawned, and blinked. "The look of the house! You've straightened up and…ah…flowers to add life to these dead halls." Smiling he took the armload of wild flowers from the second born.

"Thank you for the flowers, missy. You look positively radiant today."

The first born shot the second an evil glare, which was returned with crossed eyes and tongue, when not observable by the old man.

The first born laid hand upon his shoulder and asked, "Would you be ready for an afternoon sup?"

"Nay lassie," he answered.

"Seems cruel to awaken, find the wondrous work you have done, then boot you from my door step, but his I must do. Much is left for me to do this night, and alone it is that I must do it."

With diminutive words of goodbye, the girls pranced down the path from the house.

Targus waved a last farewell and turned to the fire. Pulling the wood from its resting place he studied it. Twas drying well, no cracks. He felt refreshed, and the worry, which originally plagued him was gone. The worry came from the realization of his own frailty. Nagging doubt as to his ability to toil all night and sleep in the day was laid to rest. The breakfast and mead had worked wonders on him, giving sound sleep with few dreams, and those he was unable to recall.

The flowers he divided into bundles and tucked them into crevices in the walls. The last bundle he scattered over his bed of straw. Turning to the door, he noted the sun's face had sunk halfway into the sea. Only a few moments remained before he could start work. Lighting his lamp (refilled with tallow by the girls) he waited for darkness.

The sand coated leather was not as flexible as he had hoped, but still and all, it worked well. The wood was dry enough that the abrasive sheets slowly contoured its rough carved surface. The edges and bottom were easy. The shallow bowl carved in the top was more difficult to force the sheets into, for they fought the bend. Using a corner, he smoothed the indentation that covered the middle.

"You still fight me," he told the carving. "Close enough you are." Laying it on his table he walked to the fireplace. The frost had returned to his chest and the flames did little to dispel it. Atop the mantel rested the final two tools for his masterpiece.

Two bronze rods, each set into wooden handles. One was thin, thinner than an awl used by the women for sewing. The other was thick…as thick as… he grinned in black humor…as thick as a man's finger. Their tips were flattened. Taking them to the table, he started with the thin.

In the bottom of the bowl he set the tip and twisted back and forth, pressing firmly. Wood curled from its motion and he stopped, blowing the particles away, before repeating his actions.

Holding the wood in the palm of his hand, he continued drilling, his thoughts drifting away to other lands. They returned when the bit slipped through the wood and plunged into his hand, pushing deep into aging muscles.

"Aye, god rot you! Already you feel the call of blood," he snarled, set the wood down and pressed an edge of his robe against the wound. When the flow had been staunched, he turned back to his work.

"A second chance I be giving you." With the thicker bit, he started the first of three holes, each equidistant from each other forming a triangle.

These holes would not penetrate the body from top to bottom, but only halfway through, from the bottom. The going was slower on these. Enthusiasms held in check and pressure less on the bit. It would not do to split the wood by hurrying.

No errors at this stage of creation.

By false dawn his chores were completed. Except for one.

Pushing the cooking pot back over the fire, he waited for the solidified pitch to soften and melt. He fingered a leather pouch that hung from his neck.

The pouch had been there for fifty years.

It still bothered him to remember. Cutting the three fingers from the body he buried had not been pleasant.

Nor had boiling them until flesh and muscle separated, leaving gleaming bone. Much later, when they had dried and the remaining marrow removed, he had bent them, separating the joints and keeping the section from first to second joint in the pouch.

Pulling the grisly necklace off, he removed the bones and placed them on the table. He picked one up and started sanding it to fit one of the three larger holes he had drilled. By the time his work was done the pitch was bubbling merrily and the sun threatened to raise its blazing crown over the hillock behind his house. Hurriedly he dipped one end of each bone into the pitch and twisted them into the planchette. The pain in his chest bothered him, but ignore it he must.

At last he pulled the parchment from the wall, opened it, and whispered one name in the stillness of the night.

The sun caught him, an old man sitting at his table with the completed carving before him.

When the girls climbed the path to the house, they knew the world had changed. From the chimney, no smoke issued. From the opened door they could see no movement. Glancing at the other, the second born pushed her way past and entered. First born followed.

At the table sat the old man, his head rested on crossed arms. Before him the finished carving; small, innocent looking and possessing a simplistic looking beauty.

With tears in her eyes, the first born walked to him and laid her hand on his neck. The flesh was already cooling.

"He is dead, is he not?" asked the second born, curiosity in her voice, but no sorrow.

"He is dead," replied her sister.

CHAPTER V
The Library

There was dead silence in the room. The ticking of a clock on the wall could be heard clearly.

"I...uh...apologize. That took a bit longer than I thought it would," said Spetzer.

"It's okay. I don't hear anyone complaining," replied Stafford.

"Do you suppose I could get another tot of that brandy?" Spetzer asked, extending the snifter hopefully.

"Bring the bottle," Stafford commanded and three persons jumped for the wet bar. "Now, while that story most definitely did get my attention, it left quite a few questions unanswered and dug up a couple I hadn't thought of before."

He picked up an empty coffee cup, owner unknown. Peering inside he assured himself it was empty and no cigarette butts hiding. "If you don't mind...Jason is it? Yes, Jason ...pour me a shot or two. Better make it two."

Raising the cup Stafford took a sip, shuddered, exhaled harshly, and continued. "Now, seven people are dead. You seem to think that this Ouiji board had something to do with their deaths. Hell, man...we aren't even sure who they were. It is thought that there was Tommy Thompson, his wife and five other people present. They probably know which one was Tom now, if they have done DNA testing. The rest is a mystery."

Spetzer fidgeted for a moment. "The body that was found away from the house. That would be Mr. Thompson. I cannot guess which remains was his wife, but I would propose that one man and one woman was his personal physician and that doctor's wife. I could be mistaken and it might not be a wife, but a nurse."

He looked around the room at the attentive eyes staring at him. "I might elaborate on this and give you my speculations, but I am uneasy doing so in front of so many people. I have not lectured to a room for many years, and even when I did it regularly, I was not particularly comfortable with the action."

Stafford looked around the room. A wave of groans circled the crowd. "Now, as your pleasant host of the evening...don't make me be an asshole. I expect everyone at the office no more than an hour late tomorrow. If you have a hangover at that time, do not try to bum any aspirin off me. I will probably need my entire stock. I am also sure that you remember the company policy for the day after consuming the boss's booze?"

Several voices answered in unison. "Use spell check often."

"You got it, and if you can't walk without stomping, take your shoes off. If you can't make it in, bring a letter from your mortician. Now hit the road."

After all had wandered out, most gulping the last of their drinks or grabbing a plastic go-cup, Stafford turned to Spetzer. "Okay, no audience now. Shall we retire to the library where it is a bit more comfortable?"

"Yes, that would be nice. Please bring the objects with you and..."

"Yes?"

"Perchance might you have a firearm?" asked Spetzer.

Stafford raised his eyebrows. "Not a question normally asked in casual conversation." Walking to the table he reached under it to the concealed Kydex holster.

"Your answer. Colt Government Model, 1911A1, 45 caliber automatic. Condition one," he looked up. "That means round in the chamber, hammer back and safety on. Does the question denote a need or a fear?"

The library was a room of modest size with no windows. Soft chairs and scattered lamps were the only furniture. Spetzer took a moment to walk the walls, examining the books stored on the shelves while ignoring Stafford's question. Grunting, he pulled one out halfway for a closer inspection.

"You have a marvelous collection. They are not exactly what I would have expected."

Stafford laughed. He laid the board and planchette on a small end table and followed it with the pistol.

"I take pride in literature. I love the classics as well as modern pulp. Not what you expected from a man who makes his living writing about Elvis being seen in a diner in Canton?"

"No, I admit I misjudged your taste in books, sir." He glanced at the pistol. "And you appear to exhibit a sense of functionality in side arms."

Stafford gave him a sharp glance. "Are *you* familiar with them?"

Spetzer smiled wanly. "I could tell you that is an enhanced Colt 1911A1. Enhanced meaning it has been reworked so the ejection port is larger. The barrel is match grade. The grip safety and slide release are lengthened. The front strap is checkered twenty lines to the inch and it all started out as a Series 70. It has Novac sights. The 1911A1 is different from the 1911 in that it has an arched grip as opposed with the 1911 straight grip, plus it has finger dishes behind the trigger and the 1911 didn't. Shall I continue?"

"That is okay sir. Not only okay but very interesting. And revealing," said Stafford.

Seating himself in a leather chair Stafford asked, "Do you want me to start off with an interrogation, ask specific questions, or would you like to tell the tale in your own words?"

Lowering himself onto the plush sofa, Spetzer glanced at the door. "A little of all, I believe. That door…is it secure?"

"It is solid wood and I took the liberty of engaging the dead-bolt, due to the fact you are making me rather nervous. I also armed the security system. If a mosquito farts in the house the alarm will sound and an automated call goes out to 911. With my job I attract the attention of many fruit loops and I don't want my writers composing my obituary – they would screw it up – so I don't take many chances."

The other nodded in appreciation. "I will throw some answers out. Some are known facts and some are guesswork. I promise even my guesswork is accurate in this instance.

One - the body found away from the house - was Thompson, as I have said. He would have been the last to die, for he was the one who 'called' or 'summoned.' Two - the board means nothing. The planchette is the source of the problem. Three - the bloodstains on it are not from the mayhem that occurred. One of the people who were killed put them there. Or at least some of them. Others have been there for centuries. Excuse me, did you hear that noise?"

Stafford dismissed it with a wave. "That was the heating system kicking on. Trust me; I know the sounds of this house. Crap. I am getting more nervous than a dog shitting razor blades, so tell me …are we in danger? Right at this moment?"

Spetzer sighed. "I don't know. Perhaps it returned to wherever it was before it was called. Perhaps it still waits. Maybe it will attempt to reclaim the planchette."

"What is this 'it' you keep mentioning?"

"Samhan. Its name is Samhan, for that is what was given it. It means servant."

Stafford smirked. "A servant. Kind of like 'the butler did it?'"

"No, not like 'the butler did it.' This servant is the servant of Morriagan. Morriagan is the one who named it, and in turn, it gave the name Morriagan to her. These names are readily found in the knowledge we have about the druids, and their religion. The actual facts behind the names are a bit distorted now, but we are talking several thousand years of telling and retelling. It is believed the names were 'foretold' in the stars."

"What exactly are we talking about here? A threat from a couple thousand years ago? What is 'it?'" Stafford asked again and waved helplessly with his hands.

"A demon," said Spetzer simply.

"Mr. Spetzer…I write about demons, vampires and the ghost of Elvis, but that doesn't mean I believe that bullshit."

"I know. That is why I have been so uncomfortable at reaching this section of the story. This is why I didn't want to elaborate in front of a roomful of people. Consider this," he said with a sweeping gesture at the books surrounding them. "In all of mankind's writing, folklore, stories and songs, certain threads run through most of them. As you mentioned…vampires, werewolves, and demons …monsters of the night.

Most of these things have been chalked up to early man's overactive imagination. I submit to you this, however, early man for the most part was illiterate, and worked from dawn to dusk eking a living from the ground. They weren't all that inspired. If their bellies were full, they were happy. No. These collective threads came from somewhere solid. I believe they all can be traced back to Samhan, and its master Morriagan."

Spetzer looked at Stafford. "If that is the heating unit making the noise, why are you holding the pistol?"

"High heating bills frighten me. Tell me more about the history of this Samhan."

Spetzer shook his head. "Samhan. The beginning I have related to you, the rest of the story…."

CHAPTER VI
The Journey of the Twins

irst and second born sat side-by-side on the beach, watching the waves crash onto the shoreline. Between them a bundle and water pouch. They had wrapped the planchette in a threadbare spare tunic of the dead master's and taken the water bag from where it lay in the corner.

"It be three days journey to reach the stones. There we will have end to this matter. Or beginning, though it rapidly begins to matter not to me," said the first born.

"We should stop and supply ourselves with food, before we begin," said the second born.

"Nay. We were instructed to begin the journey immediately after we took possession of the carving, no food to be taken, only water. If we took leisure for the day and remained close to the village, questions would be asked. As is, the death of Targus will be noted, but the missing carving will not. You did as I instructed?"

"Aye, sister," said the second born. "I took the second disk that was cut from the tree and placed it on the fire. If they look, they will believe that the old man set his project into the flames before he died." She looked at her sister's eyes for belief. "So we begin our trek on bare feet and empty belly…"

"You complain too much. When was last your feet covered by the sandals they barely know? If complaints were food, then we would be gluttons."

The first and only obstacle to their trip came on the second day, mid morning.

They walked the path single file, although it was wide enough for three to walk abreast. The ground was level, but the path's surface scarred with the hoof prints of horses that traveled the roadway. The coarse indentations in the ground came to hurt their feet; feet hardened through years of barefoot play and toil.

Rounding a corner, they found themselves nearing a camp. The camp was transitory home to five travelers. One of the campers, covered with the dust of the road spoke out, startling the two girls.

"The heavens smile and brighten the day...," he said with an malevolent grin. "Twin maidens of great splendor. Out for a stroll so far from home and hearth."

Ignoring the man, the girls did not break stride. Another man stood and walked to the center of the roadway, barring their path. "You are not the friendliest of travelers on this lonely road," he said. Behind the girls, another took to the road, barring retreat.

First born looked at second and they turned, standing back-to-back. Each felt a strange sensation where their scars were. The feeling that comes on one when too long has been spent in the summer sun. Skin feeling taut and burning.

"Gentlemen," spoke the first born. "We are on quest and have not the time to dally here. Please, let us pass so we can fulfill our vows and promises."

"Surely you lassies can spare but a few moments to...ah...brighten the day of us weary highway men," spoke the man from the side of the road.

The burning in their bodies increased. The air became dead and sullen, only to be broken by a fierce and cold wind sweeping over the assembly. The two girls stood, staring at the men surrounding them. Unblinking.

"By the gods! McCafferty...hold. Their eyes. Behold their eyes," said one who had not spoken before. Where before bright green eyes had sparkled lay orbs of black. Black as if the pupils had expanded, consuming the surface of the eyes. The cold and dead eyes one would find on the great sharks that patrolled the waters.

"They be witches!"

"Then we should slay the creatures."

First and second born laughed. First born spoke in a commanding voice. "The first that draws blade dies. By his death, he dooms the rest. Those that stay have but a hundred breaths left in their bodies. Observe - death comes to your fire...tis already done." She pointed.

Were moments before a blazing fire danced, now dead embers sat. The last vestige of smoke was already dispersing to the touch of the cold winds. When first born looked around, the highwaymen were vanishing as fast as the smoke from the dead fire.

Second born looked to first and giggled.

"Sister, could we have really killed them?"

First born shrugged. "I know not. I do not know what was happening, or even if it were us causing it."

Second born frowned. "We should have tried. We should have tried to at least kill one of them. To crush their hearts as they beat in their chests."

"And if we failed? Nay. They did no harm other than frighten us. In turn we frightened them. They were a leaf falling into the pond, and the ripple was small. Come sister, the journey is still long."

Late on the afternoon of the third day, they stood before the stones. Neither spoke at first, each wrapped in memories. The grass was tall now, and green. Foraging animals did not graze near the circle of stones, but gave them wide berth. Overhead, small clouds dotted the sharp blue sky. The gentlest of breezes played over them, drying the sweat from their faces.

Silently they walked into the center of the circle where the stone table stood. With years and daylight, it did not look as terrifying as it in their nightmares. In daylight it could be seen that it was roughly carved with chisels, forming runes that defied the girl's translation abilities. The surface of it showed the dark stains of blood, whether from the night of their ceremony or other, they could not tell.

Setting the bundle on the stone table, they hopped up and sat upon its edge. The air became chilled; shivering, they quickly jumped down again and sat on the grass, clutching their knees up and resting their chins on them.

"There is still time before we must begin." Said the first born.

"Aye and it appears we have forgotten one thing."

"What be that?"

"We have no knife or blade."

First born's eyes closed. "In our instruction, we were not told to bring one." The first born appeared tired and depressed.

"Then how shall we...?"

Tears came to the first born's eyes. "I do not know. I do not care. For many cycles of the sun we have had our lives ripped from us. Each day we live by what we were instructed to do. Each day we are cold observers of those around us dying. What good be the chance of being a demi-god, if we canna even enjoy the world of mortals?"

The second born looked shocked. "How can you ask that? For these past days we have had our every need met. We toil neither for food nor for drink. Dance is performed for us and bards sing both to us and about us."

"We have been fattened for the slaughter. The rest is to keep our minds occupied so the horror of our world does not send us into madness."

"You grieve for the old man," stated the second born.

"Aye. Aye, I do. His reward for all his toil and devotion was death."

In a rare act of compassion, the second born reached out and took her sister's hand. Thus they sat as the sun sank into the horizon.

"Sister. Awaken. The moon has risen," said the second born as she shook her sister's shoulder. Together they looked heavenward with wide eyes. Staring down on them was the full circle of the moon. Bright as it washed the ground with a silver glow. Standing on shaky legs, they approached the stone table. The glow of the planchette could be seen even through the cloth surrounding it.

"Never have I seen the brand fire this bright, except for when the tree was cut," said first born.

"When shall we begin?" asked second.

"The time we will know, and I fear the time is now."

"How are you certain?"

The first born pointed to her sister's tunic then her own. In the center of the chest on each, a small circle of blood had appeared. The same spot kissed by the Master's blade during the ceremony so long ago. Without word they pulled their clothing over their heads and discarded it. Standing naked, they eyed the wound appearing on each other's chest.

"Does it hurt you?" asked second.

"Nay. A sting, but no pain."

"So...this be why no blade is needed. This night is truly a continuation of the ceremony." Watching in wonder, more than fear, the wounds opened to their fullest extent. They looked at each other, and the first born spoke.

"It is time."

Unwrapping the planchette from cloth, the first grasped it with finger blocking the narrow hole drilled to its bottom. Leaning over, she placed it between her breasts and let the blood fall into the bowl carved into its top.

At the first drop of blood, the firebrand glow changed from blue to the color of the blood. When half full, she pulled it away and extended it towards her sister.

The second leaned over, her hair fell over the arms of her sister, while the bowl nestled to her chest. In a hundred heartbeats, the planchette could hold no more of the crimson life fluid. Standing straight, they felt a strange sense of relief.

"We begin the end of the beginning," said the first.

Walking to the head of the stone table, they found the place they had been instructed to look for. Here, on a small plot, the rock was smooth and polished. First born set the planchette down, still holding finger to bottom. She motioned with her eyes to her sister. In one motion, both placed their fingertips atop the planchette.

Nothing happened for a moment then, oozing from the hole in the bottom, the blood started dripping. Drop by drop, followed by a thin stream that fell to the surface of the rock. Without warning the planchette began to move.

"What is this sister? Do you move the wood?" asked the second.

"Nay, it moves of its own accord."

Fascinated, they kept fingers atop the moving planchette. Jerkily it moved across the stone, blood trailing where it fell from the bottom. The blood trail formed loops and spirals as well as lines.

"It be runes!" said the second.

"Aye, but what does it spell?"

As the last of the blood drained from the planchette, the wood stopped its motion. The sisters prodded and pushed, but the life was gone from the wood. The brand fire was gone as well.

"How strange," said the first born turning.

The sweep of the claws caught her, opening her from crotch to midchest.

The blow picked her body off the ground a foot and when she fell back to her feet, pink coils of intestine spilled forth. With shock in her eyes, she plopped to the ground; sitting with legs outstretched. Looking up with wide eyes, the next blow swung in ripping her throat out. Blood flowing, she fell back to the ground, her heels hammering for a minute, before death relaxed all muscles.

The shape standing before the second born was a vision from hell. It stood on all four, but had the capability to walk upright. Hips protruding, and high above a serpentine tail with spade tip. Body a dark charcoal gray, eyes of flat black, with eyelids that blinked languorously every few seconds. The heavily muscled body was shaped much as a giant cat, but no hair could be seen. Blood stained claws slowly retracted into the knobby fingers that formed a massive paw. The head moved, side to side, bobbing like a hawk's and it was flattened giving it a snake-like construct. Jagged teeth showed white and purplish-black tongue darted out, only to whip back to hide behind the fangs.

Inside her head, a voice echoed. "You have summoned and I find the sacrifice acceptable. Do you know who it is you have summoned?"

Second born's voice was remarkably calm. "You are my servant. Beyond that name, you need no other. You are to be known as Samhan. Do you know whom it is that called you forth?"

"My mistress is the only capable of call and control. Therefore, you must be my mistress. Your name is Morriagan."

Morriagan nodded. "Tis well. A question must be asked."

"Ask."

"How came you to choose between my sister and myself?"

A hissing laugh. "A sacrifice to a god, even a false one such as myself, must be pure in heart and body. While you possess the qualities needed to work with one of my nature, your qualities lack purity."

Morriagan smiled. "The better for me."

"No, the better for us. Our banquet waits." Samhan announced. Pointing a clawed finger at the now silent body on the ground.

With only a twinge of regret, Morriagan began the feast with her servant.

CHAPTER VII
Trouble Pays Its Respect

"Okay," Stafford said. "She was a bloodthirsty bitch who kept a demon, probably in violation of her rental agreement pertaining to pets."

Spetzer's face was covered with sweat and his eyes glued to the door. "I hear footsteps out there. I know you do also. Is that a silent alarm you have by any chance?"

Pistol pointed towards the door, Stafford shook his head. "Not until tonight. Look, not saying I believe all this crap, but tell me this. This, uh, creature. Well...I don't have any holy water, garlic or silver. What do you think the odds are of a 185 grain jacketed hollow point between the eyes getting its attention?"

"You mean shooting it?"

"Yeah, that's kinda what I meant."

"I think it would probably make it mad," Spetzer said. "I am sure in the past its victims did not all go quietly into that good night. Many were villains, brigands and murders, probably armed with swords, lances and clubs."

The door-nob jiggled.

Spetzer noted the pistol, and hands holding it, did not shake.

A knock came at the door.

"Are demons in the habit of knocking on doors?" asked Stafford.

"Not until tonight. What are you going to do?"

Stafford stood. "I have two options. The first is to put one round through the door at chest height, and follow it with one on each side of the door, incase it stepped to the side."

"What's the other option?"

"I was really hoping to go with the first, but seeing as how you asked." He lowered the pistol and strode to the door. Unlatching the deadbolt, he threw the door open.

"Is that a pistol in your hand, or are you just glad to see me?" asked his secretary.

"Karen?" The pistol dropped to arms length and pointed towards the floor. "You have no idea how close you came to getting a .45 caliber pink slip." He pointed to the couch and closed the door, relocking it.

"Karen, Spetzer. Spetzer, Karen. You both met briefly at the get together. Mr. Spetzer, Karen here has ah…access. Yes, access to my home." He glanced at her. "This means she also has the code to the alarm system."

Spetzer walked forward and took Karen's hand. He sized her up. She was tall and muscular, walking with unusual grace. "Karen. It is a pleasure to meet you. Do you dance or perform ballet? I could not help noticing how fluid your motions are."

Her laugh was more than feminine. "Nor how I have more muscles than a brick shit house. No, sir. I do not dance, unless you call kata a dance. I started out as a bodyguard for Mr. Stafford, here. I am fifth dan black in ranking for TaiKwanDoe, master of the katana, proficient in assorted hand weapons, and hell on wheels with side arms. I also type 75 words per minute and take dictation."

Spetzer nodded. "But you are no longer functioning as a bodyguard."

Karen shook her head, causing her short hair to halo out. "Nope. A bodyguard never gets intimate with her client. Stafford here, and I…"

"Well," Stafford interrupted. "Introductions have been made, so let's get back to business. Seats please. The story isn't finished." He stopped. "Karen, if you want a drink, you know where it is."

"Always the gentleman. That's what I love about you, Bob."

"Yeah, ain't I?" Stafford grinned. "Now, I know who was involved. I know what was involved and I know when. Give me the Reader's Digest Condensed version of why and how." He set the pistol down again on the end table.

"Yes, well…" Spetzer collected his thoughts. "The unholy trinity of planchette, Samhan and Morriagan were an attempt to obtain justice. The planchette would be filled with her blood and placed on the chest of a dead person. A person who was presumably murdered. There it would write, in blood, the name of the person responsible for the untimely death." He glanced at the door. "Or it would call her servant, who would met out 'justice' by, well, dismembering the offender in the most horrible way."

He leaned back in the chair and closed his eyes. "But there are so many things we do not know. Did the demon disappear after it killed? Did it have to be 'sent' back? What happens if someone other than Morriagan summoned the servant?" He chuckled a grim laugh. "Although I think we have a pretty good idea now of what that effect would be."

Karen walked to where the planchette and board sat. "If it spelled out any name on the board, it is too smeared to make out. It all looks pretty plain to me. Hell, I've seen better ones for less than ten dollars at the toy store." She picked up the planchette. "For that matter, it isn't even finished off nicely...if you don't count someone doing a mystic thing and painting it with luminous paint so it glows kind'a blue."

Spetzer jumped to his feet, staggered, and caught his balance. "Young lady. What did you just say?"

"I said it looks kind of cheap."

"No, no, no," Spetzer said impatiently. "After that. You said it was blue?"

"Not painted blue, but that paint that glows in the dark? It's dim enough in here that you can see it."

Stafford had joined them and looked at the old man. "I don't see it. Do you?"

Spetzer shook his head. "I see nothing. No glow. No fire brand."

They turned and stared at Karen. She backed up a pace. "Hey, now look, I didn't break your little toy."

"Its okay," Spetzer comforted. "Tell me, when you pick it up, what do you see? What do you feel?"

Karen reluctantly picked it up. "The glow is there whether I am holding it or not. It feels warm," she raised it to her face, "and it smells of...cinnamon."

"Remarkable," said Spetzer. "How do *you* feel? Not how does the texture of it feel in your hands."

"I feel a bit strange." She blushed. "It's kind of like getting horny and menstrual cramps at the same time. A burning in the pit of my stomach."

"Does it make you want to get naked?" asked Stafford.

"I hardly think it would do that," said Spetzer.

"Hey, you ask your questions, I'll ask mine. Inquiring minds want to know." Stafford returned to his chair. "So, how did the Thompsons get hold of it, and why would they attempt to use it? As a matter of fact, how would they even know how to use it?"

Spetzer sat. "You know I gave it to them, so the question you are really asking is 'why.' Young woman…Karen…please come away from that thing and join us. I don't believe it is wise for you to come into close contact with it."

He folded his hands in his lap. "I am a scholar. A scholar of the ancient myths and religions. Not just those of Celtic origin, but from every corner of the globe. I have been a student of these things for the past sixty years.

In every country I went to - in every religion I delved into - the thread of Samhan and Morriagan was present. Yes, the names were often different, but the core thoughts were there. I became obsessed with finding out all I could. For years I searched for answers, only to find them in a day.

In England, as I have mentioned, many farm sites are built upon the original druid farming plots. If one visits those farms, one is always invited in for a pint and a story. Where I started, there was no knowledge of the unholy trinity. I merely started on the beach and walked. At each house or village, I would make discrete inquiry. Some had heard 'something' but it was as dilute in substance as to be meaningless. Three days of this and I hitched a ride back to where I started and began my journey again, in the other direction." Spetzer coughed and took a sip of his brandy.

"I must mention, before you ask, I did start around Stonehenge. From the tales I felt that my destination had to be three days from that famous stone circle. Only later did I come to find there are a half dozen stone monuments scattered to the winds.

Regardless, I restarted my trek. It was like the children's game where you look for something, and people keep telling you 'warmer, warmer, colder, colder, and hot.'

Soon, everywhere I went, people knew the legend. The farther I went the more details they knew of it. Then, in the afternoon, I came upon a small village. It was on the beach. I inquired of an old man," Spetzer laughed, "although at my present age, I realize he was not all that old, as to if he had heard the legend.

He looked up from his whittling and said, 'Aye. I know of the legend, but canna help ye there. But if you look for the remains of Targus,' he pointed up the hill, 'he lies there.'"

Spetzer stopped and wiped his forehead with a linen handkerchief.

"I walked up the hill. No pathway now existed, and it was located substantially outside the village. There it was. A small stone hut, the roof gone, but walls and chimney standing."

"Hold it," Stafford interrupted. "About 2,000 years and the thing was still there, pretty as can be?"

"Well, not pretty. Weather worn but standing. As I said no roof."

"After 2,000 years? No one packed the stone off and it was still standing?"

"Yes."

"How is that possible?" demanded Stafford.

"I have no idea."

"Look boys," said Karen. "You two can debate architecture later; I wanna hear the rest of the story."

"2,000 years," Stafford said with a harrumph.

"Bob!" warned Karen. "Go ahead Mr. Spetzer."

His eyes thanked Karen. "As I was saying, after 2,000 years - or *more*," he glared at Stafford, "it still stood. The roof had decayed into mulch, dirt, or whatever it does, and the floor was grass. Of interest to me was the fireplace, and upon examining it I was flabbergasted to find the oven that the planchette had been dried in. Small it was, only about a foot and a half wide, six inches high and two feet in depth. Just to mimic Targus' motions, I reached into it, imagining what it would have been to place the witch wood into the warm oven." He stopped. "And it was there."

A heavy crash came from the door and Stafford grabbed for the pistol. As he reached, three loud concussions slapped him alongside the head.

Karen stood with legs bent, grasping the pistol between both hands. The first spent casing had not hit the floor by the time the last shot was fired. Moving to her left, she crouched down and waited.

Three small points of light shown through. One in the door about chest height, and one each through the respective walls on both sides. The three of them stood, sat and crouched without word for several minutes. Silence. No noise came to their ears.

"I hope that wasn't Billy coming back to ask for a raise," whispered Stafford.

Karen did not take her eyes off the door. "If it was, he won't be needing it now." After ten minutes, sirens could be heard in the distance.

CHAPTER VIII
Police Intervention

The arrival of the police was tense in itself. Their only report had been "shots fired." Fifteen minutes were spent with both sides convincing the other that they weren't going to shoot.

In exasperation, Karen had walked to the door and yelled, "For Christ's sake. Here!" Unbolted the door and threw it open.

A plain clothes detective stood blinking at her. Behind him were six uniformed officers with assorted weapons of mass destruction.

Voices yelled, "Make them show their hands!"

Ignoring that, the detective said, "Hi Karen. Hi, Bob. Nice night."

From his chair, Stafford yelled back, "Hey, Jerimy! How's it hanging?"

Turning the detective informed the firing squad. "The only thing he has in his hands is a bottle of brandy. We can't shoot him for that. If he had a pen and paper, I might look the other way…after the crap he wrote about me."

"Now Jerimy…that was all a mistake. We printed a retraction the next week." Stafford soothed.

"After a couple hundred thousand people read it and wrote into the station," fumed Jerimy. "May I…ah…come in?"

Karen opened the door to its fullest and with a sweep of her arm invited him in. "Do you mind if your friends aren't invited?" she asked. "They look a little rowdy to me."

Waving for the uniforms to stay where they were, he drawled, "Well, Bob, it's like this. We get a report of a silent alarm. We get here, let ourselves in - reasonable cause, you know - and find a locked door with three holes in it and the wall that look suspiciously like bullets have exited from the inside of that locked room." He hesitated, looking at his notebook. "Yeah, yep, that about covers it. I am sure there is a reasonable lie, I mean excuse, for all this?"

Stafford spread his hands and tried to look innocent. "Jerimy, it's simple. I was cleaning my gun and it accidentally discharged."

"Three times?"

"Uh, yeah." Stafford said lamely.

"That is extremely clumsy Bob." The detective swung the door slightly shut. "You know...that is one helluva pattern for accidental discharge. I would really hate to have been outside...say...trying to break in. That pattern wouldn't leave many places to hide." He turned back to Karen.

"Accidental discharge?"

"Accidental discharge," said Karen.

He turned to Spetzer, who raised a hand and said,

"What they said."

Jerimy sighed and put the notebook away. "Well, with all three of you saying it, it must be the truth. Right." He held out his hand. "I will be taking the firearm with me for a bit. You can pick it up down at the station."

Stafford bristled. "I don't like that idea worth shit."

The detective grinned. "Well, it's that, or I take both you and the gun." He turned to the men standing behind him, still pointing their guns in the direction of the room. "What do you think of that idea gentlemen?"

A resounding, "Whooo-rah!" was echoed by all of them.

He turned back. "Your choice."

Quickly Stafford picked up the pistol between thumb and forefinger, placing it in Jeremy's out-stretched hand. The detective punched the release on the left side near the trigger guard and let the magazine fall into his hand. Safety down and pulling the slide to the rear, he cupped the loaded round that had came from the chamber. Tucking the pistol into his jacket pocket, he thumbed the remaining rounds from the clip.

"Five rounds left. That means you had a full clip and one in the chamber. Unusual way to keep a handgun when cleaning. Most people prefer to unload them. Almost like you were expecting to have to use it."

Stafford started to speak, but the detective cut him off. "Yeah, I know. Accidental discharge. Well, we'll be on our way. You gave me a lot of paperwork for this little mishap." He turned, thought for a moment, and turned back. "You might want to have the exterminator come out. You have a serious mouse problem."

Stafford's eyes narrowed. "What do you mean, Jerimy?"

Without word, the detective pointed to the wall outside the room, turned and left, taking the swat squad in tow.

Walking out of the library the three stood staring at the wall. Across its surface were four heavy gouge marks, as if claws had been raked across its surface.

Stafford stared at the marks. "Grab your shit. We are out of here."

"Might I suggest we go while the police are still here?" asked Spetzer.

"Shall we lock the house up and set the alarm?" asked Karen.

"We are out of here now. If whatever that was wants to raid the refrigerator...more power to him."

Hurriedly they ran to Stafford's sedan.

"Hold it!" Stafford stood and stared at his car.

"What is it?" asked Karen.

"We are going to take your rig."

"Um...why is that?" she asked.

"Mine has tinted windows. I can't see the back seat."

"You are being a chicken shit." Stated Karen.

"Here," Stafford tossed her his keys. "Be my guest."

Catching them with one hand, she reached down. She stopped. "We'll take my car." They piled in to her car.

Spetzer was watching out the window. The tap on it caused him to jump, hitting his head on the roof. Clutching his chest, he watched as a dark shape leaned downward and the grinning face of the detective filled the window. Circular motions of his hand indicated he wanted the window down. Reluctantly Spetzer complied.

"In a bit of a hurry aren't we?" asked Jerimy.

"Well, kiddo, we have places to go and people to see," said Stafford.

"Yes...well...you didn't forget anything you wanted to take with you did ya?"

Spetzer slumped in his seat and buried his face in his hands.

"Here you go professor. We wouldn't want to leave items just lying around." He handed a bundle to Spetzer. "You know, I seem to remember seeing this at the Thompson's residence." The detective lit a cigarette. "They had a lot of marks like those you had on the wall. Of course, the marks there were on dead people. Sure there isn't anything you want to talk about?"

Spetzer shook his head. "Thank you ... Jerimy. You are most considerate." He lifted the edge wrapping the bundle the police officer had thrust at him. The planchette.

Throwing the cigarette down in disgust, Jerimy looked at Karen.

"Karen...I know you are licensed. Do you have a firearm with you?"

She shook her head.

"Crap," he said and bent down. Lifting a pant's leg he fumbled then stood. "Here." He started to say more, but quit. He reached over the front seat and placed something in her hands. "When you are ready to talk - if you still can by then - you know the number." Karen nodded her thanks.

Tires squealed as they started down the driveway, hitting the street without stopping. Karen waited for someone to give directions, but no one spoke. After a few minutes, she hit the onramp of the interstate and let the speedometer climb to seventy-five.

Finally, Stafford asked, "What did he give you?"

Reaching down on the seat she picked up the object and set it on the dash. "Smith and Wesson Model 36. Two-inch barrel. Thirty eight special."

"Is that good?" asked Spetzer.

"Not really, but it's the thought that counts." She replied.

Silence returned, and they drove on into the night.

&oon&

"While that could get you in a world of trouble, it was a sweet gesture," the swat captain told the detective.

"Ah, what the hell. She never asked for alimony. The least I can do is give her my backup."

"Do you think they know what the hell is going down?"

"Captain, we don't know what's going down. But it's bad. I know they didn't have anything to do with the Thompsons, but somehow they are now in the mix."

The captain frowned. "Official word is that it was a couple punks, stoned on PCP or something, that did it."

Jerimy smiled at him. "What do you think of that theory, captain?"

"I think someone is trying to feed me a dogshit sandwich and tell me it's Burger King." He grinned. "Two of the deceased at the Thompson's were muscle. Paid goons. I personally tagged a dozen spent casings. Nine millimeter and .40 S&W. From the casings we found, subtracting the holes in walls and furniture, something was pegged eight times. No blood."

"Do you believe in the boogey man, captain?"

"No, sir. However, I do believe in professional hit men, and body armor. I think that might be what we are dealing with."

"You might be right, captain, but I never heard of a professional hit man eating the brains of his target." He patted the captain on the shoulder. "Any chance I could get you to, uh, loan me a couple things?"

"You used the nasty word. The "L" word. What do you need?"

"Ah, nothing much. It's so trivial, I hesitate to ask..."

CHAPTER IX
Museum, Background and Betrayal

"Hey, guys," Karen said, breaking the silence. "*Hey, guys*! We are about out of gas, and I need to hit the little girl's room."

"Where are we, miss?" asked Spetzer.

"Five miles out of Tamara."

"Tamara!" Stafford roared. "We've been driving for hours and we are only twenty miles from home?"

"Do *not* give me ant shit. No one said where they wanted to go. I picked the interstate and have been driving a big circle, taking occasional exits to see if we were being followed."

Stafford mumbled something.

"Excuse me?" asked Karen.

"I said I doubt that thing checked out a car at Avis and is following us."

"Asshole! If you had a better idea, you should have said something."

"No, no. This is fine," said Spetzer. "A quick break at the truck stop and I know where to go. Half hour drive. No more than that."

Thirty-five minutes later, with the sun just coming up on the horizon, they parked in front of a large building. Getting out of the car, they looked suspiciously around.

"Okay. A museum. We all need culture, but is there any particular reason we need it now?" asked Karen.

"A thought, my dear. Just a speculation," said Spetzer. Leading them to a side door, he opened it with practiced motion and entered. Looking at each other, they followed. With Spetzer in the lead, they walked past a few people. People obviously in the employ of the museum. The workers looked up. A couple nodded, but none took much notice of the bedraggled crew wandering their halls. Entering another door they found themselves in a room strewn with wooden boxes and items covered with canvas.

Spetzer pawed through several boxes, swearing quietly under his breath. On the third try, he smiled a radiant smile and held aloft a cardboard box. His arms were tight under its weight.

"Yes! I knew it was here." Tearing the cardboard apart, a golden glow sparkled before their eyes.

"My god…that is beautiful," said Karen.

A small chest made of gold was held by the old man. He smiled wistfully. "Do not be impressed. It is…alas…fake."

"It isn't real gold?" asked Stafford.

"Oh, no, no. Of course it's real gold, but it's just a replica that was pawned off on a former curator."

"There's what?" asked Stafford. "Five pounds of gold there, and I am not supposed to be impressed?"

Spetzer sighed. "It is only about three hundred years old. A fake made in Rome and never near the pyramids."

"Then can I take it home and use it for an ash tray?" asked Stafford. Karen elbowed him in the ribs.

Opening its lid, Spetzer unwrapped the planchette and tested it for fit. The lid closed smoothly and he breathed a sigh again, but this time of relief. "I am not sure if this truly works, but I believe that being encased in gold, it shall be harder for Samhan to locate. When I gave it to the Thompsons for safekeeping, I had it wrapped in gold foil. I have no I idea if the theory is sound, but it is worth a try."

"I recommend we try to get some rest now. I can show you to a room, it's not much. Has a couple cots for our field workers." Said Spetzer.

Stafford looked hesitant. "I'm not sure it's safe to sleep. There's a whole bunch of new questions too."

"They will wait. They must wait, I am afraid. I don't think I can go on another hour," he said. Indeed his complexion was pale and his body shook. "I can offer a bit of privacy to the both of you. I will be in the room next door, should anything happen."

While the space smelled vaguely like a locker room, in comfort it wasn't that bad.

"He's right. The adrenaline is gone now, and I feel like someone has wrapped me in a blanket," Karen said, sitting on a folding army cot. "I can't believe last night. Do you think we are letting our imaginations run wild on this?"

Stafford thought hard. "Maybe a little. When you are sitting in broad daylight, and the world is 'normal,' it does seem a bit far fetched." He slipped his shoes off and lay down. "I am worried for you."

"That's sweet."

"No, really," he said, sitting up. "You saw a blue glow around the damn thing. Why would you see a blue glow around it?"

"Just lucky, I guess."

"Nah, there's more to it than that. Gotta be. Before you came along, the old geezer was telling me the history behind the twins. They could see a glow also. Plus, there is a bit of similarity in their childhood and yours."

"And what might that be? One, I am an only child. Two, I have never followed any mystical religions requiring sacrifices. Might try it some day for fun, but haven't yet."

"Don't invite to me your bar mitzvah. Actually, you sorta have. You were heavy into eastern philosophy. Martial arts. Study and practice every day. You went through a lot of pain and suffering to get where you are today. Lotta mental discipline. You even have a warped - I'm sorry - I mean set-in-stone idea of justice."

Karen laid her arm across her eyes. "That is because my childhood was limited. Not much in the line of friends to play with, video games, or wild partying."

"You were an army brat."

"Nope. I was an army orphan."

"Same difference."

"Bob, you are full of it. An army brat has parents. I never knew my parents. They were both military and died, as I was so often told, in the line of duty. I was raised by a never-ending circle of caretakers. They weren't so much interested in making me a well rounded child, as keeping me healthy and alive." She rolled to her side. "The only play toys I had were guns and knives. Martial arts?" she laughed. "There were always teachers of hand-to-hand. It was when I was about fifteen I got the urge to learn from some people who knew the philosophy behind it, not just how to break a neck or arm."

"That's kind of strange in itself. One would think the army would have shipped you off to some orphanage.

"Like I say. Just lucky, I guess."

They slept.

"Bob! Bob, wake up." Stafford opened his eyes and smiled a sleepy smile – until he noted the face looking down at him.

"Jerimy." He said, the smile disappearing. "You were following us."

Jerimy grinned. "Nope. Didn't need to. Karen's car has StarLink. I called in, identified myself as law enforcement, gave the vehicle identification number, and they told me the exact location of the rig. They even offered to unlock the doors for me." He glanced around the room. "Where is... uh...Professor Spetzer?"

"Next room - no - two rooms down the hall."

Jerimy shook his head. "Take a walk with me. Let her sleep. You and I need to talk."

As they walked down the hall, the detective questioned Stafford.

"Out of curiosity, how did Spetzer get to your little get together last night?"

"I don't know. Probably took a cab."

"Nope, checked all taxi services. Even the drunken yahoos at your party drove home. Nothing was dispatched to your house, or from it." Jerimy stopped before the door indicated by Stafford. From a holster at the small of his back he pulled a lethal looking little pistol. Stafford took a step back.

Raising a foot, the detective kicked hard at a spot just next to the doorknob. Glass exploded from the door's window as the door released and Jerimy threw himself through the sparkling hail into the room.

Stafford waited for the booms, but the only thing he heard from inside was Jerimy saying, "Well, that was fun." He entered as Jerimy was putting the gun behind his back once more.

"You will notice we are standing in this room alone. What does that tell you?" asked Jerimy.

"That you didn't need to kick the door in? It wasn't locked you know."

"One of the perks of the trade. I had higher hopes for you. You aren't a detective, but you normally don't have to be led by the hand."

Stafford sat on the edge of a box. "Well, I choose Mr. Mustard, in the library, with the rope. Okay, let me think." He stood and paced. "You say you didn't follow us, but you used the tracking system. Something must have happened to make you want to know where we were. You didn't bring a swat team with you. You are interested enough in finding Spetzer to break things and wave a gun. My final answer is, you found a dead guy in my bathroom, Spetzer ain't Spetzer, and my life is in danger."

Jerimy applauded. "I give you an A-."

"*What? I was joking!*"

"Then you only get a C+. The dead man wasn't in your bathroom, he was in an abandoned car about a half mile from your place. An old Buick. Identification on the body says he is - was - Professor Spetzer." Jerimy looked around. "And you forgot to mention that the planchette is most assuredly missing." He paused. "I take it back, just a straight C."

"But Thompson's grand kids identified the man."

"They identified *a* man. Your rent-a-cops identified *a* man. The guy who you invited into your home was not *the* man." The detective smirked. "You have a tendency to run with a story, before you make sure all the facts are right."

"Crap. Then who have I been talking to all night."

"Well..." the detective hesitated. "Are you going to give me a ration of shit, if I tell you I took the glasses from your library and had them fingerprinted without a warrant?"

"No."

"Then hopefully, in about thirty minutes, I can give you an answer to that question. I swiped a half a box of cigars also."

Two heads peeked through the door. Jerimy held up a badge and said, "Police business...send us a bill." Wiggling the badge again, he waved them away. "I suppose we should go wake Kare Bare up."

"Care Bear?" asked Stafford.

"That was a pet name he used to call me," answered Karen from the doorway. Looking from broken glass to empty room, she then stared at Jerimy. "He's gone. He took the planchette. Who the hell was he really?"

Jerimy slapped Stafford on the shoulder. "Now that's what I am talking about. That is a definite A."

Stafford flinched. "I always said she had a nice A."

"Why can't I find a guy that isn't married, and isn't a jerk?"

"You're just lucky," replied both men together.

Jerimy looked at his watch. "Let's take a trip downtown and see what we can dig up on this mysterious Mr. X."

"The body you found in the car. Was it....?" Asked Stafford.

"Did it look like steak tartar? Nope. One small caliber entrance wound to the temple. No exit."

"Then it wasn't like Thompson's." A statement, not a question,

"No, but if you want to join arms and walk off singing, 'lions and tigers and bears, oh my!' I'm game. Before you ask, Karen, I inquired around here as to who the guy was you came in with.

They've seen him around, but don't know him. When you walk in like you own the place, most don't question."

"Let's just go," said Karen. She then added, "Shotgun!"

Stafford laughed. "You can sit by the window."

Jerimy wagged his finger at Stafford. "I don't think that's what she meant. I think she wants the 12 gauge riot gun mounted to the dash."

Stafford looked at her and she nodded.

"Oh." He said.

CHAPTER X
Police HQ, Investigation

At the precinct, they pushed through the hustle and bustle of good guys and bad guys all apparently wandering aimlessly. The third floor, on which was Jerimy's office, was quieter.

"Looks like something out of the old series, Dragnet," remarked Stafford, as he stepped into the office.

"Don't start with me, Bob."

"No! I meant that as a compliment. My favorite show."

"Grab a chair, you two. I'll be right back."

When he had left, Stafford snooped the room. He picked up a notepad, huffed, and tossed it back down. Picking up a battered picture frame he inspected it. "He still has a picture of you." Stafford said.

"I never said he didn't love me," Karen replied. "He just got so jealous when I was bodyguard for you that things snowballed." She took the picture. "He wouldn't believe that nothing was going on between us." She sat it down. "That came later."

"And you still love him."

Karen smiled wistfully. "He has his good points." She turned and walked to Stafford and kissed him gently on the forehead. "So do you."

"If you had it to do over again? If you had to make a decision?"

"Don't go there. I don't know what my answer would be."

The minute hand on the wall clock swung through two circles before Jerimy returned. His swivel chair gave an alarming creak as he flopped down. Tears of frustration welled up in the corners of his eyes, and then shimmered across their surfaces.

Ten more minutes passed.

"You know, Bob," Jerimy said, speaking slowly. "I don't know what it is. For some reason – known only to God, and maybe a few select angels – every time we meet, my life turns to shit."

He walked into the beam of muted sunlight falling through a window frosted with age and grime.

"I ran the finger prints from the glasses. I got the results. I not only got the results, but I got a nice fax from Interpol asking why I was curious about a Mr. Steven Daily. I almost missed the message, because it was tucked between one from the F.B.I. and one from Quantico, Virginia. Our friends in the C.I.A. Every one of those notes had a note attached from my boss.

I haven't had the nerve to check my voice and e-mail."

"Yeah, but what did you find out about this Daily character?" asked Stafford.

"Thank you, Bob, for your warm compassion towards my situation."

"You're welcome, Jerimy."

The detective pulled a smoke and lit it. Karen eyed the action. "Jerimy," she said gently. "You know they don't allow smoking in here and get really pissed. You should at least open a window."

"If I opened a window, I would be tempted to jump."

"We're only on the third floor," scoffed Stafford.

"I'll jump three times. That makes it nine stories. Would that make you happy?" The cigarette exploded into sparks as he threw it to the floor and ground it out with his shoe.

"There, now you won't be endangered by second hand smoke." He picked up the thick stack of fax printouts.

"Most of this is telling me what they don't know about Daily." He held up another stack of papers. "This is a nice run down on the real – if deceased – Mr. Spetzer."

"Okay, let's see...Mr. Spetzer. Donald A., born 1940, Tulsa, Oklahoma. Whoops, excuse me, it is a Doctor Spetzer. Military and served Korea and then, ah...oh yes, that tidies it up quite nicely. Everything after Korea is classified. If it helps any, I can tell you he lived in Los Angeles in 1960. His college papers say he also took archeology. Not a normal minor that goes with a medical degree."

"Jerimy," Karen said, "what type of work was Thompson in?"

"Just a second," he pulled out his notebook and thumbed through. "Doctor also. Specialist. DNA research." He thought for a second, tapping the closed notebook against his hip. "Interesting."

"What's that?" asked Stafford.

"He would have been about 14 when he served in Korea."

"Is that possible?"

"Not really. If he was going to college in LA in the '60s, he was probably in Junior High then."

"So...what's it mean?"

"It means someone doesn't lie very well."

Karen spoke up, "Then what about Daily?"

"Well, I'm reading between the lines here. Professional hit man. Don't know who he works for. He's wanted by almost every country."

"He's perfect," said Karen. Old, mild, meek... asked Bob straight out if he had a gun and Bob told him. Thank god he took it with him into the library. The type of person no one would be nervous about." She stopped. "You say you don't know who he works for. What country doesn't have him on the wanted list?"

Jerimy frowned. "The U.S."

Karen grinned. "And where did you get the blatant lie from?"

"Bite me."

"Then his entire story might have been bull shit about the girls, the planchette and everything."

The detective sat back in his chair and locked his fingers together behind his head. "Maybe. But...I was the first on the scene – after the uniforms – at Thompson's. I am here to tell you...that little old man did not massacre all of them. No way, shape or form," he shuddered, "I can buy his shooting Spetzer in the car, but the Thompsons?" He shook his head.

"Something grabbed their eye sockets, squeezed the eyes from their heads doing it, and laid the top of their skulls back, like opening a carton of ice cream."

"You want to find out the truth about Daily?" asked Stafford.

"Hey, it's locked down. You think *you* can do better than my resources? Knock yourself out." He handed Bob the papers.

"I need to make a call. I'm going to use the pay phone on the corner."

"What's wrong with my phone?" asked Jerimy.

"You really want me to make this call from your office number?"

Jerimy dug in his pocket. "I'll give you some change for the phone." He held it out. "Don't use any phone on this block, thank you very much."

ငာ•ဆာ

Twelve inches separated the bottom of the opened window from the lower frame. The glass pane was age frosted, allowing only the most minimal of view.

The table was solidly build and sat three paces back from the window.

Daily leaned forward in his chair and picked up the cup of hot tea resting on the surface of the table. The warmth coming through the thin and fragile porcelain cup felt comforting against his arthritic fingers. *Growing old has draw backs in this profession,* he thought.

The cup clinked as he sat it back on its matching flo blue saucer. A troublesome set of items to pack, but one dictated by habit. Leaning he looked across the top of the rifle, pointed towards the opened window. In the fifty yards separating him from his target, the world moved as usual.

The populace of this section strolled the side-walks. Daily laughed. People that would not even look at each other wouldn't be checking out open third story windows.

He looked towards the locked door, with the body of the leasing agent lying next to it.

A shame, but a necessary chalk mark in the collateral damage column. Daily needed a platform facing the police station and this was it.

In days of old, a large wad of cash would rent an apartment or office space for a month. No questions asked. Now, there were six-month contracts, twelve month contracts, references, and credit checks. He sighed. He had started to like the real estate woman, until they had reached an impasse.

Leaning farther, he flipped the protective caps up from the ends of the scope. With thumb, he verified the tang safety was still pulled back. Even with this verification, he did not place his finger inside the trigger guard. Trust nothing, was a motto that had kept him alive for many decades in this most competitive of trades.

Through the scope, with its simple black cross hair, he could see through the window across the street. Two people. Female, the secretary named Karen.

Not a target.

Ah…possible…male…negative, the cop from the previous night. Not a target…yet. Where was the damned editor?

ငာ•ဆာ

"You want me to research data on a professional killer?" the voice was tinny in the phone's receiver.

"Yes," said Stafford, feeding more quarters into the phone.

"Knock that shit off. You don't need to put money in the phone. Trust me. It won't disconnect until I want it to. It's going through a dozen phone routers and three countries."

"So…is this going to be a problem, seeing as how his line of business is more…um…serious than my other requests?"

"No," the voice replied. "He might flame your ass, but mine is comparatively safe." Laughter could be heard behind the voice. "The fact this person is probably sponsored by a country makes it a little dicey, but no real problem I hope. I'll check out that Druid thingy also. No charge. That sounds kinda trippy."

Stafford frowned. "How much is this going to cost? Same arrangements as last time?"

"Nope. Seventy-five grand and I have my own version of Pay Pal now."

"Seventy-five grand! That's ten times what you normally charge."

The voice laughed once more. "Overhead. I have confidence, but if I'm bucking the government, and I think I am, then I might just need to relocate when I am done."

"That's still a lotta mullah," said Stafford.

"The choice is yours, and you do have to decide now. Remember, you called me."

Stafford leaned against the wall of the phone booth. "Okay, but it comes out of company funds, not mine this time. If you don't come up with anything, does that mean I get a refund?"

The voice was now dead serious. "No. It means I fucked up big time, am someone different, and will never communicate with you again. So…do we have a deal?"

"Yeah, I guess we do."

"A definite yes or no, if you please."

"Yes."

The voice brightened. "Excellent! In thirty seconds the money will be off your company's account at First State, and into mine. The bank will note a prefix of Alpha 776 on the transaction. Your accountant can off-set it however she wants to."

"Hold it!" Stafford shouted. "How am I going to get this information?" When am I going to get it?"

"Go online from your home computer tonight."

"Where do I go?"

"Doesn't matter, you'll get it."

"Good enough," Stafford said, but he was talking to a dead line.

CHAPTER XI
Confrontation, Confession and Healing

"This place brings back a lot of memories," Karen said.

Jerimy turned a critical eye on the office he saw, day in and day out. Walls that were once off white, hidden on one side by photos of the Thompson murder scene. The opposite wall blocked from view by plain gray file cabinets, some with drawers half open. The street-side wall with its narrow window and partial view of the corners of a brownstone building, and a renovated office complex.

The only decent view was the front of his office, comprised of a full vista of frosted glass, with door and matching glass inset. He had attempted posting notes and pictures on the glass, but the tape would never stick for more than an hour, before falling to the floor.

"Are those good memories, or bad?" he asked.

"Both. I remember coming in here, dusting and straightening." She swiped her finger along the top of a file cabinet. "I can tell you haven't replaced me, or if you have…she isn't much in the cleaning department."

A sarcastic laugh escaped his lips. "No, you haven't been replaced." He looked at her. "Either in the cleaning department or anywhere."

"You never even went out window shopping? You said you were going to." Karen's eyes narrowed.

"I said a lot of things. Most of them I didn't mean, and the rest I couldn't follow through on."

"Yeah," Karen said wistfully, "we probably could have handled the entire mess differently."

"Yeah." Jerimy walked to her and raised her chin with his fingertips.

With unforgotten ease their lips sought each other.

"Am I interrupting anything?" came the booming voice from the doorway. Jerimy cringed and his eyes darted to the figure of Stafford standing in the open door.

"You asshole!" he raged. "Every time I see you..." In frustration he grabbed a coffee cup from the desk and flung it hard towards Stafford.

As Stafford ducked the mug, the air sizzled and cracked next to his head, followed by a dull boom from outside. He saw Jerimy throw himself to the ground. A crushing blow hit him in the side and he found himself flat on the floor.

"Damn it, stay down," whispered a voice in his ear. Karen had tackled him and was holding him down. "I think we can safely assume Mr. Daily has not left town."

ହ•ଚ

"We checked it out," said the uniformed officer. "Third floor, right across from your office. Nothing to indicate he had been there, except for the rather obvious body of a Mrs. Irene Lufta. Real estate agent. Coroner says cause of death – probably – was a small caliber gun shot to the back of the head. That is supported by an empty .22 casing we found in the hallway. A Tenex. Target grade, subsonic, perfect ammo for a suppressed weapon."

"Well that wasn't a .22 he sent in our direction," snapped Jerimy.

"No, sir. We dug it out two rooms down. Thirty caliber, probably a .308, although it could have been a 30-06, .300 Winchester Mag, or such. I am opting for the .308, because it was full metal jacket and about 168 grains. Tactical rifle almost assuredly, but at that range anything could have worked."

Stafford looked up. He was still pale and his hands shook. "Jerimy...I never did thank you. If you hadn't thrown that cup my brains would be scattered from hell to breakfast."

"Yeah, rub it in," Jerimy snapped.

After the uniform left, Stafford asked, "Where's Karen?"

"Upstairs. She gets claustrophobic in dark, windowless places." Jerimy motioned to the gunmetal gray walls, where the concrete had been crudely painted over. "This place qualifies."

"Ah...then I am going to take this chance to say a couple things to you. I figure it will probably get me a broken nose...but I really don't give a rat's ass right now."

Jerimy turned his folding chair to face him. "Okay, big boy. Give it your best shot."

"You think I am an asshole. I probably am. Hell, no doubt about it. You, on the other hand, are not only an asshole, but a stupid mother-fucker to boot."

Jerimy turned red, but said nothing, so Stafford continued. "You drove a wonderful woman away from you by your jealousy. Hell, man, at the time, I was just a fucking client. Nothing more. I was a paycheck that came every week in the tune of $2,500. In return, Karen made sure that that psycho killer we were writing about didn't get his slimy hands on me.

In order to do that, she spent time with me. Night and day, seven days a week, for two months.

Yes, we got close. She knows more about me than anyone else on this planet. You know what? I fell in love with her. I pushed the issue. She dropped me as a client the same day you dropped her. She dropped me before you gave her a Dear John call. Or whatever you call it when a guy does it.

Therefore, I gave her a job. Secretary. Why? Because she is a damn good one. She was acting as my secretary most the time, so people wouldn't know she was guarding me. You put her in a position where she had too much pride to crawl home. You made her hate her profession, because it cost her marriage and the man she loved.

We see a lot of each other. Why again? Because I am normally surrounded by ignorant sons a bitches who can't carry on even a halfway intelligent conversation, unless it involves alien abduction or ghosts. Sometimes it is nice to talk to someone who is conversant on things like the world in general, the classic writer's, movies where there are more words than bullets, opera, and how to keep your sanity in this fucked up world.

Now the kicker. I am going to put it in nice little layman's terms for your little pin head police mind. We never fucked! We have snuggled. We have kissed. Oh, my god, we have held hands...but she ain't never jumped in the sack with me." Stafford rubbed his hands together. "Not because I am a perfect gentleman and never asked either."

Both men sat silent for a few minutes.

"Hi, guys," Karen said, stepping into the precinct dungeon. She looked from one face to the other. "Am I interrupting something?" No response. "You know I can normally read expressions, but you two have me stymied. I can't tell if you are both mad, sad, glad, comatose, or swallowed a live hamster."

"Ah...," Jerimy ventured, "Bob just pointed out a few factors on this case that I hadn't known or really thought about. I am still... ah...digesting them."

Stafford grinned. "No problem Jerimy, always glad to help out the men in blue with any observations I have."

"Yeah, um...thank you. If those facts are true ...then I might have been...crap...hasty in my previous assessment of the situation. If they are true."

"If what are true?" asked Karen.

"Oh, a lot of things," said Stafford.

"Its pretty complicated, and I don't want to go into it right now," said Jerimy.

"You two are bullshitting me right now, but I have no intention of trying to pry it out of either of you. You would just lie, get indignant when I caught you in the lie, get mad and pout."

Jerimy looked at Stafford who stood, stretched, and said, "Yep. You're right...and when you're right, you're right. So let's move on."

CHAPTER XII
Recon, Attack and Retreat

Karen was pissed. "You agreed to come to your house and check your email? Knowing that there is a guy trying to off you, and maybe a 'thing' trying to rip you to shreds?" She pulled the SUV off the road and onto a small one-lane dirt road above Stafford's house. A half mile below them the lights glowed invitingly. "Tell me this. Why does it have to be from your house? Why can't you access your email from any other computer? That doesn't make sense. It sounds like a setup."

"I agree with Karen," said Jerimy from the back.

"Well this guy is really good. He must have a reason for doing it this way."

Karen slammed the steering wheel with the palm of her hand. "If he was really good, he would have found a way to get you the info that didn't endanger you."

"Look, I don't know," Stafford shrugged his shoulders helplessly. "I just don't know. When I made the arrangement, I didn't think I would be a target who couldn't show his face."

"So now we are going to waltz into a brightly lit killing field and go surfing on the web," Karen looked at him in disgust.

Jerimy patted Stafford on the shoulder, in sympathy. "Bob, when they get like this, you need to give them some new toys and trinkets to appease them. You should know that by now."

Karen flipped him the bird. "I don't think a new dress or purse would quite mollify me at this moment."

Jerimy grinned. "I really hadn't thought of a purse. The other night, when we were here with the SWAT team, I …mmm…borrowed a few things. Nothing really special, just a couple items to level the playing field."

"You can't 'borrow' things from the SWAT lockers," said Karen.

"No, you aren't *supposed* to borrow things from the SWAT lockers. That is different from '*can't*.' You can borrow things, if you know the right people to ask, and make damn sure you don't get caught doing it."

Karen spun in the seat, kneeling and her elbows on the backrest. "What did you bring me?" she asked with excitement in her voice. "I hope it's nicer than that little .38 you gave me."

Jerimy smiled and patted two large green duffle bags and two hard plastic cases. "Well, for me, behind door number one - I have a ghillie suit and Remington Model 700 in 7.62 NATO - that's .308 Winchester round to you Bob - complete with a wonderful third generation Starlight scope."

"What do I get?" asked Karen.

Jerimy ignored her. "For you Bob, old buddy old pal…you get your .45 back with two spare magazines and a set of black BDUs."

"BDUs?" asked Stafford. "Underwear?"

"No," Karen smacked him on top of the head. "Battle Dress Uniform. Black colored fatigues. What do I get?"

"Oh, not much. Let's see…yeah, you get a set of BDUs also."

"And???"

"Well, I did manage to bum Clifford's poodle shooter off of him. He's got a new one, so he was willing - not really willing - he agreed under duress to part with his old one."

"Oh, my god!" Karen squealed with joy.

"What in the hell are you talking about?" asked Stafford.

Karen was climbing over the back of the seat and Jerimy was slapping at her hands. "No! No! You don't get it until Christmas. No opening your presents early," said Jerimy.

"Give me the son-of-a-bitch," she wheedled, half-pleading and half-snarling. In self-defense, he passed her a black, hard plastic case. Jumping from the vehicle, she had the three side snaps undone before the door was fully open.

"Holy shit!" whispered Stafford. "She really likes this crap doesn't she?"

"Always has, probably always will," smiled Jerimy.

Outside she held a short weapon. Grabbing the stock, she squeezed, pulled, and it extended to almost twice its previous length. From the case she flipped a curved thirty round magazine out and slid it home. Pulling the 't' bolt back, she let it slam home and then punched the assist rod next to the ejection port.

On top of the whole mess was a scope, the scope itself topped with a large disk almost the size of a Frisbee. Toggling an unseen switch on the side, she placed the stock against her shoulder and started swinging it in a 360-degree circle.

"That is a poodle shooter," explained Jerimy. "It's what is known as a XM-177E. A shortened version of the M-16 with collapsible stock. The barrel is really shorter than it looks. Because it is so short, the damn thing really has a bark. On the front of it is a suppressor. A silencer. It doesn't really make it silent, just quiet enough it doesn't feel like someone is slapping you on the ears when you fire it. On top is the venerable infrared scope. Similar to the Starlight, but it doesn't even need the light from stars to work. The big plate on top is like a spot-light, but it puts out light the human eye can't see. Infrared. Through the scope, it all appears green.

A sniper carries what I have. His spotter carries something like that. Works in night or daylight, and has a higher volume of fire. Not accurate to near the same range, but spits them out about 750 rounds per minute."

"And all I ever got her was flowers," mused Stafford. He looked at the .45 in his hand. "I feel kinda ripped off. Don't I get a neat toy?"

"You've got a 'neat toy.' I know your back-ground. You shot IPSC competition with that thing. International Practical Shooters Confederation. Nice. This is kinda planned out. I have a long-range weapon and know how to use it. She has an intermediate weapon and knows how to use it. You have a close range weapon and know how to use it. See how everything falls into place?"

"So what happens now?"

"Now we get dressed for the party."

⋆•⋆

"These pants are too short," complained Stafford.

"Quit whining. You have black socks on. Your ankles won't show," said Karen.

"And I don't have a holster for the pistol," he finished.

"No, Bob, you don't. You are expected to have it in your hand, in case you need to use it. Having it in a holster adds two seconds to your response time," admonished Jerimy. "Karen has point, she'll go first. We follow her."

Stafford looked confused. "Its pitch black in the trees. How will she know where she's going and how will we know where she is. Sounds like it would be easy to get separated."

Karen giggled and Jerimy explained. "Like I said. She has the infrared scope. A little hard to see things on the move, but better than showing our positions with flashlights. Every once and a while, she will turn around and smile at us, so we don't get too far apart."

"Smile at us?" asked Stafford.

He looked at Karen and she smiled. Her mouth lit up with an eerie green glow.

Jerimy smiled, but his didn't glow. "She has a small cyalume stick in her mouth. Cold light. Little plastic tube, you bend it and it glows green."

"What happens if she swallows it?" asked Stafford.

"Then her shit glows for a day or two. Other than that, non-toxic."

"Then this is going to be a piece of cake."

Jerimy shook his head. "Can't count on that. If Daily has night vision glasses or scope, the infrared on Karen's rifle will stand out like a search light. If he has a Starlight scope like mine, then we won't be able to see any indication he is there. Starlights just amplify existing light."

"Then why don't you go first with yours?"

"Ever try to walk looking through a set of binoculars? Just like that. The magnification on my scope is too high. If I had thought about it, I would have tried for some goggles."

"Then swap weapons with her," said Stafford.

Jerimy looked at Karen and then Stafford. "You want to try to take it away from her?"

"I'll pass on that," agreed Stafford.

The first half hour was anticlimactic, slow and nerve wracking. Stafford found himself drenched with sweat. While he tried to be silent, every so often his foot would come down on a twig or branch and the crack sounded like a gunshot in the darkness. Each time he would stop and a glowing mouth would turn to him, the corners of that mouth would be down turned.

Just when he thought his pounding heart would make the others stop and thump him, he stumbled over Jerimy, kneeling on the ground. Karen spit the tube into her hand, closed it tight, and whispered.

"We have movement."

ॐ∘ॐ

The night air raised hell with Daily's joints. It was not that cold, but it was humid and the dew was starting to form.

He had seen the car pull in on top of the hill. From where he sat halfway down, it was too far to risk a shot. When someone had gotten out of the car and started swinging a light around, it took him by surprise. When he raised his head from the scope, he felt a brief start of apprehension. It was night vision up there. From the way it was moving, it was probably attached to a weapon.

No problem, he decided. If he sat without moving, they would never see him. If they were coming down, he merely had to bide his time and take them when they were at spitting distance.

Patiently he watched as the infrared light flashed through the trees. They were indeed coming closer. Already they were close enough for a killing shot, but the trees...ah, yes...the trees. No way to predict if he would hit a tree instead of one of the three. Better to wait. Wait for them to hit the small clearing with a range of less than a hundred meters. Might make it a little bit more dangerous, having them that close, but ten seconds...three shots...and the mission would be accomplished. The planchette could be returned and all loose ends tied up. So he waited.

At last, they entered the clearing. Not only entered, but also came to a complete stop. How convenient! Sighting on the lead figure, he slowly let his breath out halfway. The chevron inside his scope steadied on the chest of the point man. Nothing fancy here, just a solid center of mass shot.

As his finger tightened on the trigger, the scope blurred and lit up bright green. Something was standing before him. Something big.

❈❈❈

The boom of a high-powered rifle echoed back and forth between the hillsides. The screams that followed did not.

Karen tossed the tube in a glowing arc to the ground and yelled, "Time to boogie!"

By the time the words registered, her footsteps were twenty feet away and headed for the house. Both men leapt up and gave awkward pursuit. After fifty yards, Stafford stumbled.

Hitting the ground his right arm folded under him and the .45 discharged. Regaining his feet it was another fifty yards before he realized there was a fiery stinging across the left cheek of his butt. As it didn't interfere much with running, he continued his downhill jog, flipping the safety up on the pistol.

A voice yelled back. Jerimy's. "Did you get him? Are you okay?"

"Nope…I don't think I hit him," Stafford yelled back. "Keep going."

When they hit the lawn of Stafford's house, Karen was standing there. Raising the gun above her head, it roared with a staccato booming as she emptied the thirty round magazine into the air. Turning, she ran, jumped, and planted both feet in the center of the front door. The door ripped from its hinges and folded inwards before her. Rolling to her feet, she threw the library door open and waited.

Jerimy and Stafford reached the front door at the same time. Neither looking back. The screaming sound of the alarm system was blaring, adding to the confusion and madness of the moment. Seeing Karen standing in the library, they plunged in, slamming and locking the door.

Karen reached up to the pad next to the door and punched in four numbers. Silence fell across the house.

Jerimy looked around. "Are you all okay? Any-one hit?"

Karen was staring at Bob. "Bob, you have blood on your hand. Are you hit?"

"Well…I think I caught one, but I don't think it's too serious."

Karen ran to him. "Where? Where did the bastard get you?"

"Well," Bob started, "let's just say it isn't close to my heart." He turned around.

Jerimy started laughing and Karen hit him hard in the chest. "He's wounded, you inconsiderate bastard. I'll get the first aid kit out of the bathroom here."

When she had gone, Jerimy leaned close. "Okay. Tell me the truth, hotshot. Did you shoot yourself in the ass?"

Stafford blushed. "Yes."

Jerimy grinned. "Look. Just don't tell anyone you did. Okay? I don't like you much more than yesterday, but for what its worth, sometime, I will tell you why I am missing my little toe. Just keep your mouth shut and play the hero. It won't kill you and neither will that scratch."

Karen returned with the first aide kit and yanked his pants down. Stafford grabbed them and tried to pull them back up.

"Stop that! I have to tend to it. It isn't bad, but you don't want it getting infected." She stopped. "That's strange. It's awful wide for a rifle."

Jerimy stepped closer. "Nah, the round probably hit a tree first and flattened some. Just damn lucky it deflected or it might have gotten you somewhere more serious."

Karen nodded. "Yes, it might have even been tumbling when it hit. Of course." She raised her head and listened. "Right on time."

Stafford tried turning his head to look at her. "What's right on time?"

Karen slapped a dressing on and pulled the pants back into position. "Well, I figured the phone lines might be cut. I also hoped a volley of full auto fire would attract the neighbor's attention, if the single shots didn't. The alarm was icing on the cake. You can hear the sirens coming up the valley now."

"Crap," Jerimy said. "Let me borrow the phone."

Later, the knock on the door startled them.

"Who is it?" yelled Stafford.

"Police! Open the door and come out with your hands up."

Jerimy opened the door. "Evening Clifford."

Behind the clear shield covering the officer's eyes, Jerimy could see the amusement. Behind the officer, however, the Swat team was once again deployed.

"Good evening, sir. Are you the owner or tenant of this house?"

Jerimy stared, until he figured it out. "Why no. No I am not officer." He pointed behind him to Stafford. "This gentleman is."

Stafford stepped forward. "May I help you officer?"

"Yes, sir. We had reports of automatic gunfire from this area. Upon arriving we found several dozen spent casings on your front lawn. Also, there is a trail of blood leading into this room. Did you hear anything strange, and is anyone here injured?"

Stafford shook his head innocently. "Why, no officer. We haven't heard anything. We have just been watching television."

The officer looked around. "I don't see a television."

"It's in the bathroom."

"And the blood, sir?"

"I cut myself shaving while I was in the front yard."

Clifford looked down at the blood soaked pants Stafford wore. "Of course, sir. I knew there would be a logical explanation. I will alleviate any concerns your neighbors might have."

He leaned towards Jerimy and whispered. "You bastard. I want those guns back by noon, and YOU write this damn report up for me." He stopped, then whispered again, "You need any more ammo or anything?"

Jerimy thought, then whispered back. "Naw. We're set for ammo, but could you leave a couple guys on guard here? I think there's a problem."

The officer stepped back. "Sir, just to be safe. I believe – if it's okay with you – I will leave a couple men just to secure the area. I will remove them in the morning," he announced. Without another word, he turned and left.

Jerimy stood in the door and suddenly grabbed the doorjamb. Stafford asked, "What's the matter?"

The detective stooped and picked something up from beside the door. He handed it to Stafford.

"Oh, yeah. Oh, shit. Oh...," in his hands was the planchette, covered in blood.

After a few minutes of mutual panic, Karen brought them back to task.

"Don't you think we should do what we came here for?"

Stafford looked lost. "What do you mean?"

"Well, we wanted to find out about Daily, if I remember correctly."

Stafford jumped up from the couch and threw himself into the chair at the desk. He gave the mouse of his computer a cuff and waited for the computer to come out of its sleep mode. When the monitor lit up, his face went dark. "If I had mail, it would say so."

Jerimy looked over his shoulder. "Do you have any other email addresses?"

"None." Stafford stopped. "Hold it. I don't have to check my email. I have to surf the web. Yeah, that was what it was!" He clicked at random on his favorites list.

"Isn't that a porn site?" asked Jerimy.

"How would you know from that name?" asked Karen.

Whether it was or not, Jerimy would never know. The screen went blue.

"Figures!" Stafford tossed the mouse off the table, it dangled spinning helplessly like some small creature being hung. "BSOD. Blue screen of Death." He pushed back from the table. "I spent seventy-five big ones to have my computer crash."

They jumped once more at the knock on the door. Jerimy yelled out, "Who is it?"

"Just open the door Jerimy, we have to talk," came Clifford's voice.

When Jerimy opened the door, Clifford's face was pale and grim. "Look man, I don't know what's going on here, but this isn't going to stay under wraps for more than two more minutes. One of my guys just found a body...or bodies...hell, we can't tell. There is blood and pieces scattered for thirty feet." He pointed his finger at Jerimy. "Just answer me this. With no bullshit. You guys have anything…anything at all…to do with this?"

Jerimy put his hands up. "No. Nothing. I will bet you that it's the guy who took a pot shot at Stafford earlier today. If I had seen him, I would have popped him. No doubt about that, but we didn't do it."

"I didn't think you did. I don't know how you could without a chain saw, but I had to ask. Look, I'm putting the entire squad around the house. More are on the way, including the coroner and your buddies in homicide. If they ask, you just got the weapons. You stay inside. And here…," he dug in the pocket of his jacket, "keep this handy." He a baseball sized object in Jerimy's hands. "It ain't a flash bang. It isn't department issue. It doesn't exist." He looked at Karen. "And don't let your girl friend play with it, no matter what she says." He hesitated. "You realize Internal Affairs is going to hang our asses on this, no matter what?" Without waiting for an answer he walked off.

When Clifford was gone, he looked at it. Karen came over.

"What is it?" asked Stafford.

"Whoa, you can keep that one," said Karen. She turned to Stafford. "Fragmentation grenade. Military. That's the original and industrial strength can of whoop ass."

"I guess he figured we were fucked anyway. Might as well go for broke." Jerimy smiled. "I got cute and we got caught."

The harsh ringing of the phone broke the silence. Hitting the speakerphone button, Stafford said, "Hello?"

"Listen closely and don't talk. Wouldn't do ya any good. This recording will be sent out at 4:00 a.m. If you don't answer and aren't listening to this, too bad. It won't repeat.

By now you have gone online, if you are still alive, which I doubt. You probably noticed you have some computer problems. Your computer is trashed. It won't stand up to a search for deleted files, and you don't know how to shred deleted files. Burn the damn thing if you can.

I am not here anymore. Period. Don't bother to try to contact me. I was wrong. I am good, but there is at least one person out there that is better. I wish I had asked for a lot more, because I am never going near a machine again. You, my friend, are trippin' along the edge of the twilight zone.

Your friend Daily isn't with any country you might think of. He is sponsored by the nice people in Rome. He is one of the best. He is supposed to retrieve something called, 'the planchette of the devil.'

Figures. He is supposed to eliminate anyone who was exposed to it.

Thompson was a genetic scientist. Spetzer was also. Spetzer got a hold of this planchette thing. This is crazy man, but supposedly it has a protective covering or something and they extracted DNA from it. Good DNA. They cloned the cells more than twenty years ago. Way far ahead of their times, dude. Their funding came from black ops. Somewhere there is a person floating around, likely in the military, who doesn't have a papa and mama, as we know it. No name, just a number. D-41.

The planchette does something. I don't know what. I know it scares the bejesus out of everyone who does know what it is.

My suggestion is embezzling what ever funds you can from your rag and find a third world country that doesn't have lights or phones, let alone computers."

The room was silent, except for the sound of Karen vomiting.

Jerimy put his arms around her. Stafford was concerned, "Is she okay? What's the matter?"

Jerimy looked over the top of her head. "You really don't know?"

"No, I mean its scary, the phone call and all...but, is she sick or something?"

Tears filled Jerimy's eyes. "No, she's not sick. Oh, my god. You don't know. I am so sorry. I am so sorry to both of you."

Karen was crying now and Stafford asked, "What the hell are you sorry about? I am lost again."

"I believe you now. I should have believed her before. You don't know. You just don't know."

Jerimy held Karen and rocked her in his arms. "If you had ever...if you had been intimate with her, you would know. She has a tattoo."

"Lotta people have tattoos. Hell, I have one of a spider on my arm."

Jerimy shook his head sadly. "Not the same. Below her belly button. We are talking real far below her belly button she has a little blue tat."

"Cool," said Stafford. "I would have liked to seen it. What is it? Dolphin? Butterfly? Crossed swords?"

Jerimy closed his eyes. "She doesn't know where it came from. Must have been put there when she was an infant. Just says, 'D-41.'"

CHAPTER XIII
The Jigsaw Comes Together

The mallard duck swam like a feathered torpedo. It slashed its green head underwater and grabbed at the sinking morsel. When its head came up, it shimmied, giving off a fine spray of water.

With a listless motion, Karen reached in the bag and brought out another piece of dry bread. The bench she sat on was warm. The sun shining down from the clear blue sky was warm. Her soul felt cold. She took a crunchy bite herself, and tossed the remains into the water.

The park was full of people, yet she felt so alone. Jerimy wandered up with a paper cup full of coffee.

"Sure you don't want one?" he asked.

"Naw." She looked around at the people drifting past. The bread she tossed performed its magic, two more ducks were drawn like magnets to it. "I just don't feel 'real' anymore. I guess I am even questioning if I am human."

Jerimy started to laugh, but thought better of it. "I know it opens up a lot of questions, but I think it is safe to say you are a real live human being. Is it even all true? We can't be sure yet."

"It's true. It feels true." She stood and stretched. "Where's Bob?"

"He took off for a couple hours. Making sure his magazine was going to press on time; making sure they hadn't removed his desk and name plate, all the little things he worries about."

"I have been giving this a lotta thought," Karen started, "and it all falls into place. It bothers me, but it all makes sense. I'm not sure how they would have gotten viable DNA from the damn thing."

Jerimy shrugged. "If I had to make a guess, I'd put a buck on that shitty-weird blue glow you say you see around it."

"If I am a clone...and that would account for never having seen, or known my parents, for being raised as a military orphan...which is so unusual, then I have to figure I am some sort of spawn of Morriagan. The second born."

"How do you figure?" asked Jerimy. "It could have been the first born."

"I suppose there is that possibility, but it's doubtful. If they used their blood the first time...both of them...it is just possible. The first born was promptly killed. Most of the blood that went into that damned thing was from Morriagan." She shivered. "I feel like a sadistic, bloodthirsty bitch now."

"Before you get wrapped up in picturing yourself a satanic Druid priestess, you might want to put it in perspective. At that time, the twins were raised and trained for what they...or at least one of them...became. It was part of their lifestyle and culture. It wasn't even considered bad or evil." He shrugged again. "Hell's Bells...they might have been the equivalent of Druid deputies, or something."

"That isn't a lot of consolation." Karen turned to Jerimy. He sat on the bench and pulled her back, sitting her next to him.

Holding her hand, he continued. "Okay, well think of this. Your being a 'clone' of this Morriagan, might be why we are still alive. Look at the facts.

That creature ripped up a lot of folks. It didn't touch us."

"It might not have gotten a chance," said Karen.

Jerimy did laugh this time. "Oh, I think it had a chance. It was at the house that night when you, Bob and the fake Spetzer were there, and I think the damn thing was trying to get to Spetzer then...to keep you safe.

When we went back to the house, it was out there in the dark along with Spetzer. It could have taken us out just as easy as it did him. However, it didn't. It took him out and spared us. He was trying to kill us. It stopped him. It even brought the planchette back to you and left it outside the door like a dog retrieving a newspaper."

"You might be reading a lot into this that isn't there," said Karen.

"Yes. Yes, I might be. You might be also."

"Well, this isn't one of those things where, 'it followed me home, can I keep it?'"

Jerimy grinned. "No, you are absolutely right. But since it was evidently summoned, there has to be a way of buying it a bus ticket back home. Wherever the hell home is for it."

Karen stared at him. "I think you named it. I think its home is hell." She stood once more, still holding his hand. "Let's go. I think we should pay Bob a visit at work."

❧⟡☙

The Spectral Images office was Jeckel and Hyde in its atmosphere. Walking through the heavy glass doors, the receptionist area looked quite normal and sane. Thick carpeting squished softly underfoot, muted track lighting gave all an air of respectability; in the background light pop instrumentals played.

The receptionist herself flashed them a professional smile, lacking in warmth, but not teeth. "Karen! So good to see you again, my dear."

"Morning Janice. Is the head honcho in?"

The receptionist picked up a notebook and ran her finger down the front. "Oh, yes. He's in. Strict orders not to be disturbed." She reached in her desk drawer and pulled a small plastic card. "Here, you'll need this. He changed all the codes. I had people lined up for an hour this morning, trying to get back into the zoo."

Karen turned the card in her hand. "Strict orders not to be disturbed?"

"Yes, dearie. Since he ranted and raved about that to me, and caused me such grief with the new cards...I've been sending everyone back to bug him."

"Thanks, Janice."

"No problem, dearie."

At the small, gray door in the corner, Jerimy and Karen stopped. The door had no window to indicate the world that lay behind it. Placing the card against a metal plate next to the handle, a green light lit for a moment. When it went off, a click sounded and the handle turned freely.

The room beyond was indeed a zoo. Cubicles stretched out before them like cages. Some had makeshift walls extended upwards, so none could look into them. Music blared from many. Here a ragged Hip-Hop sounded. From the one next to it, heavy metal blared. Quiet ballads were drowned out by country and western. "Didn't any of these people hear about head phones?" asked Jerimy.

"That's why it's so loud," answered Karen. "Most have head phones on, typing text from recordings. In order to hear the music over the headphones, they have the boom boxes cranked up."

In some cubes people sat typing frantically at their computers. At others, people sat under the desktops, reading. Clothing ranged from suits and ties to hole pocked cutoffs, with no shirt or shoes. While not positive, Jerimy was pretty sure a couple of the workers were naked.

Stopping at the fax machine, Karen inquired of a man with blue dreadlocks and multiple piercings, "Hey! Is the golden guru still around?"

The guy pointed with his foot towards the back of the room. "Yeah, but beware. The crazy mo-fug is wearing a pistol. He seems a bit stressed out. He hasn't sat down all morning and seems rather hyper."

Upon reaching Stafford's office, they could see him through the window. He sat in a chair in the corner with his back to the wall. *Not a good habit*, thought Jerimy. In truth, he wasn't wearing a pistol. It sat on the desktop, next to his coffee cup. Smiling Karen reached up and tapped on the window. Stafford's eyes went to the window and his hand to the gun.

"Come on in," he mouthed.

"Morning Bob," said Jerimy. He pointed to the gun. "Does this mean you need to cut back on the caffeine, or are you still worried about your health?"

Remarkably, Stafford smiled, "It's kinda like health insurance. I don't figure I need it, but if I do it's hard to call 'time-out,' and go home and get it." He shrugged. "Plus, I haven't had even one asshole come in and ask for a raise." He looked at Karen. "And how are you doing?"

Karen considered the question. "Well, let's see. I found out that I am actually someone - maybe some one vile and evil - who lived several thousand years ago. I also seem to have a pet that is either going to kill me, save me, or ignore me. Not a parakeet mind you, but something that tears people apart and then eats their brains."

Stafford looked at Jerimy. "She seems to be taking it better than I figured she would. At least she isn't armed to the teeth. That I can see." He qualified.

"I figure the guns didn't do me much good. They've been tried by others and the others aren't here anymore," said Karen.

"So you are going hand-to-hand now? That's ballsy." Stafford said admiringly.

Jerimy cleared his throat. "Not exactly." He pointed to a tightly wrapped bundle slung over Karen's shoulder. "That isn't a pool cue."

"One of those Japanese samurai swords?" asked Stafford.

Karen slid the cloth strap off her shoulder. The top of the bundle pulled off, the sound of the Velcro distinct. Her eyes narrowing, she pulled the sword from its sheath.

"No," she said. "It's *based* on the Japanese katana, but it never came close to Japan. It was actually made in a small town in Montana. A knife maker by the name of Bill Taggart." With a flick of her wrist, the blade hissed through the air and stopped in front of her. "It is Damascus steel; what's called a 'usable' blade. Probably not as good as one of the old Japanese blades, but it is definitely not for show only." Slowly she slid it back into its sheath. "Sharp enough to shave with anyway."

"What makes you think it will work better than a gun?" Stafford asked, fingering his pistol.

"I am not sure. A bullet pokes holes in things. Big holes, granted, but holes nevertheless. If something comes after me at close range, I intend on removing things like arms, legs and heads. Then I will see how it responds to that."

"The way you say that," Jerimy shook his head, "it sounds like that is a certainty, not a possibility."

"Yes," she nodded. "I have come to a decision. Not a split second decision either, I have given it a bit of thought."

"I don't want to rain on your parade, but considering the age it came from, swords have probably been tried."

Karen pushed some papers aside and sat on the corner of Stafford's desk. "We are at an impasse. It doesn't look like anyone is left who is going to willingly step forward and explain this mess. We also have no proof that the killings are finished, or that the creature...Samhan...is gone from our quaint little area."

Bob and Jerimy both spoke at the same time.

"There are still law enforcement avenues open to explore..."

"I still have some contacts..."

Karen waived the ideas aside. "We would have to get our information straight from some source, a well hidden source, inside the government, or from the Vatican. I really doubt we can do that. Even if we did glean some information, there is really no way we would be able to tell if it was bullshit or not."

Stafford stretched back in his chair. "Then what sources do you intend on interrogating?"

"I don't like where this is headed," said Jerimy.

CHAPTER XIV
Internal Affairs and a Brick Wall

The knock on the door had the ring of authority. The face in the window caused all the color to drain from Jerimy's face.

"Oh Christ," he muttered under his breath. "We have got major problems. I thought this, of all places, would be safe to hide."

"If we ignore the person, then might the person and the problem go away?" asked Stafford hopefully.

"No. That sickening visage is the head watchdog, maggot and ass kissing investigator from Internal Affairs. His name is Nathan Towbin. I didn't expect this bullshit so soon,"

"He looks happy, though. Maybe he has good news and is not here to fuck with us," said Stafford. "Look. He's holding a note up. What's it say?"

Karen leaned closer. "It's written on the back of a business card and says," she squinted her eyes, "um, 'I got your sorry ass this time you low life piece of shit, your friends and their little dog Toto, too."

"What the hell?" asked Stafford, leaning towards the card.

"I made the part up about the dog, but the rest is all there," apologized Karen.

"Don't feel bad. If we had a dog he would include it," said Jerimy.

The man grew tired of waiting for an invitation, tried the door knob, and let himself in. Stafford bristled then snapped, "I don't know who the hell you are, but I am pretty damn sure you need a warrant for something you're about to do."

The man laughed. "Nathan Towbin. You can call me Mr. Towbin. Good to meet you."

"So, does that mean you get a warrant Mr. Towbin?"

Towbin smiled. "Shut the fuck up, Stafford."

Stafford jumped to his feet.

"You want to tell the paper-pusher he better sit down, before I show him just how bad things can get, Jerimy?" Towbin smiled sweetly.

"Bob. Can it for a bit. Let's get our bearings first."

Towbin waved his hands, "It's okay. Don't sweat it." He grinned. "You don't even have to say a word." His eyes narrowed. "In fact it would be better if you didn't. Like in 'you have the right to remain silent.'"

He slowly paced back and forth. "Ma'am? Please realize that this doesn't apply in full to yourself.

Jerimy, old friend, as of immediately your badge is pulled. I could show you the list, but it just contains mundane little things like misappropriation of weapons, endangerment of officers under your command and failure to perform your duties in a timely, professional and unbiased fashion.

If you are interested, a warrant has been served at your place of residence and a truly remarkable amount of weapons taken into our possession, pending verification of legal ownership. I was particularly impressed by the grenade. I think I will keep it in my trophy collection. Want to tell me where you got it?"

Jerimy shook his head.

He held out his hand for Jerimy's badge. Jerimy held it out, dropping it to the ground just before it reached Towbin's hand. Towbin looked down at it and simply shook his head.

"Mr. Stafford...may I call you Robert?" Towbin asked.

"Fuck you."

"A short and most concise response, Mr. Stafford," Towbin said. "But I'm afraid it's really 'fuck you,' sir. You had a choice between silence, civility or hostility." He shook his head sorrowfully. "You made your choice, now I make mine. I regret to inform you that you house and its property has been declared a crime scene and it is off limits to yourself and all civilians until it has been processed. We should be done in about," he studied the ceiling, "oh, hell, let's look at it optimistically...say about two weeks."

Towbin smiled and tipped his hat.

"Well, "I think that just about covers it. I've got your badge, I need your duty weapon. SIG, 9 mm, serial number 3478, if you will be so kind."

Karen was frowning as Jerimy produced the requested item. "Are there any restrictions placed on me or my apartment?" she asked.

Towbin shook his head. "No restrictions at all ma'am. I thank you for your cooperation." He turned to Stafford. "Mr. Stafford, I'm afraid your .45 is required for inspection."

"I have a permit for it," Stafford stated.

Karen broke in, "There's no restrictions...its not taped off...I or others can go there and get things?"

"Mr. Stafford. I am aware you have a permit for your gun, and I am not interested in taking the permit. Just the gun. Now if you didn't have it you *would* be arrested. And Ma'am, rest easy about access to your place, although you should be advised, it was gutted by fire and was declared completely and totally destroyed."

He stopped at the door.

"Have a pleasant day."

CHAPTER XV
Who You Gunna Call?

"Well, I'm at a loss," Jerimy said miserably.

The three of them were sitting in the dark corner of a bar. A bar that they normally wouldn't be caught dead in.

They had separated for almost five hours, trying to regroup. Trying to assimilate all that had happened. It had been a rude awakening at best.

He sipped slowly at the bourbon and coke. "I have talked to all my buddies in blue, the crew in crime scene investigation and every marker that I had out there, or thought I had out there."

He sat his glass squarely on a damp and torn napkin. "Not only will no one help me, they won't even talk to me.

The shift supervisors, swat personnel, guys I came up through the ranks with." He smirked. "I went from being king shit to just plain shit. Anyone else have any better luck?"

"Define better luck. You know these Jell-O shooters taste strange, but they sure give you a buzz," said Karen. "I ran around with Bob. Except for the clothes on my back, everything else in my life is ashes. Bank accounts, credit cards and anything with monetary value is tied up. Seems someone reported my life as an identity theft. I have about forty dollars in my pocket."

Stafford raised his glass to his partners in salute.

"Ladies and gentlemen. Boys and girls of all ages. We have been slammed by the best.

The Federal government has clamped down on me. They have thrown paper road blocks in front of everything I can think of." He lit a cigarette and leaned back.

"The I.R.S. has locked down anything that can generate money that has my name on it," Swirling the last of his drink he downed it and motioned for another.

"I even contacted the Screen Guild, some actors and personalities to see if I could get a helping hand. We seem to have developed a bad case of the plague. Anyone that associates with us will be steam rolled." He picked up his fresh drink. "We've been shut down."

Karen attempted to attract the bartender's attention. He looked at her, looked at the clock, picked up the bar tab and scowled,

"Boys, I think we've reached the end." Karen was more depressed than anyone could remember seeing her.

"I'm a fucking clone. God knows who the hell brewed me up, and it's a monster I was cloned from. To top it off I can't get another beer."

Jerimy shook his head. "No, technically that's wrong. You weren't cloned from the monster itself, you were just cloned from a psychopath."

"Yeah," Stafford offered, "the monster is just following you around killing people."

Karen's eyes welled with tears and a sob tore from her throat. Stafford looked at Jerimy. "Crap, I don't think we're making this better."

"Ya think?"

As they sat there, each immersed in their own thoughts, a man walked through the front door. He stood for a moment letting his eyes adjust to the darkness,

His head snapped up when he recognized Stafford. He moved his hands out to his sides, specifically showing they were empty. He started walking towards Stafford.

Rob, Jerimy and Karen watched in silence and with growing tension. The person was well dressed. Not the type who would frequent a bar. A club, perhaps, but not a dive.

It was also obvious he had sized all the patrons up before he moved forward. He continued until he stood in front of Stafford.

He removed his sunglasses, revealing dead eyes. "Mr. Robert Stafford?"

Stafford didn't trust his voice, and restricted himself to nodding.

The man nodded back, replaced his sunglasses and smiled. His smile indicated it was something he seldom did, and needed practice at.

"Mr. Stafford. My business associate, Mr. Tagollini, sincerely requests that you join him for supper this evening. He wanted me to be sure and mention that your friends, the secretary and the flat foot - your pardon - the police officer, are included in the invitation. He stresses that he would look upon your acceptance as a personal favor to himself and we would be in your debt." He looked all three up and down slowly. "What answer would you like me to take to Mr. Tagollini?"

"That we would be honored, of course," said Stafford.

The man visibly relaxed and his smile looked more authentic now. "Hey," he said, "don't you mooks sweat it. When you leave here a car will take you to my restaurant. It will be closed...for private conversation you understand, and it will be informal. You don't have to dress up."

With that he turned and left.

Jerimy stared at Stafford. "I will bet it's Italian food. Is this person a um...close friend of yours?"

Stafford looked like he'd swallowed a razor blade. "No. No not exactly a friend. Just an acquaintance that I *didn't* write a story about."

Jerimy grinned. "What? A story about where Elvis is hanging out or where Hoffa is buried?"

Stafford just stared at Jerimy.

Jerimy swallowed, "You're shittin' me. Are you telling me you know where...no, wait...nothing. I don't want to hear nothing."

CHAPTER XVI
Manners

Limos would be very easy to get addicted to. Sure, stepping out of a sleazy bar and into a stretched limo gave a bit of a Fellini touch of surrealism, but that was easy to get over when your ass hit the real leather.

Jerimy watched out the tinted windows. "This is a dangerous game you're playing. You know that."

Stafford just nodded.

"Tagollini is about as big a hitter as you run across. You do a lot of business with him?"

Stafford shook his head. "I have had the honor of spending about fifteen minutes with him. Just long enough to have one drink."

Jerimy raised his eyebrows.

"It's true," Stafford continued. "I had gotten a lead about...um...something and was going to check it out. Mr. Tagollini sent for me and we discussed the alleged incident. He confirmed what I suspected. He told me he would consider it a favor if I did not break the story." Stafford smiled. "You know what, though? He never threatened me. He said he would *understand* what ever I decided.

He actually went out of his way to make sure I knew he wasn't threatening me. Seems he considers it a mortal offense to threaten."

"So, what would have happened if you printed the story?" asked Jerimy.

"Oh, hell. They would have found me with my head blown off by his *associate*, floating in the river somewhere."

"But that isn't a threat?"

"No. It's strange. He made it seem like I was being a nice guy and helping a friend out. Not a 'do it or else' situation."

"So why are we going out for dinner?" asked Jerimy.

"Beats the hell out of me."

"They might. Maybe they have a good salad bar," said Karen

&0&6

From the beginning, the meal had started with an uncomfortable feeling. No one else was present in the restaurant except them, Mr. Tagollini, and four rather serious looking gentlemen. Two of them at each door.

Tagollini was an older man, age somewhere around fifty. He was an attentive host who did not pressure his guests during dinner. Only slowly did conversation turn to business, and even then it was gently steered in that direction.

"I must apologize," he said, lighting a cigar after pushing his plate back. "I admit I am at a bit of a loss in this conversation. I sit with a man whose profession is admittedly an opposite of my own. Another man I know to be a man of his word, and a most gracious woman who is as dangerous as she is beautiful." He puffed on the cigar, then waved it in the air.

"I will tell you of the most astounding thing that occurred to me, and then some facts I gleaned through my uh...sources. Then, after my display of ah, trust, then perhaps you will enlighten me by filling in the blanks."

"Yesterday, I was peacefully doing business. Life was good and I was looking forward to treating the grandchildren to an afternoon at the zoo." He leaned back. "Then, about 10:00 in the morning, this aberrant creature pushes his way into my office, flashing some piss ant identification, whining and identifying himself as some government lackey.

He mentioned your name Mr. Stafford. He seemed to believe we were business partners, or perhaps I was going to perform some service for you. A belief I did not feel compelled to verify or disavow. Then," Tagollini looked dumbfounded, "he told me that if I *knew what was good for me*, I would offer you no assistance."

Tagollini shook his head. "I felt that it must have been a most grievous error. Surely he had misinterpreted his instructions and information. I was so sure of this that I let him live. I hope you do not mind, I had no time to consult with you. With extensive physical therapy he may even walk again." Tagollini walked to the counter and returned with a small container of toothpicks.

"Life is too short to take these things to heart, so I put it from my mind. Then," he paused, "Then I received a visit from Cardinal Bucard. Then a visit from the F.B.I. This was all followed by the D.E.A. on my doorstep.

Fuck'em, feed'em fish heads."

He raised his hands, "But still…a visit from someone representing the Vatican? You represent God, you have my attention, Paisano."

Tagollini closed his eyes. "We talked for a long time. We talked of religions old when Christ was young. We talked of demons immortal. We talked of the nice lady dining with us, and her roots. It would appear that it was a joint effort between the World Health Organization, the Vatican, and the military." He saluted Karen with his napkin. "An accomplishment. None of those three can work with themselves, let alone together.

Amazingly your freedom was assured because of your appendix. You were on an outing, a vacation, you got sick, your appendix came out at a small hospital, the surrogate parents went back to the agency that night, a piddly fire ensued; all records were destroyed, leaving only two doctors that knew the whole truth. Benson and Spetzner. You were a ward of the state for a month, Dr. Benson stroked out, died; the politicians had no idea who or what you really were, Spetzner tried to sweep the whole thing under the rug and you became a military orphan. The left hand had no clue what the right had been doing.

Trouble is, now the wheels are turning in a half dozen agencies; and they want the rug and what's under it. Namely you. Failing that, at least a most special piece of wood. They could always make another you, the planchette…not so easy."

He poured several glasses of brandy and passed them out. "Now," he said, "if you feel comfortable, please talk to me of your recent adventures. I do promise you. I will honor the trust you place in me, and who knows," he shrugged, "perhaps in some small way I might be of assistance."

Three hours later the talk was finished. Karen summed up the feelings of the group. "We all feel that we are in the right and doing the best for man."

Jerimy agreed. "Yes. Even Daily could justify killing Spetzer and lying. He even had the backing of the Vatican."

"So what the hell do we do now?" asked Karen.

"We aren't too partial to being shit on, either," offered Stafford.

"What you do now is up to you. There are a lot of options. You can turn the whole mess over to the church. You can give everything back to the military for their usage. The medical field is always interested in new things to dissect. Even if it's you, young lady. Or," Tagollini hesitated, "you could pursue the path intended thousands of years ago."

"Whoa..." said Stafford. "Just what the hell are you talking about?"

Karen answered. "I think I understand what you're getting at. This was originally a thing for good. Yeah, there was a lot of bloody deeds and sacrifice, but that really just reflected the religions of the time and the people."

"And the people ripped to shreds and their brains eaten? What exactly is the positive spin on that?" asked Stafford.

"If you hand a group of people a loaded gun who know nothing about the use and potential danger; you are probably going to see some casualties," said Tagollini.

"I know that you think I am Mafia, Cosa Nostra, organized crime or such. All I can say is I'm not. I belong to a group that started over two thousand years ago. We don't even have a name - just a symbol. Cross with a circle. Don't make me tell you more, because I can't. All from here on would be lies. It is not that I would want to, but without knowing your intent..." He spread his hands on the table.

Jerimy came up with the best idea. "We need to sleep on this and make no decisions in haste."

"The cop is right," Tagollini agreed. "I will put you up in a safe house and put some of my...security around it for your protection. You can decide what to do in the morning."

"Tagollini. What gives? Why are you even getting involved in this? What's in it for you?" Jerimy asked.

Tagollini met his gaze without flinching. "That is quite simple. I was told not to. 'Or else.' I would hate to go the rest of my life without knowing what 'or else' was." He smiled a cold smile. "And maybe I have to do something because it was decreed 2025 years ago." He smiled. "Pablo said it would bode ill if we were not to offer ourselves to you."

He raised his hand and quietly snapped his fingers. One of the men standing next to the front door approached.

"John," Tagollini said softly. "It seems our friends here are having a slight problem that we can help with." He looked up. "Is the war house in order?"

The man looked concerned. "Yeah, boss. But it's ah...fully stocked if you know what I mean."

"I am aware of that," Tagollini said.

"Might that not be a problem?" The man asked; nodding at Jerimy.

"Might there be anything there of interest to the D.E.A?" asked Tagollini.

"No sir, but the BATF and the IRS would have a shit fit."

Tagollini smiled. "I don't think our guests will be too upset with the furnishings, then. They are aware of the ways of the world." He handed a set of keys to Stafford. "These are car and house keys. They fit a Hum V out back. Pablo will be your guide and host."

He went out the front as they went out the back.

CHAPTER XVII
Safe House and the Creature

Outside, Pablo led them to the back of the parking lot. He opened the driver's door for Jerimy and cursed softly at a red light blinking on the dash.

"Quickly," he snapped, "get your butts in gear and get the hell out of here."

Jerimy called after him, speaking to his rapidly disappearing back, "What the hell is wrong?"

"That blinking light means that something very close at hand is being painted by a laser."

"What's that mean?" Stafford asked as he was bodily being pushed into the back by Tagollini's associate. The man hastily jumped in, shouting all the time, "Go, go, go, go…"

Jerimy power slid onto the road. Karen was being slammed violently against the door as she struggled to fasten the seat belt.

Stafford looked back in time to see the main body of the restaurant change to a black and yellow flash of flame and a shock wave shimmer outwards at the speed of sound.

"Oh, this sucks," said Pablo. "We've a slight change in plans. I will accompany you to the safe house. My name's Pablo, by the way. Forgive me for not introducing myself fully at the bar." He grinned broadly, "I think Mr. Tagollini knows what they meant by *or else*. That was a drive by shooting by a gang whose motto is 'Be all that you can be.'"

Swafford's mouth was dry and he had to swallow a couple times before speaking. "If that's really the government, then we are basically screwed."

"I won't play it down, but if they push us, we tend to push back." Pablo said.

Swafford managed a sickly smile; Jerimy said, "Really?" Swafford, you seem to know about these people. They have the cojones to push back against federal muscle?"

Swafford looked warily at Pablo, and semi-whispered, "Yeah, they do."

"And exactly how…" Started Jerimy.

"You ever hear of Dallas and a book depository? The view from the grassy knoll is amazing," said Pablo.

The rest of the drive to the house was in silence.

The house itself was non-descript, but very well made. Windows were small, single story structure and a large yard. A very large yard,

From the house to the nearest cover was fifty yards. Jerimy commented on that fact.

"Makes it kind of hard to sneak up on someone," he said approvingly.

"Doesn't make a helluva lot of difference if they use a smart bomb from 25,000 feet up," Karen pointed out.

"Yeah, what's going to keep them from doing that again?" asked Swafford.

"Not much, but it's kinda like this. You go outside and fire a gun in the air once, and people might ignore it or let it go with an explanation. You do it more than once and it will definitely attract attention…and reprisal," said Pablo. He shrugged, "Mr. Tagollini might let by gones be by gones when it comes to a near miss like the restaurant, but there is no way he would let another incident go by." Pablo looked at them. "Nor would I. That would be poor business judgment."

He tossed the house keys to Swafford. "Go ahead and check it out." He turned to Karen. "May I take a look at your blade, please?"

Karen eyed him for a moment, then drew the sword and presented it handle first. Are you familiar with katanas?"

Pablo just laughed. "Ah, pretty lady…yes…and no. I'm from the barrio. If it can be sharpened I've handled it, but if you mean am I proficient with it…not really. I prefer the sticks," he smiled at her again, "if you know what I mean."

He handed the sword back in the same manner he had received it.

Karen nodded, "Escrima. I have seen the style, but never ever studied it."

"No problem. You ever want to pick it up, you let me know. I teach it down at the kid's clubs. On the weekends," he pointed towards the door, "just to give a little back to my homies.

We'll take a peek at your new home." He turned and scanned the trees surrounding the yard. No homes or buildings were within two miles.

Karen whispered, sotto voice, "You are aware that there are a half dozen people out there watching us?"

"There had better be seven of them. I was supposed to be the eighth...and I will be after you're settled in.

I should tell you...they are there to stop any people. If they should happen to run across your little friend, they will attempt to give you a head's up, but they will not engage unless they are actively attacked. There is reason for this, but I can't really tell you much. You place us in a predicament," he shuddered, "we should be protecting both of you, but how does one do that when it appears one...or both...are actively aggressive to each other." He looked at her with a solemn expression. "Give that some thought."

The grins on the faces of both Stafford and Jerimy were both contagious and uncontrolled when they came out of the house. They looked like two children left unchaperoned in a toy store.

"Karen," Stafford started.

"Oh, babe. You gotta..." Jerimy said.

"Check this out." Finished Stafford.

They passed by two bedrooms and stopped in front of a third. Without speaking, Jerimy pushed the door open with his foot.

The toys were stacked all the way around the room to a height if three feet.

Jerimy waved at the neatly labeled plastic boxes, "If you can think of it, it's there. Colt, Smith and Wesson, Dan Wesson, Glock, H&K, Beretta, you name it."

"And the stack of wooden boxes in the center doesn't have the selection of handguns, but it does seem there are about fifty full auto Kalashnikovs." said Stafford.

"We got a great deal on AK-47s," said Pablo. "If you look in the closet, you will find ammunition for any or all." He finished apologetically, "It's all FMJ, but of good quality."

Jerimy looked sheepish. "I know that firearms don't have a great track record with this, er, thing, but it does make me feel better."

"Instead of thing, creature, monster or whatever; how about we call it by its name. Samhan. It makes it just a little bit less spooky and scary when you can put a name to it," Karen said.

"Sure. Why not. It works for me."

"I second the motion." said Stafford. "Is anybody here hungry? I have to admit, I'm more tired than famished."

"Well, I think we have it covered for security. Mr. Tagollini has supplied a talented group of watchdogs." He smiled. "I also noted that there are three bedrooms, and one of which doesn't have a bed, because it is serving as an armory."

He looked pointedly at Karen. "I guess you and I could double up. We do need our rest and all.

Karen's face looked amazed for a second and then a glower of biblical proportions set in place. "I don't believe it. I am with two men; the only two I can barely stand, and neither of you have the fucking slightest idea of what romantic is."

She stepped back. "Enough. Enough already. You both can have a bedroom to yourselves, and be damned." She smiled sweetly, "The couch looks comfortable. I can snuggle one of its pillows and it won't even give me a ration of shit." With that, she stormed off.

Stafford looked at Jerimy and offered, "Hell, it sounded like a good line to me." He snickered. "I was rooting for you all the way."

Later, how much later Karen did not know, she awoke. For a moment she looked around, unsure of where she was.

The images of the past days came crashing down on her and it was overwhelming. She stood and slowly felt her way towards Jerimy's room. The light coming in from the small exterior windows was intense, even with the curtains pulled. As she passed the front door she hesitated and felt an obsession to open the door. Waves of dismay swept over her, but she was compelled to unlatch the dead bolt and pull the door open.

Nothing.

A quiet evening with cool night air. The grounds were lit almost as well as if high noon. She could see vague shadows of the distant tree line, but it was far to dark at that distance to see the guardians posted there.

It seemed very anticlimactic.

Closing the door, she sat down, leaning her back up against the door and pulling her knees up and holding them with her arms.

She sat there, listening to the crickets and just feeling the night wind rustle her hair gently. At some time, unknown and unbidden, sleep overcame her.

When she awoke, she could hear breathing. Almost a heavy, deep and rumbling purr. While she didn't open her eyes, she heard the breathing stop for a beat, then start again slightly faster and without the purring throb.

"Who are you?" she asked to the darkness behind her closed eyelids.

The voice that answered was soft, silken and soothing. It echoed in her mind as well as her ears.

"Of the many questions I anticipated, that was not one of them, for I can tell from the scent of your blood you know that answer."

"You are Samhan," said Karen.

"Yes, but I am confused. You smell of Morriagan." A wetness touched her shoulder. "Indeed you taste of Morriagan and I find I accept you as Morriagan. That, however, is impossible. She died millenniums ago. I was present and held her gray head at her passing. I had the honor of eating her hot, but still, heart."

Karen opened her eyes. She gave a start, but found she was not surprised. What confronted her seemed…familiar.

Samhan was large. Larger than a black panther, which he remotely resembled.

In weight he would run an easy five hundred pounds. The body was cat-like, but crossed with man. For some reason the word werecat came to mind.

No fur. She could see no fur. Without thinking, she reached out and pulled the demon body closer. It offered no resistance as she let her hands roam the deadly being's face and shoulders as a rough tongue stroked her hair.

"I will tell you of your past life. In turn you will tell me of your present."

Just before daylight, Stafford staggered to the door and opened it. He was looking for Karen. His blurry eyes found her and more.

Sitting on the steps, with the creature's head resting in her lap, she looked up at him with peaceful eyes.

"Robert," she said quietly, "would you like to hear the story of my life? My life when I was Morriagan? I was a bitch, but an amazing bitch."

Stafford just nodded.

CHAPTER XVIII
Morriagan and Samhan

The first grisly feast was the most difficult for Morriagan, formerly the second born.

Samhan was her servant, but more. Its job was to serve, and that included serve as teacher. Plus, the teacher must perform persuasively, for the student had to agree with the rules from understanding, not fear.

"These rules are nothing without our belief and agreement," explained Samhan. "We give our actions meaning and justification by steadfastly adhering to the rules we set forth."

Morriagan's hands and mouth were stained crimson from the blood of her sister's body, on which the two had been dining.

"Then explain to me in general why the first born had to die and specifically why we disgrace her body by defiling it in eating her flesh."

"We give it not disgrace, but honor. You have certain powers. They come not close to mine, but in sharing these rituals they will be honed to their finest degree." Samhan stopped eating to lecture.

"For any action to have honor, power and legitimacy, it needs sacrifice. Earlier a goat was sacrificed, and you and your sister felt the kiss of the branding iron. Why? This was a promise of deed in the future. The sacrifice I just now took.

It, in its turn was given validity and promise by a man dedicating his life to the creation of a tool meant to join us.

The planchette can be used by anyone to summon me. They are bound by the same rules we set forth, but with exception. They know not what those rules be. By their not knowing the rules, the binding would mean little, so it is up to us to enforce the rules without mercy.

You will learn more as we go, but know this.

Blood in the planchette will summon me. It matters not whose blood. If it is yours, I will know of your desires and needs in calling. If it is another's, living or dead, I will know the truth of their deeds and action.

In being called I must serve he who called. Before service they must give my name to prove they are indeed my master. Woe to the false master.

I can be sent away only by the blood of the one person who named me. Yourself.

These are the rules in which you have no say. In all else you are master."

Samhan held the small morsel of firstborn's heart up. "The heart is eaten in honor, sparing it from rotting in the ground." He popped it in his mouth.

The brain is also eaten. While the blood gives us knowledge recent; the brain gives us knowledge past."

Morriagan's journey started quietly and not without its share of failure. Failure being measured by the attitude of the populace.

It was not obvious who the traveler was. Never did she travel *with* Samhan. Samhan returned to whatever realm he occupied when not summoned. A few times he attempted to enlighten Morriagan.

"There is a multitude of worlds with this or similar nature. They all occupy the same space, but are separated and form different dimensions. We exist in many, but not all. It would be simpler for you to take for granted that if you can think of something, then it has probably happened or exists somewhere,

By its existence, you are able to envision it. All these universes are linked by our thoughts and dreams. When you summon, I step across. When you dismiss, I step back. The ritual involved is more to focus your thoughts and bring them to my attention than anything."

Morriagan traveled light, possessing only robe, staff and bag containing planchette and knife. Latter, when her existence was better known, people she met would care for her needs. In the beginning, life was only slightly better than beggar-hood.

Fate, however, does not dole tasks out proportionate to one's fame.

In a small fiefdom her services were called upon by the local druid master.

The master greeted her on the road and explained his plight.

"Of brothers, there were two. Both of the clan O'Marha. Their ages are separated by a handful of seasons.

Upon the death of their father, the eldest was to assume the throne left vacant. This would have happened, but very shortly after the passage of the father, the eldest son breathed his last. It is generally suspect that it was not of natural causes, unless you consider the hand of the youngest natural," the master explained.

"Has the body of the eldest son been either buried or burned?" asked Morriagan.

"Nay. It is on public display."

"And will the youngest submit to my...scrutiny?"

"Yes," agreed the master. "He has knowledge of you, but not belief."

"Will all agree to my decision in the matter?" She stopped in the road. "To agree to have me issue decree on this matter, then ignore that decision would have grave consequences."

"You have more than agreement. At least on my part. It is understood that, if you so desired, you could act upon this matter with - or without - our consent."

Morriagan smiled. "But it is so much better to believe one has a say in the events of their lives, don't you think?"

"Indeed," and the master looked at her strangely.

It was only later that Morriagan realized two great truths.

With impressive ceremony, people find all actions acceptable.

When people realize they have no say in the outcome of decisions, the guilt is removed from them and acceptance assured.

At the modest castle, Morriagan gathered the new monarch, the druid master and the local cleric; all sitting spaciously around the main table of the dining hall.

On the table before her she placed the planchette and a chalice.

"The planchette is mine. A constant traveling companion. The chalice I found in the rectory, next to the body that is placed for viewing." Standing she picked up the chalice. "Please watch carefully what I do young king. I have previously performed this with your departed brother." She slowly swirled the contents of the chalice.

"The blood thickens so after death. In norm, we would add wine to thin it, but this time we have no need."

Reaching into her bag she pulled the knife and, without flinching, pulled its sharp blade across her palm. "I recommend the wounding of your hand least used. It will be sore for a day or so." Holding her hand over the cup, she allowed the crimson liquid to dribble, mixing with the thickened black contents.

Picking up a linen square from the table she clenched it tightly to the cut. Smiling she turned to the king.

"Your hand, sire, if you please," when he hesitated, she added, "t'wil sting only slightly, for the blade is keen."

Feeling his hesitation interpreted as fear, he quickly held out his hand. "Tis just the idea of drinking such mixture," he said, a sickened look crossing his face.

Morriagan smiled. "Is not so bad, but rest easy. We will not be drinking of this potion."

Returning to her seat, she admonished her audience. "Please, take care. After I start, do not leave your chair. If for any reason you do," she looked at them severely, "it will cost of you your life. It will be believed you attempt to flee justice. What you shall see is my servant. However, if my instructions are not followed, you will see your slayer."

"Very, ah, dramatic," said the king.

"The tales will become legend, if only half of them are true," replied the druid master.

The cleric sat stone faced.

Carefully Morriagan poured the mixture of three bloods into the depression in the planchette. Setting the chalice down, she reached out with one finger and laid it on the edge of the planchette.

After she let out a deep sigh, two things started happening.

The planchette started moving.

The blood started draining out of the hole in the planchette in a very thin stream.

As all watched, the hand and planchette left a symbol on the table. It appeared to be a cross or an "X" with a circle superimposed over it.

"A nice trick…," started the king.

"Shut up you fool," snapped the cleric.

The young monarch started to rebuke the robed and dignified cleric, but then he saw it. They all saw it, but not where it came from.

Samhan bent low over the table, wiped a taloned paw over the symbol, and then with long tongue, licked the blood from the paw.

The king gave a very unregal shout and rose from his chair. The only thing that spared his life was his two hands clenched on the edge of the table.

When the black eyes of Samhan met his, he slowly slumped back into his chair.

Samhan crawled to the center of the table and curled into a lethal ball. There he stayed. On occasion he would raise his head and stare thoughtfully at one of the people sitting around the table.

Twice it raised its head and stared at that which no other could see.

After an eternity it rose and laid its head on Morriagan's shoulder, where it stayed.

After a while she nodded, raised her hand and pulled the linen from it. Squeezing the cloth, she let a few drops fall into the planchette again. Utilizing a new linen she wiped the planchette as clean as possible and set it back on the table. As its three legs clicked their contact on the table, Samhan was gone.

"Well," Morriagan sighed, "that was enlightening."

She shuddered, stood, and paced the room carefully studying her injured hand.

"Where do you wish this to go from here?" asked the druid master.

"So, you knew all the time?" asked Morriagan.

"Suspicions I had. Some things do not take deep magic to comprehend. The simple facts of watching two children grow before my eyes supplied most of the answers."

"Then for what cause did you enlist my aid?"

It was the master's turn to sigh. "Knowing the truth is nothing, Knowing what to do...well, even that is easy enough. Making the decision and accepting the...repercussions, if you will... that can be a dilemma. Sometimes fate offers a way out," he sighed again, "you were my way out."

Morriagan nodded in understanding. She addressed the king directly.

"Here is what I found, and here is what shall occur. You murdered your own brother. Terrible? Horrific? Perchance.

But to define horrible and terrible we must look to your dead brother. Were he to have taken the crown the people would be raped of their land, property and dignity.

So...in part...that is the excuse you hide behind in your own mind. You cannot, however, conceal your lust for power and your jealously of the rightful, if improper monarch.

You can never hide it from your blood.

Rule you shall, but know this, a day will come when someone will approach you. They will authenticate themselves by," Morriagan leaned close and whispered into his ear. "At that time you will publicly declare them the rightful ruler.

You will then take your own life on that very night." she smiled sweetly. "Should you hesitate or delay, my servant will visit you to assist. Take me at my word when I promise...you will die badly if that is required."

The guilty king was ashen. "When will this visit occur?"

"That is part of your punishment. Each morning you will awaken to question if you will see the sun arise once more." Packing her gear, she headed for the door, stopped and turned. "Enjoy your reign, young king. Redeem yourself as best ye may. Rule well for the time given you. Die well, for the time given you."

CHAPTER XIX
The Brotherhood

'm not quite sure what to say or do," said Stafford.

"Me either," said Karen. "Do you have a pocket knife on you? I'm not steady enough to try this with my sword."

Fumbling, Stafford pulled out a smallish pocket knife and standing as far away as possible, handed it to Karen. As he reached, Samhan raised his head and stared at Stafford.

"Jesus. I have never been this scared in my life," said Stafford. "I would be afraid I was going to piss my pants, but I'm so scared, I really don't care if I do or not."

Unable to take his eyes from the creature, Stafford watched as Samhan disappeared. One second he was there, the next gone, a strange blue after image that lingered for a moment. It was reminiscent of the after glow of a flash cube.

"What just happened?" he asked.

"I...sent it away. Or released him, depending on how you want to look at it."

"Then...it's over. Finished." Stafford's shoulders slumped.

"I wish that were true. I think we'd better talk. Get all the cards on the table," said Tagollini, walking up the sidewalk.

෨෭

"Okay. Three, four thousand years ago it might have been viable. Now it's not feasible. We have countries, borders and police departments. It isn't needed," said Jerimy.

"Not to mention the flat assed paranoia of people thinking that...or knowing that power of this extent...exists. Hell, they just wouldn't put up with it," from Stafford.

"Look," said Karen, "you guys are trying to make decisions for me and most of this shit isn't needed. Can't anybody just be happy the killing is over, we are safe, and we have some answers?"

"Well," Tagollini grumbled, "if you were to think of it; Morriagan was the protector of the planchette and Samhan the servant. Isn't it remarkable your cop cars say, 'To Serve and Protect?' I wonder where that came from. As for people 'putting up with it,' they put up with nuclear weapons. They have no choice. Paranoia? You damn bet people would wig out. If they ever believed it, and that is damn doubtful."

"No," he said sadly, "you are thinking sloppily. You are thinking of this, that and everything, when you really have but two options. My little group is here to help you in either of them. Now that you know some of the details, you have to make only one decision. Do you want to live...or die?

We haven't stayed in existence through the centuries because of you. Truthfully, we never came close to anticipating the return of Morriagan, a clone or anything else. We knew the planchette existed and some day Samhan might return. We exist solely to perform damage control.

The original creators had an eye towards the future. They knew that neither the first or second born would live forever. The servant would remain."

"Is one of your chore's to protect the planchette?" asked Karen.

Tagollini looked uncomfortable. "Once we thought it was. Through an...uh...incident, we found out we didn't have to." He turned to where the planchette was sitting next to Karen.

"Centuries ago, one of our brethren decided our onus was evil. At the time we had the planchette in our control. He tried to destroy it. Hell, he did destroy it. Time after time, in every fashion you can think of. Always, at the stroke of dawn, it would reappear. If you are into quantum physics you might rationalize it as it you can destroy an object, but not the particles that form the object. And the particles contain all the information about the object. The protective aura, or whatever it is, remains and rebuilds." He laughed. "Feel free not to believe any of this. I can't prove anything except that if I burn it; tomorrow you will not only have a pile of ashes, but the whole son of a bitch like new."

"So what's this live or die bullshit," asked Jerimy.

"We can hide you. Keep you out of the public eye, but as long as you are known to be with the planchette, and Samhan, you are a target. The governments of the world can't let you live. Psychos will want to kill or control you for the power. Religions will need your head because you can produce tangible evidence of a 'god'." He coughed. "The other choice is not to live that type of existence. In that instance we can assist, making sure it is painless."

Karen walked to the refrigerator, opened it, and took a beer from it.

"It's a little early, but what the hell," she said. "Let me fill you in on some facts, and an option available that it looks like people are pushing me into."

Unscrewing the cap she took a long drink, and then set it down turning to them.

"How did Morriagan die, do you think, Mr. Tagollini?"

"We are not sure of that." he admitted. "That seems to have been lost through the ages."

"That's okay. I can tell you. She died of old age. Her 'job,' her 'purpose,' was to right wrongs. You are not aware, but there is one time and one way only, that Samhan can appear without being summoned.

At Morriagan's...and now evidently my...death, he will appear. If he were to find that death was not from natural causes...and believe me...when he ate the heart and brain he would know...he would decide a 'wrong' had been committed. He would correct that wrong and numbers mean nothing to him. One person, ten, a hundred, a thousand...probably even a million. Time really means nothing either."

"No," Karen said, setting her beer down, "we are going with a 'live and let live' policy." She smiled, "I am a bit harder to harm now. Even without my servant being here. I am...remembering things. Disturbing things, but interesting things."

"I'm not sure you can pull it of," Tagollini said. "The people you need to impress don't impress that easy. When it comes to your friends," he pointed at Jerimy and Bob, "the powers might make a show of returning their lives to normal. Then, a year down the line, a car accident, a heart attack or even a common mugging."

"I think it's time for some travel. To get back to my roots." Karen said.

"Karen," said Jerimy, "I'm a bit concerned. You aren't acting exactly normal."

"Jerimy, you are right. But I'm not Karen anymore." She held up a hand to stop any protest. "No, I am not Morriagan either. Nor, am I the one known as 'first born.' I don't know who I am, but if you love me, you will have to wait for this to take its course. If it's any consolation, I still find you cuter than Samhan." She smiled, showing dimples. "Although he is a better kisser."

Jerimy looked shocked.

"I'm joking, you asshole," she soothed.

CHAPTER XX
The Best Laid Plans

"Jerimy," Karen called. "We're having a meeting on the minds!"

"Before coffee?" came a voice slurred with the remnants of sleep.

All had returned to bed for either an extra hour of sleep or an extra hour of tossing and turning.

"Bob is making some. Tagollini is here. There have been some changes and things have come to a head."

"Well, if Bob is making coffee, and we can lure that creature into drinking some of his swill, the problem will be resolved," said Jerimy.

"Jerimy, I spent the night with the creature - with Samhan. I sent him away, but Tagollini makes some pretty good arguments that our problems didn't all go away with him."

By the time everyone had their coffee sitting in front of them, Karen had given a quick run down on the twins, the turning of Morriagan and some of the known characteristics of Samhan.

Stafford looked thoughtful. He wandered from table to different windows, carefully looking out each. Tucked in his belt, behind his right hip was a Kimber 1911.

His left rear pocket showed multiple bulges of spare magazines.

Jerimy didn't show outward signs of having armed himself, but then he never did. Show signs, that is.

"Are you inviting your new little buddy to this brunch?" asked Stafford.

"No. Samhan is not a parlor trick. It took the second born years before it was deemed she - and her sister - were ready to meet the servant for the first time. With grisly consequences. Then it took years of working together before they truly understood each other and worked together smoothly." She stopped and looked down at her healing hand. "And I am learning of myself also."

"Let's see that hand," Jerimy said, reaching out to hold it. Turning it palm up, he could see the angry red line on the palm.

"Stafford, you saw her do that this morning?" he asked.

"I know she did it, but I didn't observe it. Crap, man, I was watching that thing. Flippin' fangs four inches long and fucking razor sharp claws almost twice that long. He looked at me like I was a Porterhouse steak. A two inch penknife didn't hold my attention. Sorry."

Karen looked at them all. "I think we should prioritize our needs versus our wants and just see what is possible."

This was greeted with a variety of grumbles, harrups, nods, sniffs and snuffles. All of the sound effects seemed to be in agreement, however.

"The way I see it is this. Jerimy, you need reinstated, and the slate wiped clean. That is not happening instantaneously. It seems we can move mountains with the church and state, but the cop shop doesn't want to budge.

Bob. As Stafford of Spectral Images, you need the I.R.S. and all the other entities off your ass. And before you ask, no. No, Samhan is not going to pose for photos. He didn't even have to step in on the matter. You evidently have some decent attorneys on retainer.

Tagollini. I don't know what ramifications this has had...or will have...on your organization. I think I should make this fairly clear. I appreciate your help, but will never allow myself to come under your control. You will never, however, be cut out of the loop. Everyone else, however, *does* want to under their control."

Tagollini bowed his head, "Thank you. We are here for support. As a support system, I believe we can be a decent aide to you. And still remain objective. As a matter of fact it was pointed out to me by Pablo that the three of you should be taken into full confidence. Our little organization will be opened and explained in its entirety to you. Pablo, who you should know is really my immediate supervisor, decided all this before Samhan made his appearance last night." He motioned to Karen, then dropped his hands in despair.

"We have the, ah, clout to get things back to normal for your friends; we have members on the bench in every state and politicians up to cabinet level in most countries, but your problem goes under the covers. You were a black ops project that crossed political and religious boundaries. You disappeared off the radar until the servant reappeared. Then when you showed up along with the servant, well the lights went on all the way from the basement to the penthouse of the government.

When that happened they reopened the case. It was at their simple request your friends got slammed. When it was sure that you were the reincarnation, so to speak, people became desperate to keep you separated from the servant. Even if it meant a Stealth bomber and smart bomb.

Now you are reunited with the servant. No one had ever seriously considered that possibility. That thought even scares me a bit. It might make others contemplate a tactical thermo nuke, or serious shit. Myself, I think that we can still get a handle on this situation. In honesty, Pablo does not completely share my opinion."

Karen nodded. "Exactly. So that is why I think it time I get out of the country and away from people for a while. At least long enough for your society to find out whom I need to deal with."

Stafford spoke up. "What if they decide to take one of us hostage? To use as leverage or something? What if you get an ear in the mail? With the demand to return?"

Karen gave a grim smile. "Then I would. And you can let it be known I would not return alone, and things most emphatically would be set right."

CHAPTER XXI
Stafford

Stafford had not spent the last month sitting on his ass. He often got up and walked around. The first night he had spent with a bottle of scotch, a dozen cigars and deep thoughts. About three in the morning his decisions were made.

Through years of investigating the 'off the wall' stories he had met an amazing amount of crack pots, conspiracy hermits and just plain anti-social psychos.

A handful of them displayed a common trait. If they wanted to disappear and become invisible, they did so without reappearing until they wanted to.

Idly he picked up the phone and made a call. He knew the phone he was calling to was a 'pay-as-you go' phone and untraceable.

"Hello." A voice answered.

"Hello. This is Stafford. It doesn't matter if I use my name but I won't use yours. I'm in trouble. Everyone is out to get me and I mean everyone. I know that sounds impossible…"

The voice broke in, "Why would that be impossible? Now, shut up. Go to your least favorite diner and make a call to your dead brother," and the line went dead.

Let's see, Stafford thought. *Middle of the night, drunk on my ass, enlisting the aid of a guy who thinks that President Lincoln was from Mars and this can be proven by hidden symbols in the candy bar wrapper of the same name.* He thought about his own plight with a monster and a Ouiji board.

Okay. When I get a chance I'll buy a box of the damn candy bars and check it out.

Driving to the Denny's next to the opera house he stared at his cell phone. How was he supposed to call his dead brother? Six years in the grave it was doubtful he would answer. Hell, he never did when he was alive. Not to mention Stafford hadn't a clue what his brother's old phone number used to be.

Sitting he lit another stogie. He was starting to get the hang of thinking outside the box. It didn't mean exotic and genius, most the time it meant seeing what was in front of your nose.

After killing fifteen more minutes of brain farts, the light bulb came on.. Getting out of the car he walked to the pay phone.

Hanging beneath it was a tattered phone book. Opening it he was not surprised to find his long dead brother's name was not in it.

However, between two names where his brother's name would have been, a number had been penciled it. It looked wrong, but he tried it. A recording informed him in no uncertain terms that was not a valid number.

Frustrated he cursed. As he was cussing, a man walked by and whispered, "Try it backwards, you idiot." Stafford stared after the man as he disappeared inside.

"Fucking twilight zone," Stafford muttered as he punched the number in backward. It was answered on the second ring.

"Come in, I ordered you coffee, black, none of those C.I.A. brainwashing artificial sweeteners." And the line went dead again.

Stafford went in. It wasn't exactly crowded and only one man was sitting at the counter with an extra cup of coffee next to his order. The back of the man's tee shirt boldly stated, "The truth is out there…"

As he sat down next to the man, Robert questioned the wisdom of this action.

"So what seems to be the major malfunction of your woe-be-gone life, Stafford?"

Stafford thought for a moment then the scotch and hour of the night caught up with him and he quickly and quietly blurted the truth.

When he had finished, the man thought about it for a moment, then summed it all up, "Son of a bitch!"

He thought for five more minutes. "Okay, here's what you do. Meet me back here at six in the morning with a hundred gees and we will make you invisible and comfortable."

"How the hell am I going to get any money? I have been frozen from taking any money from the company for over a month now."

"You aren't the brightest crayon in the box, but you do have a lot of color. Your magazine buys stories on speculation, right?"

"Well, yeah."

"You came up with the outline for the story you just told me two months ago, you just forgot until right now. Now, all your contributors, do they use their real names?"

"No. Of course not."

"Okay. You get a hold of Accounts Payable, tell them to make an advance out to cash for a hundred thousand, post date it, memo for speculative book. Make that books. I know a person who will get it cashed for you...he does take 10% commission...and we will get you set up in a program that makes witness protection look like it advertises prime time and Superbowl."

"No one's going to believe that. I'm too cheap to pay that kind of money."

"They don't have to believe it, they just have to do it. It's your money anyway. Sort of."

"Will that stand up in court?"

"It might if you can say it with a straight face."

The next day was a learning experience.

"Now ya gotta understand, fifty big ones got ya a lot. It's just that some of it you can't really see."

Stafford looked at the beat up Toyota pickup parked in front of a cracked, stucco walled house. All located in a questionable border town in Arizona.

"Think of it this way. Ya got your digs you will be staying at here in Nogales. And transportation. Just don't trust the truck for more than around town.

You don't need a different name, cuz no one is going to ask you your name in the first place around here. Nor will you ask anyone else *their* name.

Now you do have a nice little condo in Colorado. It's in your name, with all utilities in your name. And a sweet little sports car; all in your name with insurance in your name.

To top it off you - well someone who looks a lot like you - took your neighbors out for one hell of a dinner party.

If someone tracks you down, which place do you think they are going to find? And if they sit for a week on stake-out in Colorado, more power to them."

They walked towards the dilapidated house. "Now when you get to the sidewalk, don't use it. Walk in the grass, easier on the feet. Plus that the alarm doesn't go off."

The interior was frightening. The furniture looked like early Meth Lab. The man frowned. "I don't recommend spending time upstairs. Try to utilize the basement."

The basement was spotless, sported new furniture and a plasma screen television. He pointed out the kitchen area. "Stocked with food for a month and a full wet bar. At the end of a month, if you need more; three homeless people will 'break in.' After a few minutes you will run them off with much yelling and cursing. They and their grocery carts will leave."

He opened a cardboard box. "Here are fifteen Tracfones. Activate one at any payphone by using the 800 number. Every week, destroy the phone and activate a new one.

Remember, these are to call out on. Do not use them for incoming. Activate one for that, give out only that one's number. If you get a call on it, limit the call to no more than sixty seconds, then destroy that phone. I don't think they can be traced, but why take a chance?

Payments and purchase. You will pay cash. You will never spend more than twenty dollars at any one place and you will never use larger than a twenty to pay for anything.

If you buy beer or cigarettes, you will never buy more than a six pack or a single pack of smokes - no cartons or cases; and never frequent the same store more than once a week.

You are never going to become a regular customer anywhere or at anytime. Need I say you don't order pizza?"

He now looked very uncomfortable. "Might I ask a favor?"

Stafford just nodded.

"Your ah, landlord. He has a business opportunity. I portrayed you as sort of an entrepreneur. He has a business investment that would probably net you some money. Would you mind if I made a couple, ah, investments for you? With the money you have left?"

"What? Oh, sure, what the hell. Invest away," Swafford said. "I hope your horse wins."

ॐॱॐ

Stafford's 'mentor' stopped back to see him.

It had been three weeks without a call,

"So, Robert…how are you adjusting to your new lifestyle?"

Stafford shrugged. "A little bit boring, but bearable. You tell me what's new. I don't get out much."

"Ah, yes. Senor Jerimy is still off the force. He spreads his time between drinking, looking for work and asking pointed questions of everyone. These questions will, in time, cause him trouble.

The nice lady of your group still wanders without apparent purpose. She is being watched, but not bothered. A nasty rumor floats about that."

Stafford smiled. "And what might that rumor be?"

"Nothing large or dramatic. Just a man was sent to interrogate her. Ask some harmless questions."

"No," Bob said, "that doesn't sound that sinister. So what's the problem?"

"He never made it there."

"That's it?"

"Yes. His car, his personal possessions, himself, everything gone. No trace found at this time."

"That is a bit strange. That's the rumor?"

"No, not exactly. At the same time, across the ocean, in Virginia, his family disappeared and his home burned to the ground."

"That is quite the rumor," Stafford conceded.

"The actual rumor is that he is the one who set fire to the nice lady's home."

"I see."

"Now, jefe…the money you told me was okay to invest. It pays returns about every five days to seven days. Depending. It has done so three times so far. You want I should pull it, pull part of it, or what?"

"Let it ride. I do not have any needs or vices I can indulge in." Stafford thought of the fifty grand. "It is quite a bit, but what the hell."

The other man wiped the sweat from his forehead. "Yes, it is…as you say 'quite a bit.' You know your safety is my concern. Should something happen to you, it would reflect poorly on myself." He thought for a moment. "Yes, I think it time to beef up your protection 'quite a bit.'"

Stafford was concerned, "What? Does anyone know where I am?"

"No. No, mi amigo. Well, there are those that know someone is here, but no one knows who you are. I will bring in some of my closest men. They will live upstairs and will not be a bother to you. This I promise."

He stood there fidgeting.

Stafford thought about it for a moment,

"What exactly have I invested in and, ah, how much have I made or lost?"

The man fidgeted some more and explained. "I don't have the exact figure, but I can come close. You pay for product and shipment. Your consumer picks it up, pays then resells it for further profit."

Stafford's stomach dropped. "Oh, Christ. What am I buying and what is the profit margin?"

"Well, the product varies, as does the profit. You are taking tremendous monetary risks that the Cartels do not want to take."

Stafford hunted for a chair to sit in. "I'm doing stuff that even the Cartels are afraid of?"

"Well, yes." The man warmed to his explanation. "You invested 50K. All worked out and you got something like a hundred thousand back. You said nothing so I reinvested it. All went tremendously. We only lost three men and one helicopter; you cleared *almost* 200K." He shrugged. "We had to kick some in on the chopper.

"When I again told them to front the two hundred thousand, they were ecstatic. That deal went like clockwork. Now you have about a half a million.

Thing is," he smiled ruefully, "if this one goes as smooth as the rest, you are going to have a cool million. Now people are getting nervous. You are getting into the big leagues. People are nervous about laundering that much. You are the new kid on the block. The cartels want to know if you want to buy in with them, if you are running competition with them, or if you are going to take the money and run."

Stafford thought carefully. "End it. I mean fucking end it. If I come through with this grab the money."

"Might I make a suggestion?" asked his mentor.

"Go for it."

"Take some of the profit on the last and send a gift to both cartels and the Pepe's. The Pepe's are the Columbian military who hunt down the druggies. Cash is always appreciated. Perhaps a note thanking all for the experience and tell them you are getting out because they are all too good for you to compete with, you've seen the light, you found god...anything. Builds their ego, gives them a day's worth of flash money...everyone is happy and rooting for you."

"As opposed to hunting me down, attaching electrodes to my testicles and then slitting my throat," finished Stafford.

"Exactly."

CHAPTER XXII
Jerimy

When Jerimy split off from Robert and Karen, it was the start of a destructive downhill spiral.

His job was gone, his ex-wife (whom he saw as having returned) and even his half assed friend and opponent were ripped from his life.

Stafford had disappeared off the face of the earth, and Karen had fled to the other side of it. Communication with Bob had severed immediately and the trickles of phone calls from Karen quickly ended. He felt abandoned.

The people whom he had called brothers now treated him as an outcast. The strange society that had helped them seemed to be slowly backing away from that position.

Now, when he talked to them, they did not inquire as to his well being, but as to if he had heard from Karen and, if so, what had been said.

The small amount of money he had in reserve would only last for one or two months. A bit less if problems were encountered or he actually paid any bills; a bit more if he were frugal and miserly.

Sighing, he sat down at the table and opened the newspaper. Time to hunt for another job. Even if only for a while. Even if only part time. 'Just until this mess sorted itself out.' He told himself.

The pull tab on the unopened can of beer snapped off before it punctured the top. He stared at it. *Fuck it,* he thought. It wasn't worth the fight this time to mangle the can to get to the beer.

He tossed the defective can back into the fridge to await a more desperate time and grabbed a new one. He was pleased when this one worked as designed.

The day before he had approached two of his retired friends. Well, one was a bona fide retirement and the other had voluntarily left the force. Internal Affairs had been breathing down his neck also; something about far too much money in the bank for his salary. Being a dirty cop never went out of style and many succumbed to the chance.

When a man 'took off the blue.' for whatever reason, but didn't want to leave the life style, there was always room for Private Investigators.

Both men were genuinely happy to see Jerimy and just as honestly depressed that they didn't have a position for him. Jerimy was too proud to ask for money, so…

That left security work.

Not an option. Not only was it looked down upon by everyone, but you had all the danger and none of the power. Face it, when a cop got shot, it was 'tragedy in the line of duty.' When a security guard gets shot, it's 'another imitation bacon gets plugged while playing cop.'

Burping beer, he relentlessly chewed a granola bar. Gotta have some nutrient for breakfast.

He crushed the can and made a perfect three pointer in the trash. Okay, then, best/worst case scenario; one month, thirty days, to investigate who or what was fucking with their three lives and set it straight, on his own.

'It shouldn't be that hard,' he thought to himself. He already had a pretty good idea who the big three were. It was just a matter of dragging someone out of the shadows, grabbin' them by the throat and getting to the bottom of it.

Jerimy's car wasn't as 'impressive' as a black and white cruiser, but it had punch. Jerimy had owned it since high school. It was a 'work in progress' and had been so for thirty years. He had bought it used and driven it into the ground. A sixty-seven Chevy Impala. Four speed with a 409 cubic inch mill.

Engine and drive train were now immaculate, visually the car was passable, as long as you didn't mind primer gray.

The headers with Cherry Bombs were iffy these days with noise restrictions, but if he didn't get on it too much, they might let him slide. They'd better. He hadn't driven it for almost a year. He could get by on the license, but if anyone stopped him, they would quickly figure out he had no insurance. No money to get any either.

Pulling up in front of Karen's old abode was anticlimactic and non-profitable.

What was once a depressingly cute, small and clean home was indeed gone. It has burned to the ground and what ashes and foundation had been left was already scooped up by front end loaders and hauled to bum fuck Egypt; or some place similar.

He amused himself by walking the area and having a smoke. The tobacco smell mixed nicely with the moist burned wood smell impregnating the very ground.

Jerimy watched to see if he attracted the attention of anyone staked out in the neighborhood. As with most neighborhoods of this status, everyone made a big point of minding their own business.

He seemed to be below the radar, beneath suspicion and beating the proverbial dead horse.

He broke down and talked to one neighbor. He didn't say he was police, but he didn't deny it either. The neighbor didn't find it unusual. Seems the police had been asking about people noising around, and it was amusing. "Why would anyone worry now? The house had burned to the ground, nothing to steal or vandalize." She had said.

He could snoop around his own house, but hell, he lived there, there was nothing to be learned by it even if it was being watched.

That narrowed it down. Stafford's digs had been declared off limits. It was big, had immense grounds, and was warranting a full fledged crime scene investigation.

At night the entrance had its own check post now. Tourists need not apply.

He looked at his watch. Four hours, give or take, before dark. Plenty of time to prepare.

Dark jeans, black shirt, gloves, black baseball cap and face paint. He looked at the Smith & Wesson 686 for a moment deciding. He slipped it into a ballistic nylon holster and added two speed loaders.

If you wanted to get nit-picky, he hadn't *actually* been fired. They had just pulled his badge and gun. Indefinitely. Without pay and or benefit accrual. It was a very fine point, but it could be interpreted as he was still affiliated with law enforcement. If you looked at the matter kind of sideways, out of focus, and with broad interpretation. A couple of drinks helped see the logic also.

Jerimy even had time to stop at the Circle K and pick up an armload of energy drinks.

How sad, he thought, *it used to be a thermos of coffee and a box of doughnuts. Now its something with caffeine, guarana, turbine, ginseng and an energy bar.*

Jerimy arrived on the dirt road high above Stafford's home just as the exterior lights of the property were coming on. It didn't mean much. Probably just his security system kicking on. He'd stood here once before. Not long ago.

From where he was, no motion was visible and the only sounds reaching his ears were the wind and occasional road noise from the interstate far away. The closest neighbor was almost a mile away. Close enough for gunfire to be heard, but even the loudest party wouldn't assault the senses.

Jerimy closed the door of the car by gently pushing it rather than slamming it. He smiled to himself. Must be nice to have enough money to live out here. The black camo paint smelled faintly of mosquito repellant and felt slightly greasy.

He pushed the cylinder release on the revolver and let the cylinder pivot out to the left. The heads and primers of six cartridges glittered back in the growing dusk.

The feeling was there. The feeling of danger lurking behind every tree. He wasn't used to this. Sure, the tension of stepping into the unknown was always there, but this was different. As a cop, you had backup. You had the knowledge you were in the right.

The creature known as Samhan wasn't here. It had been observed up close, and while terrorizing, when the unknown was unmasked, acceptance was a lot more comfortable. Yet this felt like impending doom. It was hard to shake.

Hell, so much had happened recently, this was probably a large dose of paranoia to boot.

When darkness had fallen it supplied the needed degree of invisibility, Jerimy started down the hillside.

In a straight line he was no more than six hundred yards away from the house. Between dodging trees and the zigzagging down the steep slope, it was closer to a thousand yards.

Concern that the checkpoint might pick up on his presence was almost nonexistent among his worries. It was on the far side from where he was and, having worked that type of set-up he was reassured.

Sitting, night after night, staring out into the darkness, one didn't look for problems after the first night, other than head lights belonging to a supervisor or your relief.

By the time Jerimy had reached the bottom his ankles and calves hurt from the downhill hike.

Crouching behind a large propane tank he felt he was over reacting. All he need do was stand up, walk to the front door and see if it were unlocked. That and pray the damn security alarms were off, With the amount of people who had wandered in and out, it was doubtful it would be active, but one never knew.

From where he crouched he could see the foot long wire stakes with their plastic flags; crime scene markers placed, without question, at every spot they found a piece of Spetzner/Daily when Samhan had…disassembled him. There were an awful lot of flags.

Fifteen minutes were required to build nerve to cross the well lit area between him and the door.

A door that opened easily when he got to it.

Silence greeted him. The kitchen area was vacant, as was the large living room area. Empty drink glasses were stacked in the sink and all appeared 'in order.' Almost too 'in order.' Taking a closer look it dawned on Jerimy why things felt that way to him.

In order.

He had seen it a hundred times before. This house, this scene, had been processed. Light coatings and smears of powder covered much. Looking for fingerprints. Paper products bore a pebbled appearance in places where they had been sprayed with a light mist of luminol. Looking for blood. The house had been processed as a crime scene.

That made sense. They had even told Stafford they were scouring it with a fine tooth comb. Even though Jerimy knew and understood that everybody was a suspect until evidence says otherwise, it drove home the fact that he was no longer part of the investigators. He stood with the suspects. Or "people of interest," the politically correct term.

If whoever turned this place hadn't found anything, then they sure as hell didn't leave anything.

Jerimy turned the corner and stood in the doorway to the library. *Crap,* he thought, *I missed that one by a mile.*

Sitting in a comfortable recliner was a man in a dark gray suit. He looked up from the magazine he held in front of him, but did not lower it.

"Mr.," he talked slowly and succinctly. "Jerimy Naden. I want you to know it is indeed a pleasure and honor to meet you."

Jerimy's hand slowly reached towards his right hip. The man scowled and lowered the magazine with his left hand, revealing a small Walther pistol in his right. The silencer attached to the front made it all look much bigger than it really was.

"May I call you Jerimy?" The man asked politely. "Please stop reaching for whatever it is you are reaching for." Jerimy stopped.

"I do not care, Jerimy, why you are here. I do not care who knows you are here. I find these things get sticky when people blurt this and that. So I will only ask you this. Die quietly."

The pistol coughed twice. As fast as the trigger could be pulled. Jerimy felt two blows to the chest and heard one casing bounce from an end table.

Laying on the floor his hand would no longer work. He could feel the grip of his pistol, but didn't have the strength to pull it from the holster.

He watched as the man stood over him and pointed the pistol at his face.

Damn, Jerimy thought his final thought, *a fucking professional.*

CHAPTER XXIII
The Olde Sod

Life had gone from a crazed maelstrom of death and confusion, to an idyllic vacation, where she knew people were watching her every move, but all were going out of their way to make it seem she was alone and carefree.

Britain, Ireland, Scotland and all were nameless blurs in her mind. Her belongings included passport and money - courtesy of the society - but the controlling passions were half memories that swarmed up like a shimmering haze on the countryside.

Standing on a deserted road/path on the moors, her mind told her of the home which had stood before her with welcome fire, fresh bread and soup. Her eyes showed her scattered stones that may have constituted a structure in times so far past that it fell into myth, rather than history.

She walked more than availing herself of public transportation. During the first couple weeks she stayed in close connection with Jerimy and attempted to do so with Bob. Gradually she forgot what it was she sought, and what the intentions of her travels were.

One evening, the warm day darkening into a cool dusk, Karen was attracted to the flickering light of a campfire. She wandered up towards the flames, standing at the line where darkness and light met.

Around the small blaze stood three figures, faces hidden by the cowls of their plain, but warm woolen robes.

After a half hour, none speaking, one motioned her forward to the warmth. She stepped forward and sank cross legged by the fire-pit. The silence was comfortable; the only sound the crackling of the fire and rustle as more limbs were added to it.

From time to time, minute changes in the wind moved the smoke into her face, choking her lungs and stinging her eyes till tears ran down her face.

Finally she held her hand out. The smoke stopped a few feet from her, as if a sheet of glass had been placed.

Idly she moved her hand and found the smoke would respond. With practice she could sculpt the blue-gray smoke into shapes. Each a bit more complicated than the previous.

In the morning she awoke. All her meager belongings and money intact. Covering her a worn, but serviceable robe, which she donned,

At one stage an official vehicle pulled up in front of her on the road. Police are the same in every country. The man exited the right, driver's side briskly and started walking back towards her.

When he got to her, he inquired politely, but firmly, "Miss, might I see your papers. It's a bit dicey a woman alone on this stretch."

Silently she handed him her papers. He opened the passport and read the name, verifying the photo.

"Oh. Oh, yes miss. Sorry to be bothering you. Are you okay? Might I be of assistance in any way?"

It took her a moment to find her voice as she accepted the papers back, "No. No thank you. You are very kind and I thank you."

As he turned and headed for his vehicle, she called out, stopping him. "Young man. Is this night the eve of Saturday?"

When he answered yes, she closed her eyes.

"Each eve of Saturday you stop at the market, purchase your sup, and then drive home by the fields; the better to watch the colts run. Indulge not your hunger, but head straight for the field. You uncle has been tasting of the stout and will not secure the gate. Arrive early and the young mare will not have run out before the lorry."

He stared at her strangely, but tipped his hat and drove away.

The next day found her wandering with the tourists near Amesbury in the county Wilshire. The voice behind her sounded familiar.

"Well, does it look like home, or is there anything that jumps out at you?"

"If you are asking if this is where the twins were branded, no." She smiled at Pablo. "Did you really think this all was tied to Stonehenge in some way?"

"Truth be told, yes. One likes to look to the dramatic. It would take some of the mystery away from this place."

Karen smiled. "That's not hard to do. It started ten thousand years ago. One big assed tree and four large posts planted in the ground.

Three thousand B.C. work went on in the form of earthen works and such.

About 2600 B.C., work started with stone." She nodded towards a six ton stone. "That includes the altar stone.

This was an on going work. Not all by the same group of people either." Karen reached out and pulled him towards another rock. "If you really want to tie something to the twins and Samhan, look to the bluestones. That was done about 2000 B.C. They made up the original henge I...or rather Morriagan was branded at. They were moved here to effectively keep the ceremony from being repeated. As a statement, the altar here was turned on end."

"Well," Pablo said, "that brings some truth and even a bit of closure to Stonehenge."

"But you aren't satisfied. Then consider this. Justice throughout the ages has not been restricted to the twins and Samhan. The word Stonehenge comes from the Old English word *stãn* meaning - duh - stone, and more interestingly *hence* meaning gallows. You will note that the stones have two uprights and a lintel, the same as medieval gallows. So, truth be known, there were many more things done in the name of justice at these sites than the Twins. Some of them much worse."

"Good, because that brings me to something. Truth. I was given some information, and I find it to be inaccurate. With it being inaccurate, it makes me wonder how much other bullshit I was fed. I am starting to understand there is very little magic and myth here. I know that explanation has been used even by the originators, but if you want more accuracy, substitute the word Quantum physics." She shrugged. "In another 5,000 years the two words might be interchangeable."

Pablo took off his sunglasses and moved to place them in his shirt pocket. Karen made a slight motion with her finger.

"That is interesting," he said to Karen. "It seems my arm no longer is working." He looked down at it with interest.

"I would rather you didn't reach inside your jacket. Think of this. I am not sure it would work, or that I could do it, but I just made your biceps and triceps muscles quit working." She looked him in the eyes. "The heart is a muscle also."

"Yes, well...," he put his sunglasses back on, "the arm muscles are voluntary and the heart is involuntary, but let's not check it out to see if we can get it to stop working. What exactly were you interested in information about?"

"Along the line it was portrayed that if you summoned the creature, and didn't know its name, you were in deep shit. That's a crock. It turns out that a lot of people knew the name Samhan. Spetzner, I mean Dailey, knew the name. He's the one that told me; he still got a trip through the veg-o-matic."

Pablo nodded in agreement. "You are correct. It was all a matter of impossible timing and people running into each other.

Everyone has been dancing for the prize. Control of Samhan." He clenched his fists. "The search for you was dropped five years ago. Hell, you shouldn't have been hard to find at all. You were constantly under government care and protection. But no. When the day came to bring you into the loop, shitski. Zip. Zilch. The fucking button was hit and it all came back, 'Record Not Found.'"

He stopped, removed his glasses and put them in his pocket. Karen didn't stop him. "It was then that everything fell apart. All the people who had been working together immediately blamed the next group and everyone grabbed for the brass ring on their own. Oh, yeah," he admitted, "we were just as greedy a bastard as the next.

Thompsons were our fuck up. We tried it knowing the name. Hell we called it up like a charm. It took one look around, tasted the blood and figured out our real intent, didn't see you, and just started killing."

He sat down on a bench. "You want to know how it stands now? We talk to the U.S. scientists who pushed the cloning. We talk to the Vatican who seem to have most the historical documents on it.

The World Health Organization is pulled in, in case of a pandemic.

NATO and the United Nations are both riding herd because they don't trust each other.

And everybody is wondering if you don't play ball with us, why we can't stick a gun in your ear and pull the trigger.

Have I been honest enough with you?"

"Seems like a pretty good start," admitted Karen. "Why the come to Jesus speech now?"

"Because they are tired of waiting. They think a show of force will work. They are coming after you. We aren't going to do a damn thing about it."

"Bob and Jerimy?" she asked.

"Alive because they pose no real threat. Tagollini is dead. Seems he broke acceptability by not letting you be blown to shit after pasta."

"I thought you guys would push back." said Karen.

"We did. You've been away from mainstream news my lady."

He smiled without humor. Terrible accident. Air Force Two went down. Total of twenty-five souls on board. Inclusive of the Vice President." The smile stayed cold. "We, in theory of course, are in an expansive game of chess. We will trade a bishop for a bishop, a knight for a knight, a vice president for a vice president." He shook his head. "Do you play chess?"

"Yes, I do as a matter of fact."

"What do you think the resolution of this game might be?"

Karen didn't hesitate. "Yes. There comes a time when trading pieces gets too expensive. I imagine that time has come."

"Yes. I just wanted to be totally honest about it. Not in small part because I have no desire to have something with claws show up at my bedside."

Karen laughed in spite of herself. "You are just politely saying that all bets are off and you are pulling any protection or possibility of protection."

"That and...well, like I say...giving you a warning that people are going to be coming after you hard and without mercy. You have maybe 48 hours before you become a hard target."

"Are they looking to capture or kill?" Karen asked.

"It's dead or alive baby. Your friends should be safe if they lay low and don't attract attention they should be...might be... safe." His voice changed. "Me, hey...back to the barrio and pound concrete for a while. No becoming a casualty figure for this chico. I'm going to be like your friend Stafford. He disappeared from everyone's screens."

"I don't understand. Your society isn't taking a side?"

"I wish that were the case," Pablo said. "I wasn't totally honest. The Thompson's were a part of our experiment. I told you that." He hesitated. "What you didn't know was there was video tape of the whole thing. It never made it into the hands of the police, but it has been viewed by everyone else. I am leaving the society. They will be coming after you themselves. Religions are going to be stalking you. I can think of three governments that want at least two of the three pieces of this power play. There are you, the planchette and Samhan. You are the least valuable and expendable, The society knows my feelings in this matter. I will be dead by tomorrow noon, if they can find me,"

He held his finger up to her lips. "I walk off into the sunset here and now. In the car - the red, used, compact four door - you will find some simple luggage and a thin case with a diplomatic seal. When they x-ray it they aren't going to be happy, but don't let them take it away from you.

That's what that seal is for, carry on luggage. They freak over box knives these days and your sword will have them shitting their drawers."

Her started walking off and stopped. "From here on out trust no one, but your closest friends, I think you will find...they've been busy. And from here on out, all others, and I mean all others, are your enemies. Take no captives and show no mercy." With that, he turned again and walked from the circle of stones.

Karen raised her face to the sky. The wind felt cool and fresh. She didn't let it fool her. The vaguely familiar memories were coming back to her. History was repeating itself. Thousands of years earlier corruption and greed had chased her heels for most of her life. Now was different.

Then communication was minimal. A person might live and die in one spot, never knowing what transpired twenty miles away.

Not so now.

She sighed and dug in her pocket for a faded number she hoped would still work.

CHAPTER XXIV
Storm Clouds Build

They met her at the airport, as she was preparing to leave; five men walking to her in a wedge formation. They exuded self confidence, power and control.

The lead man walked up, comparing her to the photo he held in his hand. "Well, Miss. We've been trying to meet you for quite a while now." He nodded towards a hallway leading out of the main concourse.

"Perhaps it would be better if we had privacy while we talked."

Karen smiled her friendliest smile. "That would be wonderful, but my flight starts boarding in less than five minutes."

The man smiled back, "You might want to consider a later flight. One on the weekend; a red eye, or we could even arrange transportation for you." He put his hands behind his back and rocked on the balls of his feet. "We've been looking to talk for sooooo long."

The other four moved forward taking up positions loosely around Karen. One moved his jacket back, revealing the butt of a sidearm.

Karen laughed. "You should have done that a month or two ago. That was back in my easily intimidated period."

The leader shook his head. "Don't think it, sweetheart. We know you're proficient in martial arts. Hell, it was our people that taught you most of what you know."

He nodded again at the hallway. "Here's what is going to happen. We went through your checked luggage and didn't find it, so it's got to be in carry on. Your backpack. Once we have that, we can be less formal."

They expected her to bolt and run. They didn't expect her to comply. When she started walking towards the corridor, as asked, she was five feet ahead of them before they moved.

Walking down the hallway, out of view of the public, she halted and turned.

Staring at the leader, she knew this wasn't going to be easy to pull off. She was, after all, not truly Morriagan. She might be the same right down to the cells of her body, but she didn't have the training or knowledge.

Looking inside herself she tried to focus. Mentally she reached out and envisioned his heart beating in his chest. When he was an arm's length away she used her thoughts to clamp down as tight as she could.

The man stopped with a surprised expression and his mouth half open. Beads of sweat formed on his face and he clutched at his chest.

Two of his men took him by the arms as his knees buckled, but he stayed conscious.

At that moment a man in uniform walked by the intersection of the hallway and hesitated. Karen waved frantically and called for help. She did not know if the man was military, security or police. She didn't much care at this stage.

Her attempt had knocked the man for a loop, maybe even induced a heart attack that would kill him later, but it hadn't dropped him in his tracks as hoped, and she knew she couldn't pull it off with the four remaining.

The man in uniform saw an upset woman, hailing him for help, a man clutching his chest and either being supported by two others, or attacked.

He placed his whistle in his mouth and started blowing. Another sounded in the distance, then another followed by the sound of many running feet.

In the ensuing confusion Karen headed for her boarding area at a pace just slow enough to keep from attracting attention.

She did notice the two men not supporting the ring leader glance at each other and follow her.

After she had boarded the plane, she thought the getaway had gone smoothly.

Then, as they were securing the door, the two men entered, taking seats in the back. No one was smiling this time.

Karen got on her cell phone and got lucky twice. Once in that the number she had called yesterday still rang through, and second, she was on for thirty seconds before the stewardess made her shut it off and hand it over.

CHAPTER XXV
Rest in Peace

Stafford dialed a number and waited. When a voice answered, he started.

"Hey, ya. I'd like to talk to Jerimy," he paused. "Jeremy Naden. Uh-huh, a detective," another pause. "Yeah, I know he was suspended so I can't talk to him *there,* but I figured you might know where I could reach him. He isn't answering his phone at home. What? Sure, I'll hold."

Stafford tapped out a cigarette from the pack and lit it while he waited. Finally a voice came on.

"Mr. Stafford? Mr. Stafford I am very sorry, I have bad news for you. It seems that detective Naden was having severe emotional issues with his suspension. A couple nights ago it appears to have gotten the best of him.

I truly regret to inform you that Jerimy took his own life. We, ah, have been attempting to get a hold of you, but no number was available. Would you tell me where you are, and a number at which..."

Stafford broke the connection, removed the battery and headed upstairs. At the bottom of the stairs he almost messed his pants when another phone rang. It was the one that had rang yesterday when Karen called. He had forgotten to dispose of it and activate another.

He debated answering it. When he did answer it, it was Karen once more. She quickly relayed a frightening message. He agreed to meet her at the airport and was on the verge of telling her about Jerimy when that connection broke.

He stared at the phone for a second then headed back upstairs.

Four men he had never seen before were sitting, looking at him. He had known they were there, and had been there, for several days. He had heard them moving around. They were not annoying. They moved quietly and talked the same.

"Anyone here speak English?" he asked.

One man rose. "Yes, sir. We all do. How may we be of service?" The man appeared young and clean cut.

Without thinking, Stafford blurted out his problems. "I need these two phones disposed of and a friend picked up at the airport. Not sure that will happen because everybody and the police are looking for me. They've killed one of my friends and know the other will be at the airport."

The man blinked, then spoke matter of factly. "Yes sir. If you give me the phones and a description of your friend, we will take care of these matters."

Stafford was taken back. "How would you do that?"

The man blinked again, taken back himself. "Are you sure you would want to know the details sir?"

"Why wouldn't I?"

A second man laughed, slapped his knee and stood. "I told you this jefe had balls. He does not hide behind the skirts of ignorance." The man laughed again. "I will tell you. The phones we drop in a dumpster after wiping them down. Then I pour gasoline on them and ignite it.

At the airport we have a man standing in plain sight, with a sign. On the sign is your friend's name. Never," he pointed a finger towards the ceiling, "never will a friend of our boss be made to slink around like a stray dog."

Stafford liked the man's attitude, but had some doubts. "And what if the cops or others tried to grab my friend?"

The man shrugged. "Then the dozen armed chicos and chicas we have hidden there kill them and take your friend anyway."

Yes, Stafford liked this man. "Won't you have an issue with airport security"

The first young man smiled. "Why would we? They make $8.50 an hour. They know we are not terrorists. We will offer them an envelope of gratitude. Besides," he asked, "how do you think we get your product into the states? By burro?"

Stafford smiled. "I don't suppose there is a way I could be there, is there?"

The man frowned. "Yo, man, I stand under you want to pop a cap in person, but I suggest you come and catch the show, but play it slow."

"Okay. I can do that. What do we need?"

"People. How long we got till this goes down?"

Stafford did some mental calculations. "Ten hours. You realize that the people we're fucking with are dangerous? They won't hesitate to kill."

The man motioned to another sitting in a chair still watching television. "Francisco, aqui."

"What you need bro?"

"Francisco, how old are you?"

The man shrugged, "Diez y orcho; eighteen man."

"Where were you born?"

"Bogotá."

"You ever kill anyone?"

The man looked strangely at him, "Man, what is this? I took out my first dude when I was twelve. I grew up on the streets then worked the fields. You don't keep track of the ghosts, man. That will eat you up."

The man turned to Stafford, "We are not the boy scouts."

෬෭

Disembarking from the plane was uneventful. Karen was wearing a smile, blue jeans, denim shirt, brown hiking boots, and carried her robe over her left arm. It effectively covered the 'diplomatic' pouch she cradled there.

Remarkably when she had boarded, and it had been x-rayed after tripping the metal detector, it hadn't raised eyebrows too much. A sword with a Japanese seal. To them it was like a Texan with a Stetson; a nun with Rosary beads. God bless all the stereotypical martial art movies.

The man from Saudi Arabia, behind her, had his fingernail clippers confiscated.

Entering the lobby she looked around for Jerimy or Robert. Seeing neither, her eye was caught by a young girl holding a sign. It was made from black poster board and Karen's name was in gold glitter.

The two men who had followed her on board were looking around also. Unusual. They had already picked her out, but were holding their distance. Taking a deep breath she walked to the girl holding the sign and stood there.

The girl looked her up and down, then grinned with a smile so mischievous that her nose actually wrinkled.

"Karen, I'm Carla. We *should* actually beat feet, but if you have a second I want to watch."

The grin was contagious. "What exactly are we waiting for?" asked Karen. "I assume you know those two men," she nodded in their direction, "are out to kidnap me or worse."

"Oh, yes. I've had my eye on them, I'm just waiting for the other bastards to make their move. They have been over by the rent-a-car desk for a couple hours." She folded the sign in half neatly and tossed it in a trash can.

"And we want to wait for that?" asked Karen.

The girl nodded vigorously. "The guys were here and I sent them away. They have no subtle bones in their bodies. Their idea is toe-to-toe, shoot it out, victory at any cost." She blatantly pointed at six more men headed their way. "Just like those guys. Too much testosterone."

Karen started to remove the robe from the sword. The girl reached out and stopped her. "Not needed. I called Homeland Security an hour and a half ago, describing the 'terrorists.'"

The girl cleared her throat, pointed and screamed.

Karen wasn't sure where the people all came from. The men walking their way might have been able to talk their way out, but they weren't given a chance.

Half were dropped by Tasers and the other half displayed amazing intelligence by dropping to the floor with their hands and arms extended.

The only fight was between the F.B.I., Homeland Security and the Sky Marshals to see who got the right to cuff them. There was even a cameraman from the police television show.

In the ensuing confusion Carla led her by the arm to a waiting taxi.

Robert was waiting for her and gave her a quick hug, and a peck on the cheek. She looked around the cab. "What? Jerimy couldn't make it?"

Robert sighed and couldn't meet her eyes.

"No, Karen." He slammed the door with the side of his fist. "There is no good way to do this. He's gone Karen. He's dead. The powers that be are saying suicide, but that's bullshit." Tears started forming in his eyes, matched Karen's. "It's all just bullshit."

CHAPTER XXVI
Trust Not The Horde

The taxi was dark, somber, and in its own way let them pull their sorrow out for inspection without airing it.

Karen weighed her words rather than blurt. She did not ask if he were sure. She did not rant that 'someone would pay.' She grieved and sought more information.

"How much hard fact do we have?" Karen asked.

"None. I believe that he is dead. I don't buy the part of him eating his gun.

"No," Karen said. "He wouldn't do that. He always said he would find another way, if he ever decided to. He said it gave guns a black eye."

⁂

"Are you going to be alright with this?" Karen asked.

"Define alright," requested Stafford.

"Well, I summon Samhan, we get to the bottom of this; take names and kick ass. The normal."

Stafford thought about the situation. "If it means I don't have to live the rest of my existence in this basement, I'm game."

"I am not sure what to expect, but let's have a go of it."

Pulling the small pocket knife, Karen got her thumbnail into the groove and opened the tiny blade. She looked at her hand.

"Damn, this thing just healed. This is getting old." She pulled a red bandana from her pocket, to staunch the flow of blood when done. As gently as possible, yet still slicing through the skin, she pulled the tip across her palm. The crimson welled forth, filling the cup of her palm.

She turned her hand over, spilling the red well into the hollow of the planchette. Gripping the bandana tightly she laid a finger from her good hand on its rim.

Almost immediately it moved on the table, leaving a thin, solid line of red.

Stafford turned his eyes away, bothered by the process. In doing so, he saw Samhan appear out of nothing.

It were as if the figure came into focus, rather than materialized, He found himself staring into those black, cold eyes.

"What? No camera, Mr. Swafford?" The voice was soft and feathery. "Yes, you can both hear me and understand. Do not bother yourself with the details, it is more telepathy than speech. That is how I can insure innocence or guilt."

The creature moved silently, stopped, then reassured Stafford. "You worry I will pick up on your fantasies and 'little secrets.' Do not worry about them. All humans have them and they interest me not."

Stafford noted Samhan stood upright. His rear legs had superior rotation in the hip and knee, ensuring the capability of travel on two, or travel on four. The face combined features both human and animal. The word demonic came to mind.

"I summoned you…" Karen started.

"Yes, I know," Samhan stopped her. "You summoned me for justice."

The creature looked at her with almost sympathetic eyes. "You do not understand.

You are not Morriagan. You have everything she did, down to the cellular state. You do not have her training, nor her life experience." The creature walked to her and laid a clawed hand gently on her shoulder.

"It is not meant in the negative, and you should be happy indeed. You are your own person. Yes, there is a shadow of the second born, nothing more."

Samhan paced the floor. "Indeed, your summons and my arrival means little in your world. It is overpopulated and the very concept of justice is alien to the thoughts and deeds of the horde that breeds to its own destruction."

Stafford felt obliged to speak. "You might be partially right, but our society has taken steps to insure justice or to at least exclude injustice."

Samhan actually laughed. "You have no justice, you have laws. Those laws vary from country to country; state to state, and city by city.

You have so many laws that people make a living trying to interpret them. Even they do not agree between each other and must have another party decide.

Consider this. You want me to kill the person who took this Jerimy's life?"

"Yes," said Karen.

"It will be done. How about the person who hired him?"

"Well, yes."

"And if it were done or decreed by a government, how far down the chain shall the death flow? Shall it flow to the people who elected them? Are these not the same that designed the ineffective laws to start with? Take example of the bomb dropped in an attempt to kill.

Were I to assign guilt from the age of the twins, it would be the pilot, the navigator, the people who take care of the craft, the people who trained then, the people who built everything, those that gave the order, ad infintum."

Samhan laid on the floor comfortably and stretched. "Your concept of justice cannot begin to exist with the corruption that lives. Trust not the horde, for it lies even to itself."

Karen laid her head down on her crossed arms.

Stafford demanded, "Then what? We just let them slaughter us?"

The laughter again. "No, unless that is your desire. Realize that you are not requesting justice, however. Separate yourself from the horde. You seek vengeance and retribution…"

Karen broke in, "Yes! I want the bastards to die, and to die in such a way they know what it is for, why and who."

She slammed her hand on the table, blending fresh blood with the old. "When done, I want them to cower in fear when they even consider the possibility of coming after us again."

Samhan nodded approvingly. "Now you betray a portion of the second born that resides in your soul. What you ask will be granted. In return you will grant one boon to me." He leaned forward and spoke softly in her ear.

Her eyes widened and she said, "So shall it be."

CHAPTER XXVII
The Purple Pagers

t was there, but it wasn't there. You could look on the maps all day long, but never find a clue.

To get to it one had to, first pass through the Cedar Air Center's main gate. With guards posted 24/7. The only people they allowed through were employees, or;

Military personnel headed for N.A.A.T.S., the Northern Army Aviation Training Site. N.A.A.T.S. had their own security force comprised of civilian contractors, who only let members of the U.S. military through, or;

Singapore Air Force. A foreign military contingent who purchased top line military equipment, but were banned from taking it home for five years. So, on American soil, they had their own base, training, until they could take their toys home. They only allowed their own military and a handful of American instructors, or;

The purple page gang. Tucked behind the other three outfits was a compound. Everyone in the three outfits knew the Pagers existed, but you didn't mention it.

Their vehicles would approach with a small square of purple construction paper visible on the dash. Those vehicles were not stopped. No names or plate numbers recorded.

The general consensus was that anything purple was home free. It wasn't so much security's job to protect the Pagers from intruders as it was intruders from the Pagers.

If you insisted on climbing into the gorilla's cage, then more power to you. You fuck with the gorilla and the gorilla *will* fuck with you.

And sure as hell the words black ops was *never* used by anyone in the area.

ဆစ

The pager security officer pointed to the monitor. It crisply displayed the image of a woman standing in the middle of the street, dressed in blue jeans and black tee shirt, carrying a sword. Behind her could be seen three passenger jets set to ground for antiterrorist training.

The senior officer grunted. "What vehicle did she arrive in?"

"No vehicle has cleared any of the security gates for over an hour."

"Microwave transmitters?"

"No, sir. No zone alarms were tripped. No seismic incidents noted either."

"Any aircraft in the area?"

The guard smiled. "Of course, but they are all Cedar's or N.A.A.T.S. You would play hell getting anything past them." He cocked his head at a growing rumble. "Or past the two attack choppers patrolling the area."

"So you are telling me she just appeared out of thin air? Maybe you might try something novel like sending some armed personnel out to speak with her. Go slow at first. It might just be some fucking lost D&D gamer wandered in off the desert."

"Sir?"

"Son, how many people assault a military base or such with a sword? It might have worked in the middle ages, but now we have moved a small measure beyond that."

"Roger that."

Four armed guards gathered. While they looked like security, if one inspected their uniforms, one would note the only insignia they wore was an American flag on the right shoulder and a generic patch, that only said *Security,* on the left. On their chest was what appeared to be a badge, but upon closer scrutiny turned out to be a pleasant, but meaningless, mass of silver thread embroidered in the shape of an oval.

Interestingly enough their name tags showed they all had been named after colors. S/O (security officer) Brown appeared to be in charge.

"All righty then. We go out the door, I'm lead, the three of you form a wedge on me. Two on my left side, one on my right. We walk at a leisurely pace. No hands on firearms or anything aggressive looking.

Mr. Green, when we get in range you taser her. No warnings, no 'what ifs,' should you miss it will be up to you, Mr. Black to take her out. For real. I want two shots center of mass and one to the head.

Let's move gentlemen."

The video camera caught them exiting the building; it tracked them across the grassy lawn. It happened as they crossed the curb and stepped onto the asphalt.

Even after three replays of the tape, the last slo-mo, it always looked the same. Their images smeared and streaked, rushing to a pin point at their center and disappearing completely. The only thing marking their exit was a small cloud of dust that rapidly dispersed.

The senior officer was on the phone, "Yes, sir. No, sir. It doesn't show that much." A pause. "Mr. President the cameras that recorded this can replay a bullet in flight, slowing it down to the speed of a butterfly." He listened for a while then nodded. "Yes sir, I am in total agreement. It is her and she has returned. Absolutely. Consider it done."

Reaching past the seated officer the senior flipped two toggle switches and picked up a microphone. He spoke into it without emotion or inflection.

"Shooters one and two, do you copy this transmission?"

"Roger that."

"Lima Charlie."

"Take the shot."

At the four corners of the compound stood four towers. Each held a man. The common denominator among them was that each was an exceptional marksman and sniper. Armed with a .50 caliber Grizzly rifle, topped with state of the art optics; each one could put a clean, cold shot on a man sized target at two thousand yards.

Karen was slightly less than one hundred yards from either one, or two; the snipers on the south-east and south-west walls.

The senior waited ten seconds, frowned, and waited ten more before keying up the mike.

"Shooter one, do you have a copy?" No response. "Shooter two do you have a copy?" He gently set the mike down. "Do we have video inside towers one and two?"

"Yes sir," the officer responded. Picking up what looked like a remote, he tuned a tower. The monitor displayed a red blur. Apparently the lens was covered with blood.

Tower two gave a clear image. The floor and wall it showed were both splattered with blood. Center frame showed a red, wet mass that comprised internal organs, and in the upper left corner leaning against the wall, an arm and hand still clenching a rifle.

When the view was returned to the street, Karen still stood there but now she was looking directly at the distant camera, crooking her finger, beckoning him to join her.

He did.

Karen stood smiling in a friendly manner. The senior officer approached cautiously, somewhat afraid he would disappear into a mystery dot like the last four.

"Good morning," she chimed cheerfully, "I asked you out here to answer a couple questions. Do you mind?"

"Young lady, it is good we can talk. It would appear we got off to a rough start."

"Please," Karen said. "Can it. I didn't say I wanted kisses and hugs; I just want some answers."

He nodded, he realized he was well within reach of the sword.

"First things first. D-41. What the hell does D-41 stand for?"

He hesitated. "I fail to see…"

"Just answer the fucking question," she snarled.

"Very well. Druid. Cloning attempt number forty one."

Karen reeled. "Where are the first forty?"

"Out of the first forty, most embryos were not viable or were born…defective. Those out of the parameters were terminated."

Tear welled up in her eyes and her voice choked for a second. "Next question." She held something up in her hand. "Can your camera focus in tight enough to read this?"

"Child's play, my dear."

CHAPTER XXVIII
Happily Ever After

The aide addressed the President.

"Sir, before I run it again I must impress on you; a copy of this tape was delivered by person or persons unknown to the desk of every governor in every state. In addition, it was performed in slightly less than an hour an in no case was any intruder observed."

"And this is the person that was the center of our little occult combined action?" The President asked. "You know I saw the action previous to this real time. Where the four people went down the drain with no drain."

"Yes," the aide said. "There is talk of black holes and black magic. No one knows for sure."

"This sure turned out to be a cluster fuck. To this day no one will admit who authorized a Stealth bomber strike on our own soil. What did we do about the pilot?"

"He has been removed from the equation."

"And that police detective?"

"The same."

"Good," the President nodded. "Which brings us to that editor."

It was the aides turn to nod. "That is addressed in the note which will follow the second airing. Rumors, however have him everywhere from dead to a drug lord."

The tape started rolling.

In the monitor Karen raised an object and the camera zoomed in on it. It was a stop watch and she started it with her thumb. The screen shrank and moved to the top right, where it stayed, displaying the running stop watch.

The rest of the display was a collage of death.

Two men walking down a hallway laughing. A dark blur hits them and there is an explosion of blood, arms, legs and a head coming at the camera. By the time it hit's the floor, the blur has moved on to its next victim.

The next scene shows a man reaching for a revolver in a holster. The blur jumps over the top of him; a portion of the blur reaches down and peels the top of his head back at eye level.

"What is it?" The President asked.

"You can slow it down as much as you want, it stays a blur. There is no doubt that it is a creature, being, monster...whatever, that is summoned by the girl, D-41."

The screen showed Karen pushing the button on the stop watch, then lashing out with the sword, decapitating the man next to her.

"Talk to me," the President ordered.

"From the time she started to the time she stopped was fifty seven seconds. In that time span, eighty four people were slaughtered. Not all in the same area either. Some behind locked doors and almost all armed.

It was thought to be impossible to get to this place unnoticed. It had hard security. Didn't do squat to protect them."

"The note. What about the note?" The President asked, holding it up. "I can't read one word of this chicken scratch."

"One note, you got the original, everyone else got copies. The chicken scratches turns out to be Latin. We got our initial translation on the internet.

Amazingly accurate. The note was generated by the creature, if we are to believe the words. It is a warning. More ultimatum than warning.

In a nutshell, if anything happens to the D-41 unit, what happened at the compound will happen at the Capitol here in D.C., and in the Capitol building of every state. Plus, it will all take place in just a few minutes under an hour. These people died as a demonstration of ability."

"Damn," The President said. "We definitely back off the unit. This was a comprehensive demonstration."

"More than that, Sir. If something befalls her...say...she gets ran over by a bus, it will be um...the best translation is *investigated*. It continues stating the planchette is gone. Taken by the creature when it left. It can no longer be summoned or controlled by the D-41. It doesn't care what we do, it isn't coming back, unless we go after her."

"A blood amnesty," The President said. "And we are sure this is all factual? It can really gain entrance and these notes aren't the work of a group?"

The aide moved some papers on the desk, revealing the deep gouges left by claws. "I believe it to be, Sir."

The Commander and Chief ran a finger down one of the grooves, "So do I."

෬෭

"Thank you, Robert," Karen said, standing in the doorway.

"My pleasure, kid," Robert replied as he looked down the path to the beach. "It's getting dark so I'd better..."

"I don't know if I'll ever be able to pay the money back."

Robert shrugged. "Hey, it's not important. I have, uh, a lot of money that I'd have a hard time declaring. It's got to go somewhere, and not where it has been going.

Besides, Pablo and his crew are kinda getting their shit back together. They sold it to me for a song. The contractor cleaned it up and put a new roof and floor on it. That cost an arm and a leg, but what the hell. I never gave you much, but a hard time.

This little pile of rock is over 2,000 years old. Yet it is as if the hand of God were protecting this hut."

Robert looked around a last time. "Besides, I'll see you tomorrow and we'll start a watered down version of all this. *Spectral Images* always finishes its stories."

"You can't stay below the radar, can you? I've already lost one man in my life."

Stafford lowered his eyes. "Okay, I'll keep it low key. Maybe even write it under a fake 'by-line.'"

Karen just shook her head as he walked off into the night. Turning she entered her new home.

There wasn't much for furniture, but that was okay.

She walked to the wall and pried on a stone. It came free and a soft, blue, protective light lit the room. She reached inside and brought out a circular slab of oak.

She sat it on the cheap table, next to the wood working tools she had bought the day before.

"...and toil she shall until the eye of the day returns to look upon her labor...," she whispered under her breath.

DEATH CLOUD

THE LIFE AND TIMES OF WILLIAM BUCKINGHAM, MOUNTAIN MAN

BY

W.G. MARSH

Death Cloud Notes - To start with, this is the first major, or *long* piece I wrote. As such, no matter its flaws or failings, it remains my favorite composition. Its original title was quite a mouthful.

Death Cloud - The Life and Times of William Buckingham, Mountain Man

The title itself almost needs chapters.

The story originated in the fact that at one time I was into *living history*. Also known as Buckskinning. It was in Montana, living in a tipi for a year, wearing buckskin and using nothing that was out of period for 1830. You will find my descriptions accurate. It was also because I got to thinking that man was very egotistical in thinking that alien visitation, cattle mutilation and such, was reserved for our modern time.

The story involves a notion, idea, concept, that was not written about at the time I was writing this story. Nano technology and a nano cloud. On the day I finished writing it I went to the library. I checked out a book by M. Creighton called *Prey*. It was about a nano cloud. Bad timing, I was so depressed the idea had been used I tossed the floppy in a drawer and never looked at it again for a year. No, I did not get the idea from that book.

Lastly, I know there is a disclaimer saying everyone is fictious. Sort of. The whiskey vendor in the story, and the name, is influenced by a friend I worked with at a call center. So there.

Enjoy.

- WGM
 Tucson, Arizona

Prologue

"The leaves of memory make a mournful rustle in the dark." - Longfellow

Ice cubes swirled, clinking gently against the Waterford glass as they floated in the amber whiskey.

He had been listening to the conversation, weighing in his mind whether his words would be wasted on those around him.

Normally silence would be best, with the story left untold.

As it had been in the past.

Yet these were trusted friends and business partners. All men of power and men in search of the exceptional in life, be it material or intellectual.

Besides, the glow of fine scotch in his veins lowered his guard - and raised his trust. A rarity for this man.

With a half smile he placed his drink on a leather coaster protecting the top of an ageless oak desk. The desk's surface was already ornamented with dozens of circular stains. The coaster was tradition. No new marks were permitted to join those created more than a hundred years earlier.

Rising from his chair he slowly circled the desk to sit upon its corner. From this perch he half raised his hand. All idle talk in the room ceased with the gesture, as was proper when the host wanted to speak.

"Gentlemen. You have been speaking of legends. I speak of a man. The man is now a memory; and memories - like autumn leaves

- are scattered by the wind. The leaves are fated to lie crumpled and ignored until the seasons cover them with a cleansing blanket of snow."

He hesitated. "With the rebirth of spring the dead leaves have vanished from the face of the earth, and likewise - with time - memories from the minds of men. All is forgotten and without trace."

Picking up the drink, he sipped the single malt and smiled. "So I speak of a forgotten man. William Buckingham."

He lowered his glass and stared at his friends. "But while he lived the life and times of William Buckingham had power. Power that shook the very earth."

"Refill your glasses, and listen to a tale. A tale of men and gods, of buckskin, black powder and sorcery." He stared deep into his drink. "Perhaps in a small part a story about the whiskey you drink tonight. A tale of William Buckingham, mountain man."

CHAPTER 1
Song of Death

"Death is not the greatest loss in life. The greatest loss is what dies inside us while we live." - Norman Cousins

Dying in Saint Louis was twisting what little of his mind remained; molding it into a warped and tattered mockery of what it had been.

The final act made everything vague; reality consisted of foggy images that mixed with distant memories. All floating on the horizon of his consciousness.

Reality and memory flashed like lightning, fusing, merging into fevered fantasies that served to amuse what remained of the once remarkable mind. A mind rapidly collapsing into darkness and insanity.

One of the images that flickered like a flame in the night, was of a valley. A valley that had haunted Buck through his last years of life. Now it was no longer a distant and suppressed memory. Now it was a memory standing just outside.

A memory bringing with it a feeling of dread; a feeling of standing frozen on the tracks of life while the oncoming train of death approached.

Yet even the horrifying memory of that loathsome valley was better than lying helpless, listening to the final beats of a failing heart. Lying helpless, forced to listen to a room filled with contrite voices belonging to other borders.

Sometimes the voices spoke of his impending death.

Sometimes they spoke of the strange disfigurement that branded his face.

If the borders had been able to tear their eyes from his face they would have noticed the scars covering his withered body. But such distraction was impossible. The gleaming crystal eye set next to the deep blue one stared unblinking from his death's head face and pulled their souls in for judging. For most onlookers it was not a comfortable feeling.

In the beginning the voices made him want to scream, "I'm dying, not deaf!" With passing time even the rude observations of his morbid spectators became acceptable, for he knew the soft voices would eventually fade as he slipped into unconsciousness. Once more old memories would dance on the back of his eyelid. Each slip into darkness spurred his tired heart to race in fear that *this* was the final moment. Each awakening made his heart race in relief. Relief that was quickly replaced by regret.

The valley haunting Buck's memory was years in the past and miles across the nation. A nation that had been rapidly shrinking, with vile blossoms of cities that spread along vines comprised of roads, waterways and iron rails.

This valley was a place he often thought about returning to, but even in health he had realized the journey would be in vain. But still...still it burned in his memory like a smoldering ember.

Sad, he thought, that the only journey available to him now was a journey of death. A stretch of map Buck did not want to cross, but one he knew was demanded by his unending plunge down a river of failing health.

Death cast a cold shadow across Buck's final camp, and Buck knew it to be a piss-poor camp at best.

A clapboard shack - just an impoverished boarding house standing at the edge of town and eternity.

Buckingham lay on a cobbled bed constructed of rough planks. The wood crudely hammered together in what he envisioned to be the masterpiece of some unknown and drunken carpenter. Nestled inside its splintered framework was a lice infested canvas mattress. The only bedding to cover it was a moth eaten cavalry blanket that reeked of sweat, vomit and piss.

The stench from his rack held him in a tainted lover's embrace, writhing and mingling with death's odor. A smell seeping from every pore on his body.

Too tired to move Buck shed silent tears. Tears of regret that this embrace was so very different than that of his wool Hudson. Lord, a season's pelts he would gladly give to feel the itch of his old blanket. To wrap himself in its pungent smell, steeped in the wood smoke from a thousand fires that had blazed under a million stars.

His table matched style and grace with his final bed. An old cottonwood stump, crudely hewn with a bucksaw and topped with scarred planks of varying length. Upon it sat a single kerosene lamp, its chimney blacked from sleepless nights of pain; the agony and nightmares kept at bay by the small, flickering yellow flame that stood guard.

Indeed, the chimney of the soot darkened lamp was in need of cleaning, but it mattered little. Buck no longer had coin to purchase the cupful of fuel required to feed the diminutive flame, and even if he had been rich, he no longer had the strength to lift such a cup.

Ah, money. The money was absent to pay for his lodging as well, but even his cold fingered landlord was not so glacial of heart to cast out a dying man. Particularly a man fading so fast. Death would be the great evictor from this property.

Except for one man, the same morbid audience who watched and waited called him Mr. Buckingham - or "that poor bastard." Not out of respect or sympathy, Buck figured, but out of regard for his dying. People seldom respect others, but they did respect death. They always have a tendency to respect that which scares the hell out of them. Buck no longer thought of himself by any baptismal name and had not for years. Only one man called him by a name he responded to and that name had followed him from his years in the mountains.

It was a heathen name. *Walks with Limp.*

The man from whose tongue this name fell, and without whose help the familiar wings of death would have carried Buck away years before, was friend and compadre. A compadre who had offered to move Buck from this hovel and into comfort months earlier. Only pride had kept Buck from taking the offer, and now he found himself cursing that arrogance. Buck was happy that his pride had not extended to refusing the god awful whiskey his compadre was so proud of, and grateful when his friend slowly dribbled the potent liquid into his slack mouth.

In the Rockies, Buckingham had lived as a by god, thunder'in, drinkin', fur trappin' Mountain Man.

Now he would die a derelict. A wooden plank pried from his rickety table and inscribed with the civilized name plaguing him since birth. An unwanted marker for his final resting place.

In days of old, the rocks and trees had no use of calling him by his Christian name, although they had talked to him every day. Well, perhaps not talked to him as they had his red brother, but spoken their word nonetheless. Crisp songs of wind in the mountains, the rumble of thunder in the sky - always wild and free voices. The land had known him and his heart to the fullest, and accepted him as he had accepted the wild world he loved.

Now Buck was not sure who he was, or even what he was. Existence consisted of laying in his own filth and watching a grimed view out a smudged window. Trying to think thoughts that were not too deep.

Watching the clouds gather above the skyline of roofs and chimneys brought a feeling of dread. No longer were clouds a thing of beauty. Buck shuddered and closed his tired eye.

Years before he had felt secure in what he knew. Or thought he knew. His thoughts back then had ran as deep as a spring flood in a narrow river.

Once more his heart raced as darkness poured over him. In sleep his aching muscles relaxed and his thoughts flew to a time burned on his mind, soul and body. The memory was upon him.

CHAPTER 2
Song of the Mountain Man

"Mountains appear more lofty, the nearer they are approached, but great men resemble them not in this particular." - Marguerite Blessington

The idea that the valley was holy ground - and cursed - struck Buckingham as a queer notion, but then Buck had figured out the red man had quite a few strange ideas.

As dancing flames printed flickering shadows on the lodge cover after evening meals, Buck had heard many things. Things he could nod at with a smile, but not things he took to heart.

Eyes sparkled and songs flowed from a dozen lips in turn. Tales were told of how the great Thunderbird would take wing to the top of the sky and swallow the sun. At the end of the flight, day would darken to night and blackness would cover the land.

Later the feathered God of Lightening would vomit the fiery ball from his ebon beak, unable to bear the burning ember inside its craw.

Voices murmured in agreement, heads nodding, as elders took turns telling another story.

This story of a solitary warrior stalking the high country in search of game.

After a long day of hunting, the man found a coyote standing alone and exposed.

As the hunter approached, the trickster would trot ahead; always staying just out of reach, always out of range of the hunter's bow.

Time passed as the hunter follows the coyote. The edge of the sun touches the horizon. Dusk is upon the warrior and to his amazement, gone is the coyote.

As the warrior turned, he discovers a young maiden of great beauty standing in the mountain clearing. A woman who offers him pleasure and companionship in the evening.

Long black hair and smiling lips bring the warrior near. Midnight eyes pull him into the deadly sorcery.

The next day, long after the sun had risen in the east, his bleached bones were found next to the cold ashes of camp, the empty sockets of the snow-white skull staring sightless at the morning sun. All appears as if a dozen years have passed, but strangely, no animal will approach the pale skeleton.

In mournful salute, packs of coyotes gathered in the rim rocks above the onlookers, to howl funeral dirges that echo between the mountain peaks. Their wailing songs bespoke the foolishness of man.

One coyote sat apart from the pack, in silence, waiting for the others to finish. It sat resplendent, with midnight eyes and crimson fangs.

This story was one of Buck's favorites and Buckingham had felt no shame as he sat with the children listening to the parables and stories that were passed down, generation to generation. It was part of being a family and Buck was proud to be part of that family.

What he didn't like, as he stood inside the jagged tree line watching the far flung valley stretching out before him, was a nagging tickle that ran up and down his spine.

Warm wind rushed up the mountainside from the valley below, bringing with it the smell of moist earth and pine. Trees swayed, their branches beckoning him to enter the peaceful valley. The same breeze gently pushed his tangled beard back against his face in a playful caress, while the fur of his cap flattened downward, mingling with his shaggy eyebrows.

The fur was soft and retained the beauty the mountain lion had possessed in life, but Buck had paid a dear price for the bonnet. A price not measured in gold, but scars.

Before him stood a valley much as a thousand other valleys he had come across in these mountains. It had been painted on the canvas of earth as the All Mighty always seemed to slap on His bawdy pigments. The strokes had style, beauty, and power that came from a commanding hand.

Buck wasn't a religious man, but if there was a God, He lived in these mountains.

Pines blanketed the rock studded slopes on high, while in the bottom, where water flowed, aspen flashed pale golden leaves and sang their rustling song. A song that never failed to bring a smile to his lips. The liquid gurgle of a small creek sat behind the crisp parchment sound of leaves, both tunes in harmony with each other.

From the harsh blue sky above came the sharp cawing of Father Raven.

The chill of evening had faded, leaving a neutral temperature that served to accent the heat of the sun. The warmth of the golden light made a man want to stand, eyes closed, and just exist in the moment.

Buck's eyes opened wide.

Standing with one's eyes closed wasn't a healthy pastime for a mountain man.

He shook his head and shivered, but just couldn't dislodge the damned tickle. It was an annoying critter that flitted around under his skin shirt. A skeeter that wouldn't land long enough for him to smash it.

Buckingham was thirty years of age and he reckoned and those years had not come and gone by merely trusting his eyes. If a man wanted to keep his scalp in place, he used more than the bloodshot orbs hidden beneath his fur cap.

Smell was one watchdog - even the feel of the air moving over what little exposed skin he allowed was another.

Hearing was another friend that stood by you in the day and the night. A by-god mountain man used all his senses if he wanted to see the next season.

Even then, many a good man that paid attention to the world around him did not see the thaw of spring. The Rocky Mountains were harsh teachers and mistresses. They passed out the grades without emotion.

The grades were written in blood, and ranged from a passing score of life, to a dunce cap of death.

This tickle wasn't a stranger and its touch had kept him alive countless times in the past. Times when the world put a song in his heart and some greasy bastard wanted to place a lead ball in his brisket.

"No," he thought, *"it would not do to lightly dismiss the warning."*

Moving slowly he gripped the frizzen of the flintlock, easing the curved piece of metal forward.

His fingers, shattered in the past and healed in a parody of normal, held it carefully, keeping the arched iron plate from clicking against its backstop. The sound released by contact would have been small, but there was no reason to chance the clatter might fall upon sharp ears. Sharp ears which might be listening for intruders such as himself.

Rolling his eyes downward, Buck reassured himself the small pinch of black powder was still nestled snug in the pan; a dark smidgen not caked by moisture from the air or mysteriously vanished with the wind. Just as carefully and silently he pulled the frizzen back to where the folded leaf spring held it tightly once more, trapping the vital pinch securely.

That pinch of dust was the heart of a chain of events dictating whether the rifle would roar or remain silent. Whether a man might live or die.

In the same motion, he slid his thumb across the leather wrapped flint, making sure it was clean and sharp, able to peel a sliver of metal from the frizzen in a small orange-white spark. The thumbnail sized piece of stone was held in the jaws of the hammer secure as a priceless gem in a spinster's ring. There was not a wiggle to the caramel colored rock, and Buckingham knew this was good medicine.

Something about *this* particular valley gave him the hoodoos. Buck figured that uneasy feeling held over from his last night spent in the lodges.

What bothered him about that final evening was not so much his Black Foot brothers warning against his journey to this valley to trap beaver, although they had been strong in their words that a pelt was not worth his life.

Nope.

Normally when they warned you against something, they got right riled up if you butted heads with their wishes and beliefs. No, what really wet his powder was their response when he announced he was going anyway, whether they liked it or not.

He had prepared himself for argument and for anger. He expected threats. He'd prepared himself for a rip-roar'in fight, but he had not been primed for the look of sadness in his friends' eyes.

Particularly the look in Swimming Snake's eyes. Those normally unreadable eyes were darkened with concern and resignation. Snake had turned his back and slowly stooped, exiting through the circular doorway into the night. He left no words to mark his trail and that was not like him. Snake had lectures - not sparse words - to mark almost any event in life.

Buckingham didn't kid himself the concern was about his value to the encampment. He realized that most of the tribe really didn't care he was going, let alone where he was going. Only a small band of friends had a hankering to see him keep his topknot.

The others figured the valley would take care of itself, and if the white man insisted on the trip, then the white man could take care of himself.

They would count their ponies after he left and go on with life.

In the first light of morning the campfires lay dark and cold. Silent figures huddled around frost rimed stones, while lifeless ashes stirred under the breath of cold morning breezes. Colorful blankets shrouded the figures, warding off the chill.

Swimming Snake was present and it startled Buck that a thin coating of gray ash covered Snake's down turned face. That was when the damn tickle had started. He knew the face-of-ash was reserved for the death of a warrior. Snake was already counting him gone.

Not one set of eyes met Buck's. Even the children remained hidden behind skin walls of the lodges. People had resigned Buckingham to the shadow world already, and treated the man before them as merely a phantom who stepped briefly among the living.

Buck now realized it was at *that* moment the tickle was born. The first sensations had crawled up his backbone using the bony knobs of his spine as a ladder to race up and down.

The tickle remained even now, a long two days later. Buck moved carefully back into the tree line and sat hidden amongst shadows just below the rim of the valley.

In shadow he stayed, feeling the world around him grow warm as the sun rose higher in the sky.

His butt was tight to the ground and across his lap, secure in both hands, was his rifle. His back pressed against a tree easing some of the ache it always held, while the shade in which he hid fell silently from the trees, moving slowly across rocks and ground with the journey of the sun.

In time, the shadows passed over him, theirs the only motion, until the morning sun stabbed his eyes. He squinted, but did not stir, until the need to relieve himself became overpowering.

When ignoring the pressure was no longer possible, he stood. He laughed sharply in contempt, hiked his skin shirt, pulled aside the loincloth, and pissed against a nearby tree trunk.

The amber stream darkened the bark as he marked his territory.

"Caution was one thing," thought Buckingham, *"but a man could go to his maker by being unable to spit in the eye of what troubled him."*

Habit still kept his eyes darting in all directions for danger, even as his water arched to wood.

Trails were visible across the valley and were matched by trails on his side. They wandered in and out of the trees and view. Deer and elk traveled these mountains, for they were its secluded denizens. Each day, or moon filled night, they would forage to fill their bellies, then travel to water before hiding in repose. In doing so, their travel wore down the grass and packed the earth in thin pathways. To unknowing eye and weary feet, the trails seemed to wander aimlessly, the foot wide paths scoring the mountainsides.

Any mountain man worth his powder knew that if one followed them downward, they usually led to water. He also knew that in normal times, if one valued his life – and Buck was mighty partial to his – you avoided their beckoning ease, staying many paces off that inviting smoothness.

Buck rubbed his beard and plucked out a stray twig.

This did not seem a normal time. It was improbable he would cross the path of any hunting or war parties by following the trails. From what he had been told, no one except himself was brave enough – or fool enough – to stride this particular valley in the first place.

Mentally he weighed the possibility of encountering old Ephraim on the trail.

Probably not.

The tree trunks were not scarred by claws and no stumps had he found torn asunder in the search for grubs and insects.

Buck had misgivings and knew he might regret the action, but he eyed the trail again, weighing it against the tickle. The scales in his head slowly tilted in one direction.

Grunting, he shouldered his heavy wicker pack, feeling it flatten slightly against his back. He cradled his long rifle in the crook of his arm and started down the trail, muttering to himself.

"Damn horse."

This journey would have been easier on horse back, but that was just not in the cards.

His horse had gone under more than half a year earlier; during the time the grasses were getting full sprout and fresh game had been hard to come by in the encampment. The best hunters had returned to scolding wives with hands empty and their quivers full. The winter had been mild and no reason could be found for the lack of game.

One morning, after eating a meal of what little stored pemmican was left; he and Swimming Snake decided to attempt a hunt themselves. Seemed like a good idea, for Swimming Snake had an uncanny knack of knowing where critters hid – pretty much any kind of critter you wanted.

You named it and Snake took you to it. Snake had agreed to find food and felt it better his white brother came with his rifle. The rifle had greater range than the bows of the hunters.

Besides, hungry bellies and end-of-winter boredom made both men eager to see different ground.

The horses, shaggy from the loss of winter hair, awaited them. As Buck approached his mount he reached up and gently stroked its neck in a calming gesture as he had a hundred times before.

At his first touch, the animal dropped over dead.

No particular reason for it to do so except to enrage Buck and bring howls of laughter from Swimming Snake.

After that day mothers used to threaten to have Buck touch them if children misbehaved too much.

Still pissed him off when his thoughts turned to it and Buckingham continued to take it personal that the critter had expired without thought as to the predicament it left him in.

Worse, the beast had been right tough and without good flavor. Didn't even give the satisfaction of a decent meal.

Since that time Buck was forced to ride a horse from his tribe's camp when travel consisted of more than a few minutes walk.

While he owned little, his friendship with Swimming Snake went far towards making others in the tribe charitable. For this present journey none had felt obliged to lend him a pony.

Gambling was a favored activity of the red man. His return was a gamble, but no one felt the odds of his return great enough to wager a horse.

Now Buckingham carried all his worldly belongings on his back – meager little that burden – and his own two moccasin clad feet replaced the four hooves he had grown accustomed to.

While he could walk for days on end, the miles falling away beneath his feet, it pained him. His leg served as a reminder of his introduction to Swimming Snake, and the pain in it was always there, accenting each step.

In the pack, swaying abrasively on his back, rested a battered pot serving most every cooking need where the food could not be tossed onto a stone next to open flames. A small pouch of tea, a smaller pouch of tobacco, another of salt and a handful of red seedpods consisted of most his pantry. He used the pods in small pinches to season whatever he could find to stuff his gullet.

The dried peppers would make your eyes water, your nose run, and your belly believe it was full with only a few bites. Right handy to fool one's paunch when you were starving.

A handful of jerky and a double handful of pemmican completed his victuals.

The dried meat and pemmican were gifts from Swimming Snake's mother. She felt a need to dote over someone if Snake were not available and Buck was right proud when her attention turned to him.

He smiled when he thought of the old woman. She was a figure to be reckoned with, by God; her wrinkled brown flesh like leather covered a will of steel and a heart of gold. She would have been a handful in her younger years. Still was – and he grinned broader at the remembrance of the old woman.

A mold, crucible, ladle, and a few bars of galena were packed away in the bottom – just in case – to feed his rifle. Along with the heavy ingots, a battered and slightly rusty spanner lay carelessly. Its purpose was to pull the plug from the base of the barrel. Buck had never used the spanner for such, but it served nicely as a light hammer, driving his skinning knife through the bars of lead when he needed to cut a chunk off for casting. The lead bars showed patches of shining silver where he had hewn chunks off to run balls. The silver would slowly gray with age till next it was needed.

No pistol hung from his belt, as the lock on his short weapon had broken a years earlier. It was that useless piece of metal and wood he had traded for those damn pods of the devil. He wasn't sure who had gotten the better end of the bargaining.

Setting next to all this, and taking up more than its share of space, was a ceramic jug that managed to remain intact through his travels. Crudely painted on its surface was the flaked and peeling proclamation – Kendred's Fine Whiskey. It held only a swallow or two of whiskey left over from the last rendezvous and it was a tall tale to call it 'fine.'

Even so, Buck could not throw it out regardless of the space and weight it wasted. On the other hand, no matter how tempted he was, he could not bring himself to drink the last of his fluid companion, for when gone it would be a long and dry spell.

Knowing it was there, sloshing ever so quietly in his pack was a relief. Having the godforsaken beverage he did not need it, but when absent he knew he would grieve the loss and crave its searing taste.

Midway up the pack a battered sailcloth bag encased his traps. Not many of the metal contraptions left, but enough in number to give him slim hope for the approaching season. With luck, he could replace them next year if he managed to get to the gathering.

Atop all was his prize blanket – a white Hudson with multicolored stripes, reminiscent of the hard candy Swimming Snake was so fond of. Once, when the pack was full, the blanket had ridden strapped on the top, a colorful blossom crowning a gray wicker stem. Now it nestled nicely inside the top, forming a colorful woolen cap to his belongings.

Covering Buck's body were brain tanned skins – another gift from the old woman. A gift painstakingly cut and sewn around the fire during a cold winter. A war shirt without decoration covering him to his knees, its soft golden leather was a comfort against his skin.

Morning Star had offered to relieve its plainness with some pony beads Buck had brought to her as a present. Buckingham had been tempted, but the thought of watching Snake's mother force her aged hands to work through the pain was too much. He had talked her into making a red flannel loincloth instead. Taking less physical effort to create, it would form a barricade that kept the crawling buggies from attacking his privates too much.

The plan backfired, however, as the old woman still made him a set of buckskin leggings to protect his legs from the brush. They came from the same batch of skins that produced his shirt – and if that wasn't enough, his moccasins were cut from the dark, smoke permeated leather of an old lodge, stitched by the old woman with care and patience.

She had worked with no pattern, only the memory of having looked at his feet, never letting on to him she was preparing these gifts. Preparing them after all had gone to sleep so Buckingham would not scold her and make her stop. The soles of the glove like shoes were thinner now, but still had a mountain and prairie of travel left in them.

Buck shook his head at the memory. The old woman had informed him at the end of her labor of the high cost she would levy for the goods, but she had never gotten around to charging him for the clothing.

Buck figured his silly grin and joy upon receiving them must have been payment enough for her. He had spent a week pointing out to all in camp the fact that the old woman's work and craftsmanship was far superior to all the other women. He even pointed this out to the young lassies, whose nimble fingers could not match the skill that resided in the crooked nubs of Morning Star.

It might have cost him a few smiles from the maidens, but the pride in the old woman's eyes more than made up for the frowns of the young'uns.

Hanging from right shoulder, crossing left, was his possibles bag. In it lay almost everything he might need to keep his plunder and person in right decent shape. Buckingham was not sure what hid in its dark recesses anymore for it seemed like anything he needed could be found in it.

Laid over all was his powder horn, still holding almost a full pound of powder – enough to make him feel right pert.

On the left side of his grease blackened leather belt hung a small deerskin pouch with a dozen round balls, each slightly over a half inch in diameter; caliber .54 to be precise. On the right was his skinning knife in a leather sheath. The sheath was not made by the old woman and one look would tell you that. It was crudely laced with bits of wang.

Makeshift at best.

Buck's necklace was more functional than decorative, but it served to hold his pipe and a small patch knife. The pipe was a replacement for his original, this one carved from a pale green piece of soapstone; its stem formed from a stout section of reed. The stem had busted off and the pipe was shorter than it started, but it still gave a man satisfaction around the fire at night. In good times he had tobacco. In poor times he smoked a mixture of willow bark and dried waxy green leaves of kinnickinic. It gave smoke, but little satisfaction. For now he walked in the midst of luxury with his small stash of real tobacco.

While he would not admit it, Buck secretly felt that he was as handsome as a wild flower to the maidens.

Not that a mountain man such as myself would worry about such foo-for-rah, Buck thought.

Yes sir, the old herd bull still cut a wide path – if you ignored the flattened nose and scars that decorated his body.

Buck moved vigilantly down the trail, his senses taking in everything they could. This trail would have been dangerously steep had it not zigzagged back and forth across the mountainside as it worked its way down towards the water below.

Pine needles covered the trail making for a slippery stride. When stepped on, they acted as small rollers causing his feet to slide until the smooth soles gained purchase once more in the dirt. The needles, he noted, showed signs of displacement; the underlying dirt imprinted and disturbed by various sized marks indicating the passage of mountain animals.

At one spot on the trail where a tree had fallen across the path, bark had been ripped from the topside where hooves had scraped its coarse skin – hooves not lifted high enough to clear the natural obstruction.

The morning's light darkened as clouds slipped silently in front of the sun, only to scurry on as if they realized the insolence of their actions.

Buckingham had to admit it was a right pretty day – except for that damn tickle. It was an itch that moved when he tried to scratch it, still seeming to be an inch or two away from his grasp.

The sudden explosion of sound and movement from his right took him by surprise. His heart clenched briefly in his chest. Swinging his rifle smoothly towards the unseen danger the octagon barrel collided with a thin lodge pole pine at the precise moment his feet decided to give up their tentative hold on the slippery pine needles. His eyes watched helplessly as the blade front sight swung merrily in the sky, then his butt hit the ground hard.

The impact jarred from tailbone to teeth and was the start of a short ride – a ride lasting till Buck's downhill race was halted by another small lodge pole slamming between his out spread legs.

With the sudden stop, fire blossomed in his belly, and sparks filled his eyes; tears of pain formed instantly, blurring what was left of his vision, but the salty droplets were unable to wash away the prancing spots that raced across his eyesight, nor extinguish the fire between his legs.

Try as he might, he was unable to move from this humiliating position for precious minutes. While only measured in minutes, the pain in his groin stretched them into hours.

Instinct told him to react - to move - to protect himself, but his body didn't much give a damn what it was told.

Slowly the waves of fire subsided, and with agonizing effort he regained his feet on shaking legs. Buck did not bother to investigate the flurry of activity on the hillside that started this unexpected ordeal. If something hostile *had* been lurking, he would have known it by now.

Although taking a ball or blade in the belly would not have felt much worse. He shook his head and wiped the tears from his eyes.

The Lord sure played a mean trick by putting them things on the outside of a man where they were banged around so much, Buck thought.

Made him think that the Lord was still secretly pissed about the apple incident in that garden.

Pulling the loincloth aside, Buck investigated for damage. He was pleased to note that nothing looked much worse for wear – no worse than normal anyway. A man had to count his blessings in situations like this.

He still counted two.

For this he was grateful.

Staggering slightly on pain bowed legs he continued the arduous drop towards the valley below. The mellow feeling that had formerly taken him was gone, in its place was a mood most foul. Woe to the creature or man who crossed his path. It was right strange how a man's demeanor could toss from caution and mellow to a cold and furious wind because of a mite of discomfort.

The sun had moved considerable by the time his feet secured his throbbing legs to the ground on the canyon bottom. The stabbing pain in his belly had subsided to a dull ache and his mind was once more able to somewhat appreciate the humor of current events.

The joy he could salvage was that some day – around a campfire and jug – he would regale other trappers with a colorful tale of his wild ride.

By the time of telling it would be bragged he slid a mile down the mountainside, over razor sharp rocks and cactus, off a cliff, into the arms of an enraged griz; only to come out grinning and a spittin' hair.

It was only right and fair the tale would improve with age. Most things did in a person's mind.

Standing on the lush grass of the bottomland, Buck's mood further improved with what he saw along the creek banks. His ever moving eyes took in the willows growing in abundance - and that was good. Better yet, these were not just any willows.

The densely packed green stems bore slick white scars – visible evidence that teeth of beaver had severed some of their thumb thick bodies. Where there were stubs – there were dams, where there were dams – there were beaver and where there were beaver there was money. Made life right simple.

A man left the settlements to get away from people and the need for gold or wealth. Sad to say, but the same men fled to the mountains attempting to bring back the furry pelts that one could convert so readily to money.

T'were just trading one devil for another in a way. It was just giving a man a choice of how he sold his soul.

Yes, some men abandoned all trappings of civilization, including the need and greed for money.

Buckingham knew several who had forsaken the last vestiges of civilization and gone hibernant.

Mountain men choosing this path lived a life in the mountains as alone as possible, cherishing the solitude and never returning to the companionship of fellow man; be they savage or civilized. Those men became more animal than human, passing into eternity with no more impact on the world than a creature of the wild dying in the forest.

There were worse things that could befall a man, thought Buck, but he was not sure how he wanted to die. At times he wanted the company of friends or people to ease his passing and remember him. Other days, the indignity of the final act compelled him to wish for solitude at the end. On rare occasion – generally in the company of a jug – he decided that he did not want to walk either route, just figured he would live forever and avoid the decision.

Not much chance of that.

Satisfied with his initial observation of the valley, Buck felt the need to treat himself to a day of lassitude; a reward for his pain and suffering. All would fall into place on the morrow, but for today he would indulge his lazy side - although he realized it would behoove him to set up a comfortable and secure temporary camp.

At least as comfortable and secure as that damn tickle would allow.

Buckingham would even allow himself to succumb to the urge of enjoying a large portion of the small amount of provisions he had brought in on his back. That would be a luxury, but life itself was often a luxury. Buck smiled to himself; sometimes a man had to sit back and enjoy the world around him – before he started his god-given right of conquering it.

Across the creek a small stream joined the main body of water. The stream's width was less than half that of the main flow. On the westerly bank, where the two currents collided in a flurry of white water, a narrow triangle of ground had formed from the gradual buildup of silt and sand sifting into slower eddies. Covering the far side, extending to the edge of the water, was a dense cloak of willows.

Beyond the willows, where the mass of interwoven branches met the mountainside, a thin stand of pine grew. The young trees stood like guards above the willows. In their midst was a solitary old growth tree.

Thoughtfully he made his way across the stream at a point where it widened dramatically, leaving the water only a foot deep. The water was cold and fast, but the temperature was not the burning cold that it would soon possess; when winter spit its icy slobber and the first ice clung to the banks.

The crossing went as he knew it would – as it had in a hundred crossings of a hundred streams.

Water swirled into his moccasins, depositing sand disturbed by his footsteps. There it gritted against the soles of his feet and ground uncomfortably between his toes. The clear and bright water crawled up the calves of his legs, leaving a sullen ache in its wake, the buckskin leggings clung wetly to his legs when he climbed onto the opposite bank.

The leggings would dry in time, but for the present it was a cold and clammy feeling Buck never enjoyed.

Standing close to them he realized the willows were so thick passage would be impossible. On the slippery grass beach, barely wide enough to stand on, he inspected the willows with a closer eye. At every turn they barred his way.

Buck briefly continued his search for passage before abandoning the notion all together. Giving in to the inevitable, he used the stream once more as a watery pathway to gain access to the interior of his new territory. His legs, just regaining their feeling, were cold once more and in the process of staggering through the chilled water he pinched his foot between two rocks on the bottom. The pain did not make it to his brain until the foot had warmed an hour later.

Mother Nature finally rewarded Buck for his effort. Towering in the center of this jungle of green he saw once more the single primordial pine. He had seen if from the other side, but not appreciated its true size; it was massive and out of place in the company of the lesser trees. The graceful branches stretched far and drooped low from their own weight. Jade tips brushed the ground in a circle around a trunk he would be unable to put his arms around.

Shedding his pack - and with a feeling of unease – his rifle, he pulled the hawk from his belt and carefully studied the tree.

The act of laying aside his rifle was painful to his peace of mind. If given the choice of walking naked through the streets of Saint Louis or without rifle in the mountains, he knew what his decision would be.

Hell, he had been naked on city streets several times and no harm had befallen him. Normally he was given a secure (if barred) place to sleep until sober. On holidays he was even grudgingly given a meal.

Studying the tree keenly, he noticed one side of it where bottom boughs came within the span of his hand of touching a large boulder. The boulder itself was the size of a small house, with a thin crack scarring its side. Somewhere in the past it had rolled crashing and crushing from its roost above, until it came to rest here.

It was next to the boulder Buckingham would begin.

Sliding between the rock and the limbs, the hard face of the granite scraping his chest, and boughs grabbing his back he turned, dropping to his knees, and clenched a handful of sappy needles. Slowly he worked his way in a dozen feet until he reached the massive trunk.

Dirt and pine needles coated his wet leggings, the result of wallowing through the limbs on his hands and knees, but now he found himself in a living spherical cavern extending around the base of the trunk.

Using the hawk he carefully hewed selected limbs from the trunk, expanding the cavern into a home. The trimmings Buck saved, not casting them out, but using them as a carpet for his new abode.

To take them out would make obvious the fact someone had disturbed the area. In hiding them inside the tree, the only evidence of his work was a narrow tunnel leading to the outside, opening up against the immense rock where - unless one stood next to it in just the right spot – the doorway would go unnoticed.

Construction of a small fire was possible within the green walls. If care prevailed. The smoke generated from a miniature blaze could not help but disperse as it rose through the branches of the tree.

Buckingham did not kid himself.

The smell of smoke would be obvious, as would be the drifting blue haze, but the dispersal would go far in keeping his position hidden. As it was, Buck had noticed that when the sun hit the valley just right, it appeared there was already a haze over it. A faint haze. So faint one could almost think it imagination. He thought on it.

On his way into the valley, he had sniffed the wind. No smell of smoke had come to him. Right queersome. Neither fog nor smoke. Just a haze most would not notice. He had seen it and been bothered, unable to explain its existence. It was far fainter, but reminded him of moon dogs –

the gentle radiance that surrounded the lunar disc when ice crystals were forming in the night air. Many things existed in the world that he could not explain.

No sense in dwelling on them.

He grinned to himself. If Swimming Snake were here, there would be some silly assed explanation. Probably the breath of the spirits or farts ' from beyond.

Satisfied with his work he wiped the edge of his hawk on his damp leggings and returned to the world outside his living door – retrieved his pack and rifle – and stood straight, easing the crinks in his back.

Looking skyward, the only movement picked out by his eyes was an eagle, its wings set, gliding on air currents high above the valley. A solitary master sharing its realm with dark clouds that were building in the northeast. There was a heavy sensation in the air. Feeling a stab of envy at the sight of the bird, he pulled his belongings into the heart of the tree, cussing as a jagged stub rammed into the small of his back.

Removing the once white blanket with stripes from the pack, he spread it on the pine boughs he had carefully laid on the ground. Through trial and error – plus years of experience – he created a comfortable nest, in which the sharp points sprouting from the severed boughs did not dig into his body. A tedious task that would be rewarded with comfort.

With his head high on one point of the diamond formed by the blanket he pulled the bottom point over his feet, folded the left corner across his body, and followed it with the right.

Thus cocooned he had three layers over his feet, two his body, and one padding his weary bones from the ground beneath him.

Snuggling down he noticed the one small rock that always seemed to follow his travels. It rested happily under him, poking him between the shoulder blades. Not enough discomfort to redo all his work, but enough to be an annoyance.

If annoyances were gold then he would be a rich man indeed, he figured.

With slight unease in the back of his mind, and his rifle lying next to him, he closed his eyes and listened to the faint sound of thunder starting to roll between the mountain peaks, the flashes red behind his closed eyes when the stark light broke through the tightly packed boughs.

Gradually the booming echoes incorporated into his dreams. Somewhere between the visions of killing and lovemaking, snow and warm sunshine, dreamless sleep folded him into its arms.

⊙℘

It had waited and watched for decades.

It had existed for centuries.

Its duties were many.

Simple in nature and complex in performance it was one entity – comprised of billions of beings.

Each of the individual beings was small, smaller than the flecks of dust floating in the air.

Was it alive?

Perhaps its maker could answer that question, but the makers had long since abandoned it to its station.

Would they return?

That mattered not to the watcher or the outpost.

They had their duties and those duties required performance, whether there was any to watch the watchers.

The watcher spread out over miles of rugged terrain and covered the valley from the bottomland and into the air until it almost reached the rim. With the expanse now covered, it was virtually invisible. If local eyes noticed it at all, those eyes saw a transparent fog that might glint in the sunlight at the rising of the morning sun, or when the sun set in a flare of red fire in the evening.

Normally there were no local eyes.

While the watcher might not be noticed, it noticed all – and it had noted the passage of the man descending to the bottom of its territory. A creature, bipedal – as the watcher had studied before – as it had categorized before – as it had harvested before.

No need of haste was required for examination. Creatures of this world would not flee unless danger was obvious to them.

Sometimes not even then.

There was no need for this unconscious creature to know danger loomed in the very air it breathed. It was far easier to study the subject in an artificial terrarium with no visible walls. With walls and bars, the test subject would fight to escape. Feeling secure in its freedom, the subject pursued normal habits and mannerisms. Mannerisms to be studied at leisure. Leisure was not a prime concern to the watcher, but accuracy was.

The sacrifice of a few particles was considered necessary for an initial study. They attached themselves to the moist organs the creature used for respiration. Here the particles would monitor the actions and reactions of the subject's body.

Unnoticed, but noticing and recording all.

The particles would be expelled at completion of their duties.

A pale wisp gathered in the air above Buckingham.

Small in size, no more than the brief and tiny cloud a man might exhibit in winter when he exhaled a breath into the frigid morning air. The mist moved slowly and to an onlooker would have appeared to caress the face of the sleeping subject, but there was no onlooker.

The last creature in this valley had been studied and vivisected a dozen years before.

Ⳝⳝ

When he opened his eyes again, Buckingham realized just how tired he had been. Coughing twice, his lungs felt a mite congested, but he drew in crisp air and felt his body responding to the new day.

Grunting he rose from the blanket and boughs and hunkered – taking stock of himself.

All the resident aches and pains were still there, scattered around his body. Made Buck comfortable to know he had not woken up as someone else.

The years of sloshing around in ice cold water had taken its toll on his knees and hips, he paid little heed to those aches; they were just a part of the dues one paid for a life of luxury in the high lonesome. His leg hurt at the site of an old scar, but then it always hurt there.

At its first pain in the morning he spouted his morning litany under his breath.

"Damned heathen…low life dog eating bastard…did it for my own good…bullshit," he muttered, rubbing his leg.

Movement during sleep had succeeded in dislodging his fur hat. On his second attempt he managed to snag the tawny helmet and set it atop his head once more.

Bending over to retrieve the head gear made him dizzy. He slung his possibles bag and horn over his shoulder, sheathed his knife and hawk once more, grasped his rifle and started the crawl outside. It seemed a lot farther when stove up with the night pains.

The world greeting him was green and fresh, sparkling with blankets of dew covering everything in sight with a dusting of cool liquid diamonds. Jewels soon to be stolen by the morning sun. From the depths around the trees and willows, a transparent mist billowed and hovered a few feet above the ground. A ground fog gentling the morning and taking the rough edges off.

In the cities where Buck visited, and always abandoned, they had their own version of morning mist. It was one that was not soothing. In the cities it was smoke from the factories. Smoke that choked the life from a man and stank. Smoke from the fires of black coal.

Remaining motionless, he noted a small doe rummaging silently through the mist. It appeared as a gray-brown wraith. Grazing for a moment, it raised its head and peered fearfully around, ears tilted forward to catch the slightest sound, nose flared; attempting to catch wind of the closest predator, and with each breath it was ready to flee.

Buckingham was hungry, but knew he needed to walk the pain out of his body first. From the looks of it, vittles were lined up at his doorstep and it wouldn't be a problem to bag his morning cuisine. No sense ordering the first item on the menu.

With wrinkled brow, he contemplated his course of action.

Being a mountain man, Buckingham spent a lot of time not knowing exactly where he was. Sure, he could reckon the directions without much trouble, but there were not much for maps in this part of the country. The only maps were drawn on the inside of your skull – then again, not knowing where one was made it hard to be lost, cuz you weren't supposed to be in any particular place. One could spend time being mightily confused, but only a flatlander would consider themselves lost.

Never seemed like a thing to get upset over to Buck – less you were in the high country during the winter.

Confused was dangerous then.

From the lip surrounding the valley he had surveyed the basic lay of the land. The valley was a drainage, not big enough to qualify as a hole. From jagged rim to jagged rim, it measured five miles across and just about twice that long. Its shape reminded him of the hourglasses he had seen on the desks of them high falutin' financiers in Saint Louie.

Also reminded him of the red warning sign nature put on the bottom of the shiny black spider that could kill the young and elderly, or make a man wish he were dead.

In its middle where the valley nudged together like a woman wearing one of those confounded corsets, its mountainsides turned into right proper cliffs on both sides for a spell. The cliffs were not high, but higher than he cared to climb – or fall from. Buck was not sure if he could walk the dry along the edge, but he was sure the water was narrow and deep with a current to match. A slip of the foot and injury could result. The high lonesome was not a place to become injured. If you were hurt, you had two choices – crawl out or die.

Even worse medicine, his gear could become soaked or lost if he took a plunge. A broken bone had the chance of healing. An article lost in the torrent was gone forever and replacements were just a pipe dream.

Checking his rifle he thumbed the frizzen open once more and poured the tiny sum of powder from its hollow. Making sure his finger was dry; he gently wiped all traces of the black dust from it. It seemed not to have taken moisture from the night, but it was best to be sure.

Took only a second of time and a pinch of powder to set a man's mind at ease, but he knew that soon he would have to dig out his screw, pull the ball, and dump the powder charge from the barrel if he had not fired it. The charge had been setting there for several days. Probably would set for a month and still be good, but one did not want to bet his hair on it. Many a good man had died from a flash in the pan, with no shot to follow.

Making his way through the dense willows was difficult, but he had no mind to wade the cold water again this early in the morning. Yesterday the jungle of willows had stopped him. On this day he was fresh and determined. Though he tried to move quietly, it seemed that every damned willow had green hands that grabbed at him. Bark covered fingers grabbed at his rifle barrel and possibles bag. They grabbed his fur bonnet from his head. They grabbed his goat.

Buckingham knew he was just getting cantankerous in his old age. As one aged, it seemed that most everything in life fought you.

Clawing his way to the bank of the main stream, he paused. Sitting he waited, watched and listened, his mouth half open and not breathing. Helped your smellin' some, along with your hearing, to leave yer mouth hanging slack jawed like that. It was one of the things he had learned, like not looking directly at something at night.

Nope. You looked beside it and you could see it better in the dark.

His eyes scanned the ground before him and the mountain sides beyond, not looking for anything in particular.

He watched for movement more than anything. Alternatively, anything that might just be 'out of place.' A man watched for birds flying from treetops in the distance. Might be something spooked them.

You watched for broken branches floating in the water. Something must have broken them off.

You watched the sand as the sun changed its angle over it. Shadows would show footprints of man or animal easily that way, making them stand out.

You listened for branches and twigs being snapped. There were always branches crackling, but they did not do it rhythmically in nature. Trees rubbed against each other in the wind, the sound coming from above – and it never hurt to look above either. Buckingham had learned the hard way that man was a creature of habit and seldom looked up. Buck had the lesson driven home as he lay on his back, an arrow in his leg, looking up at a red face sitting in a tree staring down on him.

His brother Swimming Snake always had been a sneaky bastard.

You listened for the frenzied chattering of squirrels. The furry woodland rats would set up a cry if any man or beast wandered past them. Less, of course, you were looking to pop one and eat it. Then they were quieter than a bunch of Crows sneaking up on your horses.

છ౭

After a half hour he felt comfortable he was alone in the valley.

Rising to full height, Buck decided to claim the valley. It was time to get down to the business of being a mountain man.

Stopping once more at the stream he knelt, and looked beneath its glistening surface. Just another mountain flow, sparkling and clear, but a might queersome. Iron pyrite gleamed at him with a golden allure. Many tin horns forked their soul over to the devil, consumed by greed, when they spied the heart stealing sparkles of yeller. Pork eaters had murdered their friends and family for a handful of sand that was worthless. It looked like gold, it glowed like gold, but it was not. Nothing but a fool's gold.

The rocks in the creek were a bit odd. All rivers and streams had stones and pebbles that were rounded and smooth. The rolling action of water grinding them together through the years did that. These were not much different than those found in other streams, but the difference was enough to catch his eye.

Reaching into the eddy of water he pulled a handful to the surface.

These stones were rounded like most he'd seen, but more so. They seemed polished and felt oily to the touch, each almost identical in shape and color. Nothing to make him want to haul a load around with him, but they *were* a might prettier than most.

He noticed another thing as he squatted there, water dripping from his hand.

All creeks had living things in them.

Normally when you crept to the bank, you would see a fish or two – at least a couple of minnows – scurry from the area. Crawdaddies would jackknife in a puff of muddy smoke as they sought deeper water. Hellgrammites and other water bugs would cling to rocks; while their distant cousins would scurry across the surface like water walking spiders. Frogs would rest, eyes above the water, and watch, perhaps dreaming of a giant fly and a meal to end all meals.

Not here. Not in this waterway.

This was emptier than a rattlesnake's heart and Buckingham could see not a trace of life in the water.

Still and all, it didn't mean much. Maybe the frogs ate the bugs, the fish ate the frogs, and the eagle ate the fish and there weren't shit left.

Nothing to get his mind constipated over – but it did not help that tickle.

Standing, he stretched and looked around once more. It was like being in a card game where you never drew a high card.

Yes, it could happen, but it always made you feel a bit uneasy.

Made a man wonder if life was on the up and up and what the next turn might bring.

Imprinted in the sandy banks of the creek prints showed life in this valley. Buck didn't remember having seen the prints the previous day.

Muddy scrapes and slides bespoke the presence of beaver and otters. Deer and elk had left their mark as they wandered the border between land and water to drink their fill.

Strange he had missed them. Wasn't like him.

He frowned for a moment over a stamping left in the mud by a bear. Bending, he studied it for a second, then smiled. The claws were curved and short. Black bear, *not old Ephraim.*

Now if it had been a griz, it would have given him pause. Buckingham was not scared of griz, but he had a right powerful respect for silvertips. One might even say that if the two met on a trail, out of pure politeness Buckingham would give way to it – just because he had manners when it came to the old rogue mind you.

Thinking hard, Buck had to admit that most mountain men he knew had manners when it came to Ephraim. Them that did not were taught proper etiquette soon enough – if they lived through it.

From his possibles bag he tenderly pulled a small square of unbleached muslin. Brown and yellow stains covered the cloth, a promise of the delight within. Carefully unfolding it, he took the crumpled and dried leaves of tobacco and pushed them between his lip and jaw with his fingers. It was dry and flaked, gagging him, but soon the spit swelled it up and he savored the juices imparted by the brown flakes.

The sun had traveled far past overhead by the time his curiosity was satisfied, and his exploration of the valley ended for the day. Leaning wearily against a rock, he scooped his forefinger along the inside of his mouth and retrieved what was left of the tobacco.

These soggy remains he carefully placed in the dwindling sunlight, atop the rock on which he rested. The sun would dry the saliva from the brown mass, and this evening he could treat himself to a nightly smoke. It did not make the best chew, (and after chewing on it all day, not the best smoke) but then one stretched his supplies in whatever way he could.

CHAPTER 3
Song of Separate Paths

"Mountains cannot be surmounted, except by winding paths." - *Johann Wolfgang von Goeth*

High above, on the windswept edge of the valley, Swimming Snake looked down into the cursed land. He knew it was not too late to abandon this foolish idea, but he also knew his heart would not let him make the verdict to walk away. That would be a judgment of death to his brother.

This was the moment of decision.

His horse had already made its decision.

There was no way Snake could coax the mount to take even one more tentative step towards the valley.

Snake reflected this horse always showed good sense, and wondered why it was he could not learn from the beast.

A few feet away the horse waited its master's choice. If he climbed onto the back of the pony he could ride back to his lodge and none would think the less of him.

Indeed most would applaud his decision as wise.

The cursed land looked the same as it had the last time Snake trespassed here with a small party of warriors. They had gathered, looking down from a clearing not far from where he now stood.

The others had been determined to journey onward. Swimming Snake had not understood, any more than he could understand the action of his white brother entering the valley.

Snake had been able to convince three of the previous party to return to the camp, not venturing further into the mouth of the waiting hell. The fourth had insisted on completing the journey.

Snake felt that he should have argued more persuasively, or at least looked upon the face of the fourth warrior harder. He could no longer remember it as well as he should and Snake had never seen that face again.

This time that would not happen – one friend lost to evil was enough.

Later the others had told of what they had seen from the rim of the valley. From their description, Snake could understand what drove them to enter the valley. He understood the driving compulsion to explore the valley. A valley of the Gods. Lush, luxuriant, teaming with game.

Swimming Snake also understood that what the others in the party saw had not been his vision of the waiting traps in the desolate hell.

Walks with Limp was his friend and brother. As much a friend as the medicine man had allowed himself for many seasons, and in truth a chance to walk with a man he could consider a brother. Walks with Limp brought him joy and amusement.

Walks with Limp was a friend who did not judge the actions of others too harshly and, although he *was* a white man, he attempted to understand and not laugh or scoff at the truths Swimming Snake repeatedly offered.

The white men, as a race, were savages Snake thought. But they had within them a quiet innocence. The white man would believe anything and shut their eyes to the reality of the world around them.

The white man worshiped their God in small buildings every seven days, and then locked the God in the building until they needed Him again. Any action was permissible in life as long as you told your God about it later and apologized. Even though they said the God already knew about the deeds.

How strange that a white man was not responsible for his actions.

It explained a lot.

Snake remembered when he first took interest in Walks with Limp. Years ago a small band of men had come into their area. As many men as the fingers on one hand. Two of the men had split off from the rest of the small band.

The warriors with Snake were dispatched to deal with the three who stayed in their camp.

Swimming Snake had skirted ahead and waited for the two men afoot. The first man he had taken in the back with an arrow. The man fell amazingly quietly and it took several steps for the other to notice.

When the remaining white man turned, Swimming Snake loosed

another arrow. This time the lower limb of his bow had been touching a wrist thick branch of the tree Snake was sitting in. The arrow did not fly true and had taken the man in his lower leg, penetrating the muscle and lodging its stone head in the bone of the man's leg. As he fell, the man parted company with his rifle and struck his head a glancing blow on a rock.

Lying dazed on the ground he had looked Swimming Snake in the eye, smiled, and made what Snake later learned was a rude gesture.

The white man then passed out.

No fear had Swimming Snake seen in the man's eyes, and for some reason a voice told him to spare the fallen man.

Roughly carried to camp, Walks with Limp had been unceremoniously dumped in Snake's lodge. In time the wound had healed, but the arrow head remained stuck fast deep within the leg, causing pain to his white brother. This injury bestowed the name 'Walks with Limp' upon him. Time bestowed the title brother.

The white man did not like the name given and held Snake responsible. In Snake's mind the name was not his fault, even though he had been the one who put an arrow through the invader's leg.

For a long time, the white man had showed animosity towards Snake and Snake found this confusing.

A day came when Snake had felt obligated to lighten the mood some. Knowing how slow mentally the white men were, he had shown the man a trick.

He had cleared a spot on the ground, placed the white man's hand over his and lowered his own hand to touch the earth. When he removed it, a small stone lay before them. The white man's eyes had gotten a bit bigger and the children watching had giggled.

He then put the white man's hand over his own again, and lowered his hand to cover the rock. When he pulled his hand away, a lizard was there and gone was the stone. The white man had pulled his hand back as if burnt and moved quickly away from Snake.

The children laughed.

Outside he preened with pride as the giggling children surrounded him.

"Are you not proud to have such a powerful medicine man in your midst?" he asked.

One boy answered, "That was not magic. You had the rock in your hand."

Frowning, Snake asked him, "So you believe ...but what then of the lizard?"

A girl reached out and touched the sleeve of his buckskin shirt. "You picked the rock up and the lizard you had hidden crawled down your sleeve."

Another chimed in, "Lizards do not live in rocks. There is no magic like that. Spirits live in rocks, but not lizards."

Yet another said thoughtfully, "Maybe the white man thought it possible, because lizards are always sunning themselves on rocks."

Children were so hard to fool these days, not like when Snake had been young. Moreover, the songs they now sang – he cringed.

While some people received their names through deeds of great bravery, others were given their names from things that occurred around them.

Snake was unique in his name – as befit a medicine man.

In youth he had been tagged with a childhood name. What that childhood name was is not important at this time, but it had been a peculiar name, as befit a peculiar child.

Everyone has habits that are a bit difficult for others to understand and Snake was no different – although his habits were.

For some reason, known only to him and never shared, the young boy had found his own way to relax and meditate on the great mysteries that surrounded him.

A small rivulet of water ran by the main encampment where the lodges were set, their entrances facing the morning sun. It was too small to be a stream, but too big to just be run-off from the hillsides. It was only five feet wide and one foot deep, but it moved along right smart, and its waters were always clear and cool.

On hot days Snake would strip and lower himself into the water, laying on his back with his head cradled on an old horse skull he carried everywhere. Why he carried the skull was never explained. No one ever felt the need to inquire.

As he lay comfortably in the water only two parts of his body stuck out above its surface. The tribe was not all that impressed with his solemn face staring up towards the heavens, eyes unblinking – but that swimming snake dangling downstream impressed them mightily.

CRBO

By mid-afternoon of the third day Buckingham was tuckered out. He rested in the shade beneath the green willows and let the wind play over him drying the sweat from his brow and cooling his face. His mind was tired and foggy. He knew he wasn't as alert as he should be and he had difficulty remembering everything he did the day before. His belly was tight and he didn't remember eating either.

In the distance, above the rim, clouds were building and thunderheads were growing once more. That bothered him because most things in nature a person had control over. Lightning was not one of these.

Buckingham had little book learning in his life. For this he felt empty and a bit cheated when he was in the cities. Most of Buck's knowledge had been passed on to him by his mentor – LeBlanc.

When it came to lightning, however, Buckingham felt his schooling was right prime. He knew what he had observed over the years in the mountains. He had watched the blue fire crash down on trees, rocks and just about anything it took a mind to. When a man was caught in the middle of an electrical storm, it was like living inside the Old Testament that his daddy had spoke about.

Fire and brimstone.

Swimming Snake schooled him proper also, when it came to thunderbolts. Many a winter eve, sitting in Snake's lodge around the fire, he absorbed the tales offered by hushed voices over the evening meal.

The mountains pushed up into the sky, crowding it, intruding on territory not its own. The sky became angry and lashed out at the mountain peaks. Likewise the trees – particularly the tall ones – attempted to claim space that was not theirs. For this they were punished, splintered and broken, forced to bow beneath the power of the sky.

One lesson of Swimming Snake's he had not put much store in. That story was about the white man's rifles. Swimming Snake was of a mind that the boom of the rifle was too much like thunder, and for this reason Swimming Snake never used a smoke pole.

He solemnly said, when bored, the sky would take offense at the rifle and strike at it, and the man who wielded it. Just to teach a bit of humility to the offender. This part seemed a bit tall to Buckingham – until he was forced to think about it later.

During a rendezvous, Buck had been enjoying life to its fullest. Arriving at the festivities which blanketed the prairie, he had quickly converted his plews into provisions for the next year, foo-for-ah for presents in the tribe, and credit for use at the rendezvous.

Buck realized that the price he had been given for his pelts was low. He also realized that had he bargained a bit harder – and longer – his gain would have been substantially more.

But the thirst was upon him.

Each moment that he stood and argued over the quality of his furs was a moment denying the rare sport of drinking. Almost in a panic, he had taken the offer before him and bolted from the tent.

Buckingham's first view of the whiskey wagon was not exceptionally reassuring. In a world of bright colors and banners it stood dark and unadorned. A simple wagon burdened with barrels and casks; coarsely burned into the plank side the information –

'Kendred Sterling Whiskey.'

Oil lamps were spiked to the side, their chimneys cracked and blackened, waiting in anticipation of nighttime customers. A lure to pull moths to the flame. Moths who had worked so long and hard for this moment.

Two other whiskey wagons stood near, both doing brisk trade in their fiery beverage; drunken mountain men surrounding them. Some men he recognized, some he did not. This particular wagon, however, had no lines of thirsty patrons. Two men were visible, one leaning against the wagon (grasping a rapidly swelling arm) groaning and rocking in pain; the second – face down – a few paces from the tongue of the wagon.

Giving careful consideration, Buck stroked his beard, contemplating the other two wagons with the impatient customers jostling and pushing in the long lines. The thirst was strong and it would not hurt to investigate the path less traveled.

Striding forward, he stepped carefully over the man lying motionless on the ground. In passing Buck noted that the man was not breathing.

Could be a coincidence, not having anything to do with the quality of whiskey provided by this vendor. Five paces from the wagon a voice called out to him.

"Aye and good morning, sar. Can I be of assistance to ye?"

Looking around, Buckingham spotted the man sitting quietly amongst the barrels in the bed of the wagon.

Buck stopped. "A prime morning to you. Do you have whiskey?" he asked, pulling his sleeve across his parched mouth.

"Uh-yep. Whiskey I have, but I am not open for business at this time." The man carefully lifted a round cover from a barrel, peered inside and hastily slammed the cover back down.

"Be about thirty minutes, I recon." He smiled brightly at Buckingham. "It ain't rightly whiskey yet, but it will be shortly."

Buck was confused. The man appeared sane and rational, dressed in clean, but mended clothing. The vendor had medium length dark hair and a set of pince-nez glasses resting atop his nose. He did not look like what one would expect of a store clerk in the east, nor did he quite look like a man used to spending his time in the mountains.

Perhaps a figure taking sabbatical from an asylum, thought Buck. As Buckingham stood, turning his eyes on the other two wagons, the whiskey trader jumped lightly from the wagon.

"Now, as ye may have noted, I am not accosted by a multitude of patrons at this moment. If ye have a powerful thirst, we can sit a spell and taste of me personal jug. After that, this vintage of fine whiskey should be completed."

He moved farther down from the man writhing in pain and held aloft a jug in one hand, patting the ground with his other.

In one graceful motion Buck sank cross legged to the ground next to the man, his eyes stuck on the jug like a starving dog would watch a bone.

The man handed the jug to Buck and turned to retrieve two tin cups from the wagon. Turning back he found the mountain man drinking deeply from the jug. Shuddering, he tossed one cup over his shoulder where it rattled noisily into the dark shadows of the wagon bed.

Remembering his manners, Buckingham handed the jug back to the man. The trader carefully decanted a small amount into his own cup and handed the jug back, returning it to the grasp of the thirsty mountain man. Taking another pull from the jug, Buck sat it on the ground between them and looked back to the vendor.

"I don't rightly wish to be too inquisitive, but I notice our companions," Buck gestured towards the other two mountain men, "appear to be in some distress."

"Aye, you notice correctly. Me name be Kendred. I assure you that my whiskey was not to blame for their conditions." He looked at the two men, now both on the ground. The man who had been grasping his arm was now quiet and appeared to be sleeping.

"Well, perhaps inadvertently it was, but they were given fair warning." Kendred took a small sip from his cup and placed it on a level spoke of the wagon wheel he was leaning back against.

"In the old country, me family made a verra fine whiskey. A good and true Scot's Whiskey. Here," he shrugged, "one must settle for a lesser quality. Aye, here it is but swill compared to the old sod's drink."

Kendred reached out, grabbed Buck's sleeve and looked him in the eye. The strength in the grasp surprised Buckingham.

"Do ye know what I have been reduced to in this heathen land? Do ye have any concept?"

Buckingham simply shook his head no. Kendred rubbed his hands together and warmed to his tale.

"On the far side of the Mississippi I took my last savings and made purchase of this decrepit wagon against which we now rest.

Then, through the last of my cash and promises I must fulfill, I obtained twenty barrels. Five of them filled with straight grain alcohol and the rest empty."

With a tear in his eye, Kendred stopped, took another small sip, and continued. Buck wasn't sure if the tear was from emotion or the god-forsaken liquid they were drinking.

"The trip was fearful. At one time I thought that these red men were savages, but after the company of the ruffians and hooligans I traveled with, I find the red man to be well mannered and of superior social and moral quality."

Buck nodded silently in agreement, dividing his attention between whiskey and host.

"When I arrived here, I distributed the alcohol evenly amongst the barrels and filled them almost to the top with fresh spring water." Kendred hesitated. "Aye, at least that was me intent. I could only obtain the muddy discolored water of the misbegotten stream that flows through this camp. Taking the last of me tobacco, I carefully dispensed it into all the barrels." He cocked his head and reflected for a moment. "It gives the liquid a beautiful golden color, although it does give it a wee bit of an off taste.

For a cupful of the straight alcohol, I had traded for a bucket of these things." Kendred pointed to a wooden hopper filled with dried red pepper pods. "Seems people actually consider them edible." He handed one to Buck and turned to his cup for another sip. "Be careful that ye…oh my…."

While it looked a bit like some kind of jerky, when Buck had bitten half of it off and started chewing he found it was like trying to eat glowing coals from a campfire.

Kendred shook his finger at Buckingham.

"Ye should only take a pinch of it and crush it between your fingers and sprinkle it on your meal." He pulled his finger back and looked at it. "Aye, and then do not put those fingers near yer eyes for a couple days." He thought, then added. "Or near yer privates."

Buck sat, tears streaming from his eyes, spitting fragments of the pepper and snot running from his nose as he gasped for air. Kendred continued his lecture.

"I take a handful of these and place them into each barrel. The other traders advised me to make two more additions. I add in several scoops of molasses to give it some sweet and further the color."

Kendred stopped once more to peer at the motionless men.

"And the final ingredient I am not sure was required, but they told me to place a couple rattlesnake heads into the barrels – to give it the bite that you mountain men seem to expect." He sighed.

Buckingham nodded his head. The recipe sounded about right to him.

"Took me most of two days to gather enough serpents to do the job. Verra dangerous, I might add, but I did so, so not to disappoint my customers." Kendred shook his head and spoke in soft admission.

"I am not a hardened man, and I admit that my heart is a mite more tender than most. I just could not bring myself to kill the wee poor serpents, behead them and toss them in."

Kendred looked again at the motionless men.

"I opened the lids and placed the wee wigglies into the whiskey alive."

Raising his hands to the heavens Kendred asked, "How were I to know that the critters could swim, and swim so well for so long?"

Pointing to the two corpses Kendred said in explanation, "I told them it were not ready yet, but would they believe me? *No!* They were brutes, forcing past me to dip their cups deep into my barrels." He paused and lifted the jug, "May I offer you another refreshing sip?"

Somewhere – about four days into it as far as he could remember – and what he could remember was not much, Buck found himself sitting with Swimming Snake.

They were planted on their butts in a clearing overlooking the lodges and wagons. The first thing Buck realized was a hellish storm was going on all around and above them. But that did not seem to matter much.

He had been drinking Kendred's whiskey steady, and the world was a blur. He did note he was not sitting on a blanket, but both were comfortably sunk in six inches of mud, as if waiting for roots to grow.

Swimming Snake was sitting there, dignified as ever, solemn as ever, holding a large stick of hard candy in his fist, taking small bites from it. The rain was melting it, covering his hand with sticky goo.

This mystified Buckingham somewhat, but not as much as the fact Buck himself was naked. Well, not totally naked. He still had one moccasin and his fur cap. For the life of him, he could not remember what had happened to his garments, and he was more than a little afraid to ask. Snake did not seem to notice Buckingham's lack of apparel.

While he sat there trying to sort it all out, Spider Web Johnson came roaring through the mud on his horse.

Course he wasn't known as Spider Web yet, but that name was a comin'.

When Spider Web hit the center of the clearing, whooping and a hollerin', he raised his rifle to the sky.

The sky must have taken offense, because the next thing anybody knew – after the brilliant flash – was the smoking carcasses of the horse and Johnson laying there in the mud.

Swimming Snake had turned to Buck with a pleased expression, pointed to the steaming bodies with the hard candy and said, "I spoke of this."

Exceptionally pleasing to Johnson was the fact that he was not dead. Addled and changed a mite, but still alive and kicking.

Now from his right wrist, up his arm, across his back, chest, and down his left leg, was a curious pattern of fine lines – looking essentially like a spider web.

Sometimes the lines were red and sometimes they hovered indecisively between black and blue. Overall the new decorations were pleasing, and a matter of great pride to Johnson's two wives. They would drag other women into their lodge and display him proudly; careful to point out that as he got hot or cold the lines would change color.

The lines did not bother Johnson much, but he was becoming annoyed at his wives.

After that, Buck did take the rifle business a bit more seriously.

❧

Buckingham's thoughts returned to the tasks at hand. It had been a hard day, it had been a long day, and now, with satisfaction, Buck was ready to relax.

The meager supply of sets were planted and staked; nothing remained for labor in the area of trapping. He had placed his bait prim and proper, as he had so many times before, and soon he would be pulling in the pelts, scraping and stretching them.

Life would fall into a satisfying routine for the next several months. All seemed good and even the nagging tickle subsided some.

During the day, events passed that perplexed Buck. Actually the events had stymied him, causing great concern.

In the early afternoon Buck had watched a nice doe come to water and decided she would make a fitting supper; the remainder of the meat to be jerked for the uncertain future.

From where he was, she had been no more than seventy paces off. He had pulled the wiping stick from his rifle, planted one end on the ground, and used it as a monopod upon which to steady the heavy rifle. Pulling back the hammer, he squeezed the set trigger nestled inside the trigger guard. When pulled to its fullest, it set in action a mechanical series, whereby all the cogs and sears aligned, and only the slightest touch of the next trigger would fire the rifle.

When his finger touched the second trigger a gratifying 'pssst' and cloud of smoke from the pan sent a tongue of flame through the touch-hole, caressing the main charge in the barrel. This ignited without hesitation and the rifle boomed, sending a cloud of smoke and linen wrapped lead ball to its target.

Now Buckingham was not the best shot in the world, but he was no slouch either. The thought of missing at this range never crossed his mind. In his mind the meat was already in the pan and his mouth was watering in anticipation. When the blue-white smoke had cleared, he strode forward to claim his vittles. To his surprise the doe was gone and upon inspection, no sign of blood wet the sand.

Buckingham blew down the barrel, pulled the plug from his horn, dumped a charge into the cylinder of carved antler hanging around his neck, and poured the measured charge down the muzzle of the rifle.

With his hand, he smacked the side of the rifle right smart to set all powder to the bottom, and from the possibles bag he pulled a small piece of linen. Sticking a corner of the wad in his mouth he let spit soak in while he rummaged in the bag once more for a galena pill.

Putting the soggy linen over the muzzle he placed the gray ball on top of the linen, drew his knife and used the handle to start the lethal package into the barrel. With the honed blade he cut the linen flush with the muzzle, sheathed the knife and returned the rest of the linen to the pouch.

Retrieving his wiping stick from the ground, he pushed and tapped the ball and cloth to the bottom of the barrel. Eying the stick he noted his mark on the rod, indicating that the entire mess was seated as far as it could and should go.

Pleased with his efforts he replaced the stick into its thimbles on the underside of the barrel, where it slid home into the stock.

Pulling the fur cap from his head he wiped the sweat from his brow once more and frowned.

There were not any way he could have missed – but he had. He looked at the front blade and then the rear buckhorn sight. All looked right and nothing had moved or been jarred out of place. The scratch mark he had made when it was sighted still met its twin on the rear sight. He knew the deer had not moved nor had he flinched. Maybe the cloth patch holding the lead ball and conforming to the rifling had blown out or torn in its fiery rush down the barrel.

Even so, it probably would not have made the flying piece of lead miss its mark by that much.

It confounded him, but there was not much to do about it. There was always next time, and his supply of pemmican and jerky would have to suffice for the evening sup. It was a hard pill to swallow, but at least he could have a bit of tea to make his belly think it was getting a hot meal.

After retrieving a bit of food from his pack he gathered twigs and branches next to the creek and set them in a pile to build his fire. Pulling his flint, steel, and a piece of char cloth from his possibles bag, he set them down and looked for some dried grass. Finding a fine handful he set to work.

Laying the char cloth over the flint he struck hard with a C-shaped piece of iron. The spark caught on the cloth and expanded outward in a glowing orange ring. Poking the smoldering char cloth into the wad of dried grass he blew gently on the tinder.

A small amount of smoke issued from it, but did not take, no matter how tenderly and carefully he blew on it – it did not sprout the small feathers of flame he expected. He had performed this act countless times. It was more surprising for it not to work than if he had woke up in the morning to find the Queen of England under his robes.

He checked the grass. Perhaps it had been damp and he had not noticed, but to his chagrin it was dry. Dry as his throat five months after rendezvous.

"Cannot put ball in a deer and cannot put fire in dry grass. Enough to cloud the nicest day," he muttered, but Buck was not without cunning and there was more than one way to tie a horse to a tree.

Trudging back to camp he pulled a length of rope from around his pack. Cutting four inches off the end, he grunted, retied the rope, and returned to the intended site of his campfire.

Pulling apart the three main cords that twisted together to form the main cordage, he set one down, and tossed the other two in his possibles bag. The one he had saved he pulled apart, fluffing it up into a ball of fibers as billowy as the down from a milkweed plant.

Digging out more char cloth he set ember to it, put it in the nest of rope, blew on it gently and in a few seconds was rewarded with a flare of fire. Grinning he set it on the ground, covered it with a small handful of tiny dry twigs, and felt his grin slip away when the twigs refused to smolder.

Cursing a blue streak he stood questioning the heritage of the twigs, the father of the tinder, and his own capabilities of making fire. With his leather covered foot he kicked the ill fated start of his campfire to the winds, stomped on the ground where his fire pit should have been, and stormed back to his tree.

"Fine," he bellowed to the sky. "I wanted a cold camp anyway. It matches the vittles."

◌◌

Swimming Snake was not happy. He had hurriedly planned for this journey and brought with him what he figured he needed. Now, having time to consider more carefully, he thought of a lot more things he could have brought.

Some more herbs. Some more items of power.

Perhaps a war party of ten heavily armed men.

From what he had seen already and from what he feared he would find, none of that – even the warriors – would be of any use. Carrying his bundle under his left arm, he reached up with his right, and fingered the medicine pouch around his neck. He carried no weapons as such, although he did have three Medicine items in the bundle that would serve as armaments.

He did not unwrap the bundle. The unseen eyes watching him had no need to see what he carried, either in the bundle or in his heart. They would have to wait just as he had waited, hoping that his Brother Walks with Limp would return without having entered the valley.

That had not happened and Swimming Snake felt responsible. Yes, he had told the white man the valley was not to be entered, but the white man – all white men – were so stubborn in their ways. You could sing them the songs and warn them of the danger, and it only served to pique their interest. If you flat stated that they could not go, then they looked on it as a challenge, and would continue their actions, just to prove that no man had control over them.

Snake shook his head. He knew Walks with Limp and knew him well. Were it just other men he would be confronting, Swimming Snake would still be at home flirting with the young girls of the encampment.

Walks with Limp was a creature unlike any other Snake had met. He was perceptive in the ways of the forest and the animals. When provoked he was easily a match for any three, including the warriors of the village they both called home.

At rendezvous Snake had watched Buckingham, so drunk he could barely stand, pull a knife and dance the death dance with another; stand over the body of his enemy at the end with no regret in his eyes, and no gratification over the bloody deed.

Halfway down the valley slope Snake stopped. He could easily see through the trees around him. Each was barren and stripped. No pine needles hung from any bough and the ground itself was sterile dirt.

Neither a sprig of green could he see, nor the track of any animal other than the moccasin prints left by his brother.

Looking to the heavens he shivered. "Great Father, I know I am wrong to be treading this path. You created this ground and you destroyed this ground. I come not to take or give, but only to lead back a man. He knows not of your ways. He knows not the true legacy of the valley."

He stopped and looked around once more.

"It is clear to my heart he knows not what he is doing. Forgive him. There could be many reasons he does so. He could be filled with greed or ignorance. It could be to prove his bravery. Perhaps it is just because he is a stupid white man." He shrugged. "The last is probably the case, but he is my brother."

Snake sat and waited. He watched and waited with the rising sun, until movement in the valley rewarded his patience.

℘℘

Buckingham woke to his cold camp. His mood was not improved and while his belly was not as empty as it had been in the past it felt right cheated.

A momentary fear swept over him that he was loosing his touch. Loosing those skills that he had learned and earned at a high cost of year, blood and friends.

His eyes were gritty and his mouth was shitty, as one of his old (may he rest in peace) trapping partners used to say. Overall, he just felt worn, tired and confused. The normal aches were still there, but even they were dulled as if his body and mind were winding down. As if something was sucking the very life and vitality from his body.

It was not the lonesome either. Sometimes in the mountains a man hit a spell where the lonesome set in on him, grabbing his heart and spirit and giving a squeeze.

It was not that. He was too fresh from the lodges for it to be that.

With slumped shoulders he hoisted his possibles and rifle, setting out for the creek. Buck prided himself in his bathing. He bathed right regular, every month or so, and sweat baths every couple of weeks. While he was afraid that it might weaken him to bath more often, he decided to chance it this time. Often, after scraping oneself off and washing, a person felt right pert. Seemed to give a man a new outlook on the world.

Swimming Snake spent most his time in the water. Never seemed to hurt him. Well, truth be told, he was an eccentric savage, but the water had not hurt him – at least not physically. Mentally? Who knew what had set the Snake's mind on the paths it followed.

With heavy footsteps he made his way to the creek. For some reason he seemed to remember something different. Something used to make his passage to the creek more difficult. He could not remember what it might have been. It seemed miles and the journey felt like it took hours. Once there he started the arduous process of removing his skins.

It took a while to adjust to having the skins off. The sunlight felt very strange against the bare skin of his back and chest. Buckingham turned and studied the creek with a slight anxiety.

Carefully he reached out one toe and touched the water. Sure he had been wading around in it the past couple days, but it did not make no mind not to check it out again. It was cold and wet, much as he expected it to be. His toe did not fall off neither and that were good sign.

Another thing that he did not expect was the knife stabbing him in the back.

CHAPTER 4
Song of the Brothers

"We few, we happy few, we band of brothers. For he today that sheds his blood with me shall be my brother..." - William Shakespeare

The pain was not much, but a knife cut seldom is – at least during the fight. It would hurt like the bloody blazes later. This knife had taken him right below the shoulder blade on the left side. He did not know how much damage was done, but it had either kilt him or it hadn't. In either case he was still moving, and it was time to do something about it.

Unfortunately his rifle lay back in the direction the blade had come from. He threw himself forward into the creek where he did a watery forward somersault and came to his feet.

He whirled around to face his attacker.

"You no good, back stabbin,' sneaky low down piece of buffalo turd! Why for did you go and stab me?" He screamed at the Indian.

Swimming Snake was standing there.

In his right hand was an ornate knife with an intricately carved antler handle and long thin blade. The first half inch of blade was crimson with Buck's blood. With thumb and forefinger Snake wiped the blood from the steel, raised his hand to his face and sniffed the blood carefully. Then he frowned and touched his bloody finger to his tongue. Smiling with satisfaction he wiped his hand on his leggings.

Snake raised his hand to the white man.

"I had to be sure. I thought you were a spirit."

Pulling from behind him a wooden handled stone club he showed it to Buckingham.

"At first I was just going to smash your spirit head and set you free.

Then I thought – what if my friend and brother Walks with Limp is not a spirit. If I should release him with the medicine club and he is still of this world, then I will have been responsible for making him a spirit. I felt you might not like that, so I decided to check first."

As if lecturing a child he finished. "As you know spirits do not bleed real blood. I have spoke of this."

"And are ye satisfied that that is real blood?"

"Yes, but if you are still concerned," comforted Swimming Snake, "we can check again."

"No, damn you!"

Buck shook like a dog spraying the excess water off him. He then went about collecting his skins and putting them back on. It was obvious to Snake that Walks with Limp was in ill humor again – for some reason.

Pulling on his shirt the first words out of his mouth when his head popped through were, "What in blue blazes are ye doing here in the first place? Other than stabbin' me in the back for my own protection?"

Snake settled cross legged on the ground.

"When you left the camp I was concerned. I waited for many days hoping you would return. When you didn't I decided to come for you."

Buckingham looked at him with disbelief in his eyes. "I don't know what you have been smoking in your medicine pipe, but you had better go back to kinnic-a-nik. I have only been here a couple of days. Hardly had time to set up camp and get my sets out."

"Brother...you have been gone from the lodges for the time it takes the sun to rise and set the number of fingers on both ones hands twice."

"Now that is plumb crazy."

Swimming Snake thought for a moment.

"You remember my brother, just before you left, we had a feast. It was in celebration of Small Rock becoming a man."

Buckingham laughed. "Sure I do. It was hard for me to forget. He spent almost a year leadin' up to it practicing stealing horses. Most the time he practiced on yours."

Snake smiled also in memory. "Then you remember that evening, when I was making the monument for the medicine pouch he was to receive?"

Buckingham squinted and thought for a moment.

"Yep. I guess I do. You and I hauled some river rock to build it. As I rightly remember, the ones close to the camp weren't the *right* ones, and we had to haul them from a hellacious distance away."

Snake shook his head. "Yes. You remember the slight bit of trouble we went through to get the proper stones for the ceremony, but do you not remember my grievous injury?"

Buck nodded. "Yeah, if'n you mean your pinching your finger and howling like a baby. That I remember."

What had actually occurred during the time was Snake had slammed a rock the size of his head down on the growing pile. In the process he had smashed his finger between the rocks. It had been a mighty blow and severe enough to remove the nail from the finger.

By Buckingham's remembrance that had been about six days ago.

Without word, Snake held his hand out for Buck's viewing.

Buckingham looked at it and then took the hand in his own. "Okay, let me see your other hand." Snake held out the other hand.

"That's right peculiar."

Buckingham could see injury to one finger and it was almost totally healed.

"But you always were right good at healing people. Maybe you just had some good herbs and grasses for it."

"You know that is not the truth."

Buck looked around for a spell. "Then maybe you could tell me the truth – without making me drag it all out of ya. Now, I am not promising I will buy it, but I would like to hear the story. I admit there have been some mighty perplexing things happen here." He held up his hands.

"Nothing dangerous, but just mighty peculiar." He plopped down on the ground.

"Here is as good a place as any to tell it."

Snake looked around. "There is not any place in this valley that is good." Seeing the look on Buckingham's face he hurried on. "Then when no place is good, they are all the same." He sat on the stony ground facing Buckingham.

CHAPTER 5
Song of the Valley

"I tell you that the cloud of murder hangs thicker and lower than that over the heads of the people. It is the Valley of Fear. The Valley of Death. The terror is in the hearts of the people from dusk to dawn. Wait, young man, and you will learn for yourself." "Arthur Conan Doyle

"Many years ago, my people came to this area. Not to this valley, but to camp near where we camp now. This was in the days of my father's father. When my father's father was young." He grinned slyly. "You might remember the time."

Snake looked at Buckingham innocently, waiting for a response. When none came, he continued.

"Game was plentiful then. The hunting parties were short and always returned with meat for the tribe.

The land was good and blessed by the spirits. Not as you see it now." Snake looked at the countryside then at Buck. "Or as I see it. You and most others see it as it was, not how it is."

"Then the stars fell from the sky and came to rest in this valley. We no longer sing the songs telling of it. It is bad. We do not sing of this bad thing.

One night the entire village watched. From the heavens the stars came down and spread their wings over the countryside. They crossed the sky – back and forth – each night for several days. During that time we guarded our families and horses." Snake hesitated. "We tried."

"During the day we would wander. Close to camp at first, for we feared the stars might return during the day. Then we went farther searching for game. We found animals – deer, elk – even some of the horses that had wandered.

They lay dead. Drained of blood. Parts of them had been …removed. During the night we would watch the stars fly. In the day we would walk the ground beneath where they had flown and find the carcasses of the animals." Snake looked on the face of Walks with Limp, searching for belief.

"A few warriors went out to learn of what happened during the night. They did not return. The tribe went out during the day looking for them. We feared we would find them as they found the animals, but that was not to be. They simply were not found."

Buckingham raised his hand and started to speak, then thought better of it and motioned Snake to continue.

"Finally one night when the moon was gone the stars all came to this valley. From the camp all could see them. They came from every direction and stayed over the valley for a time. It was said that the night was as day around this valley. Before morning they descended, fell as the hawk does upon his prey, into the valley.

There they did stay for six risings and settings of the sun. People went out – it was impossible to forbid them – to look upon the stars come to earth. Those that were near said the valley was afire with a light the color of new grass tufts in the spring.

Those that went over the rim and down into the valley spoke of it briefly. They became ill. Sores and blisters as if the pox appeared on their bodies. Blood came from their eyes, ears and noses. Before death they spoke of what they had seen in the valley."

Swimming Snake stopped his lesson. He looked to the sky and then down to the earth before looking his brother in the eyes.

"What I have said has been told to me. What I have to say now will be difficult for you to believe. This I know. I did not see it with my own eyes and it was difficult for me to accept. Many times I wondered if the songs were wrong. If they had been embellished for the entertainment of the tribe. If they were intended only to scare the children in the late nights around the fires."

He continued doggedly. "Having seen the valley – having talked to others who have seen this valley…I must accept. You must accept also if we are to leave this place together.

The dying ones spoke of the children. Children not of the skin you call red, but of gray. The gray of smoke from the campfires. On their heads they bore no scalps only more skin of this gray. They had heads of the buffalo. Not shaggy and with horn, but large when set atop their bodies. Eyes big and the color of the night sky.

They spoke that they had gotten close to the children. Close enough to see all this with certainty. The children knew of their presence, but ignored them, much as we ignore a cur slinking around the camp. In the morning the children would gather in a circle – there were many of them. Facing inwards the morning sun would rise in the middle of them. It made no sound, but they looked upon the light for as long it might take a man to eat his fill."

Snake looked at Buck again.

"Then they would separate wandering in and out of their lodges the color of polished iron."

After a time the stars rose back into the sky and the children walked the valley no more. The valley died. All trees gave up their spirits as well as the grass. No animal walked the valley. It is as it is today. Barren and dead."

Snake looked at Walks with Limp a final time. "I have spoken the words of my grand father and my father. I have spoken."

CHAPTER 6
Song of the Search

"The search for truth is more precious than its possession." - *Albert Einstein*

Buckingham looked around him before daring to speak.

"Swimming Snake…I have heard the words you have spoken. I can tell you mean them from your heart. By the heavens man – look around you! This valley is not dead. The trees and grass grow and critters wander its length. Do you not see this?"

"No, my brother," said Snake. "I do not see what you or most see when I look upon this valley. This I cannot explain. Do you not have things about this valley that you cannot explain?"

Buck thought for a moment. He remembered missing the doe and the fire he could not build. These memories were faint and fading quickly.

"Well, there are a few things that took me by surprise. Nothing, howsoever that is strange and dangerous. I do know that I ain't seen any strange children running around. Besides," Buck continued, "I for one see some holes in your story."

Buckingham pulled his pipe, loaded it, and set on his own yarn.

"All this would have happened some fifty, maybe sixty years ago. That be a long time. Anything that was hoodooing this valley would be long gone by now." He pointed the stem of his pipe at Swimming Snake. "In your lifetime have you ever seen the stars come down and fly around?"

Snake thought for but a moment. "No."

"Have you, or any of the current tribe, ever seen these here children you spoke of?"

Swimming Snake started to speak, but Buckingham broke in. "Now in person, mind you, face to face, not in your dreams."

"No," admitted Swimming Snake.

"And," continued Buck, "do you see any difference in me since I have been in the valley?"

"No," said Snake. "You are still the same stubborn and unbelieving white man you have always been."

"Now, you know what you see. I know what I see, and you say it is not the same. Who is to say which of us is right? But I will make you a deal."

Swimming Snake grimaced. "I know how most deals work with a white man. Why does my heart not sing to hear of this deal?"

Buckingham frowned. "You are an astute man."

He saw confusion on Snake's face. "That means you see a lot of what is around you. You cross the trail of a badger, weeks old, and are able to tell the tale of its passing. You have been to encampments long abandoned. You were able to tell me how many people were there. Men, women and children. How many ponies they had. How long they stayed and in what direction they left in. Do I speak the truth?"

Snake smiled in modesty. "Yes, this is true. I possess the knowledge of reading the past through sign." He was quite pleased that his brother had noted his skill.

"Then it would not be a problem if you and I looked around this valley. You seeing what you see and me seeing what I see – and between the two of us we should be able to find sign of these children having been here. Even if it were a bit ago."

Snake fumed. "Your heart is black and your skin is white. You complimented only to get your way."

"But it be the truth, is it not?"

"Yes," said Snake.

"Then tomorrow morning we set out. We find the truth."

"No," said Snake. "Tomorrow it will not be. We must do it now. Today. While this sun still stands in the sky. Tomorrow – with or without you my brother – my feet will not walk this ground."

It took little time to prepare. Snake had only his medicine knife, ceremonial club and bundle. Buckingham grabbed his rifle, crammed a handful of jerky into his possibles bag and rejoined Swimming Snake.

Swimming Snake had stood and watched as Walks with Limp went to get the small amount of food.

He watched as Buck went through elaborate motions getting to the trunk of his tree. A tree – for all that Snake could see – that was nothing but spindly barren branches one could push aside and walk through. It was obvious, however, that to his brother it was a full and living tree.

"Now I will have you know," said Buckingham, "I walked pretty nigh this entire valley the first day I was here. Not to spoil yer hopes, but I didn't see anything much out of the ordinary."

Together they walked towards the middle of the valley bottom to an area next to the creek and about a quarter mile downstream. There a small mound of earth stood. From the slight additional height it gave, they could see well. Climbing to the top both surveyed the landscape around them with careful eyes.

"It might be farther downstream to the south, after the valley tightens up. That may be where yer little children had their playground," said Buckingham.

"No. It was said their encampment was at the end from which the cold wind blows."

"Well let's get on with it. That tickle I had has come back and it is worse than before."

Buckingham eyed Swimming Snake, waiting for him to make the first move. Snake stood fingering the medicine pouch around his neck. He started walking.

For almost three hours they crisscrossed the valley floor, carefully looking at everything there was to see. They studied the ground. They studied the rocks on the ground. They studied the sky. They looked to the tops of the ridges and rims around them. Their journey led them in a large circle by the time they were finished.

Sitting atop the mound that they had started from they planned their next move.

"Well, that weren't all that fruitful," said Buck.

Swimming Snake merely grunted. Holding his medicine bag he alternated between grasping it and letting it dangle and swing.

Reaching into his possibles bag Buck pulled a piece of jerky and twisted it in half. Assuring himself both portions were about equal he offered a gnarled brown slab to Snake. Snake accepted it with another nod then lifted it to his nose and carefully smelled of it. Satisfied it was not tainted; he ripped a hunk off and started chewing it thoughtfully.

"My brother, tell me this. When you look across from here, what is it you see and hear?" asked Snake.

Buck thought for a moment then studied the view.

"I see the willows yonder. The wind is blowing and moving them some. Makes a whispering noise, it does. Always liked that sound."

"Now close your eyes," commanded Swimming Snake.

Buckingham did so.

"Tell me – do you hear the wind now? Do you feel the wind?"

Buckingham sat for a moment then quickly opened his eyes. After a second, he closed them and sat motionless. A few minutes later he opened his eyes once more.

"This is right strange. When I close my eyes, I can no longer hear the wind. It just sort of fades off. What's stranger, when I close my eyes I can't feel the wind on me anymore," said Buck.

Swimming Snake nodded, rose to his feet and pointed. "It is time. We walk this way."

For another two hours both men walked the floor of the valley. They searched anything and everything that they could think of. Again they observed, they listened, and they even smelled everything in their path. Again rocks were pulled up from the ground and inspected.

Snake thought it perplexing, but Walks with Limp even inspected some things that he himself could not see.

Thus it went.

No contentment was found for either man.

As they rounded a bend in the creek Buckingham pointed out a deer with fawn grazing peacefully on the grass. Snake looked, but did not see the deer. When he pointed this out to Buck, the man cursed, asking him if he were blind.

"Then shoot the animal. This will be proof," said Swimming Snake.

"You know I do not kill for sport or fun," snarled Buckingham.

"I do not ask you to kill for pleasure. If indeed you kill the animal, then I am wrong. If I am wrong, then we spend the night – we spend many nights here in this valley. We will need food." Swimming Snake stared at Buck, waiting for his words to sink home.

Buckingham thought about it and raised his rifle, took a fine bead on the animal, then lowered the rifle.

"Nope," he said. "You know darned well that I would kill the mother for food. If I was starving and of a mind I would take the fawn, but just to prove a point – right or wrong – this I will not do."

Swimming Snake sighed. "You are afraid that I am right. Think of this.

We stand here talking; they take no notice if your eyes are to be believed."

"Yep. Been known to happen."

"In which direction is the wind blowing then? The wind that you feel?" asked Snake.

Buck thought again, raised his rifle in one smooth motion, and fired when the sights came to rest just behind the deer's front shoulder. The blast rocked the valley, blue-gray smoke drifting slowly before him.

When the sound had died and the smoke dispersed, silence reigned over all.

From the look on Buck's face, Swimming Snake knew the answer, but asked anyway.

"Did you kill it with your rifle?" asked Snake.

Buckingham looked down at his moccasins.

"Nope." He slowly pulled the makin's and reloaded his rifle.

"Well, Swimming Snake…you made your point. The wind – if there is any wind at all – is coming from our backs. The deer should have bolted long ago. They might ignore noise – would not be normal, but they might – but they wouldn't ignore our scent."

He did not speak again until his ramrod was set back in place.

"When I fired they weren't there. The instant I pulled the trigger they were gone. Not like they had run off – they was just gone."

Swimming Snake waited.

"Okay," Buck said. "I owe you an apology." He grinned. "You ain't gunna get it, but I owe you one."

They wandered slowly back to the mound and sat cross legged once more. One sat with heavy heart from truth learned, while the other sat relieved that truth had been accepted. The sun beat down on both, but neither man moved.

Finally Buckingham spoke.

"At least we found proof this valley is hoodoo. Might not have found anything else, but I am a believer." He looked around. "It all looks real. You can reach out and touch it. Now I don't know what to trust."

Snake looked up. "We have found more than what is *not* here. We have found what *is* here."

Buckingham tossed a handful of dirt to the wind and asked, "And what did we find? I admit the deer were but a dream in my eyes and did not exist. What exactly is it that we might have found?"

"There are places. Places with power." Swimming Snake responded.

Buck tossed another handful of earth and looked around. "I am sure that has some deep meaning. Howsoever, at this time that meaning escapes me. Perhaps in your infinite wisdom you would enlighten this pilgrim."

Snake rolled his eyes to the sky. "Always you need an explanation. Always you need the white man's proof. Power places exist in many lands. How they come to be is mystery. It is enough to know that they exist. By their existence, they draw people to them. They draw happenings."

Snake stopped and looked at Buckingham. "Does this help you my brother?"

"Yep. It's a start."

"You feel...what was it you said you felt about this valley?" asked Swimming Snake.

Buck replied. "It's like a tickle. Just a feeling that seems to crawl over yer skin. I had it before I even got here, but...," he paused, "...since I got into the belly of this valley its been worse."

Snake nodded. "Yes. A tickle. For me I can feel it in my medicine bag. When I am near a place that has this power, the medicine in the pouch moves. It quivers. Watch..."

Swimming Snake held the medicine bag by the thong, letting it dangle from between his fingers. Buckingham watched as it slowly swung back and forth, and then stopped its pendulum motion. Even as it stopped swinging, he could see the slender piece of leather that suspended it seemed to vibrate.

Snake stood and spoke softly. "Now watch."

Slowly – barely moving – he kept the bag dangling and started walking down the side of the mound, his motions smooth and graceful.

As Buck moved with him, Buck kept his eyes glued on the bag. His head mere inches from it.

When Snake moved from the top of the mound the bag no longer hung straight down. It seemed to angle out of plumb. The pouch seemed drawn to the mound; perhaps the center of the mound.

"That be right strange, too," said Buckingham. "How you doing that?"

Snake stopped and gave Buck a dark look. "I am doing nothing. This is not by my hand. I just spoke of this. How it is doing so, I know not. Why it is doing so, I know not."

"This isn't another of those lizard things is it?" asked Buckingham.

"No, this is not a trick. Remember when we started our search? Here is where we started. Then we ended our search here. We left again and we ended again," said Snake in disgust. He looped the medicine bag back over his head.

With the side of his foot Buckingham kicked half heartedly at the side of the mound.

"Then what do we do now?"

Swimming Snake stared at him as if he were insane. "We leave."

"That just don't seem right," said Buck. "Don't you think we should explore some more? See what is causing this? Don't seem right not knowing what it be that is here."

"My brother, when you find the bear sleeping, do you stick your hand in its mouth to see it if has a tongue and teeth?"

"Nope. That sounds a mite risky to me," answered Buckingham.

Swimming Snake nodded towards the sun that was starting its drop towards the rim of the valley.

"We must start now. It will be dark by the time we make the top of the rim. In the day there is danger, but it seeks us out not. To remain while darkness covers this cursed land is to stab our own hearts. At the top we can spread our blankets. It will be a long walk back to the village."

Buck asked, "Didn't you bring a horse? As I remember, you are not that fond of walking."

"I brought a horse. I believe he has left by now. He is a smart animal you know."

Gathering their meager belongings they started the grueling trek towards the top of the valley.

CHAPTER 7
Dance of Escape

"You cannot escape the responsibility of tomorrow by evading it today." - Abraham Lincoln

By the time they had reached the top of the canyon the sun had set behind the horizon. A dull and sullen blue coated the world around them and clouds glowed as if afire, illuminated by the sun they could no longer see.

Pulling the fur cap from his head, Buck wiped the sweat from his face with a leather sleeve blackened from years.

"Bout time we took a breather."

Swimming Snake looked at the almost black sky, at Buckingham, and then the valley behind them. He motioned with his hand.

"No. This is not a place to rest."

Buck squinted and peered back on the path they had come. "I know I am tired. I figure you must be a mite winded. Any particular reason we can not sit a spell?"

"It follows," Snake said simply.

Buckingham swung his rifle towards the canyon.

"What follows?"

Snake shrugged. "I do not know."

Buckingham kept his eyes on the canyon rim behind them. "Do we want to know?"

"I do not think so," said Swimming Snake.

Buck gave his brother a hard look in the growing darkness. "Reckon that's good enough for me."

The two men started walking once more, through the clearing of a saddle separating the canyon from the shallow draw next to it. They walked silently into the night, looking back every few steps.

∞

Buck awoke to the morning sun. He sat up, the blanket falling from his chest and looked around, his hand instinctively feeling for his rifle. The morning pressed a light chill against his face.

Swimming Snake sat a few paces away, watching the sunrise forming in the east. Buck knew without asking the man had sat all night without sleep.

Rising to his feet he turned towards Snake.

"Reckon we should get on our way."

Swimming Snake shook his head. "There is no hurry now, my brother."

"What ever it is, or was, isn't following us anymore?"

Swimming Snake looked towards the ground.

"No. It is not following us. It past us in the night and has moved on before us."

"Why in tarnation didn't you wake me?"

Still staring at his feet Snake spoke, "I was afraid. I was afraid to make a noise. I was afraid to move. It was out there and watched us for a while. Then it moved on."

Buck looked at his own feet and could think of nothing to say. Snake had never used the word afraid when speaking about himself.

They walked single file, five paces separating them from each other. Each man looked to the sky, the ground their feet were traveling, and the countryside around him.

Occasionally they would stop – listening and smelling, searching for anything out of the ordinary. Buck's thumb stayed on the hammer of his rifle and his finger inside the trigger guard. The long stock cradled in the crook of his left arm.

Words spoken were clipped, quiet and rare. The tickle that Buckingham had felt was gone and slowly fading into memory. Halfway through the day, when the sun had risen to where it beat down on them, they found the first sign.

Swimming Snake stopped his stride and raised a hand halfway up and out to his side. When he heard Buck's footsteps cease, he slowly moved his hand forward and to the front. Pointing.

Buckingham's eyes searched for a split second before he saw it. A gray form lying in the sagebrush. From years of hunting he knew it was the shape of a mule deer.

224

Deer were unpredictable critters. They might jump and run when you were a half mile off. If you caught them off guard, they might lay in wait, not moving, hoping that you would walk past them – then bolt to safety.

But this didn't feel right.

He slowly raised his rifle to his shoulder and sighted down the barrel. Setting the blade in the rear V-notch he took a coarse sighting picture. His thumb pulled the hammer back – its click reached his ear. His finger pulled the rear trigger and he felt the set trigger engage, hearing the sears click into place. He then touched – ever so gently – the front trigger. He held the rifle on target waiting. He was not sure of what he was waiting for, but he felt danger.

After Buckingham had stood so long the heavy rifle started wobbling, he placed his thumb back on the hammer and lowered it. Both men looked at each other and started walking towards the deer.

Standing across from each other – the carcass of the deer between them – Snake motioned to the body and said, "My grandfather spoke of this."

There were wounds on the body of the deer that would cause death. None of these wounds were such that the animal would have stood still while they were being performed.

On its muzzle, skin and tissue had vanished from a section shaped like an egg and teeth were visible. A couple of teeth were gone. Buck knelt and examined the wound closely.

From where Swimming Snake stood he could see that its ass hole had been removed. No blood had flowed from any of the wounds he saw.

On its belly a "T" shaped incision had been made and innards fell out in pink and purple coils. With a cautious hand he moved the guts around and peered at it again. Moments later he repeated the action.

While kneeling Buckingham pulled his knife and made a cut on the neck of the dead animal. Looking at the cut he shook his head, wiped the blade on his legging, and returned it to its sheath. He stood and motioned to Snake.

"Snake…look at this." He pointed to the cut he had made, and to the cut where the flap had been removed from the deer's muzzle.

Swimming Snake knelt and stared at both.

"I see, but I do not understand."

Buck grinned broadly, gleeful that he was now the teacher.

"The cut on the deer's mouth…when you look at the hair on the border of the cut…then compare it to mine. You see? You know I keep my blade sharp, but look here," he pointed to both again. "When I made my cut it was clean and deep. Nevertheless, even the sharpest blade moves some of the hairs aside. Rolls them away. It does not slice through them all when you cut."

He pointed to the original wound. "See here? The hairs – every individual hair – is cut in half cleanly."

He stuck his face down close to the cut and inhaled. Raising his face he exhaled, performed the same motion and inhaled again.

"And it smells...well...burned. But it doesn't appear scorched or blackened."

Snake waved his hand in agreement. Pointing to the bowels lying on the ground he said, "Yes, and things are missing. Things one would not normally take as prize eating. The heart is gone, but also those vines and artillery you told me of. Those are missing."

Buck looked over. "Vines and artillery? Ah! Veins and arteries. Ya mean veins and arteries. I had a book learned doctor tell me about them. They carry the blood."

"They are missing. One does not generally eat them."

Buckingham stood. "Do ya think the spookums you saw last night did this?"

"I do not know." Snake looked at the body laying there. "There is much meat here. There is much death and waste."

Buck's shoulders slumped. He looked towards the sky once more. Even the vultures had not gathered over this hunk of dead meat.

They resumed their trek until they hit upon a small stream that still bore water this late in the year. Its clarity and pureness slaked their thirst and pulled layers of fatigue off their spirits.

Their bellies still hungered for food.

Digging in his pack Buckingham pulled forth his jug. Swirling it in his hands he reflected upon it. Pulling the cork, he drank what he felt to be about half. It burned as molten fire in his mouth and seared his throat going down. When it hit bottom it exploded into heat that burned away the hunger.

Turning to Swimming Snake he offered the jug.

"This will take the edge off the hunger for a while. Besides – I need the jug."

Snake took it without word and drank deeply, finishing the last of the whiskey. He shuddered and handed the jug back to Buck. "Only the white man can bottle his evil."

"You never complained about it before," said Buckingham.

"It is good to know the heart of your enemy. Before I drank only for knowledge."

Buck took the jug and put a small amount of water in it. He swirled it and drank the lightly flavored water. No sense in wasting any drops of the liquor. He then filled the jug with water, corked it, and replaced it into his pack.

CHAPTER 8
Dance of the Cloud

Clouds symbolize the veils that shroud God. - Balzac

Morning in camp was uneventful.

The sun rose, as always, upon thirty lodges; all erected with their doors and smoke flaps facing the rising sun. When the false dawn started (the period of time when the new day was but a faint light in the east) a few people were up and about their early morning tasks.

Ashes in the fire pits scattered gently at the touch of probing fingers. Cold hands searched for glowing embers that rested beneath the powdery gray blanket. When small sparks of red appeared, dry grass was set atop them. The old women starting the morning fires gently blew life into them again; small tongues of red and orange blossoming as dancing flowers, growing to warming blazes that shot sparks into the still dark heavens.

In the distance, a coyote howled briefly, to be answered by its pack mates across the prairie.

Overhead bats fluttered here and there through the sky, picking the occasional insect from midair.

The sky itself – the very air around them – had a dreary and numb feeling. The feeling one would find just before a storm. Eyes scoured the brightening heavens, but only one small cloud was visible, glowing on the farthest horizon.

Children snuck quietly from the lodges, so as not to wake their elders. Mischief was the order of the day and it would not bode well to attract attention, or awaken those that might dampen such plans.

Morning Star had risen early, started one fire and was now contemplating gathering water and bringing it back to the lodge. A chore performed each morning that stretched back in time so far she could no longer remember when the task had been laid upon her shoulders.

Her eyes still sparkled with happiness at the new day. She heard the young ones planning their day of secrecy and adventure. In her heart, she would have given anything to join them. She sighed. The problem with growing old was not in growing old itself. No, the problem was the requirement of dignity. Elders were to be respected. She laughed. As such they were supposed to act with dignity and wisdom.

Morning Star thought to herself that she was indeed an elder, but dignity and wisdom were overrated.

It was always difficult when the body was eighty, but the heart was twenty.

Sighing again, she picked up two skins and began her slow walk to the creek bank, upstream from the animals.

Hearing her footsteps and labored breathing, the young boy and his sister who had crept silently from their lodge gave pursuit. Moving like shadows they followed the old woman with stealth. Darting from sage brush to rock. From rock to tree.

Morning Star noticed her companions immediately but could not bring herself to ruin their fun by acknowledging their presence.

છ૪

In the distance the cloud from the valley moved leisurely from west to east.

When it left the valley its movement had been slow, no more than a fast walk.

For years it lay scattered throughout the valley, spread so thin it was invisible. Even spread thinly its power had not diminished, nor had time reduced its lethality.

At the start, it had gradually flowed together over the mound. As more and more of its bulk congregated over the site it became visible.

If there had been an unfortunate onlooker, they would have seen a light fog appear, a fog slowly twisting and turning above the ground, extending to a height ten feet above the dome of earth.

If there had been an onlooker their life would have ended then.

As the shadows of sunset fell over it, and it gained in size, a gentle luminosity appeared.

Not a glow, but the merest hint of a radiance.

When this bluish tint formed, the cloud began its journey.

Flowing over the ground it moved towards the surrounding mountainside and started to climb. Behind it the bulk of its nature flowed, a diaphanous tail stretching back – fading slowly to invisibility – chasing the growing glow and following the path taken by the two men.

As it crested the containing walls of the valley, the leading edge of the cloud stopped, while the rest caught up. It boiled in a low spot on the ground, tendrils stretching outwards as if searching, and then falling back into the main body. As it grew in size the glow increased.

The glow concentrated in a small ball of electric blue in the center of the billowing mass; then expanded outwards, starting bright and dimming as the light spread until it touched the farthest boundaries of the cloud. The color changed slowly to green and the glow contracted back upon itself, growing in intensity until it was a small ball of intense, unearthly green. The cycle repeated – it changed to blue and started its outward migration once more.

By the time the farthest particles had joined the body proper it stretched a hundred yards across and fifty feet high. The grass and brush beneath it began to dry and char. The cloud slowly started moving once more.

Flowing across the ground the cloud flattened, dipping into depressions that pocked the earth. When it reached a rise or hill, it would slow and part, flowing around the obstacle, only to rejoin beyond it.

After several miles it lifted from the ground and hovered at a height of a hundred feet, from where it would occasionally drop to the ground, stop, and then regain its motion, rising back into the air.

In its path nothing was readily visible as to changes in the terrain it covered. The ground held a lingering dry smell and radiant heat came from the earth. Energy was being used.

The exorbitant expenditure of energy was wasteful and programming quickly changed to seek only movement beneath the death cloud. Movement equaled danger.

Passing over the burrows of a prairie dog town it leisurely descended, attracted by the movement of a lone sentry. Blanketing the ground, the glow changed from its color of blue to purple, then from purple to a brooding red. The dog standing guard fled to the supposed safety of its burrow.

Tentacles stretched from the main body of the cloud and invaded the mouth of the burrows. Each tentacle the thickness of a man's arm. The ghostly snakes followed the twisting tunnels to scores of chambers hidden below the surface.

The small creatures that were asleep awoke, setting up a chatter of fear. En mass they fled the chambers, scurrying down tunnels. As they fled they ran head long into the probing fog.

Above ground, the cloud retracted its misty serpents, the scarlet color faded back to blue, the blue contracted and it rose back into the sky, resuming its voyage of death.

On the ground silence reigned. Empty tunnels stood as mute witness to the passage of the death cloud.

An hour into its trip the world put forth its first resistance. An impediment to the death cloud's progress. From the east a brisk wind sprang up.

In the mountains winds are more often than not predictable. In the day the air is heated and moves up the mountains in a rising wind. At night the cold air returns to the valleys dropping down the mountainsides in a chill breeze. The flats of the prairie catch the eddies that spill out from the mountains like ripples in a lake.

This wind was subtly different. It did not vary in its strength or speed. No gusts punctuated the moving air.

It did not generate from thermals or weather fronts for it came from the soul of the earth.

When it hit. the wind slowed the progress of the death cloud to a halt. Streamers flowed backwards from the top and sides. Pale ribbons that stretched and fluttered, but never detached from the main core.

The color migrated forward until the light centered and focused on the front of the cloud. The back grew dark – a dull gray like the bottom of a thundercloud.

The cloud moved forward once more.

For an hour the wind blew unwaveringly, halving the speed of the cloud. Then – as quickly as it had begun – the wind died.

The first battle had been lost, *but the sleepers had awakened.*

Without pause the cloud reclaimed its wind tossed streamers.

Now it moved with caution.

Something had confronted it. Something it could not analyze.

Three quarters of a mile farther the cloud halted once more. Hovering above the ground it waited and *sensed.* As it waited it took note that there was no noise. It noted that there was no motion. In its own way the cloud was patient. It had lain for decades in the valley and an hour here would be but the blink of an eye in its measurement of time.

On the ground, in the darkness, Swimming Snake had sat with his fear. Unmoving. Unblinking. Hoping that his brother would not awaken. Thus he stayed until morning, assessing his fear and wondering at the wind from the heart of the world.

Long had it been since he had felt the earth sigh.

The awe and fear balanced each other.

Rising back into the air, the death cloud moved on with no wind to help it, but none to hinder.

A half hour farther in its trip it passed above the next creature in its path. A young mule deer sprang to its feet and stood silently, studying its surroundings. It sensed danger, but could not identify from where. Ears stood straight seeking the slightest noise. Nose twitched – it snorted and sniffed again. It stamped a hoof, attempting to induce the unseen to show itself, but time had run out for the animal.

Its standing was more than enough motion for the death cloud to track.

The killer cloud settled over the deer.

Since its creation, the cloud served many functions.

Primarily it was an information gatherer.

It would evaluate the forms of life it ran across. It would *sample* them, cataloging this information and saving it for future reference. At other times it would *gather* the life form, taking them whole for processing.

Slowly it encompassed the deer. At its touch, the deer became motionless. No longer did it search frantically for danger, for the danger was upon it and the option of flight was no longer available.

The cloud could perform muscular paralysis with life forms not possessing a sophisticated enough nervous system to override the basic program. The involuntary muscles still worked. The heart beat frantically in its chest, but not even its eyes could move. The deer had become a living statue awaiting its fate.

The death cloud recognized this life form and found the required information nestled amongst thousands of other bits of information. This would not be a gather, merely a sample. Perfunctory. A double check of existing data.

From the outer edges of the cloud thin threads of crimson light grew – each no thicker than a human hair. Around them a corolla of pink glowed as the bright strings harshly illuminated the fog around them. They extended towards the trapped animal.

After a dozen had grown in adequate length they wove a precisely patterned web around the deer, flitting close, but not touching.

Two threads darted forward to the same point on the deer's face, landing in a slight puff of smoke. They separated in opposite directions, curving, till they met once more outlining a precise oval on the jaw.

At the same time two other strands were at work.

One writhed under the deer to caress its belly and the other snapped to the tail of the creature.

Less than a minute elapsed, and the threads retracted back to the outer edges of the cloud and faded. Muscles relaxing, the deer sank quietly to the ground. Death claimed it as the cloud rose and continued its inexorable motion east.

CHAPTER 9
Dance of Decision

"In the words of the ancients, one should make his decisions within the space of seven breaths...when matters are done leisurely, seven out of ten will turn out badly. - Hagakure, Book of the Samurai

To the west, Buckingham and Swimming Snake continued their forced march.

The ground of the prairie was easy walking and, while never flat, the falling and rising of the earth was gradual and not steep. Sagebrush had to be avoided and sporadic islands of young trees by passed. Their pace was not of a laid back walk – or a hurried lope either. It was a quick step without breaks that would rapidly eat up the miles.

A pace that would not allow for idle chatter, but not causing the lungs to heave for breath.

After some hours the pace had taken its toll on Buckingham; his limp became more pronounced.

Swimming Snake looked to the face of his brother, but knew it was a wasted effort.

The pain that was undoubtedly growing in his brother's leg was reflected in his eyes, but complaint would never pass his lips. His brother reserved complaining for unimportant times.

"Ya know Snake, I am a might confused," said Buckingham.

No response came from Snake who kept his steady pace.

"I mean, I know we are headed for the village. I know you think that...well that whatever it is...it's headed for the village. I am a might confused as to what we are going to do when we catch up to it."

He stopped talking to catch his breath.

Several minutes later Snake replied.

"I have given that much thought. We will fight it."

Buckingham grimaced. "That might just be a tall order to fill."

"We will not be fighting it alone." Swimming Snake reassured him.

Buckingham perked up. "Now that be good news. I figure there are about a dozen first class warriors in the camp. If we can get some of your neighbors – the ones we ain't stolen any horses from lately, anyway to help us, we should be able to field a decent little army. Say fifty men or so."

Snake kept walking but spoke. "No. There will be no warriors in this battle. I do not believe a hundred seasoned warriors could count coup on this enemy."

Buck stumbled once as his bad leg caught a rock.

"If the warriors are not going to help us, who is? I mean I realize that a couple of the women in camp are meaner than badgers, but that doesn't reassure me a lot."

Swimming Snake shook his head without breaking stride and said, "No. That is not of which I speak. I will call upon the spirits to help us. They are awakening. They fought the evil last night."

Buckingham came to a dead stop.

"Snake, we have to palaver here some before we go any farther. I know you have given this much thought, but I think I would really like to know what those thoughts are."

Snake stopped and looked at his brother.

"We loose time by stopping."

Buck pulled his sweat drenched cap from his head, the fur now matted and dark. He nodded to himself.

"Ayup, we do. Now the faster you explain a few small details to me, the faster we will be back on the trail."

"What questions do you have this time, my brother?"

Buckingham took a deep breath and then blew it out between pursed lips.

"Oh, Lordy. Where to start," he bent and placed his hands on his knees, catching his breath while searching for the words.

"Okay. What are the spirits that are going to help us? Where do they come from? Ever fought with them before? What can they do? How come I ain't never heard or seen'um before? Why am I headed east when I should be making tracks in any other direction?"

He paused.

"Guess that will do for the first round of questions." He took a deep breath. "But I got a bunch more left to ask."

"It must be difficult being a white man," replied Swimming Snake.

"It has its moments."

"You know I am a medicine man." Snake said. "You are familiar with us as you have lived among us and other tribes before. There are medicine men and there are shamans. All medicine men have their beginning in nature.

From a young age we study the world around us and our elders teach us. The Great Spirit teaches us the ways of the animals and the ways of the plants. We learn what is useful…what can heal and what can harm. We also study the spirits and honor them."

He thought for a second before adding. "There are medicine men…and then there are medicine men."

He hesitated and looked around the area they sat.

"At a young age this is how I began my study. On my first vision quest – you are familiar with these quests – my learning was," he paused, "slightly exceptional. My quest led me to the mountains north of where our camp lies.

It was there I waited and fasted. It was there my quest was answered. In a quest one is sometimes granted audience by a spirit who becomes their totem. I know you believe this to be a madness that is brought on by hunger and exposure."

Buck spread his hands out, fingers splayed, in agreement.

"For me a spirit appeared. Not the spirit of the eagle or owl. Not the spirit of any animal. It was the spirit of the earth itself. Behind it stood all the other spirits. It did not seek to teach or instruct me. It stood in judgment of me. It measured me. If it accepted or rejected me, I do not know. At that time I realized that the spirits had been with me since I was a young child.

One of the gifts given that night was of vision. I could see the world and all things in it. How they nurtured, or destroyed each other. Why they nurtured. Why they destroyed. All things – even the blades of grass on the ground – are connected.

Laces of silver light connect all things to each other.

These laces can be broken. They can be mended sometimes, but of this I was given warnings.

How it works I do not know. Why it works I do not know.

Since that time I have been able to …do things. I am not sure why." Snake extended his hand, palm down facing east. He slowly turned a complete circle.

The next words were addressed to that broad circle and not Buckingham.

"I have not practiced these things. They frighten me as they are things of power, and I do not feel I am worthy of them. I do not feel that any man is worthy of them."

Swimming Snake lowered himself until one knee rested on the ground. "Even speaking of these things make me feel unease." He lowered his eyes to the grass beneath him. "I am just a man. I am not worthy to stand next to the spirits. Through the years, I have thought of how much power and respect I could demand, if I so chose. Women to pleasure me. Great deeds in battle. To be leader to many people. These thoughts prove my unworthiness." He looked up at Buck. "So I play the fool and the medicine man."

Buckingham was speechless. Snake had always treated his station in life with humor, and to see him kneel and speak of his life and inner thoughts with such seriousness was unnerving. It saddened his heart to see how much belief Snake placed in his "spirits," and his lack of acceptance for feelings that came to every man.

Standing, he told Snake, "My brother, you do not need to trouble your heart. I know you are a good man, but to place our faith in these…um…powers, that is not something we can depend on.

You know me. You know I have heart for only those things I can see and feel. I am not sure I can come across for your spirit friends. If they believe in me as much as I believe in them, we might not make such a good band. After all. I am just a white man."

"It is good when a man can admit his failings." Snake's eyes lit up. "Is that all it takes to remove your fear? More proof?" He laughed. "I should have known. When you had the arrow in your leg, my heart told me that you must live. That our lives were twined together. That your deeds would be great. That is why I took you to my lodge." He laughed again.

Buckingham was touched, but not much persuaded.

"I appreciate you saving me." He frowned. "Even if'n it were your arrow in the first place. The fact you let me live is appreciated, but it don't reassure me right now. I need…"

"…proof." Finished Swimming Snake.

"I understand. The gift of life was long ago. It was a gift I gave because I felt it might help me later. As such, it was tainted." He nodded.

Snake raised his right hand to his chest and then his brow. Holding his hand to his head for but a moment, he lowered it and blinked.

"Now I give you a gift. This one is not for my gain. This has no requirements. This is for you, in sorrow of the pain I inflicted on you. A gift long overdue."

Raising his hand he pointed towards Buck. A warm wind blew against Buck, rocking him back a step.

Snake turned his back on his white brother and started walking.

Buck paused, started to call out, and then tentatively followed Snake with mixed emotions. Sixty paces farther it dawned on him. The pain in his leg was gone and the muscles felt tight and strong. No longer did agony spear up to his hip with each step.

His leg felt – good.

Swallowing his questions and doubts, he followed. He was still concerned, but he needed to see what happened next. He called out to Snake.

"Snake – that thing you did with the lizard. Were that…?"

"No, it was hidden up my sleeve."

Buckingham slapped his knee and grinned. "I knew it."

Swimming Snake turned.

"But before the lizard…I had no rock in my hand."

Buckingham stopped grinning.

CHAPTER 10
Dance of Death

"Death smiles at us all; all a man can do is smile back." -
- from the movie Gladiator

The cloud rapidly approached the village.

From its height, the village was sensed as a multitude of cones entrenched on a morning landscape. On the western side, nearest the cloud, sunlight struck the tops of the first lodges, the rays cresting the distant mountains with its golden illumination.

The tops glowed in sharp contrast to the bottoms, and in a few heartbeats the light cascaded down the sides bringing them to sharp relief – surrealistic against the brown and green of the prairie.

Smoke spilled from the tops of the lodges, their morning fires all ablaze. The blue haze rose straight up in the morning sky, only to strike a layer of cold air and flatten out into a blanket that covered the village at a height above that of the death cloud.

Morning Star felt the warmth of the sun as it laid golden hands on her old body. The gentle warmth brought a tremble of pleasure.

Matching giggles rang out from the brush, telling her of the joy morning brought to her hidden companions. The two children moved slightly in the bushes, shielding their eyes from the intense light, but allowing it to cover their bodies.

Star smiled. The children felt hidden as long as their faces remained concealed. They gave no thought to their bodies left exposed. The innocence and games of youth.

Taking one of the water bags, she moved carefully to the water's edge. The grass gave way to dirt and the dirt to rocks. The rocks were damp, a coating of green algae making footing treacherous. With caution, she planted her feet on stones she knew would not shift beneath her weight, and knelt next to the flowing water.

A small pool formed behind three of these rocks, the water was clear, cold, and deep enough to submerse the skin without disturbing the bottom, muddying the water. One hand forced the neck below the surface while the other prodded the body under. Protesting bubbles spewed forth, for a time, and then the crisp water flowed smoothly into the skin.

Her hands were numb and cold by the time the pouch could accept no more. The pain of age would return shortly, bones generating the ache that always appeared upon contact with frigid water.

Morning Star rose slowly, no hurry investing itself in her this morning. It was just another day and not one to rush forward through; she leaned, set the skin securely on the bank, and looked around at the new day.

Star's hands moved to the small of her back, pressing firmly, helping to remove the kinks her kneeling position had placed under the skin. In ritual, she turned to the east and greeted the morning sun. Slowly she turned, following the path the sun would take, first looking to the south. The world was warming to the slow heartbeat of day. As she turned to the west, she stopped.

Her eyes spotted the cloud, filling her with a sense of dread. The children and the water bags forgotten, she climbed the bank for a clearer view.

Morning Star reveled in nature. Born on the plains, and gradually moving to the mountains, nature was a foundation of her life, and in her own way she studied it, not for gain or knowledge per se, but for the secure feeling it gave her to know her place in the scheme of eternity. Upon the birth of Swimming Snake, it pleased her to see this wonder of the world passed on. As Snake grew, his wonder at the world – both seen and unseen – had exceeded her own. Her son warmed her heart more than the morning sun.

Eyes shaded with her hand, she studied the cloud.

It was wrong. Her eyes told her it was wrong. Her heart told her it was wrong. It was the only cloud in the sky and it moved towards her and the village – yet no wind fell against her face.

Her eyes were old, but still sharp at distance and she looked below the cloud to the landscape. No wind moved the grasses or leaves. The cloud had shifting colors. This in itself did not bother her as she had seen clouds flash with every color of the rainbow, reflecting the rising and the setting sun, but this bluish-green was different. Its rotted colors were reminiscent of the iridescent bottom of a toad stool.

Poisonous.

Deadly.

In her mind unheard voices told her to run. With the water skins forgotten, with the children forgotten, she stood...waiting. Watching.

The children in hiding noted the change immediately. They watched the old woman freeze and stare. Their young eyes searched the horizon for a problem, but saw nothing. In the east the sun was glowing, to the north and south, the countryside itself was starting to shine with color and life. In the west, the last darkness of night faded, blue sky appearing behind a lone cloud. No sign of trouble connected in their minds.

The cloud began its descent, not slowing its forward motion, it swept downwards, until the bottom glided over the ground. A figure stood before it unmoving, and at the last second, the figure turned as if to flee.

"Run children!" screamed Morning Star, her eyes searching for the children. The pair looked at her, eyes wide and mouths open. In haste, they turned and ran, but they turned to each other – running only into each other's arms. Falling to their knees, they watched the cloud approach, billowing over the figure of Morning Star.

As the death cloud swarmed around Morning Star, it knew disappointment.

This creature was old, offering no new information.

Perfunctorily it took a few samples and left the carcass, its attention now on two remaining figures in its midst. These were young. Nothing new was immediately noticeable, but it had been so long since samples and study of this species that the young posed the prospect of new data. No simple samples here, this was a possibility rating a full gather.

The red threads wove around two small figures, never quite touching them, wove themselves until the forms were totally covered, existing as blood-colored silhouettes. As quickly as the threads had appeared, they were gone – as were the two children. Footprints of the children ended at the spot they had clung to each other.

The people of the village observed the events.

Not all camp's occupants, but enough. They watched the cloud descend upon the old woman. They saw the cloud pass, leaving only a dismembered body lying on the ground.

Life was harsh for the small band of Indians and they had learned to react quickly and without question to a thousand things that could threaten. In case of a raiding party, the warriors would strike back immediately, buying time for the women and children to escape. In time of storm, when the black funnel clouds formed, they would seek shelter.

This was different. This threat was new, and in their actions, they splintered. The warriors grabbed weapons at hand while the women searched for children and provisions.

In every mind was the imploring voice of an old woman. A voice that was familiar. It beseeched them to abandon all fight and possessions and flee. A few – a very few – paid heed to the ghostly voice and taking nothing, scattered to the winds.

Six warriors faced the oncoming demon. Two on horseback, charged bravely towards the death cloud, lances at ready. They yelled at the enemy, challenging it to battle but fifteen yards before contact the horses – eyes wild and rolling – skewed to a halt throwing the veteran riders. In panic the horses fled, one cresting the rise to the creek, tumbling into the stream in a watery curtain, its left foreleg snapping.

It lay thrashing in the water - until the cloud passed over it.

Of the two riders, one lay dead, his neck broken upon contact with the unyielding earth. The other ignored his cuts and shattered ribs, jumping to his feet. His lance had been lost in the fall; he turned to face his enemy, drawing his knife. Around him the cloud gathered.

The doomed warrior noted the cloud did not feel damp or cold, as he had expected.

He chanted his death song, swinging his knife in short arcs before him.

The red threads gathered around him. Swinging his blade to meet them, one crossed his thrust, catching his arm between wrist and elbow. The severed limb fell to earth. Still singing, he secured the arm to the ground with his foot, and with his other hand pried the knife from the quivering appendage on the ground. The threads flailed savagely at him. His song ceased.

The remaining four warriors could see only a shadowy picture of what was happening, but that was enough. As one, they fired a volley of arrows towards the cloud. Each aimed true, but there was no effect. The same was true on their second attempt. Realizing the futility of their battle, they turned and ran en mass.

Three of the four warriors were engulfed, the cloud swirling around them. The fourth saw the others swallowed by the cloud, and another flurry of red ribbons dance around his brothers in battle. At his feet landed a bloody leg. He stopped chanting and reserved his breath for a mad dash of salvation.

The women of the village fled with the children. Those children old enough, and fleet of foot ran with the women. Those too young to run were unceremoniousiously yanked from their resting places, tucked under arms, and carried.

Some ran for the low lying hills to the south and some ran for the brush and rocks to the north. A few ran to the east, fleeing on the bare and open grounds towards the sun now sitting above the horizon.

The remainder of the men circled the cloud and taunted. There was no fear now, the anger and pride far overwhelmed the fear.

The cloud flattened and took those that stayed.

The cloud pursued the ones that fled.

CঙEO

As Buckingham and Swimming Snake stopped, the white man held his hand to the horizon. At arm's length he could place two hands between the morning sun and the horizon. Each finger one could fit was about fifteen minutes.

The sun had been up two hours.

"Okay Snake, how long do you figure we have to the village? We have been moving right along. The ground looks plumb familiar…."

"Half a day. Maybe a little more. When the sun is just past overhead." Replied Snake. "If our pace were a bit faster."

"Seems a long spell," said Buck.

"It matters not. It is already too late."

"What do ye mean?" asked Buckingham.

"I mean that it is too late."

Snake slowly pulled the medicine knife and placed it behind his head. With a slow sawing motion, he hacked through his flowing hair, letting it fall to the ground. Then, as Buck watched dumbfounded, Snake grasped the blade between thumb and forefinger – the sliver of exposed edge extending between them – and drew it across this chest three times, starting from left shoulder and angling downward to the right. Blood flowed coating his chest and belly.

"For Christ's sake man, what are ye doing?" shouted Buckingham.

"I am mourning." He stood facing the sun, his expression showing no emotion, nor pain.

"There is death. There is death of my friends and my family. The Morning Star burns no more."

Three fingers of each hand were drawn through the blood flooding his chest. Three fingers were pulled across his face on each side. Crimson tracks in their wake.

Swimming Snake turned and faced Buckingham, but it was not a face that Buck recognized.

"My brother...I told you that I am unworthy. I am unworthy because I have been tempted to use my power for my own gain. Always I desired things. Distinction amongst my brothers. Wealth...women. Of this I have spoken.

Now I have another desire. A desire that claims my heart. A desire I *will* use my power for, whether honorable or not. I desire *revenge*. I will not let my heart stop beating until I have that in my grasp."

Swimming Snake faced the morning sun once more, raised his hands, and cried a wordless scream. Beneath Buckingham's feet the ground trembled. The air around them dropped in temperature, as if a winter breeze had fallen upon them.

In the sky an eagle screamed back at Swimming Snake.

Buck stepped back a pace and looked at Snake. "You be scaring me some."

"As am I afraid," said Snake. He looked at his white brother. "No, I fear not my death. I fear what the world has become here. I fear what I shall become. I fear my death will be a failure to my people. His eyes burned deep in their sockets and though slight of stature, he now seemed broader than the sky.

"We part ways now. The battle we fight will be the same, but we will not stand together, except in our hearts." Reaching into his bundle he pulled forth the third item. A pouch a foot deep and a foot across.

"I do not know why I brought this, but it is yours. It is the white man's medicine. It is for you to use." He handed the pouch to Walks with Limp.

Buckingham took the pouch and peered inside.

"Good god, man. Where did you get this?"

Snake replied. "I have had it for – forever it seems. It was taken from the white men who were traveling with you when we first met."

Buck looked into the pouch again. "There must be ten pounds of powder in here. You are lucky you didn't blow yourself to kingdom come."

Snake looked to the horizon where the village would lie, then back to his brother. "You must return to the valley. It is defenseless now. You must remove its home as this evil has removed our home." He paused. "I must go and face the evil, but if I fail, it must not have a place to return to."

Buckingham felt ill. "What am I supposed to do with this?"

"I do not know. This you must decide," replied Snake.

Buck thought about it for a moment.

"There is only one thing, Snake."

"What is that?" asked Swimming Snake.

"Why the hell did you let me walk this far only to tell me to turn around and go back? That is downright mean. You are acting more and more like a savage every day."

"And you like a white man."

"Take care my brother."

"And you, my brother. We *shall* meet once more.

CHAPTER 11
SONG OF BUCKINGHAM

"Is not the sky a father and the earth a mother, and are not all living things with feet or wings or roots their children?"
"Give me the strength to walk the soft earth, a relative to all that is!" -Black Elk

For the first mile, Buckingham walked a plodding march back the route he had came. His heart was heavy, and he knew in his leaden heart what Swimming Snake said was true. The village was gone. With each step, the gravity of the loss weighed him down more – a depression he had not felt for years.

For fifteen years he had wandered the mountains. A decade and a half into his life he had left from 'back east.' He had left a past he could not stomach, trading for a future he could not guess.

When he left, he had not known where he was headed, or what he hoped to find. All he had known, at the time, was that anything, even an unforeseen death, was better than the life that lay in store should he stay.

From a barefoot-poor rock farm he fled. Never knowing his mother, who died giving birth to him, he had only his father for companionship; a father he felt resented Buck's very existence, blaming him for the loss of a wife.

Looking back with a wisdom that comes with age and experience, Buck realized what he had taken as punishment was probably not. The toil and struggle from sunrise to sunset was not a punishment, it was merely the requirement of making ends meet in an attempt to stave off famine and destitution.

The distance imposed by his father was not out of anger, but fear. Fear that came from loosing a loved one and the fear that he might loose the offspring of that loved one.

Now he wondered. He wondered what had become of the tired man who had sired him. The work of the farm had been enough to kill two healthy men, let alone a single man who would now be old and infirm. The guilt of his youthful actions had always been carefully shielded – blanketed by day-to-day needs and requirements.

The need for a full belly. The requirement of shelter.

The actions of his life, and the decisions made, came crashing down on Buck. He found himself weeping in sorrow, guilt, and self pity as he walked.

Until now, he never thought much of his past decisions. Each day was a new day and a new life. Sleep at night was death of that day and morning a rebirth. It kept life simple.

At fifteen, he traveled hungry and alone, wearing only the rags on his back until he hit the Mississippi River. There, in a town – he could not remember the name – he lived on discarded scraps and handouts from those who would condescend to feed a homeless waif. He remembered fighting packs of dogs wandering the muddy streets for what bits of food might be found in the garbage.

As life was about to drag him into the folds of madness, he wandered into the midst of some men. Not ordinary men, with jobs and security, power and wealth, but men who stank of skins, whiskey, and bait.

Mountain men.

In the year of 1800, he found companions. Men who looked upon him with cold eyes and warm hearts.

Pierre Leblanc was the first of the mountain men he met. He still remembered the first words spoken by the man who was to become his mentor.

Pierre had smashed Buck's nose flat against his face and was holding a knife to his throat. The blood was running freely down Buckingham's face, coating his throat and sticking the torn shirt to his chest. LeBlanc spoke to him in a voice soft as silk and a breath that reeked of rotten meat and whiskey.

"Young puppy. Before I slit your gullet, I must ask. Why? Why did you feel you could take of my possessions without asking this one for permission?"

A grim smile was set on LeBlanc's face. "Come now. Go to your maker with the truth on your lips."

Buckingham no longer cared. He was too tired and hungry for death to frighten him. He welcomed the thought of a night never ending.

He said simply, "I was hungry."

LeBlanc's drunken eyes sharpened for a moment. The knife was still held to Buck's throat, but the pressure was less. Then the eyes lost their focus in thought.

"You were hungry. Yes. Hungry. Hunger can bring a man to do many things."

He lowered the knife. "It can do many things that do not make a man proud." LeBlanc looked squarely into Buckingham's eyes. "Are you so hungry you would do anything? Are you so hungry you would sell your soul? Are you so hungry you would eat your best friend if he were dead?"

Buck thought. "No. I do not think I could do that."

LeBlanc laughed. "But you had to think about it. Therefore, I think that you are truly hungry. A hunger that a man should not feel." He slipped the knife under a red sash lashed tightly around his lean waist. "Pray you are never so hungry that you must do that which can never be undone."

The world had gone to a soothing black and thought fled. When he awoke it was to a new life.

The blood on his face and chest was still there. It was no longer fluid, but caked and flaking. Rolling his head to the side, he saw three men hunkered down around a campfire in the early morning light. One he recognized – LeBlanc. Two he did not know.

Without turning his head, LeBlanc called out, "So. The puppy is awake." Taking a slab of wood, his knife reappeared as if by magic in his hand. With the bare blade he scraped the surface of the wood until it was fresh core. The blade then disappeared.

With careful fingers, he pulled a chunk of meat from a rock inside the fire pit and placed it upon the wood. Lifting a battered and bent tin cup, he filled it with something ladled from a blackened pot hanging over the fire. Both these he set next to Buckingham.

Charred meat on the outside and blood ran from the center. The cup steamed and Buck did not know what it contained, but it was the finest feast he had ever eaten.

No words of welcome were spoken. The only welcome was a meal that stretched the skin tight over his stomach.

No words of gratitude were spoken, except for tears of joy that dripped from his chin, seasoning the roast of dog he ate.

Over the next year, he learned of the men who had accepted him. No, they had adopted him as one of their family, not accepted. One was named Pourelle, and of the same nationality as LeBlanc. Pourelle was a man well educated and quite insane.

A man who at times unpredicted would recite poetry and song to the land around him. A man who LeBlanc never turned his back upon.

The other was a man unnamed. Never once did Buck hear his name spoken, either to him or about him. Should the man speak, it was only in grunts or motions of his hands. At first, Buckingham thought the man impaired and unable to speak.

After months of companionship and travel, he realized that the man spent his time listening and observing, rather than expounding on matters that may – or may not – have been important to those around him.

At one time, high in the mountains and months after they had met, Buck and the man with no name sat on a hillside looking at the world.

The man turned to Buckingham and asked, "Did you see that? Did you hear it when it fell?"

Buck had been startled and shook his head.

The man looked saddened and shook his head in return. "It is not important."

Those were the last and only words that Buck ever heard him speak.

LeBlanc was the undeclared leader of the group. After time, Buck found that the man could read and write. To what extent Buck never knew. He did know that people feared LeBlanc. When they entered the taverns and inns, the sea of people would part, eyes would cast downward, and when addressed – it was with respect.

As leader of the group, LeBlanc outfitted Buck for his first trek to the mountains. He supplied Buckingham with the bare minimums. A small caliber rifle and a handful of powder and balls. A rusted butcher knife without a scabbard.

What he did not supply in material items he made up for in knowledge. He taught Buck to shoot, and to shoot to the mark. He taught him that any caliber rifle was worthless, unless the ball was placed in the right spot. He taught him to take the rust from the blade of his knife by rubbing it in the sand, and to sharpen it to an edge that could shave hair by stroking it on a flat river rock.

The man with no name taught Buck as well. He taught him that one learned nothing, saw nothing, and heard nothing if one was talking and thinking about himself. By walking in silence with the man, he learned to listen to the wind, see the flight of birds in the sky, to notice the danger that lurked motionless in the shadow.

From Pourelle he learned that nothing mattered in life, unless one placed value on it. He learned that anything one owned could be taken at any time, except for the values of the thoughts in one's mind. If singing brought joy – you sang. If linking words together, and by doing so, it painted a picture in your mind, then indeed, it was a masterpiece, even if unappreciated by others. He learned the boundary.

An area created in your mind and surrounding oneself. If another forced entry into that space, you attacked. You attacked like a wild animal until the other was driven from your space or was dead. That space was yours and the only thing you could ever own in your life.

For five years he traveled with this family, until death collected its debts.

One spring morning they had awoken missing the man with no name. Searching they found him. Silent as always. Looking out over the land, sitting with eyes open and unblinking. They did not bury him, but left him as they found him.

Silent.

A few months later Pourelle stood up from the campfire, raised his voice in a tempest of rhyme and prose, and walked into the night – never to return.

On the morn, they searched in vain. His possessions were left at the campsite in the event he should return. If he did, they never learned, although they waited for three days.

A year after that, LeBlanc died as befitting a man of his character – and in a fashion he would have appreciated.

Buck and he had returned to a settlement; to winter in comfort and warmth. A night of entertainment was in order and by the dawn, Buckingham had learned the fate of his last friend.

LeBlanc had been stabbed through the heart with his own knife; by a whore he had purchased in the evening.

When asked why she had performed the deed, she replied, "Because I loved him."

CHAPTER 12
Song of Snake

When it comes time to die, be not like those whose hearts are filled with the fear of death, so when their time comes they weep and pray for a little more time to live their lives over again in a different way. Sing your death song, and die like
A hero going home. — Chief Aupumut

As Swimming Snake walked, he too reflected upon his own life.

Never in his life had he been consumed by the desire for revenge. Far from it. His life had been balanced and – for the most part – serene.

At the time of his birth, he too was deprived of a parent, his father. Not through any glorious act of battle or bravery, but through accident. While on a trip to the mountains, his father's horse spooked.

What it was that caused the horse to bolt, no one was sure, but what was known was that his father was thrown from the horse, breaking his right leg in the fall.

A splintered end of bone protruded forth from the skin, and bright blood pumped in arcing jets. It had severed an artery. All that remained was to watch as the man quickly and quietly bled out.

Morning Star entered a period of mourning, then set it aside, to care for her son.

Death was an unpleasant fact, it was something to be mourned, but not kept to one's breast for eternity. Life went on, and while the memory of her man never faded, the pain did. The pain eased each time her eyes fell upon her son.

Snake, then known as Runner, was much as other children in the tribe. He had energy that would not end, inquisitiveness that grew each day from the time his eyes opened in the morning to the time they grudgingly closed at night; always there were questions on his lips.

A swarm of biting gnats was an aggravation, but an annoyance that would gladly be taken over the company of this young one.

While he showed respect to all elders, he plagued them – with every breath.

"Why do the birds not fall from the sky?"

"Why does the snake not have wings?"

"We eat sweet grasses, but some make us ill."

"Why is that?"

"Why does an arrow miss?"

"Why…why…why?"

Moreover, from morning to evening, he never stopped talking. He talked to the elders. He talked to the other children. He talked to the horses. Then – when his first decade had been reached – he talked to things that others could not see.

It was common to find him engaged in conversation with the very wind sweeping across the prairie. Elders of the tribe became worried. Children always have make believe friends, warriors of the imagination, a bevy of imaginary friends to occupy the day, but this went beyond normal in their eyes.

After a time, they chided him, and scolded his behavior.

As one morning a person awakes to find ice on the stream, Runner's behavior changed. No longer did he speak aloud to friends that could not be seen, in fact, no longer did he talk at great length to any.

Except for Morning Star. To her he would speak, and speak only the truth, though he knew at times her eyes showed disbelief.

Swimming Snake never questioned the reality of the voices he heard. If one sat inside one's lodge, talking to another outside, the two could not see each other, for they were separated by a thin piece of tanned hide. You could not see the other person, but they were real. There was no doubt of this.

He could find no difference between that and the voices he heard, for he and the voices were separated. This he understood.

Not by hide, but by something else – a veil imposed by the world. These voices gave him answers.

The hidden ones would answer any question he asked and never did they seem annoyed. If anything, they were joyful to have someone ask and seek their knowledge.

When he asked why the eagle did not drop from the sky, the voices explained.

They told of how the animal worked with the sky. The wings beat against the sky and pushed the animal away from the earth. More than that, the sun worked with the eagle. Snake did not fully understand, but the warmth of the sun would cause the air to rush upwards, supplying a wind from the ground allowing the bird to rest its wings and float.

All of his new knowledge he poured forth to Morning Star. She listened carefully to all things that her son repeated to her. Not fully accepting the existence of these voices, she realized it did not matter.

If the voice came from within Snake's own head, or if the voice indeed came from something not seen by others, the words that Snake repeated were wise.

Nothing he described could be found to contain fault or harm.

As he grew, Swimming Snake occasionally caught glimpses of...things. Never quite plain, they were as shadows or flickers in his eye. Once he felt the presence of a horse, and when he looked, he could almost see the shadow of the beast on the ground. He knew that it stood, head bowed, grazing on the grass. When he looked at the ground, he could see the grass was unmoving and untouched.

Immediately the question was silently placed by young Runner.

"What is it I am seeing?"

"You are seeing nothing and you are seeing the world around you."

Snake thought for a moment. "Then what is it that I am almost seeing? What is it that I am feeling?"

The voice laughed quietly. "You are almost seeing the horse. You are almost seeing a horse that has moved on in its existence."

"You mean dead?"

"Yes," the voice replied. "That is a word you use. Look at your feet. What do you see?"

Snake looked at the ground. He saw nothing out of place at first, but then caught a glimpse of it, hidden under a clump of sagebrush. It was a skull. The skull of a horse.

Picking it up, he held it high. The shadowy flicker that was the horse turned briefly to stare.

"Is this the...?"

"Yes, it is," said the voice.

"Does he miss it?"

The voice paused before answering. "Yes, he misses it. He has moved on and left it behind, but a part of him misses it. That is normal. That is the way of man and beast."

For days thereafter, Swimming Snake carried the sun-bleached skull around with him and thought on the matter. He would follow the phantom around, carrying the skull carefully, and in what he felt was a respectful manner.

When the horse went to water, he would accompany it. While the phantasm would stand in the creek drinking, it never seemed to get its fill of water. Tiring of waiting, Runner would lay in the water using the skull for a pillow. On occasion, he spoke to the horse and asked questions of it. Never did the ghost answer.

Unable to let the matter rest, he asked aloud why the horse did not answer. The voice answered quietly in his head.

"Perhaps the spirit does not wish to. For most of its life, it existed as a beast of burden. It existed for barter. In its time it was treated well, in its time it was treated badly, but always it was a slave to its owners.

After its death, it found that others had no further use for it.

No more did men brush it, feed it, or water it. No attention was paid to it. Now you follow and ask questions of it. Perhaps it is not paying attention to you."

Snake rose from the water for the final time. He looked at the skull in his hands and gently set it on the bank of the stream. Without looking back, he walked from the water's edge.

CHAPTER 13
Return to the Valley

Battle not with monsters lest you become a monster, for if you gaze into the abyss the abyss gazes into you. -Nietzsche

Buckingham cussed the ground that made him trip. He cussed the wind that could not ease his troubled lungs. He cussed Swimming Snake for sending him back. He cussed himself for starting this god-awful mess in the first place.

He had no idea of what he was going to do once he had returned to the valley. The only thing driving him was the obsession to get there. To stand where it started. He was a man with demons that pushed him from behind and would stand in his path when he arrived at his final destination.

Buck had started out without looking back, a gentle but fast walk eating the miles. An hour into the return, he had broken into a lope – half-run and half-trot. A pace that not only ate the miles, but ate what little reserves of strength and stamina he had left.

He ran until he could run no more, then walked until he could catch his breath enough to run again.

No longer did he carefully watch his path and select the most comfortable ground. Cactus punctured his moccasins, embedding in the soles of his feet. The blood slicked the inside leather and, through the pain, he could feel the moccasins move and slide, lubricated with his own red oil.

In a way, it would not have bothered him if his pounding heart had given up and stopped. It would be a relief in its own rights, for to fall dead would mean that he no longer would have to make painful decisions. No longer have to face the wave of guilt and despair. To no longer have responsibility fall on his weary shoulders.

This was not to be. While gaining in years, his body was used to harsh climates, stress, and extreme physical exertion. The pain and weariness felt like companions well met.

After an eternity and a minute, he stood on the valley rim for the second time.

An appalling view lay before Buckingham's eyes. This was not the lush, verdant crease in the earth that he remembered. It was a view of hell.

When Buck arrived at the rim of the valley, the immenseness and reality of his goal brought him to his knees.

His breath caught in his throat and his heart hammered in his chest.

Mirrored in the vista spread before him was the desolation of his spirit.

Years he had spent in God's mountains. He had seen the brilliant fire of the morning sun reflecting off glaciers, a hundred thousand years in the making; rivers of ice that defied the blazing sun of mountain summers. Frozen beauty that defied description.

He had watched as boiling water erupted from the ground in an immense geyser, spraying the heavens with steam, and mud pots bubble in an area known as Coulter's Hell.

His eyes had taken in layers of destruction left behind in miles of prairie, blackened by flash fires sparked by thunderstorms; setting the world ablaze for as far as the eye could see, but nothing he had seen prepared his heart for the panorama extending before him.

Life was stripped from this valley, stripped as the hide ripped from an animal before butchering, but it was more than that. It was as if the very soul of the earth had been raped and thrown from the basin, leaving only the naked and humiliated corpse of what once was. A graveyard – shunned by both demon and angel alike as unclean.

As far as Buckingham could see across the valley, down its slopes and scattered in the bottom, dead trees stood in a surrealistic caricature of a cemetery scattered with stark tombstones. Each second he looked, his eyes picked out more – still more – of an unearthly devastation.

The trip down the side was far easier than he anticipated it would be. His heavy heart pulled him downward. Buck could no more stop, or return uphill, than a river reverse itself and flow backward.

Tattered remnants of trees stretched out before him. The boughs were tangled, snapped, and broken. Stripped from branches were all pine needles and leaves, leaving only gray skeletons visible. Those that had the dignity and grace to fall to earth were reduced to dust and decay.

The ground held neither moss nor grass, only a surly brown dirt that could hold no life. With no ground cover, the rains had furrowed it, leaving a texture that screamed of giant claws rending the surface.

From his vantage point, he could see the creek in the bottom, not sparkling and clear, but flowing with the same color as the ground. A mud choked stream that reminded him of a coffee colored serpent winding slowly through the lifeless land.

With a feeling of dismay, he continued towards the bottom. As he placed his feet on the first few steps leading into the barren ground, the air around him changed. Sound became dull and lifeless and he could feel his little remaining vitality slip from his body. The wind did not blow and no breeze was present to waft through the tops of the goblin trees.

As he walked and slid, he followed the tracks left where he and Snake climbed up out of the bottom. These were the only tracks he saw. Remembering his initial jaunt, and the sign he had seen – or thought he had seen – made him appreciate even more his brother coming after him. It had taken a lot of bravery to go after a foolish white man who had not listened. Swimming Snake had walked into the valley with his eyes unclouded.

In his mind, Buck had a revelation. It hit him hard. He faced that which he already knew, and had to accept the enormity of it.

If he had not gone to the valley in the first place, then whatever had followed them out would have stayed planted. If Snake were to be believed, about the village, and Buck believed him now with all his heart, then Buck himself was responsible for the fate that had fallen on the small tribe.

Buck had brought on the destruction of the people he had grown to love. It caused his chest to tighten and remorse to flood his being again. When it had almost brought his progress to a halt, he remembered something from the past.

Something LeBlanc had said in one of his lectures to a young and frightened boy.

"Little one...you sit and think of your past. Put it aside. It means nothing. Yes, you have done things that were wrong. You have made decisions that you wish you could go back and correct, but you cannot."

LeBlanc slowly stirred the campfire with a stick the length of his arm until a cloud of sparks danced up into the night air. They spiraled up for a ways then blinked out of sight.

"The past is like those sparks. It follows you for a while then goes black. It is still there, but you do not see it. Your mind will quiet and hide it. The good you will remember. The bad you will forget. If you do not..." He pointed towards Pourelle with the smoking branch, "then you will end up like our friend. Madness will consume you. Each day you will make decisions. Some will be good decisions, some will be bad. However, you will make them. When you are happy, you will make them. When you are sad, you will make them. When you are wise you will make them as well as when you are foolish.

If you come to a place where you refuse to make any more decisions, then you will be like our other friend." He pointed to the man whose name was not known. "He stopped making decisions. Now he only watches and listens. He travels the mountains with us, because I tell him to. He eats, because I tell him to."

Holding the branch by both ends he sat it across his knee and pressed both ends until it snapped, then he threw the pieces into the fire.

"Some day you will make a very bad decision. Maybe more than one. I know. I have made these. Your mind will not be able to ease the pain of those decisions. Then – and you will know when – you must act. You must do what you can to make amends for the decision. The decision will follow you, nipping at your heels and your heart until you do this."

The young Buckingham looked at LeBlanc. "You have done this? You have made a decision that haunted you?"

LeBlanc laughed until tears cut swaths through the dirt on his cheeks. "Yes! Once I made a bad decision. On one side I would die. On the other – well it does not matter. I chose the other and the memory of that haunted me. It chased me...through the day...and followed me into the nights. Then I acted on it."

"What did you do?"

LeBlanc looked at Buck and blinked. "I fed you."

"You fed me? And now the memories are gone?" asked Buck, fascinated.

"No, the memories are still there, but they do not chase me during the day." He looked at Buck and winked. "Only at night and their teeth are not as sharp now, but their eyes are still ferocious. One just does not look them in the eye."

Now that he had grown, Buckingham understood it more. He also understood that now was a time that he would do something to remedy, or at least atone, for his decision.

ᕶᲖᕶᔕ

He walked the bottom at last.

Under his left arm was pinned the pouch Swimming Snake had given him. He still did not know what he was going to do with the powder. It was a right large amount, but even with the additional powder he had in his horn, it was not enough to affect the valley. There was not enough powder in the world to erase a ten-mile long scar from the face of the earth.

When he had left Snake, he had felt guilty. He had felt that Snake was racing into the teeth of danger and he was going the other way. Now – looking at the terrain around him – he wasn't so sure.

Kneeling he set the pouch on the ground gently.

Leather thongs, wrapped around the bag, prevented its explosive stuffing from spilling out. He undid the knots and carefully opened the bag to look once more. With thumb and forefinger, he gently spread the tattered canvas top.

Powder – nothing but plain old black powder. It was coarser than that which he carried. It would not do for priming, but might do in a bind to use as the main charge for his rifle. Dipping his finger in, he felt its texture for moisture.

Halfway through the swipe, the tip of his finger touched something. Frowning, he dug deeper until he could grasp it and pull it from the charcoal hued grave. Looking at it, he raised it to his lips and blew on it, scattering the last grains of powder from its soft surface.

It was a leather pouch, grayed from immersion in the gunpowder. It looked familiar to him; then he knew for sure where he had seen it.

It was Swimming Snake's medicine bag.

The temptation was on him. With all his heart he wanted to open the plain buckskin bag and explore its contents. For years he had wondered what Snake had in it that was so all-fired important.

Buck had asked Snake a couple of times what it contained. Each time he had asked, Swimming Snake appeared insulted. The final time he asked, his brother had taken the time to explain to him the error of his ways.

It seemed that what goes into a medicine bag is quite personal to the man creating it. It could be – does not mean there was – but could be things like a particular rock, twig, feather or whatever; anything that held 'power' for the owner.

One thing you did not do was let another open it and paw around. Just was not done. Buckingham reckoned that it would be similar to asking a man if he would have his wife undress so you could have a look see. Just not socially proper.

Buck no longer asked Snake what was in it, but he did offer guesses – just to annoy Snake – not that Buckingham really thought Snake would stuff horse dung or gopher peters into the bag. This was his chance to find out once and for all. Probably just a couple of kernels of corn, a shiny coin...or such.

Buck slowly grasped the top of the bag. As he did so the skin of his arm grew the biggest mass of goose bumps he had ever seen. It was like the coldest winter snow on that arm and someone walking over his grave at the same time.

He pulled his hand away with a start. Slowly his arm began to warm and tingle, returning to normal.

Buck shook his head, and then looped the bag around his neck. It did not bring on another attack, but instead felt warm. That were right strange in itself, as it did not touch his skin, but rested on his buckskin shirt.

Buck took stock of himself.

He was exhausted and bleeding from a dozen shallow cuts. The stock of his rifle had cracked somewhere towards the lower end of his slide into the valley and his cap was missing. He grunted.

The cap might be missing, but so was the guilt and fear.

In their place there was anger.

A cold red rage keeping him from feeling the sting of the cuts or the puncture of the cactus.

He was a by god mountain man – here to demand an accounting.

CHAPTER 14
Return to the Village

"Celebrate your success and stand strong when adversity hits, for when the storm clouds come in, the eagles soar while the small birds take cover" - Anon.

Swimming Snake saw the lodges long before he heard the wailing from the handful of survivors.

Smoke no longer rose into the sky from the abandoned lodges, the fires had burned down and were now as dead as the bodies lying scattered on the ground. Here and there, a few women and children clung to each other while watching the sky fearfully. No comfort could he give, so he did not attempt to give consolation.

Slowly he walked an ever expanding circle around the lodges.

Here lay the body of a warrior, dismembered with parts lying on the blood soaked ground. By the creek he found a horse. It was flayed with a thousand cuts. In any direction he turned, he found death.

Farther up the creek, he stopped – finding that for which he searched – turned, and went to his lodge.

Drawing his knife he slid it through the tough hide cover and sawed downwards until he had reached the edge next to the ground. Moving over he repeated the cut, then severed it across the top. Carefully folding this into a tight bundle, he slung it over his shoulder and returned to the creek.

There he laid it on the ground and tenderly wrapped the body of his mother in it. With rocks he weighted down the edges, not in burial, but to keep the prowling creatures from performing the acts that came naturally to them.

Returning to his desecrated lodge, he entered through the opening and walked the path of the sun in proper fashion, until he was at the rear of the lodge. There he stripped off his clothing and stood naked. From a par fleche bag he pulled a simple loincloth and plain moccasins. These he put on, sank to the ground cross legged, and opened a second par fleche bag. From it he pulled a twist of dried sage.

Starting the smallest of fires in the fire pit, he felt the smoke burn his eyes until the flames took hold. Dipping the end of the twist into the flame, he withdrew it and waved it around, stopping at each of the four points of the compass. The sweet smoke of the sage filled his nostrils and was calming. When the ember had burned out, the remainder of dried sage he sat on a rock next to the fire.

Slowly he closed his eyes.

"It has been long since you sought my counsel."

"It has been long since I have felt the need to question the world around me." Snake replied aloud. "You have seen what has happened here. You know what is in my heart."

"You will fail."

Swimming Snake's eyes closed to slits.

"There is nothing I can do to stop this evil?"

"You know the answer to that. You will fail. That is not the same as being unable to stop that which has passed through here.

When it came time for you to take your next steps in learning, you stopped talking to us. Let me ask of you a question. Can the worm fly"

Swimming Snake thought. "The worm cannot fly, but the worm can fly. That is not the answer I am seeking."

From the unseen, the voice said, "Then you will fail. You know the answer. You have spoken it. You know what must be done. Recite your lesson. In it is the answer, and it is the only answer you need."

Snake closed his eyes once more. "The worm cannot fly, but if it lets nature take its course, it becomes the butterfly, and being one and the same as the butterfly, it will take to the winds." He opened his eyes once more and asked, "If this thing I do will I be able to avenge my people?"

"No, you will fail."

"Then what is the purpose of my allowing this change in me?"

"For years you learned what it is and what it means to be one with the spirit of the world. To be one with the world. Even if you take the next step on the pathway, if you reject all and stand alone – you will fail. If you are one with the great circle, then *we* will not fail. I know this for truth. Earlier I stood before the evil and tried to stop it. I could not. I failed, but if all work together, nothing can stand before us."

"If this thing I do, would it be possible…"

"*No!*" The voice was shrill and firm. "That must *never* be done. It is against the way of nature. The people you loved have moved on. Would you restore them to butchered and decaying bodies?

Would you hear their screams for eternity when they cannot die, and cannot live? Of this we have spoken before. Now you must decide."

Swimming Snake spoke. "I will do this. I fear for those of my tribe that are left."

"The creature has left. Others are watching it, it will not return for a while. There is time. There is always time. You have one more question. It is on your lips, but you ask it not. Now is not the time to deny such question."

Swimming Snake stood, fists clenched before him. "Why did you not stop it? I know you tried, but why did you not band together with the others? Why should this depend on me? Am I so powerful that you need me to do this thing?"

The laughter was as silver raindrops falling around Snake. "You ask. This is good. Nothing should be hidden.

We are old. Older than you can imagine. More moons have passed since our birth than stars in the sky. It has been so long that we do not even remember our birth.

The fire and passion has passed from our memory. Now, we go on set paths and let the burden fall upon what you call the way of nature. Death is the way of nature. It is not evil. It is not good. It is. What has happened to your people strikes your heart, but in the great circle of life, it is nothing.

My brothers and sisters give it no more notice than you would leaves falling from a tree. We are old. We are sleepy. You are needed. You will supply the passion. You will supply the anger.

If you gather wood all day, lay it in a pile, stand, and look upon it – what happens? Nothing. The wood lies there. It does not grow, it does not burn.

If a small spark is applied to it, a flame is born. The flame grows until it reaches the heavens. You will be that spark."

The laughter pealed out once more. "Believe in what I say. When the fire is ignited this time, nothing will stand before it. It will flee or die. A death that will not be moving on, but extinction."

"What should I do?" asked Snake.

The voice hesitated. "You must go to where you stopped. The path goes on, but you must start again from the place at which you stopped. You knew this also, for you have cloaked yourself with the same items you wore when you stepped from the path. The only thing missing is the stone that you took before you fled from your future and placed it in the medicine bag."

Swimming Snake lowered his eyes to the ground. "The stone is now with another. Will it…"

"No. One pebble does not make the path. It will not be missed or hinder you. You have moved far beyond that. In some way it may help the other, but if it does not do that – it will do no harm. You worry about the man you call your brother. If you have question, ask."

Snake contemplated the question. "What is happening with him? What will his fate be?"

"A worthy question. You ask not what will become of you. You inquire as to your friend."

A pause. "At this moment he digs in the earth like an animal. Before," the laughter returned, "he attempted to open the medicine bag. We were gentle with him. It is not time yet. Ask not the particulars, for they matter not. It is his fate. As to the future, that is different. His fate winds into a pattern even we cannot foresee – as if he will be the one to decide his destiny. How strange."

A wind rustled fiercely around the lodge, turning into a dust devil jumping across the plain. The voice was gone and Snake felt no need to call out to it for its return.

He knew what needed to be done. A part of his being rejoiced and a part of it feared, but he knew in his heart it no longer mattered. He was the worm, and a worm neither knows nor cares of its future. His wings awaited him. Behind the fire pit, he dug in the earth searching for an object long from view and memory.

Stepping from the lodge Snake looked around him a last time. The small handful of survivors worked together to pack and carry what they could. Without word they turned and walked for the horizon. No song or chant filled the air. Their grief now went unvoiced, the only sound the muffled footsteps fading into a dark future.

Swimming Snake turned and looked to a hill in the north. It was too large to be rightly called a hill and too small to be a mountain. Even if he hurried, it would be nightfall before he stood on the top. That was good. It had been night when he left the path leading up it, and would be so when he returned to it.

◌◌◌

The darkness enfolded him as he sat on the rock outcropping that crowned the hill. Snake let his mind ease. His anger was still there, but in the swirling mix of anger and hatred, serenity for his coming actions was mixed – calming the rolling emotions. Gradually his ears once more registered the small sounds around him. Slowly his eyes picked out the small sparks of fire in the sky; stars standing crisp and clean in his vision.

They seemed to be watching him. Waiting.

Snake set the small leather pouch on the ground before him. He had been worried when he had first dug it up. Worried that time, dirt or moisture had destroyed that which he so desperately needed now. His concerns were unfounded. When Morning Star had buried it, protection had been provided; the package carefully wrapped with greased leather. Layer upon layer he had peeled from it.

The first layers decayed and falling to pieces in his hands. Subsequent layers remained firm, and finally when he had reached the heart of it, his search was over.

Morning Star's father had left nothing for his family but this pouch. No words had ever been spoken between Snake and his mother about its existence. None were needed, as it had never been hidden from him. She had been told to save it for her son. She did.

His grandfather's medicine bag rested gently in the grass at his feet. A gateway to a future only slightly understood.

Loosening the drawstring that held its mouth tightly puckered together; he cautiously emptied the contents into his hand. Setting the bag back on the ground, he brought his hand closer to get a glimpse in the darkness. There lay six small objects. They were as hardened pellets or nuts.

Swimming Snake knew that at one time they appeared differently. These were the dried buttons of a cactus used by shamans and medicine men. Snake knew that much of his grandfather's peyote. He had never used the buttons before and was not precisely sure of what it did, or how it was used. Snake knew there was ceremony involved, but not the performance of the ceremony.

Mentally he shrugged; the spirits must forgive some things.

Placing one in his mouth he tasted it on the tip of his tongue. It felt dry and wrinkled; the taste was a bit dusty. Gently he bit upon it and was surprised by its resistance. Biting harder it slowly flattened between his teeth like ancient leather. Suddenly his mouth was filled with a bitter taste and saliva flowed like a river. Gagging slightly he continued chewing. When that morsel could offer no more, he moved to the next, until he had completed all six of the buttons.

Sometime during his magic meal he vomited. It was not an unpleasant experience, more a flow and purging of his body. When all was done, he sat quietly and waited. His body felt numb. Not a numbness of illness or injury, but a numbness that bordered on emptiness. He felt himself a container awaiting something to fill it.

As he waited he knew he was being filled. The night around him entered at the top of his head, flowed freely down his neck and seemed to coat the inside of his chest. It kept a steady pace down the inside of his body, through his hips and into his legs. He could feel the stars sticking to the inside of his body and when he looked at his chest and legs, he could see them. Small specks that glowed through his skin, as if he were covered with fire flies.

Moving his hands before him in the air, the stars beneath the skin left long trails of light that glowed in the air after his hands passed. They did not disappear and soon an intricately woven net of light surrounded him. He found that by sitting silently and still, they would gradually darken and disappear.

As the lines vanished, his vision was drawn to the darkness around him once more. As his eyes adjusted he found the darkness had a subtle glow. This one more familiar to him.

Tiny threads of light were once more connecting all things together. He could see the grasshopper connected to the rock it was sitting on by a small, bright thread of silver. More than that, he could see another, but much dimmer thread, leading off into the night. As he watched, he saw the grasshopper take flight and followed that dim thread. As it traveled the path of the thread, the thread brightened and the insect became a comet heading off into its own personal future.

From his own body, from the stars embedded in it, a thousand small strands flew out in every direction. Instinctively he knew they were his attachments to everything in his life. His decisions made – and decisions about to be made. While all of the input should have been overwhelming and incomprehensible, it was not. It all made perfect sense and made him feel at ease with himself. Even the voices made him feel at ease.

Sometime during his study of the threads, the voices had appeared. Not directed towards him, he had not responded. Now the hundreds of voices, all speaking at once, assailed his senses. Placing his hands to his ears did not seem to deaden them.

When he could stand no more he had yelled to them.

"I am here! I am ready to learn!"

Silence blanketed the landscape for a time, and then the voice he was familiar with spoke to him in a tinkle of laughter. The laughter grew as hundreds of other voices joined in the mirth.

"You are ready to learn?" The laughter grew in volume. "There is a lesson to be taught here tonight, but you will not be the student. Indeed, you shall be the teacher.

All things gather here tonight to learn. Except you. It is from you *we* will learn. It is you we will study and learn – or more precisely – remember. Let us begin."

The voices faded to whispers and the lesson began. Snake understood finally what was happening. It was not comforting, but at least he possessed understanding.

The creatures, the spirits, the sprites surrounding him, disassembled his life, from the time he was born onward. They were like wolves devouring Snake and his past. Every moment of his life was pulled forth from him and examined.

Never before remembered was his birth and the light that shown on his eyes, forcing them to clench tight. The discomfort, the feeling of slipperiness, the fear at birth; lapped up by the surrounding entities. They took the emotion into themselves and it swirled among them. The happiness and revitalization of the first time his lips suckled at the breast of his mother was relived and shared with the throng.

Through this, they felt the same happiness and security. It swelled through the surrounding beings, amplified by each until emotion coursed through the very earth upon which he stood.

Thus it continued for a time without end. The eternity of Snake's lifetime. An eternity that lasted the blink of an eye. All the deeds performed through his youth. The happiness, the shame, the sadness, the fear, the anger, the dreams. All multiplied in sharing. The time when first he felt love – both mental and physical. The stars embedded in his body expanded outward and the very air was a dancing kaleidoscope of light and emotion.

The sharing continued through the death of Morning Star, the friendship of Buckingham, and the cloud. By that time, the emotions were more powerful than a thousand suns blazing on a desert of white sand.

A silence brought Snake back to his senses. At the final sharing of the end of his tribe, all was stillness. He sat, feeling the world and spirits around him, for they were still there, but silent.

They were different now. The calmness was gone, even though silence reigned. The world was now still. The world was now listening. The world was now deadly.

A voice came to him. No laughter in it. A voice sullen and flat as the still before the storm.

"You lead us. We will follow. We will hunt, bring forth the enemy. His death song will be trampled beneath our feet and hooves."

Swimming Snake rose to his feet as the first rays of the morning sun rose in the east. The light was blood red. The world rose with him. Where he walked, the earth trembled.

CHAPTER 15
The Death Cloud

The hunting ground of the Indian is yonder, among the purple clouds of the evening. The stars are very thick there, and the red light is heaped together like mountains in the heart of a forest. - Anna S. Stephens

The death cloud reached the maximum distance it could safely go from the Valley. Fear was not an emotion it recognized, but it did know its limitations.

Its boundaries.

Boundaries controlled by the power source emanating from the valley far behind. As the cloud moved farther and farther away from the valley it became increasingly difficult to maintain the energy required for proper and efficient function. In emergency situations, power could be pulled directly from the light of the sun, but this was neither efficient nor adequate. The solar radiation was enough to maintain existence, but not perform its duties.

The death cloud was not designed as an offensive entity, but it was not without offensive programs.

By design, it was built to accommodate almost all situations, and in proof, throughout the course of an hour, it had evolved into a battle posture.

The cloud modified its shape to configure to its new objective – survival. It understood in a way that it was facing a danger. This was novel in itself and not treated lightly. Seldom would such a machine face danger or the requirement to respond to that danger. The bilious cloud shrank into itself; the puffy but dangerous billows flattened in shape and spread out. Soon it covered an area of over three hundred yards in diameter, but with a thickness of only one foot.

No longer did it appear as a cloud. From below, what could be seen appeared as the bottom of a large leafy autumn tree. The leaves composed of glass. The exposed surface was shiny and hard in appearance. The leaves glowed and pulsed with hues of red and orange, reflecting the blood red light of the morning sun. The branches, veins of energy, connecting the leaves were a stark and ghostly green.

Air currents no longer pulled from its body streamers and banners; in its battle mode the particles compressed against each other to a degree giving it substance and protection. It became its own armor. Lowering to a constant twenty feet above the surface of the ground it turned and began its flight back to the valley.

Beneath it – once more – the grass and sagebrush charred, and areas broke into flame. The wake of the cloud was marked with the smoke and fire of an alien hell. Small animals that had previously gone unnoticed, not betraying their position by not moving, were incinerated as a matter of course, not detection.

The expenditure of energy was calculated to increase as the distance to the Valley's power lessened.

Here, two jackrabbits froze in the brush.

With an electric blue flash, their flesh charred and crumpled into the pit of molten glass formed when the sand under them melted and flowed together.

A colony of ants received similar treatment, although not warranting the same amount of effort. Their bodies sizzled and popped in a shimmer of heat waves that seared the life from the thousands of bodies.

Another deer – a white tail – shrilled a whistle-like scream as its body ignited from within, flames bursting in jets from its hide, the smell of burned meat permeating the air.

The death cloud did not consider this a senseless slaughter. It knew not from where danger was coming and no chances would be taken.

Anything perceived as living, or in its path, would be extinguished in self preservation.

For the first five miles of travel back towards the valley, the destruction was centrally located beneath the cloud. As it closed the distance, its area of destruction fanned out, encompassing an area not restricted to its shadowy footprint on the ground.

Flares of energy, small lightning bolts, sparkled outward claiming anything that was near its path. Spidery webs of energy hunted down even the insects fleeing in the air, in a never ending flurry of tiny, lethal tendrils.

Nothing would be allowed to stand in the path to safety.

CHAPTER 16
A Mountain Man Stands

"When their adventures do not succeed, they run away. It was the mark of a brave man to face things that are, and seem, terrible for a man, because it is noble to do so and disgraceful not to do so." - Aristotle

Buckingham stood in the valley. Not just anywhere in the valley, but by the mound that he and Swimming Snake had sat upon. His chest had stopped convulsing with the effort to regain his wind and the searing agony from his over taxed lungs had faded to an ache that grew and shrank as he pulled breath into his body and expelled it.

Standing there, he realized he had absolutely no idea of what to do. He felt right foolish; his anger had supported him thus far, but it too was fading.

All he could do was stand on this cursed ground and look around. Nothing seemed available to vent upon what remained of his rage.

Settling his limited possessions on the ground he took stock. From his jug, he drank his fill of water and emptied the remainder on the ground where it splashed and slowly sank into a patch of mud and muck. Pulling the wiping stick from his rifle, he took a swatch of linen used for patching the balls of his rifle, and poked it down into the jug. With the end of the ramrod, he worked it around; absorbing what was left of the water inside.

Scowling, he opened his possibles bag and removed a worm jag from within, screwing it onto the end of the hickory wiping stick.

The rod was blackened from being rubbed with coal oil.

Poking the contraption inside the jug he twisted a few times and removed the now damp cloth.

The damp rag he tore into a long and narrow strip, stopping just short of the edge and tearing it across – repeatedly – until he had a thin strip almost six feet long. Opening the bag of powder he pulled a handful forth, and setting the end of the strip into his powder filled hand, slowly pulled the cloth through his clenched fist.

When done, he had a powder caked wick to use as a fuse. Setting it aside, in the sunlight to dry, he turned back to the jug. Using one hand as a funnel, he filled the jug to the brim with powder.

"There," he said to the world, "Got myself a right fine little package. Not sure what to do with it, but by God, I bet there is something here that needs its attention."

Stymied as to his next move, Buckingham sat once more. It felt good to rest his body, though he knew there was little time left for action. The ground was hard and brown, and his eyes still drawn to the forest of lifeless trees around him. Placing his hands behind him he leaned back and looked skyward. Bright blue stood out more intense than he could remember, a sharp counterpoint to the desolation around him.

"Well…" he spoke idly to the sky. "If'n ya got any suggestions, now be the time. This pilgrim is lost."

Around his neck, the medicine bag began a gentle vibration. Without thinking he pulled it from his neck and cradled it in the palm of his hand. Felt in his hand, the vibration increased and before his eyes he saw the tawny buckskin disintegrate into powder, falling between his fingers. Among the powder lay the objects he had wondered about for so long.

When Buck finally saw the contents, he was not all that impressed. Here lay the claw of a hawk. Next to it a tiny square of thin parchment that appeared blood stained. Beneath all, a stone. Nothing that really instilled fear or confidence. Nothing that could explain the previous effect on his arm.

The mystery was not finished.

As he watched, the parchment burst into flame, turning to ash in an instant. It happened so fast that his hand was not burned. The claw glowed briefly…and…was gone. No dust, no flames, just not there anymore.

Buck fought the urge to fling the rock away, before something else happened. It was dusted with the fines from the powder left from the medicine bag. Carefully he wiped if off on his skin shirt, half expecting his shirt to go the way of the bag.

Holding it to his eye, to inspect his handiwork, he was taken by its beauty. No ordinary stone was this. It was a crystal. Nature always created nice baubles, but this one was special. Clear, clearer than window glass in the cities. A bluish tint when the light struck it just perfect, six sided with faceted ends that tapered to a needle sharp point. In his wanderings he had found many pretties, but none so nice as this.

Looking through it gave a comforting view of the world. The sky was still a smothering blue, unaffected by the tint of the sparkler. The hillsides, with its death and decay, was mellowed some, the stone making even that desolation look somewhat more acceptable to a man's soul. As he turned, he stopped dead.

Through the crystal the mound appeared different. Rising off it was a mist. Through the almost undistorted picture he perceived the mist swirled in small vortexes across the surface of the mound. In an area on its near side, close to the top, they seemed more concentrated.

Lowering the fragment from his eye, he looked at the mound unfiltered. Without the unnatural lens between him and the mound, it looked as it always did. Just a rounded pile of earth about fifteen paces across and twice the height of a man.

Lifting his fragile monocle between him and the mound, he slowly walked towards it. As he approached, he could see the small whirlwinds more clearly.

They definitely were concentrated in one area. As he drew near the mount the crystal seemed to vibrate, tiny sparks jumped from its tip to sting his fingers. It was as if the rock itself did not want to go near this place. As if its purity would be sullied by proximity to the earthen mound.

Buckingham tried to walk up the side of the hillock, but could not do so. The crystal was doing something in his hand. It was a feeling that he had once in his life.

At a traveling medicine show they had displayed what they called a Leyden Jar. From a container rose a metal rod, ending in a small brass ball. When you touched it a spark would jump and if the person grasped it firmly, the muscles in arms and chest would quiver and convulse. The closer he got to the mount, the greater the intensity, until – when he reached the side and started to ascend – he had almost no control of his body.

Flinging himself away, he rolled in the dirt until he was far enough away that his body would respond to his commands and he could rise to his feet. Staggering back to his possessions, he laid the crystal on top of his possibles bag and stood, heart pounding. Steeling his will and controlling his fear, he returned to the mound without the crystal.

This time he approached with caution. His caution was for nothing as when he arrived at the side and started moving to the top, there was no discomfort or pain. The sun shown down on his back and he stood atop the mound. Unharmed. Looking at his feet, to a spot a step or two away, he could see neither sign nor trace of the small whirlwinds he had viewed through the crystal. With his foot, he kicked and scuffed the earth. Nothing unusual, merely dirt, loose on top and hard packed an inch or two under the surface.

Nevertheless, something was here. Something that drew his mind and being; something the crystal let him see.

Sinking to his knees and facing uphill, he pulled his 'hawk from belt and pounded the blade into the ground, cutting and breaking the compacted soil into clumps. With his other hand he pulled them back between his legs like a badger digging a den. Buck concentrated his attention to an area two feet by two feet. Hacking and scraping in the limited space made it so he did not have to move and could devote full effort to the chore.

After a half hour, his mind drifted while his body continued the mindless task.

◌◌

Buckingham's first season in the mountains with LeBlanc had imprinted a dislike of digging. The high country had seemed like a dream to Buck. The warm summer nights, lying on the ground, blanket pushed aside, watching the stars burn far above. A full belly and friends, comfort and security – it felt like it would last forever.

Then came the first fall nights and the bite of mountain air chilled as a fine wine.

The blanket was now carefully tucked around the body, the body shaped into a crescent, facing the fire to catch all the heat that flowed from the flames, then radiated from the coals glowing orange in the darkness; when the flames died.

It was still a sense of well being, but halfway through the night, the cold crept into the small pockets of warmth nestled between blanket and body.

For a time the cold could be ignored, but when the shivers scooted across the skin, it was time to rise, toss twigs onto the coals and slowly feed the fire back to its former intensity. When the shivers subsided, Buck would lay back down and catch an hour of sleep before starting the cycle over again.

As the newest member, that was his job. The cold was an omen. An omen of approaching times.

Summer had gradually slid into autumn, but there was no easy slide into winter. A man went to sleep one night expecting to wake up to a familiar world next day. He awoke to find the world a frightening wall of white and freezing cold. In the morning the sun came out feebly, but the world of white refused to melt and did not flee from the specter of the sun.

Buck had felt sure he would perish from the cold in the first week, but LeBlanc showed him the path of survival. In the afternoon, when the party made camp, a roaring fire was built, but with differences not found in any fire Buck had seen. Now the fire was built over a floor of rocks gathered from around the area. The size of the stones ranged from a man's fist to the size of his head. Buckingham remembered that now, more than ever, the fire was both friend and enemy.

The rocks, in their bed of fire, would pulse red from heat and some would explode, sending sharp fragments through the air, seeking blood from those who huddled close for warmth. When the fire was blazing enough to dispel the cold from the body, each man would return to the cold, just away from the fire and begin digging with his hawk. The frozen ground would grudgingly break into chunks and these were carefully set aside.

Labor continued until frozen hands refused to work. Each would return to the fire. Numb hands warmed slowly, until they tingled, then burned with the circulation returning to them. When fingers would bend once more, each returned to his personal hell of digging.

After the ground had been moved in an area the width of a man's body and its length, to a depth of eight inches; the super heated rocks would be carried between two sticks or rolled along the ground into the shallow nighttime graves. The earth that had been removed was placed back over the rocks and the frozen and tired bodies of the mountain men carefully lay atop all; covered with all the blankets available.

Rising through the ground and around the sleeping figures, captured by the blankets and held in a tenuous grasp, was the heat that kept a man neither cold nor warm, but in a purgatory in between state that would last until morning.

ભ৪৩

The memory of the cold had returned to Buckingham at the same time reality returned. He found himself kneeling beside a hole in the ground that was almost as deep as his hands could reach.

His fingernails were broken and bloodied, but never had he noticed the pain. With a start, he realized he would probably still be digging, but he could go no farther.

Carefully sweeping the remaining dirt in the bottom of the hole aside, he peered in, eyes widening in amazement. The bottom of the hole was a sheet of metal. Dark gray, almost black – with a shine to it that reflected the image of a man possessed. Buck recoiled in horror, unable to stop himself even though he realized that it was his own image. Cold emanated from the metal, piercing his buckskin shirt, his flesh and threatening to freeze his heart.

Slumping to his side, he rolled to the bottom of the mound, unconsciousness taking his remaining scattered thoughts from him. Thus he stayed, in a sleep bordering death, until he awoke to a morning sun.

◁◎▷

Three entities formed three points – equally spaced – on a line stretching from west to east. At one end, in the east was the death cloud. At the western end of the line, Buckingham. In the middle was Swimming Snake. At this moment in their lives the trio shared the crimson morning sun. Their goals, though intertwined, were different. Ranging from repentance, vengeance and survival.

◁◎▷

Swimming Snake stood facing the morning sun. The night's activity and lack of sleep left him drained, emotionless. It felt the spirits surrounding him in the night had sucked all emotion from his mind and soul. Now, in the morning light, he could not feel the spirits' presence. Their power – the power that had surrounded him during his walk from the mountain was gone. Gone from his world, the spirits had disappeared into the void, taking with them a large portion of his life and spirit.

Snake stood at the edge of the deserted encampment, oblivious to the flies and vermin that had gathered to feast upon the remains of his loved ones.

Even this did not evoke any strong feelings in him. Thought flashed in his mind that he was now less than human and a twinge of regret flared over his callousness of the moment. This was instantly blanketed and swept away by the dead feeling seeping from his mind. Unbidden, his feet propelled him forward to the east. A slow and unhurried shuffle.

◁◎▷

In the morning sun, the death cloud continued its destructive journey to the west.

During the night, it had grounded and flowed outward, dispersing until next to invisible. This was the best mode to conserve energy, with an added plus of being protected by its vast expanse.

Reforming, it configured to its battle structure once more. Yet again the death it dealt as it traveled was as final, but now – total. The air below it shimmered as the flickering one sees on the desert as the sun pounds down. No longer did it seek out and destroy every life form. The concentration and memory that required could be used elsewhere. Now it sterilized. It sterilized the ground below it in a fan of death that radiated forty-five degrees from the edges. No animal or insect could live beneath its passage. The ground was as the ground of the Valley, devoid of insect or plant, the remains already brown and decaying. Worms, seeds and roots dwelling below the surface were just as lifeless, all dead to a depth of fifty feet.

Above the death cloud no shimmer exposed the danger. Any bird that happened to pass above was marked and painted as a target. On the top surface of the cloud a small blister the size of a walnut would appear – bursting open – a glowing ball rivaling the brightness of the sun sprung forth, flying unerringly towards the predetermined – and doomed – target.

Upon contact the small sun expanded, taking the shape of the object it targeted, and a gentle rain of gray ash floated downward from the sky.

ଛଓଈ

Buckingham awoke to the sun in his face and for a moment his thoughts were lost, confusion claiming his thinking. All too soon reality flooded back. His mouth was dry and lips cracked.

Starting to look and reach, he remembered he had poured the last of his water from the jug the previous day. At this instant, he would have sworn celibacy of the whiskey, if he could have but one drink of plain water.

Buck's hands ached and were stiff. To straighten his fingers, he laid his hands on his chest and pressed them flat, until they no longer looked as claws. Then he worked them together and flattened them once more, until he could force them open and closed on their own.

Sitting, his stomach lurched and he folded to his side heaving. No food remained in his paunch, and the best he could bring forth was stinging bile.

Wiping it from his lips and chin, he crawled on his knees to begin this final day's work.

Now Buck had a plan of action, he just wasn't sure how to initiate it.

The black powder charge in the jug was fairly powerful – but not powerful enough.

As the powder 'blew,' it would shatter the ceramic of the jug and make a mighty 'puff' of smoke – give a fair amount of shock, but probably not enough to do any real damage.

If he covered it with the earth he had so painstakingly removed, it would increase the power of the explosion tremendously. Trouble being, if he buried the jug, the fuse he had prepared would hit the ground, being smothered before it came close to igniting the charge. How to get the fire to the jug. Therein lay the confounding question.

Buck set the jug and the fuse next to the hole and slowly walked back to his pile of possessions to study them. Not much there. Nothing that he could see that would solve his problem. He was just plain and simple trying to make the powder do what it was not intended to do.

If it were in a rifle, pushing a bullet, it was one thing. The fire was contained behind the ball and expanded explosively, driving the patched round ball from the muzzle. This was different. There was just no way to let the small amount of air needed remain around the wick while it passed through the ground.

Well…he could stick the muzzle of the rifle in the jug, bury it, and then touch off the trigger – firing the rifle, but that had a tiny drawback. Would not be real healthy to stand on top of the jug when it went off. Might ruin his whole day.

If he had enough cordage, rope, twine or such, he could tie a hitch around the trigger and set it off from a distance. Taking into account all he had for hemp, sinew, thread and the like, there was no way for him to get much more than a couple paces from the explosion.

Taking off his war shirt, he pulled his knife and studied it for the best way to cut it into an endless strip he could use to pull the trigger. Buckingham had almost started cutting when it came to him. He rifle was already busted up. There was no sense in him loosing his shirt also.

Raising the muzzle to the sky, he reflexively looked for clouds and possible lightning. No sense ending up like Spider Johnson. Seeing nothing, he gritted his teeth and pulled the first trigger, then the second. With a "pfft…" from the touchhole and a roaring boom from the muzzle, the rifle discharged into the sky; a rising cloud of smoke declaring the passage of the .54 caliber ball.

By the time the echoes of the shot had stopped their reverberations, he had sat himself on his butt next to his gear. With his knife, he pried the tenon pin from the side of the stock and pulled the wiping stick from its hardware. Lifting the muzzle of the barrel away from the stock, he extracted it from its rear mount. Setting the stock aside, he turned his attention to the octagonal barrel.

From the bottom of his pack, Buck pulled forth the shabby spanner that would supposedly fit the square hook protruding from the breach plug. It was with contentment he found that it actually fit, and fit quite snuggly. His smile of pleasure turned to a frown when he was unable to hold the barrel in one hand and unscrew the plug with the other. His grip was not firm enough to keep the barrel from twisting in his hand. Switching hands, he found the results the same.

His cursing turned the air almost as blue as the cloud of smoke that had dissipated from firing the damned rifle. Once more, he sat on his rump and contemplated the situation. Reminded him of a story once told to him by a fellow trapper around a forgotten campfire.

Seems a man had lost everything and was crawling across a burning desert. His luck had been on the tramp for some time and just kept getting worse. Finally, when he could bear no more, the man looked to the heavens and beseeched, "Oh, Lord! Why me O Lord?"

After a few seconds, the Lord's voice boomed down from on high saying, "I don't rightly know, compadre…just something about you pisses me off."

After another ten minutes, a halfway smile returned to his lips and he rose. Gathering the barrel, hawk, and spanner, he headed towards his old camp in the tree.

At the boulder that sat adjacent to his now exposed former camp, he found what he hoped he remembered. A large crack ran down the side of the rock in one spot, starting out four inches wide at the top and tapering to a hairline at the bottom, about five feet down. Setting the muzzle in the crack, he worked it down as far as it would go, then tapped it solidly with the back of the hawk. The octagonal barrel wedged solidly in the crack, holding it as if it were part of the stone.

T'were a good thing, as it took the strength of both his hands and arms to force the barrel plug to turn. Once it started, and he had forced it three quarters of a turn, he was able to twist the crude wrench and plug with one hand until the plug was out. With both hands, he pried up and down on the barrel until the rock relinquished its hold.

Curiosity, more than anything, made him raise the barrel to the sky and peer through it. Darkened with the residue of his final shot, he could still see the rifling spiraling down the length of the tube. One full turn for every sixty inches. He noted it still looked sharp after he last had it freshed back in Saint Louie.

Them Hawkin brothers did shining work, no doubt about it.

Turning, he strode back towards the mound, pausing only to pick his wiping stick from the earth.

At the mound, he tucked the end of the fuse on the wiping stick. Carefully he poked it through the length of the barrel until three inches remained exposed from the muzzle. With his finger, he worked the wick into the neck of the jug. Setting the barrel inside the mouth, he felt it come up against the lip tight, when the front blade sight refused to go any farther. Setting all into the hole he had dug, he started back filling it with dirt. Now he wished he had not scattered it down hill quite so far.

Sighing mightily, he pulled his shirt off his back once more and set it below, where the dirt had accumulated downhill. With both hands, he pushed the dirt onto the shirt and dragged it back uphill, depositing it in the cavity. It took twenty trips with the shirt before the hole was filled to the top once more, and only the breech end of the barrel stood skyward, an iron flagpole missing its banner; not totally missing, perhaps, for it still bore three feet of blackened cloth that remained of his impromptu fuse.

Buckingham rested. Nothing remained except to light the damned thing and see what happened. He found himself hobbling back to his gear once more and retrieving his flint and steel. Slowly, painfully, he walked the short distance and climbed the side of the hillock again.

Holding the stone close to the fuse, he struck it a glancing blow with the steel. A shower of sparks sprang from contact and danced off the wick.

Nothing.

A second time he laid steel to stone with a cascade of sparks bouncing off the fuse.

Nothing.

Not even an ember taking to the cloth. He closed his eyes tiredly.

On the third time, his weariness vanished as a foot of the cloth disappeared in a sizzling puff of smoke that raced towards the breach of the barrel.

Damn! It moved far faster than he had ever envisioned it would. Flinging the steel and flint away, he ran from the mound.

It took less than a second and a half for the hissing flame to consume the remainder of exposed fuse and hit the barrel. The barrel slowed the burn some, but not enough that one would notice. Buck had barely hit the bottom of the mound when the package detonated.

A dull boom, with the undertones of a gigantic bell being struck one time, rang out. Dirt blossomed into the sky, followed by a puffing ball of fire, surrounded by a bloom of blue smoke. All hung in the sky for a heartbeat.

At the base of the mound, a ring of dirt humped slightly from the ground, spreading like a ripple that follows a rock being tossed into a pond. Behind this ripple chased a hazy curtain, extending out of sight into the sky. If Buckingham had been facing it, he would have recognized it as similar to an intense display of northern lights, expanding outwards in a curtain.

The dirt ring wave overtook him, forcing his running feet forward, and spilling him backwards – into the ring of lights. When it hit the walls of the valley, it disappeared. No trace of it remained, nor did any trace of Buckingham..

The hole Buck had burrowed in the side of the mound was back. It was larger now and its edges ragged. The smoke clinging to the side of the mound and filling the hole slowly floated off into the surrounding air. The shiny surface of cold, reflective metal at the bottom of the hole was still there, but now blackened and dull. It had not dented and no gaping hole adorned its surface, but marring it was a crack. A crack that bled hissing white mist from damaged innards.

જટ

As Swimming Snake walked, his pace gained a rhythm, a rhythm duplicating his heartbeat. His steps became shorter with each foot placed firmly. Not a stomping of the foot, but a firm and solid stroke that struck the ground hard, with each step his moccasins displaced a small puff of dust. Snake's eyes remained fixed on the horizon, his attention on that which lay before him. Not once did he turn and look behind.

Clouds appeared in the sky, sparkling white in the sunlight, now that the sun had risen far above the eastern edge of the world. The cirrus clouds floated together in thin chevrons, all pointing in the direction of the medicine man's travel. As they formed, they started moving with him. Following. Far above and silent.

As one took shape and started its migration, another would slowly spring to life, form its aerial arrowhead, and follow.

In the myriad of gullies and washes crossing the land, dirt and sand dislodged from the walls, trickling downward. From deep in the earth, Snake's footsteps echoed as the heartbeat of a behemoth, buried beneath the skin of the world.

The breath of the world flowed from behind also. One moment hot with dust devils spinning away from him and into the distance – the next cold, a wind flat to the ground, brushing the grass down and holding it pressed to the bosom of the earth. Snake realized a power was there, but a power held in check.

Waiting. Watching. Challenging. Following. Growing.

ଓଃଽ୨

The cloud stopped suddenly and hovered. For an instant, the power radiating from the valley had ceased. All communication from its host had halted, leaving the death cloud lost and alone. A feeling that it had never encountered before. Finally, the power was back, but at a reduced level. Communication was back, but whereas before interchange and interface had been instant, there were now pauses in the exchange of data. Pauses that would not constitute the blink of an eye, being measured only in milliseconds, but pauses present before.

For every blast of energy the cloud expended, a rebuild period was now needed to charge back to its original strength.

It shared with the valley the knowledge that the capability to send information outward, to its origin in the stars, was gone. The original code, requiring it to return to the valley, download its information, and transmit all details to its distant home was derailed.

The destruction inflicted on the landscape beneath the cloud ceased. Power levels were brought back to maximum potential – and the death cloud resumed flight. System analysis was performed, because of the sensor data the death cloud was receiving. The sensors sent out signals that returned to the surface of the cloud with information. Between it and the valley, seismic activity was increasing.

This was abnormal.

At any other time, this would warrant a full investigation. No tectonic plate activity, nor geothermal activity should be occurring in this area and the odds of such activity were minuscule.

Additionally, unusual weather formations were gathering. It sensed the high pressure and low pressure systems in the surrounding region, studying and evaluating them. The weather formations were in no way generated by those pressure systems, in fact they seemed to fly in the face of all influence that existed.

This was extraordinary.

This was impossible.

This was danger.

Once more, the cloud changed its shape and composition. Hovering, it flowed together forming a huge ball in midair. The exterior collapsed inward and the center flowed outward, forming a hollow shell – the outer body only two feet thick. The eastern surface shrank, moving its mass into the western surface and soon the shape was that of a teardrop. A teardrop lying horizontal with the ground. In size it had condensed down to a hundred feet long and fifty feet at its bulbous head. Color disappeared from it and it became almost transparent.

Through it the countryside appeared distorted, as the bottom of a stream might appear through water. In its hollow center, bolts of violet lightning formed and grew to a tapestry of light that danced to an unheard and alien song.

◌◦◦

In the valley, the mound was undergoing changes as well. To look upon the interior of the mound was to look upon a geode. The shiny metal casing enclosed and protected a mass of crystals growing upon its inner surface. Crystals ranging from the size of a cigar, to the height of a man. No world had ever created these crystals through fire or pressure. These were grown in an environment where gravity held no sway.

In color, they resembled the pink quartz that decorated the mountains in some areas, except quartz did not have that subtle inner glow or clarity. The energy the crystals created, controlled, and stored was vast – but fragile. Surrounding the pink crystals – protecting them – was an inert gas, now tainted by the oxygen rich atmosphere that was slowly seeping into their quarters with its caustic oxidation. Near the offending crack, the wall dulled and the surfaces of the crystal spires turned a cancerous, milky white.

A crystalline cancer that slowly spread across the gemstone brain, madness running before it – the precursor of death.

The explosion had done more than cause a crack in the shell.

The shock of the explosion had caused the inner depths of the crystals to pulse in unison. The invisible energy formed by the shockwave had poured forth in an expanding circle – radiating its power through soil, rock, metal, and flesh. It displaced physical elements to a small degree, but it stretched the fibers of time and space to the verge of ripping.

⦈⦉

Buckingham did not know if he were alive or dead. If he had to place money on it, he would have to believe dead – and not gone to his maker in good graces. He knew he still had a body, for he could feel it, although not see it. He just knew it were there after a fashion. That he could not see it did not cause him great distress, because what he could see was beyond his grasp.

Buck had lived with good vision, but that vision had been restricted to what he could see before him and what he could catch out of the corner of his eyes. Now that was changed. He saw everything.

His view exposed that which lay before him, behind him, above him, and below him all at the same time. He was hard pressed to explain it, just as his mind was hard pressed to absorb the information.

Colors, as such, were gone, but everything had shape and vibration. The vibrations were too rapid and minute to fully 'see,' but it was there. Nothing appeared solid, and the vibrations of things and shapes behind the foreground blended through. He could 'see' in a full spherical circle around him, and in turn through everything.

Worse, he was not alone.

The other person…creature…entity, existed around him as well as his mind could figure out. Nothing you could pick out, but it was there, whether you liked it or not. It was akin to when a cloud passed over, and the shadow covered you. You could feel its passage. This 'other' was random vibrations that flitted here and there, not quite seen, but disrupting the vibrations of all objects it passed between. Seemed like it was controlling some of those objects.

More frightening was the fact that he could not only look outward in every direction, but inward.

When he looked inward – that were the wrong word, but the only word that he could think of – he saw his essence swirling down into a dark point. Concentrating on that dark point was like falling through a funnel. The dark vibration opened up into a new surrounding of vibrations, a new self. That essence had its own 'inward.'

This continued on, much like standing with a mirror behind you and one in front, watching a thousand images of yourself stretch off into infinity.

Looking 'outward' again, he was slowly able to gain a perspective of the valley. After study he was able to identify trees and rocks. The trees he was able to interpret as the barren skeletons he had seen before. Idly he wondered what they might look like if they were alive and vibrant. As he wondered, they slowly changed and became a vibration vision of what they might look like if located outside this cursed valley.

Not precisely, but as if a demented artist had set a pane of glass between the bones of the tree and the viewer, painting the difference on the glass so it overlaid the truth. In realizing this, he understood the trickery that had been thrust on him when he first entered the valley. In a second – if time really had any meaning here – he transformed the valley into the Garden of Eden it had once been. Immediately sickening of the lie, he let it slide back to reality.

A blast of intense pulsation slammed into him and threw him from the mound in what was readily interpreted pain. Buckingham found that anger was quite possible in this altered state. Buck also found that what he knew about the vicious tricks and tactics of fighting did not translate well to his newfound existence.

Reflex told him to drop and spin into his attacker – trouble was, if you could 'see' in all directions, it was right hard to figure out which direction you were facing in the first place. The reflex of dropping and spinning translated into staying in one spot and vibrating like hell. To his good fortune, whatever had booted him from the interior of the mound did not seem set on pursuing him.

Buckingham had been unceremoniously tossed from an occasional drinking establishment in his time. All the forced departures had ever succeeded in doing was to rile him up; resulting in a wood-splintering reentry – with an accompanying war whoop that normally froze his evictors long enough for him to set his attack into full effect.

Here, there weren't no wood doors to bust through, and there weren't no way to give a respectable battle cry. This was down right frustrating. Buckingham felt like a schoolboy who had been insulted and bullied, unable to make a decision on what to do, except stand there and be pissed.

Lord, this was one helluva day. Buck decided being dead was not very much fun.

In the effort Buck put forth to try to control his essence, he found motion was possible. No legs were involved, no putting oneself out of balance, falling, catching the fall on a foot, and transferring it to forward motion. To move, one simply picked a location – and was there.

'Looking' down the valley, Buck picked an area next to a bend in the creek. No sooner had he picked the area, but he was there, the new area opening up to him. The transition was as if he had blinked, only to find when he opened his eyes he was in a different location. The novelty of the experience entranced him for a spell, and he spent some time blinking/moving to random places in the valley.

At one stage, Buckingham blinked next to his gear. It was recognizable to him, and fascinated him in that he could see inside the pouches, recognizing the contents as well. On the ground next to his possibles, a spot glared. It was not a vibrant light he saw, but rather a vibration that was rhythmical and intense. Unthinking, he reached for it and with a reflex blink, it filled his world. The shimmering vibration had six ribs that appeared more intense than the sun. At the ends, the six lines of force flowed together to a point that gave off a secondary vibration that surrounded the object with smaller rays.

The shape leaped to him, blending into his own vibrations, and becoming a part of their pattern. Buck's pattern intensified, pulsed, and bonded.

On the valley floor – Swimming Snake's crystal was gone.

The feeling was unnerving, but not totally unpleasant. The tiredness, aches and pains in Buck's new essence were gone. He felt...energized, with strength flowing throughout his being. The uncomfortable came from feeling...bloated. Something new was added to him and it was slowly melding with Buck, becoming one and a part of him – and ever so slowly growing, displacing and changing him. Buckingham could not find a way to control what was occurring, so he did the only thing he could.

He ignored it and hoped for the best. Looking inward, he saw the new vibrations flow into the multitudes of other Buckingham's continuing its passage into the infinite other versions.

Activity had returned to the mound. The small vortexes were visible once again, and as the air passed into the crack in its shell, it displaced the inner atmosphere, spilling it into the valley air. It also appeared as a vibration. Long wisps that snarled like snakes leaving a nest. Snakes made of mist.

Concentrating on the mound, Buck 'blinked' and was there. 'Looking' at the mound, he realized this was one object he could not see within. When he had been inside, looking out, the shell had been transparent. Now it concealed a shadowy world where only hints and flashes of the interior broke through. Another 'blink' and he was inside once more.

Buckingham knew immediately that a warm welcome was not in store.

Mentally he hunkered down – a split second before he was slammed again. This time the world around him rocked fiercely, but he remained inside the mound. Buck felt surprise around him, followed by a much more violent attempt to expel him. When the universe had calmed and vibrations returned to normal, he remained where he wanted to be. Inside the mound.

The two opponents sized each other up. As brute force would no longer function, communication was in order. Words could not be passed, but basic feelings could, and those feelings translated into words familiar to Buck.

"Go," chimed the mound in a wave sweeping over Buck.

"No way in hell, here I stand and here I stay," thought Buckingham.

"Unacceptable. Intrusion. Dismay."

"Tough shit," thought Buck with some satisfaction.

"?"

"Means it ain't gunna happen," Buck thought back.

"Imperative."

"Tough shit."

"Understood," the response, and the pain began.

The mound was forced to improvise. This incident had not been envisioned, and never before had such an occurrence happened. Hundreds – no millions – of samples had been collected. Those samples reduced to individual molecular vibration patterns and those patterns condensed and archived inside the crystal jungle of the mass.

This was an error of incredible magnitude. When the explosion had occurred and the wave warping time and space had gathered Buckingham up, it categorized him into a vibration pattern. It did not know what else to do with him. That was well and good. What had not been done was the completion of the job, condensing him down and storing the replica inside a crystal. Rather, it left a pattern mimicking in form and function that which controlled and oversaw the mound.

The mound's first response had been to cast the foreign body out. This it had done. If programming has a virus, it isolates the issue and removes it from the system. This virus had survived outside the mound when expelled – and possibly worse – acquired a secondary vibration from what had originally been assumed to be a harmless crystal structure of this world.

The only option left was to dampen the annoying vibration until it disintegrated, existing no more.

Buckingham was no stranger to pain.

Most of his life he had struggled with pain in one form or another. Pain ranging from the day-to-day aches, cuts and bruises; to having his belly ripped open by a cat he mistakenly assumed was dead. Of the cat, he remembered little but the pain.

The pain and fear had possessed his mind, and somewhere through the ordeal, he remembered LeBlanc standing over him while the others held his arms and legs. LeBlanc had looked at the pink ropes spilling from his belly and done the unthinkable. He had pissed on Buck.

Later he explained he did this to clean the wound, having no water. He then carefully placed the handful of guts back inside and stitched Buckingham up with sinew.

For three weeks Buck had fought the fever. LeBlanc later admitted that he contemplated placing a ball in Buck's head to end his suffering.

Buck still had the memory of the pain and a nice cat fur cap to crown his head, but even that pain was a lover's kiss compared to the molten wave of agony coursing through Buckingham. Just as Buck's newfound 'body' seemed to stretch on into eternity, so did the pain. Putting salt to the wound was the fact there was nothing Buck could do to fight back.

CHAPTER 17
Battle Joined

When such men, who are beyond hope and fear, begin in their dim minds to see the source their woes, it may be an evil time for those who have wronged them. The weak man becomes strong when he has nothing, for then only can he feel the wild, mad thrill of despair. - Sir Arthur Conan Doyle

In the distance, the horizon blended with the sky. The scattered scrub pine painted a fuzzy border allowing the eyes to define the horizon, but not pick a clear line of demarcation between sky and earth. Standing, Swimming Snake shaded his eyes and searched the world before him. His eyes were sharp – not as sharp as the hawk's or eagle's, but trained from hunting to identify any movement or object that was out of place. By the time he spotted it, his heart had returned to a slow beat in his chest. It was there. A small point on the horizon. Moving slowly now, ever so slowly. The thrill of discovery sent his heart racing once more. The small, lethal point was moving towards him.

Snake waited with a patience born of his acceptance of past and future. His eyes remained fixed on the cloud until the hair on his arms stood out on their own and the nape of his neck bid him turn. In fear, he turned to see what danger lay behind him.

The sky behind was alive. The lead "V" of clouds had stopped and was now spinning in one place. As Swimming Snake watched, the following formations collided with the edge of the spinning circle and became part of the churning mass. One after another, they joined in the ever darkening storm growing larger over Snake's head.

No air moved on the ground and no wind swept the grasses. Above, the world's cloud moved with ever increasing speed. The center of it opened into an eye of blue, while the iris took the gray-black color of a thunderhead. From nowhere other bits of cloud appeared, billowing out of points in the sky at the edge of the monster and throwing themselves into the storm. The storm now covered the sky behind and above Snake almost from horizon to horizon.

Large sections of it began to light brilliantly as lightening flared through the body of the tempest.

In the blue center of the storm, Snake saw the sun. Even it was touched by the magic of this day. From its edge, a crescent was chewed, the bite turning black.

Swimming Snake laughed. Even the mighty Thunderbird had taken wing this day, ready to consume the sun. The medicine was strong.

Snake turned to face the death cloud to the east.

Raising his arms, he cried out beseeching. "Come to me. Come let this day have end. In your death, I will sing to you the names of those you have taken from me. Together, we will sing of them and give them the honor you have removed."

The blazing sun, now half gone, still gave light to see the cloud. No longer did the cloud drive on relentlessly towards Snake, but slowed and stopped.

Swimming Snake fell to his knees and screamed wordlessly in frustration.

From the sky above, laughter burst forth with the thunder.

"You thirst for blood, little one."

Without looking up, Snake snarled with clenched teeth. "It stops. It shows cowardice and has no honor. It is nothing more than a beast."

From beside him a quieter voice agreed. "It has no honor. Indeed it is a beast, but why do you throw yourself to the ground as a child might?"

"You see for yourself. It shall run. It shall escape," said Snake.

"Ah…" replied the voice, now from behind. "This you believe?"

"Yes. It stands before us and you do not fight."

Patiently the spirit explained. "You have hunted the buffalo. Can you run as fast as the buffalo?"

"No, I cannot."

"Are you as strong as the buffalo?"

In spite of himself, Swimming Snake laughed. "No, but…"

"Then how is it," the voice asked merrily, "how is it that you have ever tasted of the creature?"

Swimming Snake knew the answer. He had known this answer since he was a child and watched the hunt played out. In a small way he had been a part of the hunt, even as a child.

Hunters on horse back carefully chose a place. When buffalo herds were near, charging horsemen would set them in motion. Once in motion, it was necessary to direct them. Natural objects were used, small hills and such. Then, bands of men, women, and children formed lines, waving blankets and yelling. All to direct the running and panicked herd to its death. They were channeled to the edge of a cliff from which there was no escape.

A buffalo jump.

By the time the herd realized the earth had ended, they were in midair and falling to the hard ground below.

"I understand," said Snake. "This is merely to set the evil one in motion, directing him to where you will fight."

The spirits around him hesitated in embarrassment. "Yes ...and no."

One voice rang out from the multitude who all spoke at once. "Your passion has awoken us. This is as it was planned. What had not been considered was that when our passions were set aflame, it would awaken yet another. We now play no more a part in this than do you."

"This I do not understand," said Swimming Snake.

"The Old One has awoken. This matter has been taken from our hands."

"You will send the enemy fleeing into the arms of the Old One?" asked Snake.

The spirits around Snake shuddered and the air itself quivered.

"Yes, but now it is a game. The Old One does not need to have this enemy driven to it. There is no place on the world that it – or anything else – could hide from the Old One."

"No..." the spirit said thoughtfully, "for a time we were called from you. There we had to account for our actions. Actions we have performed, or failed to perform, for countless centuries.

It was the whim of the Old One for us to drive the enemy before our gathering. Perhaps it was a reward, a chance for us to count coup, as the battle has been taken from us. Perhaps it was merely a way to teach the enemy fear before his death. Perhaps it is a lesson to remind us of our place in the circle of life."

"Who is the Old One?" asked Swimming Snake.

"The Old One is the Old One. The One who was here before. The One we serve and honor. The Old One is more powerful than you can imagine. We control some power. The Old One is power. Therein lays our origin. The Old One does not concern himself with trivial and small matters. We were given form so we could work as the fingers of the Old One. Our purpose was to perform the delicate matters of work." The spirit shuddered once more. "The end of this day will not be delicate, I fear."

Day has darkened revealing a night sky in the eye of the storm. A circle of fire showed, surrounded by stars. No longer could Snake see the death cloud plainly. Around him the world held its breath – waiting.

Swimming Snake looked to the heavens and into the dark world of the spirits, all swimming in the churning thundercloud. The dark world exploded into blue fire once more and the air surround him became a living and solid force.

"He calls. We must obey." Tolled the voices as one.

Snake knew instinctively he stood at a wall of death. Were he to take fifty paces forward, or backwards, into the world of the spirits; his life would be snuffed with no more thought and effort than an insect would be crushed, unknowingly, beneath his feet. He held his own breath as he waited for the storm to move and pass over him, sealing his fate. This happened not.

૯ଇ

The death cloud was no longer interested in engaging combat with creatures in its path. Something was amiss in the valley. Something that caused intermittent communication and direction from its primary programming source. While it was capable of functioning independently from the power source in the valley, this was not normal protocol. The advanced nano technology allowed the cloud a semblance of life, but it was a symbiotic life, dependant in majority on the controlling central mind and power of the valley.

For a time, information had passed normally with the valley, and then the data being transferred was corrupted. Information would come in that could not be processed. Contradictory. Meaningless. Instruction paths that lead around in spiraling circles performing no meaningful task. Now the only option available was a quick and direct approach to the valley to attempt to ascertain the problems that had arisen there.

Separated, neither the cloud nor the mound was capable of the massive repair that was so obviously needed. The mound was the brain, but the cloud performed as the peripheral nervous system and the hands of the whole.

Compounding the problems that lay at hand was the celestial event that was known and expected.

The solar eclipse was easily predictable, it merely happened to fall into a window of time that was inconvenient. What could not be explained were the unusual electromagnetic fields that were forming in the earth of this area.

The sunlight dimmed to almost nothing, but visible light was not a requirement for the cloud to verify the occurrences around it.

To the area laying north by north-west, unusual weather phenomena had formed. Phenomena the cloud had easily detected and avoided. The detection was not a problem. Massive thunderclouds gathered. The electrical discharge inside the weather cell was impressive. At any other time, a careful observation would have been performed. Massive bolts arched throughout the cloud formation. On top, blue jets and red sprites danced in rampant abandon.

Microbursts, amounting to upside down tornadoes, lashed from the storm smashing into the ground, as if the cloud had sprouted a dozen feet and was stomping the earth below into submission.

From the top, rain fell through the black and rolling mass. As it approached the ground, the temperature – which had dropped dramatically – froze the droplets, then violent updrafts hurled the ice crystals upwards towards the top. They were recoated with water, fell again, and after a few passes were small hailstones. The process continued repeatedly, each time the hailstones grew with the coating of water that froze on its downward plunge. When they reached the size of a man's fist, their weight was enough to break the cycle; they plunged to ground battering all upon which they fell.

The gigantic hailstones were but a harbinger of the future. From the side of the thunderstorm came a popping noise. A globe of blue fire the size of a pony was birthed, shooting away from the storm and stopping. More popping and yet more balls of intense blue-white crackled from the interior of the storm. Each aligning with the first, not touching it, not quite standing still, but dancing around the first-born.

On the ground, just outside the radius of destruction, stood Snake. He was lost in the fury of a world gone mad, unnoticed by cloud or storm.

When a hundred of the spirit balls had formed in the sky, the world was no longer dark. The sun was still swallowed by the Thunderbird, but the powerful light given off by these mystical spheres lit the countryside; to look upon their faces was impossible.

Turning his back to them, he stared at where the cloud had last been. He could see it, reflecting the light radiated by the blazing orbs. It looked closer.

Before him lay his shadow, pointing like an ominous finger towards the cloud. Even as he watched, hands cupped around his face to shield his eyes from the fury of the light behind, the spirit balls moved.

They moved as a pack of wolves might, leaping to the chase, scattering across the prairie in their pursuit of a lone animal. Tightly grouped at first, they slowly scattered apart, forming smaller groups.

Some branched out to the left, another cluster of a dozen veered to the right – by the time they had covered half the distance to the cloud they formed a gigantic "C" shape, the horns of which pointed towards either side of the death cloud.

Inside the death cloud, internal alarms flashed across every synapse it possessed. In a flash, the immensity of approaching danger overwhelmed it.

What was taking place was impossible, impossible contradicted by the fact that the situation and environment was present and developing, it flew in the face of everything the cloud knew and understood.

It flew against all the data that had been stored through millennia of information gathered across thousands of light-years of study – and it flew straight at the cloud. Nothing gathered during its stay on this world had presented an inkling of this possibility or capability.

Attack was imminent and not by the creatures of this world. Attack was forming from the planet itself and appeared – more than appeared, was irrevocably indicative – that this was a logical and tactical assault by one or more thinking beings.

In desperation, it fled from the oncoming attack.

The arms of blue fire contracted inwards upon the cloud. The first globe touched the side of the cloud with a resounding '*bang*,' exploding in a coruscating display of electrical energy spreading out across the surface of the death cloud. The second, third, and forth impacted the same area, with explosions of sound merging into one drawn out peel of thunder. This time the released energy traveled far, washing over the top and bottom of the cloud, penetrating inward as well.

The cloud gave a soundless scream of agony. Never before had it been introduced to something that could be interpreted as pain. The concept of pain was memorized and not foreign, but this was an introduction into the reality of definition.

In defense, it threw out its own streamers of electrons in pencil thin ribbons of energy. The ribbons formed instantaneous connections with a dozen oncoming balls. The moment they touched the spheres, pathways formed back into the cloud and the energy of the ball lightning raced down the pathways.

The previous pain was nothing compared to this. All systems shut down and the death cloud – drifting slowly at first, then picking up speed – fell to earth.

CHAPTER 18
Collateral Damage

"Over my dead body!"
"Okay, but it's going to hurt."
- movie, Last Man Standing

Buckingham did not know how long the pain had lasted. Might have been a minute. Might have been a year. Did not much seem to matter, what mattered was the pain was gone. For some reason, whatever was in the mound had turned its attention away from Buck.

Buck was not a man to run from a fight, but this were not rightly a fight. More like being held down and having boiling oil poured over one's privates.

No one was ordering him from the mound anymore – but the idea seemed right pleasing.

Buckingham's thoughts turned to the top of the valley, the rim rocks overlooking it, and instantly he was there. Still seeing all around him, he realized there was trouble. Buck had used the phrase, 'trouble in the air' before, but now it was not just a saying.

Far to the east was something the likes of which he had never witnessed. As quickly as his attention was focused on it, he was there, stuck in the center of a tempest of unearthly proportions.

The world went silent around him, and Buck could feel the thoughts and eyes of a hundred beings turn towards him in shock, amazement and anger.

Grabbed by unseen hands, he was held immobile. Buck knew those invisible hands were about to rip whatever he was to shreds and shit on the fragments.

Made the mound seem right hospitable.

The emotion surrounding him turned to amusement and recognition. Buck felt himself being tossed from being to being in a playful game. Each spinning him and flinging him to the next; in his mind he heard voices and they addressed him.

"What is this morsel that throws himself into the pack?"

A second voice, catching him, and looking into his essence replied, "Ah, it is the white man – the unbeliever – the brother of the one called Swimming Snake."

"Do you believe yet?"

"You are not a spirit, you are not a man. You are a spirit man. How came this to happen?"

Another voice cut through his mind. "He has not passed on. He is not a spirit." The spirit became thoughtful. "Should we not allow him to pass on?"

"Whoa!" said/thought Buckingham. "You and Swimming Snake think a bit too much alike. If'n I still be alive, lets let it stand as such.

Don't much like what I am right now – whatever the hell it is – but I am not that much partial to another change, if'n I can help it."

"IT IS NOT FOR THEM TO DECIDE."

This voice silenced all around him. The sentiment coming from this being held neither anger, fear, or humor. It held judgment and decision. The silence grew and Buck felt a need to dispel that silence.

With what he hoped was respect, he said/thought, "My name be William Buckingham. Might I ask who you be?"

"MY NAME IS LEGION, BUT NOT THE LEGION THAT IS SPOKEN OF IN YOUR BOOK. YOU KNOW THE NAMES BY WHICH MEN CALL ME. IF YOU DO NOT CARE TO ACCEPT THOSE NAMES, OR RECOGNIZE THEM, IT MATTERS NOT TO ME. THE QUESTION IS…WHAT SHALL BECOME OF THE MAN NAMED WILLIAM BUCKINGHAM?"

Buck thought for a moment, then gave an answer he would wonder about for the rest of his life.

"If'n it is up to me, I guess I would just like to go on livin' and die of old age somewhere far from this campfire."

Silence.

"A REQUEST NOT SHOWING THE HONOR OR SPIRIT I HAD EXPECTED, BUT GRANTED."

Gone was the voice, and the spirits surrounding Buckingham regarded him with disappointment.

"What just happened?" asked Buck.

"You were given a choice and it was granted," replied one voice. "You were given the chance to grasp a roaring river, and you chose a handful of water to drink," stated another in amazement.

"I don't understand," said Buckingham.

"You are either very wise, or very foolish. Being a white man, I fear that your wisdom is in question.

Never have I heard a mortal given the chance to pick its destiny."

"Come," said another, "the least we can do is give you what understanding we can. You shall watch and choose your own song to sing about this day and this battle."

The spirit could be felt shaking its head. "I, for one, stand in awe and respect of you. You have no greed. You have no selfishness. Indeed Swimming Snake was right, you are a man of power."

Buck was carried to a position he could watch the battle. He was moved not by the 'blink' he was just getting accustomed to, but in a massive rush of wind streaming past him. Its howl would have deafened him, were he still saddled with ears. The position was not one he would have though of, but one far above – above where even the eagle could soar. A vantage point reserved for the gods. In this place the spirits held him. Held him on both sides, much as a child tethered between parents to prevent him from wandering.

Above him, the sky was dark with stars shining brighter than he had seen before. His vision was now different, yet again. Whatever it was that had merged with him was allowing him to see as he had with the vibrations, but now colors were discernable. Below, the ground was a blur of blue, green and brown. The horizon was curved and misty. All this he could still see at one time.

Words failed Buckingham.

The insignificance of himself and his plight was brought home in a chimera of understanding. When he concentrated on the ground below, it rushed to the fore, and the clarity was flawless. The vision of not an eagle, but the legendary thunderbird itself.

With the guardian spirits he waited.

꙰꙰

When the death cloud fell to earth, its shape slowly changed. No longer did it retain the hard and compact teardrop shape it possessed during the short and decisive battle. Now it morphed into a semblance of its original form. It existed as a ground hugging mist, slowly spreading out across the prairie. Around it, in a circle, were the remaining balls of lightning.

Watching…waiting…hoping the cloud would attempt to flee.

Function and consciousness returned to the cloud as its systems rebooted. The ghost image of pain still overlay the functions and memory of the death cloud. As programs responded once more, its shape started to contract. It was cognizant of the circle and limit set around it.

It was respectful of that loop.

When it started to flow back together, the circle around it began to contract. When it ceased its movement, the contraction halted. The cloud was an intelligent being. It did not need to have additional punishment to reinforce what it had learned.

Quickly it stopped its reformation and let itself flow back out into a vapor. As it did so, the circle expanded. This was just as the cloud knew would happen, and as it feared would happen. Sequential events could be predicted, and it knew what was expected of it.

Allowing itself to fully reform into a bilious cloud once more, it returned to the air. When it had done so, the perimeter around it opened in one area. The death cloud studied the exit with resignation and slowly moved forward. As it did so, communication restored with the valley, and the situation was transferred in full.

In the last vestige of sanity, the mound received its warning. Unseen in the air above the mound a signal beamed skyward. A signal that moved with the speed of a beam of sunshine, until far from the earth it entered a blackness complete – a blackness the size of an acorn – and disappeared, only to appear in an area of space so far away, the distance would be incomprehensible to a man.

The cloud continued its journey, meekly and passively. Resistance could gain nothing. In its alien mind, it plotted and pursued a thousand scenarios. Each ended with the same result. Defeat. Destruction.

The blue-white balls surrounded it once more, stopping its forward progress, while the sun reappeared in the sky and light bathed the world once more. The brilliance of the returning star dimmed the presence of the lightning surrounding the cloud, but did not dim the danger. When the sun had fully reappeared, an opening presented itself once more to the cloud, and it dutifully resumed its journey.

ଔଓ

Swimming Snake blinked his eyes with the return of the sun. Wheeling, he faced the gathered assembly of spirits and watched as the thunderhead above thinned in the middle and the eye of blue shown through. In a rush, the earth's clouds shot forward in wispy threads into the eye and darted upwards to dissipate and vanish. As it did so, the voices vanished – one by one – from his mind. In the space of twenty breaths, all were gone but one.

"Wait," cried out Snake.

A tinkle of silver laughter.

"I go no where."

"Where did they go? Why have all left?"

"We have been dismissed. Our presence is no longer required. To stay after dismissal would be to speak that we do not have confidence in the Old One."

"Is he present?" asked Swimming Snake.

"He is always present."

"No," said Snake. "Not the Old One. I felt the presence of my brother."

"He is near."

Swimming Snake implored of the spirit. "Then let me talk to him once more."

The spirit silently considered. "This is...allowed. It is allowed only because it is not forbidden. Written upon the picture of life is his future. To bring him here will smudge the picture, but not alter it greatly."

Three whirling gusts brushed Swimming Snake's face. Two of them left, followed by the spirit Snake had been talking to. The remaining spirit swarmed around Snake in happiness and confusion.

"This is you, my brother?" asked Swimming Snake, wonder in his voice.

"Good God, almighty! I can see you, hear you, and feel you. Kinda, sorta."

Snake pondered. "How came you to be this way, my brother?"

In a wild babble of explanation, Buck tried to educate Snake. The answer came as a rush of emotion, images and more. It fell upon Snake, pushing him to his knees. In a split second he had relived all that had occurred to Buckingham, and knelt dazed on the ground.

"Stop my brother. It is too much," Snake shook his head to clear it. When he raised his head, there was a sad smile upon his face. "You have power. I knew this, but did not realize how much power you have." He stopped and frowned, qualifying his statement. "For a white man, of course."

"Of course," replied Buck in a voice lacking the pure tones of the spirits, but fitting Snake's memory of his brother perfectly.

Swimming Snake spoke. "I stand in fearfulness of your decision. You were offered whatever you could conceive, yet you chose the path of a common man. I know not if I could have chosen so wisely.

The Old One was wrong. It has honor. It has humility without greed."

The spirit that was Buckingham chimed out, "You know – I ain't rightly sure what you are talking about – nor what choice I made. Or even when I was asked to make that choice. I feel mightily confused right now."

"It does not matter. You made the choice that befits a man of honor."

Buck hurried. "I ain't sure how I know, but I know the candle is burning out on our time. What are you going to do now? What the hell is happening?"

"This day comes to a close. All must walk the path laid before them."

"That tells me nothing. What are you gunna do, Snake? I have a right uneasy feeling about this."

"My part is done. I was but a spark. I sought vengeance, but have found something better. I have received acceptance of what has happened," said Swimming Snake.

Buckingham was grabbed and ripped skyward without the chance of reply or question.

"Stop," screamed Buck to the spirits transporting him aloft. "Taint neither right nor fair. I got no chance to say goodbye or ask what he were planning to do."

The two spirits spoke as one, comforting the man-spirit. "Why do you feel farewells are required? Your brother will do as it has always been written he will do. He shall return to his village."

"But his village is gone. Everyone is dead!"

"You see," said the voices, "you do understand. You just do not accept."

◌ᴈᴇ◌

In the mound, activity was anything but meek and passive. Safeguards were incorporated in every monitoring station to prevent their overrun or external detection. The safeguards ranged from innocuous to total erasure of the crystalline complex. Operating procedure in this situation – although this situation had never been envisioned – would normally be the erasure of all physical evidence of the station. The artificial intelligence controlling the mound was not functioning on a normal level. It was insane.

The original intruder entity/vibration was gone.

This fact barely registered in the maelstrom of data flowing into the mound. It was aware of the capture and servitude of action placed upon its airborne counterpart on this world. Steps would be taken to include all entities in the erasure of recent events.

In the fragmented mind of the mound crystals, two events were set in action at the same time. Surrounding the mound materialized a sphere. Its surface was reflective, mirrored to the nth degree. Covering the mound like a dome, it extended beneath the mound in a continuation, forming a mathematically precise and perfect shell. Through it physical matter could not pass. Radiation of any nature was not allowed passage either. Sound, light, air, *everything* was barred from both entry and exit. Should the enclosed mound be set on the surface of the sun, nothing would be noted inside.

Inside the mound, a second sphere of the same nature formed. It was small – three feet across. Inside it was the corrupted air filling the mound. Dust particles, smoke, anything that existed in that space the split second before it formed. And something else.

A program. A program of destruction.

Systematically all that existed inside the miniature sphere disappeared from our universe. The air, the particles of dust flashed into nothingness – until all that was left was a hard vacuum and the program. Then the program itself vanished, leaving the process it started to continue on its own.

The next to go was space. No longer did the inside of the sphere have volume. Time followed quickly, leaving a status existing as was before the creation of the universe. Into this total emptiness bled a single drop. A droplet from nowhere. It started growing, the sphere now an egg of both creation and destruction. An egg envisioned by the creators of the mound, but a program never ran. The result of the program could not be totally evaluated, but those that wrote it, held it in fear. What it would create was primordial. Energy from the beginning of time. An energy that could not be predicted or controlled.

The instant the sphere formed over and beneath the mound, the Old One howled in rage. No longer was the Old One satisfied to choreograph the spirits in battle. Its patience at an end, the Old One stepped onto the killing ground. With his entrance, the spirits vanished from the ground and sky surrounding the battlefield. The only spirits left hovered nervously – far above, to bear witness to the battle.

At the four points of the compass, slightly more than a hundred miles away from the mound in each direction, the earth cried out and split asunder. Four cracks formed. At first, they were but a dozen feet across and a hundred feet deep. Rocks, sod, and trees fell into their abyss as they widened and deepened.

Rapidly their depth increased until the skin of the earth bled forth molten blood – the magma trapped below the crust. The cracks extended, jagged rips in the face of the world that raced forward, all toward the silver ball that dared exist on the visage of the world.

The death cloud hovered, dazed. Its captors had vanished. As it started to move, the back of the floating mist glowed crimson with the reflected light of the onrushing river of fire. Sensors detected the skyrocketing heat, and for an instant, it hesitated – deciding between dispersal and whole mass flight.

Sheets of liquid rock shot into the air, blanketing the cloud. A billion individual nanotech particles died as one. The cloud's passage into oblivion was not even noted by the crystals in the mound, from which it had been cut off without warning.

From above, Buckingham watched as the red snakes in the earth converged upon the sphere, forming a cross, the sphere a silver jewel set in its center. Magma struck the sides, erupting high into the air as molten tidal waves washed over its surface. Where it struck, it flowed down the sides, leaving it unmarked, a pure and pristine reflector of the hell surrounding it.

Inside the sphere, no knowledge of the event was known or felt. When the converging rents struck, no notice was taken. No vibration. No sound. No effect.

Meanwhile, inside the primary sphere, the secondary sphere continued to fill. It would continue until the force growing exceeded its nonexistent capacity. How long it would take was a meaningless question. Inside the small sphere, time did not exist. When ready, it would hatch as an egg immortal.

In brief periods of lucidity, the mound crystals were horrified by the action they had precipitated. Energy from the creation of the universe could just as easily destroy it. Solace came to the crystals as psychosis reclaimed its thought process and even the need to rationalize was negated.

Far above, from his restrained observation point, Buckingham commented to his guardians.

"Appears that yer Old One might have bitten off more than he could chew."

"We do not know the mind of the Old One," responded one of the spirits.

The second spirit added despondently, "Yes, but no matter the outcome, the damage *we* will have to repair. The battle is not delicate. Of this I spoke to your brother."

The first continued, "Disturbing this is, but – do you not sense the amusement in the Old One."

The second spirit seemed to think for a moment. "He beats his shield, waves his weapons, and cries insults to the enemy, but there is laughter in his song. I do not understand."

"Don't get me wrong, I am right impressed by the show that the Old…" Buckingham stopped short. In the blink of an eye – it was over.

Inside the mound, inside the sphere, the crystal had been waiting over its creation.

Slowly the surface of the egg-sphere began to change color from its silver to gray. It started to dissolve.

A pale light, not seen since creation, seeped out in rays that sparkled and bounced from pink crystal to crystal.

With the light, there was laughter.

"IT IS A GOOD DAY TO DIE. AND SO YOU SHALL. LONG HAS IT BEEN SINCE I HAVE HAD SUCH A PLEASURABLE ENEMY WITH WHICH TO PLAY. AN ENEMY WHO BUILDS A FORTRESS UNBREAKABLE THEN OPENS THE GATE AND INVITES ME IN."

The mound could only watch as the Old One selected a small crystal from the wall. It wondered how this being knew the exact crystal to select, but it was no longer amazed. The tiny crystal powdered under the attention of the Old One, and the silver sphere protecting the mound vanished falling into the event horizon.

As Buck watched, the entire valley was engulfed. The thick lava rolled and bubbled gently, the excess flowing off through the same channels as the water had once flowed. Though distant, he imagined he could feel the incredible heat radiating against him.

And the world stilled.

With passing time, the lava crusted over. The next change was restoration and repair.

Work to be performed by the spirits. The lava filled cracks that had opened up – swallowing all in their path – had larger cracks open around them, swallowing the still burning fires back into the bowels of the earth. The lake of smoking rock that filled the valley quivered and sank abruptly, until it was only half filled. The earth then shook, the mountains broke apart, and all fell into the valley.

Nothing was as it had been, but the horrendous scar that had branded the earth had been removed. Looking to the east, the site of Snake's encampment, all that remained was a shallow depression in the earth.

Buck spoke to the spirits who had now released him. "It happened – it happened so fast. What will the Old One do now? What will happen and become of us…you…me?"

The spirits replied, almost as an afterthought. "Your questions begin to sound like your brother's used to. So fast? This was nothing. It was but the slightest display of the power of the Old One. Now he will return to where ever he goes, and do whatever he does for the ages between his appearances.   However, we know he headed for a blackness in the heavens first. He follows something spewed forth by the enemy.

We are empowered to perform our work now. We will rebuild the earth, regrow the plants, trees, and reset the rocks. When done, the circle will be complete. Perhaps we will honor this battle.

As for you? You have made your choice and it is now out of our hands – or yours. Know this, however – never shall you return to this valley."

William Buckingham was cast down from the sky.

CHAPTER 19
Dies are Cast

"The countenance is the portrait of the mind, the eyes are its informers" - Marcus Cicero

The Bible said that Satan was cast from the heavens. If Buckingham had to compare, he figured Lucifer got off pretty lucky. As it were, Buck was cast from the heavens two hundred miles from the battle – and ten years later.

The first day was a blur of hunger, agony, and disorientation. Lying on his back, he saw steam rising up from around his naked body. None of this made much of an impression on his wretched mind. The hunger he felt deep in his soul. It was the need for food. Thirst was past. His mouth was dry and his tongue lay as a lead bar in his mouth, welded to the side of his cheek.

The agony was a pleasant companion to remind him he still lived. Most of it was concentrated in his head. Fluid had streamed down his face, around and beneath his right eye. There it caked, collecting the red dirt that he rolled in with his throes of pain. In a rare lucid moment, he raised his hand to his right eye. It was not there, but it was. In place of the soft, squishy ball that granted him vision was a hard round lump. It did not give him vision, only pain.

The first day passed in joy, he was still alive.

On that first day, he felt the sun pass over his body, reddening his skin and burning all that was exposed. With the passing of the sun, he felt the passage of insects. They crawled over every square inch of his body. Some in travel uncaring and others to stop briefly, making a meal of the exposed flesh. One he felt crawl to the edge of his eye, then nothing as it traversed the globe that had replaced his god-given eye. Then its minute footsteps continued as it crossed the bridge of his nose. His good eye shut in reflex as it continued its journey across his face.

The onset of evening filled Buck with bliss, the night air bathed his burning body with coolness, and sometime in the darkness, sleep overcame him and only the stars remained to guard Buckingham.

Morning found Buck just as hungry and thirsty, but refreshed somewhat in physical strength. He took stock of his surroundings. Trying to sit, waves of nausea forced him back to a prone position.

He called out to Swimming Snake, but there was no answer.

He called out to the spirits, but no voice rang through his head.

With his good eye, he scanned the ground he could see without having to move. It was not his eye that gave him hope, but his ears. Behind him, he heard the song. A song sung many times, but not one he could even hope for right now. It was the song of water. Not the chorus of a river, but the tiny, gentle hum of a stream.

Rolling to face it was one of the most exerting actions he had ever performed. After he managed to lever himself over, he lay disheartened. He could see willows rising above the hidden banks of the creek. With only one eye, he couldn't tell exactly how far it was. It was a ways off and any distance crawling on his naked belly was a far piece. It might as well been across the continent to Buck and no matter how he tried, he could not 'blink' himself to it.

At first, he tried counting how many times he laboriously raised himself on his elbows and pushed himself forward with his legs. That was just depressing as hell, and once again, his body took over while his mind fled.

The sharp rocks that opened the flesh on his chest went unnoticed.

Whether death would come to him on the open or in the wash did not matter. It would come. Buckingham was just too damn ornery to lie down and peacefully die.

His wandering mind did not even realize it when his body continued its bloody crawl over the edge and fell ungracefully in a tangled ball of arms and legs in the muddy water.

CHAPTER 20
Savior

"We are all travelers in the wilderness of this world, and the best we can find in our travels is an honest friend" -- Robert Lewis Stevenson

Kendred's thoughts swayed in unison with the wagon, its team plodding across the open prairie. This was his last trip through this god-forsaken land. That fact brought no small happiness to his heart.

The last decade had brought him money. Indeed, he was to a stage where he could consider himself wealthy. That was a nice feature, but one that did not bring him as much pleasure as he had once thought it would.

The gatherings, outposts, and settlements that dotted the land west of the Mississippi were sponges that soaked up his whiskey. Once he had found he could set near any price on his goods, greed had set in for a spell. People might grumble, but that did not stop them from paying.

The greed was short lived, and he had lowered his fee to a figure he felt just and fair.

Yes, ten years of hard work had set him comfortable. With a distillery of modest size and a family large.

Citizens had taken note of his Scotch. Soon it had become a matter of pride to drink a "local spirit, the like of which cannot be found in Europe."

Now the time spent apart from his children and wife wore heavy on his heart. Independent haulers would take over the trips to supply his original customers, and Sterling could become the family and businessman he had always dreamt of.

As he drove, listening to the creaking of the wagon, the squeaking of the seat springs, he looked down the valley to his right. It was a smooth and broad belt of ground that slowly dropped in elevation until it was sharply brought to a halt by the beginnings of the mountains. Many times he had pushed his way down that valley to rendezvous, but no more. Beaver were mostly gone, and the trapping was rapidly becoming a thing of the past.

About to turn his gaze from it for the final time, a spark of light caught his eye. He waited, but it did not repeat. Just as he moved to seat himself, the bright white glare shown forth once more – then vanished.

Pushing his silk top hat back upon his head, he wiped his brow with a square of fine linen.

Could be a thousand things, or naught.

Picking up the reins, he put in motion his team, only to stop again. For no particular reason, he turned into the valley and headed for the flash.

Latter he would admit to friends that he really was not sure why he stopped and turned. His curiosity was not that great, and his desire to continue home a driving force – but he turned.

It took the better part of an hour to pick his way down to where he thought he had seen the flash. Kendred knew he was close, but he could not pinpoint the site. Setting the brakes on the wagon, he spryly jumped to the ground and walked to the bank of the stream. The small creek had cut deep into the earth, but where he now stood the banks were only three feet high. With the undulations of the land, they grew to almost ten feet.

Resigning himself to task, he started walking upstream on the small waterway. After five minutes of walk, he felt nervous. His rifle remained in the wagon. It was not far, but it was not in his hand. His mountain customers had impressed the importance of that. Indeed, he had learned a lot in these mountains and become hardened in body and spirit.

Three paces farther, a sage hen erupted from the brush next to him, almost giving him a heart attack. Standing, shaking, he leaned forward and rested his hands on his thighs, gulping for breath. Enough was enough. He would head back towards the wagon.

At the wagon, he regained his rifle and decided to invest a few more minutes looking downstream.

This decision bore fruit.

Standing on the crumbling dirt bank, Kendred was not sure what he was looking at. Might be a critter, might be a man. Looked kind of like an injun, red, naked, sprawled in the water and probably dead. He was not even sure if this was what he was looking for. With apprehension and a cocked rifle, he half strode, half slid down the embankment to the side of the – now known to be fact – man. The poor fellow was burnt to a crisp from the sun, scrawny with ribs accenting the torn skin of his chest, and half drowned. With one hand on his rifle, he used the other to roll the man fully onto his back. Looked somewhat familiar. Half starved and half dead, the man's face stared up at him. The stare would give Sterling nightmares for years to come.

The man's face was drawn and the skin tightened across the cheekbones and facial structure like the head of a drum. But his eye. My god, the eye.

One eye was half open, staring with blue iris at Kendred. The other eye – the skin had pulled back, as if fearing to touch the eye itself.

The eye had neither iris nor pupil. It was a finely polished crystal ball. A sphere that reflected light from the sun as a diamond – blue-white and intense.

When his shadow fell across it, it glowed with an internal fire.

Taking his canteen, he gently poured a few drops between the slack lips. Rewarded for his effort, he leaned close to understand the whispered words.

"Been lying in water for days. Ain't got no more whiskey?"

CBEO

The final day passed easier for Buckingham than it did for the onlookers. His body still clung to its final ember of life, the mind was ready.

Shallow breathing was punctuated by gurgles and desperate gasps for air.

One observer commented. "We might as well haul the old carcass to the undertaker now. Will not be long."

Another onlooker, elderly and dignified, spoke. "You touch that man before he breathes his last and I will gut you. You are not worthy to clean the shit from his ass."

Turning to face the old man in anger, he saw something that made him lower his eyes and leave the room. Beneath the top hat, he saw a visage that was printed on men who had spent their lives in the mountains. This man was a respected businessman, but underneath the polished exterior lurked something primitive and deadly. Something better left untouched.

When the detractor had left, Kendred soothed the dying man's brow with a damp cloth.

CBEO

Buckingham had been wrong about one thing. No crude cross was placed at his gravesite. Sterling was later questioned about the fact that no cross or monument was erected to signify the last resting place of William Buckingham.

His only reply was to smile and state, "The earth knows this man and needs not a reminder of who he was."

EPILOGUE

The awakening of the Old One did not go unnoticed by man. Thousands felt the battle, even if they did not witness it.

Some did see the side effects. What they saw was the earth heave and the great Mississippi run backwards; for a hundred days thereafter, they felt the ground tremble from the Old One's footsteps. Boats tied to the bank of the Mississippi were found forty miles away – upstream.

Bells adorning the white man's churches rang out in the town known as Boston; the tremors of the Old One's passage caused them to dance in their mounting.

In what is now the capital of our country, walls split, and windows shattered. The elite, the noble, the powerful people trembled in fear of the unknown.

The Indian tribe we know as Cherokees fled the area the white man called New Madrid, realizing that the Old One had awoken and feared his anger.

At the base of the Rockies, far to the west – where the battle took place – mountains bowed before his power, falling into valleys, leveling the earth of high and low in places.

The one man left alive who knew the truth – Buckingham – spoke not of the matter. Even on his deathbed the story did not pass his lips, although it passed before his eye once more.

How do I know of these things? Have patience.

If survivors of Swimming Snakes tribe still exist, never has the legend passed on in song.

If it is for the site you search, there are signs. Massive hieroglyphics mark the ground in our country. They contain indicators that point the way. In our simplicity we assume Native Americans placed them. Look to the scope of the hieroglyphic's construction. Ask why a tribe would bother with such a tremendous chore. Ask instead if perhaps the servants of the Old One did not mark the path – so they themselves would never forget the forging of man, spirit and Old One in battle.

The one man possessing knowledge that the life and times of William Buckingham had power pieced the story I have told together from the addled ramblings of a man half-dead and mad.

A man he accompanied back to Saint Louis, caring for him until the stricken mountain man was once more healthy, in body if not mind. They remained friends and companions, and that one man was present at Buckingham's death bed.

The man passed the story down to his children and them to theirs, until it fell upon my ears. A story to be told when names such as Boone, Crockett, Johnson, Bass, Coulter and Bridger are mentioned in awe. A story to set legend into perspective.

A story told over a fine glass of scotch whisky that my family has made throughout the years. May I offer you another drink?

Enjoy the whiskey. It is far smoother and comfortable on the palate than that my great-great grandfather made almost two hundred years ago. Moreover, I promise – none of the ingredients we use now slithers."

THE ATTORNEY AND THE WEREWOLF

BY

W G MARSH

"**L**adies and gentlemen, boys and girl of all ages, step right up and enter a world trapped inside the mind of a demented author, with a warped sense of humor.

Watch as its denizens dance for you. Werewolves will cavort at their favorite bar. Vampyres can be seen eating popcorn and watching television...all while the secrets of Stone Henge are revealed..

View the most frightening beast of all - the attorney..." - *W. G. Marsh*

The Attorney and the Werewolf Notes -

This is a strange one…even by my standards. It was started "long ago" and in truth was not intended to be a full blown book. It was written in installments - short stories. Why? Because it was written by me, for me and because it was so damn much fun to write.

I just couldn't say good bye to the characters. It was getting to be unwieldy, so I took all the components and stitched them together. Did it work? Well … yeah. It did not work seamlessly, but it worked. Is it done? Well this phase is done, but the characters are still very much alive.

Where did the names come from? Crank, Skank and Rank. Three names picked at random that rhymed. Skank was originally a guy. J. Rank is based, in part, on a gentleman I used to work for. Yes, he is an attorney.

So feel free to howl at the moon.

- WGM
  Tucson, Arizona

CHAPTER ONE
CRANK - SKANK - RANK
C.S.R. - ATTORNEYS AT LAW
I

"No. Oh, hell no. We do not do pro bono; I wouldn't do Sonny Bono if he were alive."

My partner slammed the receiver down on her princess phone, which served as our link to the world of high finance and clientele - also good for ordering pizza when we had money.

I counted to ten before gently reminding Skank, "You know we really could use some money right now. If that call you just did a cluster-fuck on was an open and shut case, we might have made some chump change out of it anyway. Not like winning the lottery or having a real client, but you know, grateful relatives buy dedicated and hard working attorneys lunch; let them borrow young sons and daughters for the evening without pressing charges - that kind of thing."

I raised my hands to the overhead light with its smoldering ballast, and cried, "We have to work on your customer relations skills.

It's *thank you, ma'am*, not *bite me, bitch*. Even if it's your ex's new girl friend.

We strive for *have a nice day*, although I admit *watch your ass* comes in a close second. It's the finer points we need to work on, Skank."

The chair groaned in protest as Skank leaned back, staring at me like I was an ex-husband. Skank fired up the butt of a cheap stogie she had found in the street, and waved it in the air for emphasis.

"Oh yeah, smartass? It was open and shut all right. They open the door to the gas chamber, kick his guilty little ass in, and shut the airtight hatch just as the warden punches the button on his industrial sized can of Raid. Seems the prospective client you want so badly bumped off the District Attorney's squeeze. I got that straight from my sister. She was the maid that found her."

She coughed twice, savoring the foul stench from her cigar. "Maybe you would like to go down in history as defending the man who massacred the main mistress of law enforcement, but it could be a bad career move.

Some of these cops know where we live, you know. At least I'm supposed to let my parole officer know if I move.

I realize Lady Justice might wear a blindfold, but you aren't supposed to strangle her with it. Case closed."

She thought for a moment. "Has Crank got anything on the back burner that might make us some moolah? If memory serves me correct, he won the last case and it's about time he pulled his own weight around here."

I shuddered. "He won, but we sure as hell aren't going to claim credit for that one. Seems all the witnesses for the prosecution were found floating in the river.

Well, not all. Some were found on the bottom, tied to concrete blocks. When that fact was introduced in court, it pissed the judge off to no end, but there was nothing he or the prosecutor could prove. Let's hope it stays that way, cuz the rope used looked suspiciously similar to the jump ropes we bought in our 'get healthy' phase."

Skank shuddered and I continued.

"Would have been okay, but Crank jumped on the table when they announced it, screaming, "so there asshole," at the prosecutor.

It was his ex-brother-in-law, you might remember him. He's the one that took the compromising pictures of you last New Year's Eve. They were posted on that porn site and the cruelty to animals society.

For an encore and finishing argument, Crank flipped the presiding judge the bird. He says he doesn't remember doing it, but it was on live court television with a feed going out to 3.2 million viewers.

They didn't get a chance to cut to commercial."

"Contempt of court, eh?" Skank said before asking the important question. "Probably a hefty fine, to boot?"

"You could say that." I agreed. "He will need a new sun tan by the time he gets out. Unless we want to take a quarter mil out of petty cash and spring our esteemed colleague."

"That's more than most murder bonds."

"And it's cash only. Crank's last check came back insufficient funds."

Skank was wearing her hand-in-the-cookie-jar face. "I took the buck ninety-eight out of petty cash yesterday and bought a hamburger. Petty cash is extinct."

She pulled an I.O.U. from the desk and held it up as proof. It had ketchup on it.

"I thought I mentioned it.

"How about you?" she asked. "You got anything on the docket? Know any good horses at the track?"

"The last horse I bet on broke its leg coming out of the gate."

I rummaged through the stack of mail on the desk, looking for anything that might have the potential of being converted to currency. All were bills, except for receipts from the local pawnshops. Then it came to me.

"Uh, yeah. A possibility. I got an e-mail from some guy asking us to defend him. Said cost was not an issue. I didn't get a chance to reply before they cancelled our DSL."

Skank's feet hit the floor with a solid thud, ending the life of a passing cockroach. I had her attention for sure and her bloodshot eyes warned I had better not be joking.

"You didn't mention this before?" She demanded. "It just slipped your mind? You thought it might be spam sent to the entire internet? 'Represent a cyber-punk today...receive a free lap-top for your participation?'

What did you have? A day to respond? Too busy surfing the porn sites?"

"He's up for murder, Skank."

Skank smiled. "Murder, manslaughter... shop lifting...Its all in the presentation. We're attorneys. We don't pick and choose. They are all innocent, until their DNA is found."

"He says he killed the other guy. He put it in writing. You know, it's called a confession."

Skank frowned. "A confession makes it a bit harder to obtain an acquittal, but not impossible. We can always look for the angle. There's always an angle. The right jury will believe anything."

"He says it wasn't his fault." I offered.

Skank stabbed her cigar in my direction. "See what I mean? Mitigating circumstances. There's always another side to the story.

The guy he killed was banging his wife. Maybe the defendant was possessed by demons caused by listening to rap music. Moreover, his childhood – whoa, don't get me started. I can find three witnesses to say he was raped by his animated teddy bear and one shrink to say he was scarred for life by the incident."

Skank stopped and practiced letting a single tear skate down her cheek.

She was getting good at that.

"He asserts he is a werewolf and couldn't help himself."

"You are shitting me." Skank frowned. "Okay, no problem. It's a challenge, but we live for challenges. We are the professionals. We go with insanity. Worst comes to worst he gets fifty years in the dog pound and we get paid. It's win/win buddy."

There was righteous fire in Skank's eyes now.

"Where's our prospective client at now? He needs CS&R, Attorneys at Law, and he needs us bad. And that's exactly the kind of service we provide."

"Twenty-Ninth Street Precinct, midtown division."

Skank grabbed her purse, stuffing in some rolling papers and a suspicious plastic bag.

"Did that say 'evidence' on the side of that bag?" I asked.

Skank smiled awkwardly. "It's on loan. I am running an analysis on it, checking purity and so forth. Favor for uh, some CSI friends. No money involved, but all I can 'test' in one night. You want to help me analyze it tonight? Been a while since you let your hair down." She opened the cupboard and peered into its depths. "Let me grab a chew toy for this unjustly accused person, on the off-chance it was a full moon last night and the bastard is telling the truth."

"Not a good idea, Skank." I shook my head. "I haven't been able to quash that warrant on you."

Skank looked confused, or maybe just tweaky.

"Ah, *that* little incident. It was just a joke, a harmless prank – nothing more. They need to lighten up down there at the Fifth Superior."

"You stole a squad car from the parking lot to get home. No bus fare, remember? What on earth possessed you to take a cop car?" I asked.

"All the motorcycles were gone." Skank waived the cigar again; its noxious trail of blue smoke was mesmerizing.

"I know, I know. I'm sorry. They even want to hold me responsible for the cruiser being stripped by the street kids on my block. Hell, the department has insurance on their vehicles. It was a lapse in judgment, that's all."

"Strange. The police called it grand theft auto. Be that as it may, I think you should lay low for a while. Unless you want to share a cell with Crank, and I know he's been off his medication for at least a week.

You remember what he did with my hamster last time he was off the little pink pills for just two days? That rated way up there on the scale of unnatural acts. Hell, Jerry Springer wanted to talk to him."

Skank sighed. "Well the emergency room doctor found it humorous even if the rodent didn't, but I guess you're right. I'll pass this time. You keep me posted on what you find out. Call me. Let the phone ring three times, then hang up and call again. I'll answer it the second time. I'll lock the door when you leave."

◁⊱⊰▷

The morning sun shown brightly, revealing a balmy summer day in Tucson. Ambient temperatures in the shade were in the low three-digit category; as witnessed from the quantity of prostate bodies sprawled on the hot gray concrete.

The cement might be littered with unfortunates who succumbed to heat stroke, but the weather *was* helpful in lowering the violent crime rate.

Junkies could lift the wallets of heat victims at leisure - no guns, knives or Tasers needed to induce compliance.

I couldn't help but notice the similarity to a large scale Easter egg hunt. The children replaced by dozens of crack-heads running from body to body, searching for brightly colored plastic and cash.

The precinct was exactly as I remembered it; I've seen smaller crowds at rock concerts. Indeed the lobby was wall-to-wall humanity at its worst, but no music at all, except for the rhythmic vomiting of a drunk in the corner.

Envisioning a three-hour wait I pulled from my jacket a personal *calling card*, kept there for occasions such as this. Unfolding the paper bag with bright blue lettering on the side, I inflated it with two breaths and spun the top tightly closed.

Holding it above my head, I waited until all eyes in the room were drawn to it like a magnet, and then shouted, "DoughNut Deli delivery! Make way please. Hot and fresh, as you've come to expect from DoughNut Deli."

I got the idea from The Idiots Guide to Pavlov Action and Response – available at your local library. Do not try this with Highway Patrol or FBI. For that you need a pizza box.

Two police officers immediately pulled riot batons and beat a bloody pathway to the inner sanctum. The rest drooled enthusiastically.

The jail proper was nothing more than a dungeon with a fresh coat of cheap gray paint (slapped on by the inmates) and tastefully aged vomit (slapped on by both the inmates and the employees).

The species and phylum of this vile and nauseous realm were unshaven characters reeking of whiskey, urine and worse.

Skank enjoyed coming down here. She always found a Friday night date. Me, I just prayed I wouldn't run across Crank.

I approached the least fragrant member of law enforcement I could find, that was still standing, and inquired, "Officer? Can you tell me where I can find a Mr. Vladimir Lupes?"

Blurry eyes moved slowly and I imagined a grating, grinding noise; the blood shot eyes focused on me before a practiced smile appeared, teeth the color of a men's room urinal on New Year's Eve.

"Not sure, but we do have a wide selection of criminals and felons for your viewing pleasure. Was there a particular style or model you were looking for? In the off chance we can't find the exact felon you seek?"

Pretending to give his words heavy consideration, I waited a full three seconds before answering, almost exhausting the man's attention span.

"Well gee, officer, I haven't really given it a lot of thought. You know how it is...wife sends you out with a list... pound of butter, coffee, non-fat dairy creamer, someone who's a werewolf... it wasn't all that clear..."

The jailer belched, scraped some of it off his badge, and interrupted. "Him. The howler. Follow me."

He stopped after a few paces.

"We put a flea collar on him. I hope that don't violate any of his precious rights."

I waved the idea off cheerfully to put him at ease. "Nope. It's been written in the Miranda laws, an addendum I believe. You have the right to remain silent, you have the right to have an attorney present at questioning, and you have the right to pet supplies of your choosing. If you cannot afford any of this, we will provide it grudgingly."

He nodded sagely. "Yeah, I knew that."

Vladimir was not what I expected. I've read the books. I've watched Lon Chaney on late night television. When one thinks werewolf, one thinks vicious fangs, rending claws, and the standard hulking monster ready to rip the guts from the innocent passerby.

A horror from Hell.

Vlad was not the expected norm. A disappointment to be blunt.

Yes, he was truly a werewolf and I give him credit, he was worthy of note. The undeniable proof was there, Vlad in his bestial form, pacing the cell; yet he did not look unerringly like a creature from hell. With pink flea collar and thick wire-framed glasses he was more an overgrown dachshund from Kansas.

I had a hamster once that looked more lethal, may he rest in peace. I'll never forgive Crank for that.

My heart went out to this creature - against my better judgment - and I knew I would take the case, no matter what. After all, anyone who wagged their tail and licked your hand deserved the best defense attorneys that money could buy. It was a shame he was getting Crank, Skank & Rank instead.

I scratched him behind the ear until his hind leg thumped on the cold concrete floor and he piddled just a bit.

I turned to the officer. "Can you tell me if he has displayed any signs of aggression that you are aware of, or at least to the best of your knowledge?"

"While he's been a hairy little varmint, you mean?"

"Exactly," I replied.

"Nah, no real problem. He tried humping the animal control officer's leg, and pissed on the water cooler, but he ain't bitten anyone that I've heard of."

He scratched his chin and neck, eyeing Vlad's flea collar wistfully.

"He had a collar and tag on him when he came in. We took it so he wouldn't hang himself or anything."

"And then you turned around and gave him another...never mind. Would it be possible to see the tag?" I asked.

"Yes," the officer replied. He continued standing like a statue.

"Would you take me to see the tag or bring it to me?" I hoped to activate some brain synapses in the dormant organ. It was mildly productive.

"Oh, yeah. Sure. Follow me." He started a zombie-like walk to parts unknown and I followed.

ଔଓ

The address stamped on the cheap metal tag he showed me wasn't hard to find.

Tucked into a quiet cul-de-sac next to a cemetery, was a house whose number matched the numerals on Vlad's tag.

It was a bright and cheerful ranch house nestled amongst a forest of For Sale signs posted by neighboring properties. Properties that were vacant, displaying jungle-like yards.

In front of one of the realty offerings a cat clung to the top of the telephone pole. I called to it, then realized it was dead. Still frizzed up its sharp claws were embedded in the wood, even after the passing of its ninth life.

A traditional white picket fence, neatly manicured lawn, and meticulously kept flower gardens surrounded Vlad's home; the house was painted a happy sunflower yellow - not something out of a horror show, as I had anticipated.

It was more a dwelling in which one could find a Martha Steward clone. At least an Oprah wanna be.

The latch on the gate worked perfectly and the white washed pine swung open with nary a squeak.

I walked the narrow sidewalk, admiring the gorgeous flowers and noting their beds, unmarred by the digging of dogs, or their use by felines as a litter box. The care bestowed upon these pedigreed weeds was impressive.

On the porch my hand reached out and touched the textured stained glass that formed the insert in the door. Textured, with colors that would blaze from the sunlight, when viewed from the inside.

I rang the bell. I could hear its cheerful chirping. When the door opened, it wasn't Martha that greeted me.

"May I help you?" asked the luscious, six foot tall Amazon answering the chimes. I was stunned as she was stunning; all she needed to be a centerfold was a staple in her navel. It took me a few seconds to compose myself.

Rising up to my full height of five foot eight, I inquired in my best baritone, "Are you Mrs. Vladimir Lupes?"

"No, I am Vlad's sister," she said with a smile so brilliant I instinctively grabbed for my sunglasses. "I'm a Miss or a Mizz. I always get them confused."

"Oh...," I said, my mind going into melt down and my mental thesaurus losing fifty pages. "I'm sorry. I was just confused for a moment. I guess I didn't see the family resemblance and assumed..."

"Understandable. Vlad was the runt of the litter," she said, her breathtaking smile marred by large canine fangs. They appeared a touch sinister.

"I apologize. I forgot my manners. Would you care to come in?" Reaching out, she tucked me under one arm like a football and carried me to a plush couch where she gently deposited me.

Alpha female, I thought.

She sat on the floor in front of me; legs crossed, back straight, head erect, waiting patiently for me to speak.

I slumped on the couch in front of her, a bit wrinkled from transport and delivery, patiently waiting for her to speak.

Overall, it was a comfortable silence.

She sat, staring at my throat, a small bead of saliva forming on the tip of her left fang.

I sat, staring at her see-thru tank top with twin, rosy - well, let the court note, as I said, it was a comfortable silence.

The ringing of my cell phone ruined the mood, bringing me out of my dreamlike state.

She growled softly at the noise.

I reached for the cell phone, smiling in apology.

She growled louder.

"It's only my phone," I explained and continued reaching, but slower now.

She snarled and her head bobbed instinctively in my direction.

"It's okay, I have voice mail." I pulled my hand from my jacket.

In response, she stopped snarling and this was a good thing. A happy thing.

"You are no doubt aware that Vlad is in jail?" I asked warily.

"Oh, yes," she said in a cheerful tone that was not matched by the look in her eyes. "A police officer - the one that arrested him - came by and told me all about it. He decided to try to search my home. Sadly, he didn't have a warrant."

"Did he get what he was after?" I inquired.

She laughed, her smile widening and reaching her eyes this time, as she licked her lips. "No. No, I seriously doubt that."

"Oh...." I considered those canine teeth once more, and quickly asked, "Did I mention I am here to help Vlad and that I am his attorney of record now?"

She sighed, "I see."

I could swear disappointment flashed over those lovely features like a cloud before the sun. "May I offer you some coffee then? Or perhaps a drink?"

"Sure. Whatever you have containing alcohol would be great." Nerve builder, 101, nectar of the gods; it's not just for breakfast anymore.

She smiled, sans fangs, and disappeared. I heard rustling and a clatter. I seized the moment to wipe an accumulation of cold sweat from my face and neck with my sleeve.

Five minutes later she returned and handed me a battered clear plastic tumbler (that appeared to have been chewed on) filled to the brim with an anonymous liquid and an olive. I took a healthy slug to steady my nerves.

"Sweet gods of tainted passion...," I choked, tears streaming down my face. It felt like my lungs were pissed and kicking the shit out of my stomach, while my liver cowered in the corner.

She looked concerned. "I don't know the exact formula for making a drink, but I have all those little bottles they give you on airplanes. I opened them and poured them into the glass. I think it is what you call a mixed drink. Was I wrong to use an olive?"

An avid fan of distilled spirits, I could vaguely identify gin, tequila, whiskey, rum, vodka - could have been Everclear - and a large quantity of scotch and peppermint schnapps. I could not detect coke, 7-Up, tonic water, club soda or mixer of any kind.

"If it isn't any good, I can dump it out," she offered. "You don't have to drink it."

Pulling the drink out of her reach, I told her, "No way. It just went down the wrong pipe. It is excellent. Just what the doctor ordered." Doctor Kevorkian perhaps.

"Kind of like a buffet of booze. I like it very much, and the olive gives it body." Taking a smaller sip, I smacked my lips and continued. "You should know that Vlad admitted to killing the man in writing."

"Where's Writing?" She asked.

"No, I meant he signed a confession. He wrote it down."

She nodded her head, her beautiful hair flaring with the gesture. I was starting to like her, again.

"It is possible, I suppose. It is that time of the month, and Vlad was displaying signs of P.M.S."

"P.M.S.?" I asked. I am not a doctor, nor do I play one on TV, but I do watch commercials.

Her hair tossed again with the nod. I was falling in love.

"Male werewolves have P.M.S.?" I asked again to confirm.

Again the golden ripple of hair. If it wasn't love, at least it was good, honest lust.

"Of course," she said. "All Lupes have Preternatural Moon Syndrome.

It makes us cranky and irritable. We have a tendency to become moody and chase cars."

She shrugged in embarrassment.

"Occasionally we snap and attack a mail man, but not so often now that they carry mace." She rubbed her eyes. "That shit really stings."

"And during this P.M.S. you turn into the wolf state," I finished.

"No, silly. That stereotypic profiling has been tagged on us by writers and movie directors. Although I do love Lon Chaney. People think that we only change during a full moon."

She laughed softly.

"That is like saying you change into a lawyer during a full moon. No," she said thoughtfully, "if one is a werewolf, one is always a werewolf. You can change at will." She waved her hand. "And it's not like in those awful movies, with people screaming and writhing on the ground in pain, fur sprouting out, bones creaking and snapping."

She looked sad.

"Then the town's people hunt the poor werewolf down at the end of the movie, just for eating a villager or two."

"It's not like that?"

"No," she giggled. "You can eat almost anyone you want, as long as you are discrete. No one seems to mind much."

She looked out the window at the For Sale signs.

"Of course, if a person gives in to temptation, and eats just one of the neighbor's cats, they try to burn you at the stake. Another misconception from the movies, cuz I think that is supposed to be reserved for witches.

We don't take kindly to fire.

The people with gas cans that survive normally move out in the middle of the night. The same night if they are smart."

"No, I meant the change. Where you become a wolf. It's not all bloody and grotesque? I've always wondered - in the movies now - why people didn't run like hell when the person starts to change."

"Cuz it's not in the script, silly." She turned her back to me, pulling off the transparent tank top.

God, it was a wonderful, naked back.

In the time it took to think that, the back changed, becoming a sea of spiky, reddish blonde hair. She turned towards me. I realized I would need to change my underwear.

Now this is a werewolf, I realized, as I went through my mental checklist.

Vicious long fangs that thirsted for blood? Check.

Massive, rending, saber-like claws? Check.

Muscular, hairy body that exuded violence? Check.

Eyes that peered into one's soul and worked better than ex-lax?

A horror from Hell?

Check and double check.

Lon Chaney eat your fucking heart out.

I closed my eyes and waited for the pain. All I heard was silence, and all I felt was squishy. I slowly opened one eye. She was standing there, human again, with wrinkled nose.

She pointed down the hallway. "Second door on the left."

I nodded thankfully, waddling with dignity towards the bathroom.

"I'll refresh your drink," she promised.

ଔୠ

We spent the next two hours getting to know each other. I asked questions about her parents, she sniffed my ankle. I asked her favorite colors, she licked my arm.

Most questions she answered without hesitation, but there were some I could tell she was uncomfortable with. By the same token, there were certain areas she sniffed and licked that made me uncomfortable.

We were off to a great start, and I was becoming quite fond of her. This was not a monster. This was a wonderful woman who was sorely misunderstood.

After considerable discussion, she convinced me to give her a ride to the police station. (Okay, she asked one time.) There we could question her brother together.

She offered to bring a rubber hose and I found that both thoughtful and sweet. (Skank had borrowed mine.)

The ride itself was moderately uneventful. Sarah had the disconcerting problem of being ill at ease riding in a car.

She mentioned this could be resolved by sticking her head out the window. I agreed with this remedy when she informed me, "I'll barf if I don't."

The idea of Sarah up-chucking parts of blue uniform and badge from breakfast was not an endearing vision, so I cheerfully concurred.

"Hey, not a problem. Fresh air is good for you."

I was only startled once, when Sarah snarled and made a slashing grab for a Garfield toy, stuck with suction cups to the inside window of an

SUV. I managed to grab the waist band of her pants before she toppled out.

Sarah apologized to the white-faced driver, explaining it was reflex and recommended an alternative Scooby Doo figure to prevent future misunderstanding.

While I found the "head out the window" endearing, others found it a bit odd, as might be expected.

We laughed when one pedestrian was silly enough to kid her about it while stopped at a red light. No harm, however – the paramedics arrived at the scene quickly and life-flight was able to land in the intersection without problem.

Later, we stopped for ten minutes at a local park to give Sarah the opportunity to run around and calm down.

Long trips without a carrier would be out of the question. At the park, I found Sarah to be a girl of many talents. She is excellent at climbing trees, much to the chagrin of the cats that used to inhabit the park. She offered to share, I declined, as did the ducks that preferred bread crumbs. I was happy cat parts sink rapidly.

"Sarah," I told her when we arrived at the station. "I want you to be on your best behavior here. It's very important."

I looked deep into her eyes.

"This is a hall of justice. Of law enforcement. It runs on protocol and manners."

She didn't blink.

"Sarah, they have guns and will use them without provocation."

No blink.

"They carry mace."

There was the blink of understanding I was looking for.

"I promise," she said, coughing up a soggy lump of tabby fur. "I won't do anything to embarrass you, Mr. Rank." She smiled so innocently.

A new metal detector was in place. It hadn't been there that morning. It seems someone had stolen the entire machine the previous day and they were just getting around to replacing it.

Kids these days. They will steal anything. What can you do about it?

The current consensus was to shoot on sight.

We passed through the shiny new metal detector without incident. I had placed the car keys in the little Tupperware basket and left the brass knucks in the jockey box of the car. Nary a beep, blip or buzz heralded our passage.

The guard dog was a bit trickier. With all the terrorism in the world today, since 911, poochy had been pulled from working with the blind.

His new job was to sniff for "explosives."

Thankfully the pooch agreed I was non-flammable, but when he sniffed Sarah, she sniffed back.

Damn.

The Sergeant of the K-9 Corp was having limited success trying to persuade the German Shepard to come out from under the desk, where it was alternately whimpering and howling for his previous, sightless master.

Vlad was "human" when we arrived at his cell. He was a small man, early twenties, meek and unpretentious.

If I knew then what I know now.

He smiled and wiggled when he saw Sarah.

She smiled and waggled her finger at him in admonishment, "Bad Vlad!" she said, but there was pride in her voice. "Going hunting without the pack – and getting caught. Next thing you know you'll turn into a lone wolf."

"I'm sorry," he muttered contritely, but he didn't sound sincere.

"Now who exactly did you kill and eat? You should be careful. You know the vet has you on a strict diet."

"Taka Hunt," he answered softly.

Sarah gasped, reaching out to steady herself against the bars of the cell.

"Taka Hunt? You have to be shitting me. Taka Hunt the executive?" Her eyes narrowed. "Taka Hunt, living Master of the Undead?"

"One and the same."

"That's impossible," she snarled.

"No its not," he snarled back. "Furthermore, I didn't eat much of him, like some people I know who binge on anything that walks or purrs. So there!"

"We're finished here, little brother." Turning to me she said, "We need to talk." Over her shoulder she spoke to Vlad in a severe tone, "Vlad, I am disappointed. You are lying to me and I don't know why, but you are. Come here."

Vlad approached the bars. If he still had a tail, it would have been tucked between his legs. Reaching out, Sarah grasped the chemically impregnated, pink nylon flea collar between her thumb and finger. The sound when it snapped was loud and she let it fall to the floor, grinding it beneath the sole of her shoe.

"The next time I see you with a stupid flea collar, I will snap your neck and not the collar. Don't you have any pride? What would Papa think?"

Not waiting for a response she walked away.

"That's it?" I asked. "We came all the way down here for a thirty second conversation?"

Sarah stopped at the door to the lobby. "I learned everything I needed to know. He is innocent. There is no way he could have done it, even if he had the balls to hunt on his own."

"He's never aggressive?"

"I mean he's been neutered." She smiled sweetly. "He was the runt, remember? It's standard procedure with the packs." She frowned in thought. "Grandma had a better idea, but it's too late now."

A curious officer, who had been listening in, picked this time to interject, "Hey, lady. We got a confession from the dirty dog. He's…"

"…innocent until proven guilty," finished Sarah, who was holding the officer by his throat while his feet kicked midair.

I felt this might be an appropriate time to intervene.

"As an attorney," I said to the officer, "I recommend you blink your eyes twice if you are in agreement with this young lady, who also happens to be the defendant's sister."

His eyes blinked twice, before rolling up in his head. Stepping over the body, I asked Sarah, "How can you be so sure? Let us keep moving. People are starting to stare."

The growl was soft, but audible.

I held my hands up. "I mean, I believe you honey, but I need to convince a jury of twelve."

Oops. The word just kind of slipped out. A pet name. Common pet name, but a pet name anyway. Sarah's eyes widened and her pupils dilated, but that was the only response, other than a quick, random looking sniff.

"A couple reasons. The first is I know the scent of Taka Hunt. The smell was not on my brother.   Nor was the smell of the truth. Yes, he had some Undead smell on him, impossible to miss, but he slums with those creatures. Says they are his homies.

We all know Taka very well. Or knew him. There is no way Vlad could have attacked him, even if he wanted to."

When we reached the car I opened the door for her as she explained further. "We need to go to the body of Taka Hunt. There I will demonstrate and prove my point." She looked ill at the thought.

"Is there a problem with that?" I asked.

"Can't you just take my word on this one?"

"Sorry Hon," I told her. "I believe you, but a court of law discounts personal beliefs rather severely. They prefer eyewitness accounts, tangible objects, or paid informants. If you say, 'believe me,' they look to see if you're holding a jar of Vaseline. They are gun-shy of that particular phrase."

She looked so down; I thought I would try to cheer her up some. "It's getting on in the day. Would you care to stop somewhere and have a bite to eat?"

"Who do you have in mind?" she asked thoughtfully. "I love Italians. Chinese are okay also. Germans give me gas. You decide." She sneaked a peek at me and added, "Honey."

"I thought we might go low key and generic this time. The House of Ronald."

She smiled and laid her hand on my leg.

I sighed.

Our first date.

I attempted to explain fast food to Sarah while we drove. After we got her past the initial misconception that fast food consisted of people who wore running shoes, she was intrigued. (She admitted she didn't get out much socially.)

"I would like six Big Rons. One loaded, the special meal. The other five regular, hold the sauce, lettuce, cheese, pickle, onions...um...and the sesame seed bun. While you are at it, don't cook those five either."

The voice came back through the tinny speaker of the drive-thru without hesitation. "You want fries with those?"

I looked at Sarah, she shook her head. "Nope," I said. "That should ought a do it."

"Pull around to the first window, please. Your order comes to ten dollars and twenty five cents, plus tax."

Sarah turned out to be a perfect date. She was cheap; no expensive restaurants. She was courteous; she didn't make fun of my eating habits - quite the contrary, *she* licked *my* fingers clean.

Sarah was all smiles by the time we had finished, and I think she even wiggled once.

"Wow," I said. "You really wolfed that down."

She cocked her head and looked at me.

"I mean you seemed to enjoy it. You gulped it without chewing."

"Yes." She laughed. "It was wonderful. Pre-chewed. It didn't have any fur, or bone – and it didn't scream before I ate it."

She whispered confidentially, "When I want a quiet, sit down meal, it hurts my ears when it squalls and carries on until its half eaten. This meal was wonderful. Well, part of it was kind of tasteless, but it had a nice crunch.

Normally I don't get that unless I'm at mom's. The quiet part, that is. Crunchy comes if father cooks."

"I had a Smiley Meal," I explained. "You ate my toy."

"Is that bad?" she asked.

"Not at all. I already have two clowns. I'm holding out for the ring-master toy."

We held hands on the way to the morgue.

CHAPTER TWO
ଔTHE MORGUEଓ
ଔTHIS PLACE IS DEADଓ
ଔIIଓ

In your mind, picture a bad motel. Now imagine it with limited parking. Conjure up an image of it being made out of marble, with no swimming pool, Jacuzzi or ice machine. Remove the signs and windows.

That is what the morgue looked like.

"Stop here." Sarah demanded, while we were still a half a block from the entrance. I pulled hastily to the curb and killed the motor.

"What's the matter?" I asked.

Sarah pointed. In the afternoon sunlight, there was quite the crowd gathered in front of the structure. More, say, than you would see at a theater, opening day of a new Star Wars movie.

"Undead." She said simply.

"How can you tell from here?" I asked. I wondered if we were talking about the same thing. The only Undead I'd ever seen were in B movies.

The people surrounding the entrance weren't tap dancing, but they were all in an upright position.

"Well, from what I've been told – and please don't take offense," She patted my hand once more, "I can see about five times better than you can.

And my sense of smell is unimaginably better. Under the right conditions I can get a whiff from about one and three quarter miles. Given time, I could tell you everywhere you've been in this city in the past four months."

She kissed the hand she had been patting.

"Your hearing tops out about 20 kilo hertz. Mine around 80. It must be so hard for you, being restricted in all your senses."

She then pointed to the crowd.

"Those bastards smell dead. I got a whiff of them two miles back."

I thought of the hundred plus weather and my sweat soaked shirt. "I probably smell dead to you too," I said in embarrassment.

Sarah grinned and gave an obvious wiggle. I live for those wiggles.

"You smell wonderful. I am not sure why it is you non-changers insist on polluting your scent with chemicals. Sure, everything needs washed off once and a while, but you could just go out and run naked through a lawn sprinkler.

I love it. Vlad does too, but he rolls in cow shit afterwards."

She frowned.

"He's such an imbecile. Momma used to get so fed up she would toss him in the washing machine." She smiled again. "He used to howl during the spin cycle."

She giggled.

By now the undead had all turned and were facing us. I expected them to start lurching towards us, but they remained where they were.

"Are they dangerous?" I asked. "I mean like night of the living dead dangerous? They don't seem to have a lot of get up and go."

"Yes. They are slow, they are uncoordinated, but for god's sake…they are dead. What are you going to do to them? There are only about a hundred of them. I could probably dismantle them into parts that couldn't harm us, but god, they taste terrible. Kind of like a five day old diaper, from a kid that's really sick."

She looked at me sheepishly.

"Okay, so when I was a pup, I used to rummage around in the neighbors garbage cans. I outgrew that."

She shook her head and pointed at the crowd.

"I would have to eat a bunch of grass and puke my guts out for a week to get rid of the taste of these sleezeballs. Besides," she gave me a quick hug, "you aren't as fast as I am and you don't heal hardly at all. They might hurt you. My god, they might *turn* you. I couldn't bear that thought."

"So what do we do? Why are they here?" I was frustrated. "I wish the morgue had delivery."

Sarah opened the car door. "Come with me and stay right behind me. I am somewhat well known in certain circles. They might decide to let us pass. As to why they are here – I don't know. Their Master is dead. Maybe they are waiting to see if he returns as an undead. Maybe there was nothing on television and they decided to all gather at the morgue for fun and conversation."

I laughed. "Excellent. My love, I didn't know you had such a sense of humor."

"What do you mean?" she asked.

"Well, you know. Nothing on television, gathering at the morgue..."

"I'm lost," Sarah admitted. "Where do you go when there is nothing on television? I mean, the cemetery gets old fast."

She tucked me in behind her. "Never mind, I guess I have to learn to take a compliment. Just stay close."

Walking behind Sarah was delicious. I had never noticed how she walked before now. Her gait was smooth and flowing; almost a lope in slow motion. It wasn't just the legs that moved, her whole body swayed. As we got closer, the crowd parted like the Red Sea.

Except for three Undead.

"Evidently these three don't...uh...know you," I whispered. They stood staring at us, then their arms slowly raised and they made gurgling noises.

"No, they know me. It's you they don't know. They are hungry and their hunger outweighs what little common sense they have left."

"So, basically, they want to eat me?" I asked. I was close enough now that even I could smell them and their intentions concerned me more than a little.

"Just your brain. For some reason they only eat brains."

Sarah fluttered her hands and acted exasperated at the thought.

"Sure, they will gnaw on whatever part they can get a hold of, but they are very wasteful."

"Perhaps we can reason with them," I suggested, "or maybe just run like hell."

Sarah whooshed as she took the three steps forward, blurring like a bad photograph, laying one hand against the first zombie's chest and grabbing his wrist with her other hand. With only the slightest grunt and a look of revulsion, she ripped his arm off and started screaming in a shrill voice.

"Don't make me morph, you piece of shit. If I morph I will end up biting you and that will piss me off. You icky, nasty, filthy, slimy, un-fucking-dead lumps of cat turd..."

She repeated this dialogue with various styles, vocabulary, and tempo - all the time beating the creature before her into a pile of bloody jelly with the detached arm.

When the mound of splintered bones, muscles, and goop showed no sign of movement, she tossed the arm into the crowd and said, "Ca-ca. Oh, I hate even touching them. They are sooooo gross."

The other two Undead had drifted back into the gathering, demonstrating they did still possess some reasoning skills. I pulled the handkerchief from my pocket, spit on it and gently wiped her hand as clean as I could get it.

It was still aromatic, but at least I made the attempt.

"There. It's better now. I know how much it must bother you," I said.

Sarah snuggled up against my shoulder, flipping a piece of Undead confetti - part of an ear I think - from my lapel with the tip of her finger before bending and laying her head against me. "You are so sweet and thoughtful."

Inside the front door we were greeted by the secretary from hell. If it didn't say that on her nametag, then the printer got it wrong.

"May I help you?" From a five foot tall, white-haired grandmother type with horn-rimmed glasses.

Add in the fact she was wearing a cross-braced shoulder harness with two Colts, had a flask of holy water on her desk with sharp wooden stakes soaking in it, and a lapel pin stating, "I'll Be Back." (Small print under it, "You Won't.")

"Yes, ahem, I mean yes, we would like to have a viewing of Taka Hunt's body if at all possible and at your convenience." I smiled my 'business as usual smile.'

She returned it with an 'I've heard it before smile.' "Do you have an appointment?" She asked.

"No. I'm sorry. I didn't think to make one. I didn't figure Mr. Hunt's day planner was filled up at this point."

"What is the purpose of your visit?" She asked with a lemony puckering of her lips and tapping the toe of her combat boot on the slick tile floor.

"Excuse me?"

"Sonny, we get a lot of weirdo's and kooks in here."

She looked me up and down.

"They like to look at the dead, perform unnatural acts, try to resurrect them, and take souvenirs from the corpses. That is *strictly* against the morgue's policy."

She hesitated.

"Unless you sign a waiver and make a donation of fifty dollars or more to our fund." She pointed a gnarled finger to a battered coffee can with note scrawled in magic marker.

Morticians Have Needs Also…Give to the Needy.

"Then you would automatically become a sponsor. We ignore the habits of sponsors a little more than the common tourist."

Sarah stepped around me. "Hi, Emma." She gave a little wave of her fingers.

The secretary stopped. "Why Sarah, dear. Whatever are you doing here? Nothing on television today?"

The hag's smile blossomed to a true and happy grin. "Are you picking up..." she stared at me, "or considering dropping off?"

"No, Emma. That was an accident last time. They have Vlad in jail. They say – well Vlad said – that he was the one that killed Hunt."

"Well that's just ridiculous sweetie. I've know Vlad since he was just a pup, he doesn't have that killer instinct in him, sad to say." Her hands moved farther away from the butts of the big forty-fives, and she settled into her chair. Her eyes looked haunted.

I couldn't tell if the creaking and groaning came from the chair, or from her aged bones.

"Mr. Rank here is Vlad's attorney." Sarah smiled lovingly at me. "He needs proof positive that Vlad couldn't have done it. I brought him here to give him that proof."

She looked at the old woman piercingly, "He will be leaving with me."

The old woman looked at me like I was a new species of insect. "Well, dearie, I make no bones about liking even the undead over an attorney, but I don't have to sleep with him." She looked at Sarah over the top of her glasses. "Have you done the deed with this gentleman? Did you decide to...?"

"Emma!" Sarah blushed.

"It's okay sweetie. I was just asking. Good gossip is hard to come by, but you don't need to answer. Time will tell."

She hit a button under her desk and I heard a buzz. "Through the main door, down the corridor, door marked, 'road kill.' They found him in the ditch, down Highway Ten. No tire marks, but you have to classify them some how."

Emma moved from her desk. "I think it's time to disperse that crowd out front. They're starting to stink the place up." She looked hesitant.

From a file cabinet she pulled a couple objects that looked remarkably like fragmentation grenades or kumquats. "You two kids just run along and let an old lady get her chores done."

The corridor walls had been painted white, at some time in the past.

They were now a creamy ivory from age.

The floor was not spotless, but showed patches of mud. I hoped it was mud.

Sarah and I walked down the passageway, holding hands and bumping hips every once and a while, in time with our echoing footsteps.

"So, do you come here often?" I asked, half joking.

"Oh, it's like…you know…non-changers, NCs we call them − go to libraries, museums and places like that. We don't fit in well at those establishments.

I mean, we would like to, but half the people don't believe in us to start with, and the other half treats us like we are monsters or something. I do miss libraries."

She waved a hand at the surroundings. "Here people pretty much take us for granted and we are welcomed. Not with open arms, but we are accepted. Sometimes in life acceptance is all you can ask for."

The sadness was obvious in her voice. "NCs have domesticated almost every life form on the planet. They talk about saving and protecting just about every one of those species, except for mine." She looked up at me with accusation in her eyes. "Yet you eat damn near everything on the planet. Whether it is animal or vegetable. Sometimes you kill the creatures just for fun, without any intention of eating it, or needing to eat it."

We continued walking.

"We eat one species. Sorry it just happens to be yours.

Well, then there are cats…cats are like chocolate to me. Can't help it. Just a craving, but I do try to control it, so don't judge others by my flaw."

She looked up at me again.

"And for that I am a monster?"

I was speechless. "I'm sorry. I guess until this morning, I didn't believe either. I do understand. At least I think I do.

If it's any consolation, I hate cats. You can eat as many as you want and it won't bother me."

She squeezed my hand back.

"You know," I confided, "I like chocolates myself. I like them because I can poke my finger in them first, to see what's inside. Then if I like it I eat it. If not, I leave it for the next person. Isn't that terrible?"

Sarah laughed. "I understand. I do the same with cats."

ᗧᗤ

"Sarakasha. She has taken up with a non-changer."

"It is nothing to worry about. She will either tire of his company or consume him."

A hesitation. "No, Anastar. Nothing is ever so simple with her."

"Then challenge her and place your demands upon her."

Another hesitation. "I think not. I am well aware of her strengths and stubbornness - your sarcasm is not lost. A third option exists."

"And that is?"

"Remove the problem ourselves."

"You believe she would merely let that action slide? I recommend the pack let the matter evolve. Perhaps the problem will go away at the hands of the Undead. We still do not know what has happened in their infrastructure. Whatever was powerful enough to take out Hunt is more than powerful enough to snuff a simple mortal who meddles in its affairs."

"I am not sure. I smell danger. Something is not as it appears."

"We shall sleep on it."

"You mean we will ignore it."

"No, I mean we shall sleep on it. Remember, Vlad is still in jail."

"We should have put him to sleep."

"Hindsight, Padarsky my love, hindsight."

CR80

One dead body looks pretty much like another and Taka Hunt was no exception. A little better dressed than most corpses - but dead is dead - even for a past Master of the Undead.

The room was small, fifteen by twenty, with three elevated tables. Only one was occupied, and that by Taka.

The other two gleamed of stainless steel, unadorned by blood and body fluids. I approached the body in question and noted that Sarah did not. She remained by the entrance.

My curiosity was high. All day I had been imagining a face to go with this dreaded Master of the undead image people were giving me.

"Well, this sucks." I said.

"What?" asked Sarah from the door.

"How am I supposed to tell if the guy was dignified, ugly, handsome, or looked like my ex-wife. Something ate his damn face off. Just one poached eye staring at me and it isn't in the best of shape either."

I realized I was becoming a bit more callused about blood and gore. "I want my money back."

Sarah moved a step to get a better look. "You didn't pay anything to get in. You are still classified as tourist."

I grumbled some more. "I know - that was a figure of speech." I turned to her. "We came all the way down here, ran the gauntlet of undead, and you are going to stay over there? I thought you wanted to inspect the body."

"No, I wanted to prove to you that Vlad couldn't have done it. More precisely, *you* wanted me to prove it." The hair on her neck and arms was standing up.

Our first spat.

"I'm sorry, honey. I didn't mean to sound harsh."

"It's okay. I can smell that this whole thing has you upset also. Let's just get this done with." She covered her eyes with her hand.

"All right. Take Taka's clothes off."

"Excuse me?" I said. "Is this one of those things where I'm going to have to upgrade to sponsor and donate money to the needy when we leave?

I mean, I will try almost anything you ask, but I need some advance warning here."

"No, my dear. Just do as I request. If we do anything weird, it will be later, but business before pleasure, as you NCs say."

Undressing a corpse is not an enjoyable pastime. He wouldn't bend where he should and he was still leaking.

By the time I had gotten his jacket off, I realized a few hard facts.

Cause of death. A gaping hole in his chest. He was indeed a heartless bastard. I had no idea where it had gone, but it wasn't where it was supposed to be.

The face removal evidently occurred when his chest did the Grand Canyon imitation. Unless someone had visited before us and took a souvenir.

There were no bite marks on him. No teeth lacerations. It appeared that he was just ripped open and his face blasted off.

His clothing was antiquated, but very nice. Looked like theater wear from the 1700s, but it was heavy. The jacket ungodly heavy. The pants were of the same material while his shirt was, (what remained of it) silk. He did not wear underwear.

When I had a naked body on the table and a pile of sticky clothing on the floor, I called out to Sarah.

"Okay, that's that. Now what?"

"Now you take your clothes off."

"Oh, hell no. No, no, no." My heart was racing and my mind envisioned a hundred perverted and unnatural possibilities. Mentally I filed a half dozen for future reference and consideration.

"I only want you to put on his clothing."

"That's it?" I asked. "He was a big enough chap that his clothing would fit over mine."

"Well, I wanted to see you naked, too," she pouted.

"Business before pleasure," I replied, but I was secretly pleased - and hopeful. Two dull thuds resounded from somewhere beyond the walls.

Emma wasn't into kumquats, evidently.

Wearing the deceased clothes was not all that bad.

Sure, they stunk to high heavens of things that normally stay inside the body, and they weighed about twenty pounds, but when clean and pressed, I was sure they added a great degree of sophistication and elegance to the person wearing them. Good haberdashery had a tendency to do that and never went out of style.

I looked up to find Sarah crying.

"What's wrong honey?" I asked.

She sniffled. "Now, in order to convince you, I have to kill you. It's going to hurt sooooo much."

"*What*? Noooo, I'm a believer..."

When a heartbeat lasts an eternity, it has no meaning to say something happened in a heartbeat.

One moment she was standing there crying. The next there was an explosion of clothing, a flash of fur, claws, teeth and death in the air hurtling towards me.

No life flashed before me, just three truths. I was me, she was a werewolf, and I was going to die.

Period.

The fourth truth, and I took her at her word, it was going to hurt sooooo much.

The jaws opened, head turning sideways to grasp my throat. The arms reached out in midair to trap me.

The powerful flash of electric blue light blinded me.

What the hell?

A dancing image glowed red on my retinas and jumped in front of me everywhere I looked. A terrible odor of burned hair and flesh filled my nose.

Slowly I was able to see past the flash impressions once more. Sarah, still in wolf form, lay in the corner curled up in a fetal position.

The hair and flesh on the front of her still smoldered. The eyes the eyes above her muzzle looked at me in shock and pain. Slowly she reverted to human form.

The beautiful body I had envisioned for so long was scorched and blackened. I could not bear it.

She could kill me if she wanted, but I had to hold her in my arms and offer comfort. I stepped forward.

"No. Please. For god's sake don't come any closer." The words were slurred with pain and came in panting breaths.

"I don't understand." I blurted.

"The clothes. Take off the clothes," she whimpered.

Quickly I started stripping off my clothing. Emma came to the door, found me half-naked and Sarah curled up in the corner in a medium rare state.

"Oh, sorry kids. Didn't mean to interrupt. We take check, cash and major credit card, stop at the donation box to upgrade to sponsor," and was gone before I could explain.

Sarah's body felt hot, feverish, and her face was burned and cracked. I held her in my arms. Slowly she relaxed.

"The clothes," she whispered, her eyes clenched in pain. "Taka's clothes have silver threads woven throughout them. Vlad couldn't have done it.

You see what would happen if a werewolf tried to attack? Even if one of us were able to break through the army that protects him, there is no way for us to touch him.

The wars between werewolf and undead ended centuries ago, but Masters of the Undead never take chances. They always go clad in silver. Even at night their bed clothes are woven with that cursed metal.

I never could have hurt you if I wanted to. I knew that, but you needed your proof positive."

In a slightly petty voice she added, "I hope you're happy now."

I stroked her hair. "I'm so sorry. I believe you that Vlad didn't do it. I wish we could get him out, if only for a while to get to the bottom of this, but bail is set at two hundred and fifty thou. I don't have that kind of dough." I laughed involuntarily. "If I did, I would go the extra two fifty and get Crank out also. He could be useful for a change."

She whispered back. "You mean with money we can buy Vlad?"

"It's not like going to the pound and adopting him. It's called bail. You put up the money to prove you are honest and going to show up in court."

"So if you are rich, you are honest. If you are poor, you are dishonest?" she asked.

I nodded. "Yeah, that about covers how the legal system works."

"How strange. If I get lots of money, can we stop at the House of Ronald again too?"

"Of course. If you get the ring-master, I will trade you a Siamese for it."

"Deal. Kiss me and make me better."

CHAPTER THREE
ରGET OUT OF JAIL FREEଚ
ରCRANK - CON AN BARBARIANଚ
ରIIIଚ

"Okay, let me get this straight. You have enough money to spring me, if I can turn or convert *how* much gold into cash?" Crank spoke quickly, his eyes darting to every corner of the holding cell. No one was close; although there was a chance the conversation was being recorded. He was a tall, thin man who looked like a weasel.

Not meant as an insult to the weasel species.

When I told him the quantity of gold, he held up his hand, his other was no doubt behind him with fingers crossed. Crank is like that.

"Hold it, hold it. I make ya a deal. You don't ask where the money comes from and I won't ask where the gold comes from."

He looked insulted for a moment. "But it ain't right you been holdin' out on me. Me being a partner and all."

He thought for a minute. "How long do I have to convert it and what are you using it for?"

"Twenty four hours and it's to get a client out on bail."

He shook his head. "No can do, Kimo Sabe. It would take at least a week for the boys - I mean my contacts - to process that amount of bullion. There is another way and much less expensive I might add."

"Is it legal?" I asked.

"Depends on what country you are in." Crank hedged. "Let's just say, I can have yer boy sprung in four hours, he will be delivered to the steps of the jail house. After that you have eight hours to find him a place to stay. On the ninth hour, there will be some - we will call it controversy - over what his mailing address should be."

"How much controversy?"

"Do the words 'aiding, abetting,' and 'harboring' sound familiar?"

"We will do it," said Sarah. She appeared much better this morning, her skin having a bright pink tinge that looked like nothing more than a bad sunburn.

Sarah looked at Crank. "But do I have your word on this? It would be very disappointing to me if you reneged. You smell like a person who cannot be trusted."

Crank smirked. "Is yer girly friend for real?"

Sarah's hand flashed out and the bullet proof Plexiglas separating us and Crank developed a nasty crack across its width.

She sniffed. "He smells like he can be trusted now."

"Then we have a deal," I concluded.

C3∞

Most people's closets become catch alls for unused clothing, bowling balls, and boxes filled with do-dads we can't remember, let alone use.

Sarah's was different.

"Where did you get all this?" I asked in awe.

"Here and there," she said, "Gramps and grandma gave it to me. They didn't have room for it anymore. Vlad used to play with it out in the yard, but he never picked up after himself, so I just dumped it in here."

"Did gramps live in a place called Fort Knox?"

"Nope," Sarah said. "Little town in Massachusetts named after a cigarette, I think. Salem or something like that. They moved to the West Coast after a disagreement with the townsfolk in which great-granddad was the main attraction at a bar-b-cue."

She sat back down on the couch.

"Take what you need. I never use it, but you'd better hurry. I smell that man. That Crank. He's outside and he is getting scared." She frowned. "I am glad you don't smell like him."

"You aren't thinking of eating him are you? We gave our word."

Sarah grinned. "No. I wouldn't eat him, but I might bury him in the back yard. People like him make great fertilizer."

I thought of the lush flower beds that surrounded the house.

Taking a serving bowl that weighed over five pounds, I carried it to the back porch and set the golden treasure on the deck. Without looking around, I turned and went back in the house to join Sarah on the couch.

C3∞

The gray dungeon of the jail felt like a second home to Crank.

In a way it was.

Most of his time was spent talking to the inmates. Sometimes he was on opposite sides of the bars; sometimes they shared the same side.

"Dooley," he said, tapping a large uniformed cretin on the shoulder.

"Yeah?" The eyes focused on the insolent civilian that that was addressing him. "*You*. How did you get out here?" Hands reached for the night stick.

"No. Hold it big fella." Crank started backing away. "I made bail. You know, on the up and up. Legit."

"Really?" The blue behemoth asked. "You can do that?"

"Yes," Crank said, warming to his story. "You can do that. It's a great new legal concept, and I will explain it to you. In fact, you can get in at the ground floor of this novel new idea."

The cop looked suspicious.

"No, really," Crank reassured him. "This isn't a scam. I've turned over a new leaf. I found God. He told me to go forth and sin no more.

Hey! I finally picked the right voice in my head to listen to.

Not only isn't it going to cost you anything, but I am going to modify the ground rules a bit, so that you will benefit immediately, just to prove the point."

"How?"

"Well, normally I would have to go before a judge. Talk my head off for an hour, just for the chance to give the court some money. You know, the same court that pays your wages."

"Yeah."

"At that time, the judge will let me give him some money and in return he releases a prisoner of my choosing. Are you following me?"

The cop nodded.

"You work down here, working hard I might add, and every two weeks or so, the court gives you a little bit of money."

"Yes. My paycheck." The cop agreed.

"And I bet the government takes what they call taxes out of it. A lot of taxes."

The cop scratched his head. "Um…yeah. I never understood that."

"Me either, Dooley. That's why I quit paying them, but you know, this is America, my friend," Crank said, clapping the officer on the arm.

"And in America, we have the best business systems in the world, and with those systems come what I fondly refer to as, 'loopholes.' Repeat that word after me, Dooley - *loopholes*."

"Loopholes." The cop repeated dutifully.

"What we are going to do is streamline the process and cut out the middle man, Dooley."

"What do you mean?"

"If I give the judge a shit pot full of money do you ever see it?" asked Crank.

"Um…no."

"Do you ever get to touch it?"

"Um…no."

"Do you ever get to spend it, Dooley my man?

"Um…no, but my paycheck is taken by the wife and I do get ten dollars a week for an allowance.

That doesn't cover booze and smokes.

I shake the prisoners down for that," he said proudly. "Is that like one of them loopholes?"

Crank nodded in agreement.

"Yes. The administrative costs of handling that money I give the court are tremendous. It goes through accountants, clerks of the court, other jailors, well you get the idea." He pulled the cop close and whispered, "And just between you and me, I think some people are dishonest and even - well I hate to use the word - *steal* some of it."

"No!" Dooley said horrified.

"That's just my belief, Dooley. I can't prove it, but it uses up damn near all of that shit pot full of money I give to the judge. I want to change that.

Wouldn't you like to get a little extra in life? Own a little piece of the local loophole?"

The guard thought a moment. "Yeah, but dey warned us about that. They said if we took money it was called a bride."

"You mean bribe, but I understand. I would not insult your integrity. Money does not have to be involved. Money can be taxed. You are a smart fellow indeed. Let me tell you about what we, in the legal community, call 'perks.' Dey is a whole lot like loopholes, only bettah." Crank pulled him to the side.

"What type of car do you drive?"

og⁊ဆာ

"I don't know, Sarah." I said. "Crank just said for us to meet him in front of the cop shop, and we could collect Vlad."

"Why did I have to smear mud all over the license plates? Is that like a ritual?" She asked. It was hot in the car and she was starting to pant.

I liked that about her.

She never broke a sweat, just panted in a cute little way with that pink tongue going in and out, in and out…

"With Crank it is. He recommended removing them completely, plus filing the VIN number off the engine block. That, I believe, is over-kill."

I thought about it.

"Or maybe not. Crank is very savvy about these things. He says his whole family is, and that he comes from a large family. Very tight knit. All his relatives are named Don something."

"I smell him," said Sarah.

"Crank? You smell Crank?" I found myself sniffing the air. Sarah's habits were contagious and I was even starting to imagine that I smelled new things.

"No. Vlad. There he is."

The revolving door had spewed out two persons. One was a massive figure who was leading a second, and by comparison tiny, figure down the steps.

The small figure flinched under the grip of the jailor. Sarah growled and her hand went to the door release.

"No, honey. Please don't. We have to see how this goes down." I pleaded.

"He's hurting Vlad. That's my job."

When they were halfway down the steps, I noticed a whistling rumble coming from the street behind us.

In a flash of red, a shiny Ferrari whipped by us, slammed on the breaks – its tires smoking – and slid neatly into the parking spot at the bottom of the steps.

Crank jumped from the driver's seat and made a beeline up the steps. He tossed the Ferrari's keys to the man holding Vlad, grabbed Vlad's hand and pulled him in a half drag, half sprint towards our car.

Opening the door he barked, "Go. For all that is holy, go."

"Where?" I asked.

"Straight ahead. Step on it, it's the slanty pedal on the right. About three blocks I will tell ya what to do then."

I did as directed, ignoring Crank's pleading to run the red light. In three blocks he instructed me to pull over.

"Okay," he said breathlessly. "Everybody into the white van."

"But if we leave the car in this neighborhood it will be stolen." I complained.

"God I hope so. That would give us plausible deniability."

We hopped into the white van that was conveniently equipped with a driver.

"Honey, why is the driver wearing a nylon stocking over his head?" Sarah asked.

Crank answered for me. "He's uh...bashful."

Sarah's eyes darkened and she sniffed the air. "You are lying," she said flatly.

"Okay," Crank admitted. "How's this. He doesn't want us to know who he is or he would have to kill us all."

Sarah's face lit up with a smile. "Oh, okay. Why didn't you just say so?"

"You okay with that?" Crank asked incredulously.

"Of course," Sarah said, showing her fabulous dimples.

"Sarah," I asked in a whisper. "If by some chance the gentleman decided to do that anyway - do you think he would succeed?"

Sarah whispered back, "You have to be joking."

In a louder voice, she said, "Vlad. So nice to see you again little brother." She stuck her nose in his ear and sniffed. "We need to have a long long talk."

She slapped him on the back of the head.

"Can you get youse friends to pull their heads back in?" Asked Crank.

Sarah and Vlad both growled at the same time.

"Or not," Crank finished.

Three hours of driving and two vehicles later, we were unceremoniously dropped off alongside the road, about a mile from my apartment. Near where the Master of the Undead was found.

Coincidence, I am sure.

Before Crank drove off with the teenage driver in the Volkswagen that was our final transportation, he pulled Sarah aside.

"Okey dokey, miss. I have delivered unto you yer brother. As we agreed. I have retained, as my fee, the remainder of the money from the little object you parted with.

I might use it to relocate when this is all over. Somewhere far away. Somewhere that doesn't extradite."

He looked at her intensely. "Are we good with this?"

Sarah stared back just as intensely. "You are being exceptionally straight forward on this, Mr. Crank. I am 'good' with this."

As he pulled his head back in the window, Sarah asked, "But what is the one thing you are forgetting to tell me? Something has you scared, and it isn't me."

Crank kept his eyes straight ahead, ignoring the sweat rolling into them. "I had a visit from a friend of yours. He suggested I not become involved. I have fulfilled my obligations, but I will entertain no further involvement.

A Mr. Padarsky sends his regards to you." With that, the car sped off.

CHAPTER FOUR
ଔAN EVENING AT HOMEଞ
ଔ~~NO~~ PETTING ALLOWEDଞ
ଔIVଞ

Dogwood Estates. The apartment complex in which I live is called that, but not very often.

Normally the tenants change the name to suit their mood, as normally it has the word 'slum,' 'project,' or 'dive' associated with its local name. A quiet little community of misfits, psychos and drug dealers. A place to call home.

We were greeted at the locked entrance by the property manager, Mr. Brungfoal.

"Good evening, Mr. Bung Hole," I waved enthusiastically.

"No, you know better. Name Brungfoal. What you want?"

I looked at him and I looked at the gate. "Well, I live here. I rather wished to go home and relax, after checking for major vandalism and break-in."

Sarah voiced a deep throated growl at him. He stared at her. I realized she was an instinctively good judge of character.

"You have guests. You know better. No extra people living in apartment."

I slumped against the gate which was still locked.

"Look Brungy. They are guests, visitors, or friends, pick your own term. They are not going to be living here. They are not tenants"

"You know better. No extra people living here."

Vlad even started to growl.

Sarah was visibly upset now. She wanted to get out of the open. Something that Crank had said to her had her worried.

"What if I told you I was a werewolf?" She asked him menacingly.

He turned to me. "No pets. You have pet, must pay pet deposit. No deposit, no pet."

Vlad handed him a card. He peered at it before handing it back and saying, "Ah, sorry. You enjoy your stay." He punched a code into the display on the gate and it swung open. He held it for us

As we walked, I asked Vlad, "What the hell was that you gave him?"

"My business card. I work for the city as a health inspector. I only check those little fans they have above grills in restaurants, but it doesn't say that on the card," he explained.

"You have a job?" I asked.

"Of course," he said defensively. "We aren't bums. You have to have at least an appearance of normalcy."

He pointed to Sarah. "Even my sister used to have a job. She blew it though."

"What do you mean?" I asked.

"She was a librarian, but they fired her."

I turned to Sarah who blushed. "I told them to be quiet. I told them they were disturbing others. They just wouldn't listen."

Vlad elaborated. "They didn't prosecute. They were too afraid. It's a shame the surgeons couldn't reattach the tongues." He leaned closer and said, "They were missing one. I betcha she ate it."

Sarah slapped him across the back of his head.

"Stop that, it hurts," he whined.

I opened the door and motioned them in. They entered and just stood.

"It's okay. Make yourselves at home. I'll see if I can scare up a stray cat."

Vlad turned to Sarah. "He's joking right? You really haven't got him fetching you cats now, have you?"

Vlad is quick himself. He easily ducked Sarah's swat.

"No, Vlad. He's joking." She turned to me and the frown turned to a smile. "It's nice here, it smells like you."

"Oh, yeah. Hey, sorry about that." I picked up the dirty socks and threw them in the direction of the bathroom.

We sat there, no one speaking, and this time it wasn't a comfortable silence.

"Well," I said, trying to break the ice, "we have so much to discuss. Would anyone like to start out?

How about you Vlad? This weather has been something else. Have you been coping with the heat?

Any idea who really killed the Master of the Undead?"

All I got was a defiant glare.

I am glad I didn't have new furniture. The coffee table shattered when Sarah picked Vlad up and body slammed him down on it.

I revised my assessment of how fast Vlad was. He couldn't hold a candle to Sarah when the chips were down.

"You will not look at him like that," she snarled in a voice promising impending doom. "You will answer him when he asks you a question. You don't want to talk, I can help you. Your tongue might grow back, but I can keep pulling it out."

She turned her face to me, "It's hard after they are neutered. No place to kick them that really has an effect. One has to improvise."

I looked at Vlad. "Would she really pull your tongue out?

He grimaced. "Hey, it's her specialty. Remember the library? Two days, four hours to grow back. Another week before you can talk right and things taste funny for a month," he offered.

He turned back to her.

"I hope the cats in this neighborhood have distemper."

"Settle down all. It's been a rough day and I think we'd better get some rest. If we continue on this way - well, we're just fighting ourselves." I tried one last question. "Sarah. Crank said something to you that got you upset. Can you tell me what it was?"

She burst into tears. Vlad rolled away from her and watched her like she had rabies.

He blurted, "Wow. That's a new one. I never saw that before." He put his hand out towards me in warning. "It might be a trick."

Sarah ran instinctively towards my bedroom, slamming the door behind her.

Vlad was hot on her tail and pulled up short, against the door, singing merrily, "Sarah has a boy friend - Sarah has a boy friend - Sarah has *ARGHHHHHH*…"

The hand punched through the door and grabbed him by the throat. It pulled violently, smashing his head against what remained of the door a half dozen times.

It then released him and he slithered to the floor in a heap.

He coughed a few times, spitting something out, and then rolled facing me. "She's always been a little sensitive to kidding." He grinned a grin that was missing some white. "She likes you."

I stared at him without blinking. "I like her." I stretched. "Vlad, I will tell you this one time. I like her a lot. If you give her a bad time again, I will hurt you."

Not quite a sneer, he replied. "You. A NC, going to hurt me? Hey, I appreciate you helping me, but honestly man, you don't put the shakes in me, dude."

I smiled sadly. "I see." I turned for the kitchen. "Excuse me a moment."

In the kitchen I had to rummage around. I knew it was there somewhere. I had picked it up at the second hand store years ago. Not in the forks, not in the knives...ah, it was mixed up with the spoons. I palmed it and went back to the front room.

When I got there, I held it up for his inspection, and then started towards him.

"What? Like you're going to poke me with a pickle fork? That's pathetic man."

I kept advancing. The fork became hotter in my hand. Two steps away, his eyes got big.

"Whoa dude. What the fuck. That's silver." He backpedaled.

"You don't know what you're doing man."

"Oh, yes. Yes I do. I saw a graphic demonstration. Here's how the program works. Sure, you can morph and take it away from me. Your are going to get hurt in the process, but you can no doubt kill me. What happens then?"

A scary hairy arm ending in a hand with massive claws poked through the hole in the door and flipped Vlad the bird. Sarah had been listening.

"That's right Vlad. You would be fucked." I agreed. "I am not sure your sister could kill you, or if she would..."

Hoarse, maniacal laughter came from the bedroom.

"...but I have a sneaking feeling that it is a possibility, or she might come up with something worse."

I lowered the fork.

"The thing is, I won't let you do this to her. I may just be an NC, but you will treat her with respect, or you will have to answer to me."

Vlad sat on the couch with his hands folded in his lap. "Done deal, man. I'm like sorry."

I walked to the bedroom door. "Sarah? It's okay dear. Why don't you come out now?"

The door opened and she flung her arms around me in a hug that left me breathless. Possible rib fractures as well. In my ear, she whispered with sweet breath, "The pickle fork was fantastic. You might try a rolled up newspaper as well. Scares the shit out of him."

"Really?" I asked.

"Yes. I had to quit using it for punishment, Vlad started eating the paper boys in self defense. They quit delivering after the second kid disappeared, told me to read the paper online."

She sighed.

"Grandma wanted to put him in a gunny sack with rocks at the lake, but mom wouldn't let her."

I was worried about the next question, but I asked it anyway. "Is your mom - you know - is your mom still alive? Your dad?"

Sarah laughed with pained eyes. "Of course. I will take you to meet them soon. You aren't quite...ready yet. Lupine families are not exactly like NC families. There are different etiquettes involved."

"Well, whatever and whenever you think I'm ready. I look forward to meeting Mr. and Mrs. Lupes."

The eyes grew more haunted. "We don't go by family names. The names change with every generation. Clan names stay the same. Their name is...Padarsky. Padarsky of the Clan Black Forest." She smiled a faint smile. "Vlad and I are Lupes of the Clan Black Forest."

She gave me a kiss on the cheek, thought about it, then laid a good one on my lips.

"It's bedtime now. Maybe all will be better in the morning."

"Okay," I said. "Good night Sarah. Sarah?"

"What my dear?"

"Nothing." I said.

She sniffed and the sadness washed over her.

"You are lying to me. It is not nothing."

I felt the blood rush to my face. "No. It's really not important."

She sniffed again and a tear formed in her left eye. "You are doing it again."

I turned to Vlad. "Would you mind stepping outside for a moment?"

"Why dude?"

I picked up the Sunday edition of the Daily Ledger.

"I'm outta here," he said, followed by the front door slamming.

"This isn't the way I wanted to do this," I confessed. "It doesn't have style or class."

"Just say it. Anything is better than a lie," she said.

"I want to sleep with you." There. I had blurted it and it couldn't be retracted.

"OH!" Sarah smiled graciously. "I didn't know you were cold. You don't need to be embarrassed or bashful about that." She headed towards the bedroom. "Come on, we can snuggle until you get warm."

Sarah lay on the bed and I sat on its edge. She looked at me quizzically.

"This isn't going to work," I told her.

"Sure it will. You lay down, I flop myself over you, my body heat is greater than yours anyway, you will be toasty in no time."

"That's not exactly what I had in mind. I was thinking a little more...intimate."

You could see the lights come on in her head, and her eyes got big. Her mouth opened in a little "O" and she sat straight up next to me. She grabbed my hand.

"Well," she said slowly. "That would solve a lot of problems."

"Say what?" I asked.

"I am going to ask you some questions. Please answer them truthfully." She nestled next to me and set her nose in the hollow of my throat.

"Do you realize what a big step and commitment this is?"

"Yes," I replied as she inhaled deeply.

"Do you realize if people find out, you will be shunned by NCs? They might even try to hunt you down and kill you?"

"Well, yes. I can handle that, but you might be blowing it out of proportion." Her sniffing was tickling me.

"You realize you will be subjected to the scrutiny of the clans, and you will *have* to meet my mother and father?" she continued.

"Yes."

"Do you promise not to hurt Vlad or kill him, no matter how much he deserves it?" She raised her eyes to mine before sniffing and said, "You can lie about this one, I won't mind."

"No. I promise. I won't hurt him. I might go through a helluva lot of newspapers, but I won't hurt him." I said solemnly.

She moved back. "Okay then."

"Aren't you going to ask me if I love you?" I asked.

"Um...I am not sure how that...well, no, I don't need to ask. I know you do."

I pushed on. "Aren't you going to tell me you love me?"

"I love you? Yes, I love you. We can talk more about that in a month or two. We'll see if you still love me afterwards. Maybe you won't like the way I smell." She pulled me to her.

ࡓࠞ

I awoke in the morning to a knock on the door. Opening it, I found Brungfoal standing over Vlad, who was curled up on the mat, blinking sleepily.

"He sleep on mat all night." Brungfoal said.

"Oh, yes. I forgot to give him permission to come in." I said.

"He stay there, no permission?"

"Yes." I replied.

"Remarkable." Brungfoal said with respect in his voice. "Have nice day."

"Vlad, come on in. We have a lot to do today."

Breakfast was difficult. The two of them were not particularly interested in sugar frosted flakes, but they contented themselves by sharing bites off a three pound chub of frozen hamburger.

In the middle of our little breakfast, Vlad leaned over to grab the salt shaker. He stopped in mid reach and froze like a pointer who has found a pheasant.

Slowly he turned to Sarah and sniffed again.

"You didn't. Oh, Christ. You didn't."

"Didn't what, Vlad?"

Vlad stared at her in horror. "You did."

Sarah wiped her lips with a napkin and smiled. "It was his idea. He asked for it."

"But did he..." Vlad started.

"Yes, I made sure of it. I asked him first."

"And he..."

"Absolutely," Sarah said. "I told you, it was his idea."

"Then..."

"You damned well better believe it," Sarah finished.

"Am I missing something here?" I asked.

Vlad turned to me quickly. "No sir. I'm sorry sir, if I was speaking out of turn."

The puzzle pieces just didn't fit, so I did the only thing I could. I shrugged off my confusion. "Don't worry about it, Vlad. It's a free country. Talk when you please."

"Yes, sir." He said meekly.

ࡓ367ࠞ

CHAPTER FIVE
ෆOFFICE CALLෂ
ෆFATHER KNOWS BEASTෂ
ෆVෂ

No way around it. I wasn't hoofing it to the office and a taxi seemed logical.

I sat in front with the driver. Vlad and Sarah sat in the back, both hanging out the windows.

I turned to the driver, "Look, don't ask and don't comment on it. If you just ignore them there is an extra twenty in it for you."

"Ignore who?" he asked. I peeled two tens out of my wallet.

"Good man," I told him.

Three blocks from Broadway the trouble started. I had turned to make sure Vlad's tongue wasn't hanging out and that he hadn't slipped and fallen into traffic.

He was still there, wind blowing his hair around, and staring steadily at the police cruiser that was keeping pace alongside us. The cop in the passenger seat was holding up a photograph; looking from it to the taxi and back again.

He motioned to our driver and yelled, "Pull over."

The driver talked to me from the side of his mouth. "For ten bucks more, I don't speak English."

I scrounged two more fives.

"Lo siento. Me no hablo englash."

"I said, pull over."

"Quein es?"

The cruiser pulled behind us and the blue lights came on. "Sorry," the driver said, "universal language there. I can't ignore it."

"Any chance you can out run them?" I asked hopefully.

"I don't know. How fast do radio waves travel?"

"I get your point," I said. "It was just a thought."

Sarah had reached out and grabbed Vlad by the back of his shirt, cramming him down on the floorboards. He didn't fit well, but with some violent reconfiguration on Sarah's part, he fit into a much smaller space than I thought possible.

His screams couldn't be heard over the siren that was now blaring.

"Is he okay?" the driver asked as he pulled to the curb.

"Yeah. They are brother and sister." I explained.

The driver looked at Sarah who had her feet on top of Vlad, holding him down.

"He looked at me, then he got on my side of the seat," she said righteously.

The driver looked back at me. "Yep. My sister used to do the same thing to me. My kids are going through that stage now."

"What happens now?" Sarah asked.

"Hell. They have a picture of him. He matches the picture and description. They will verify it when he gets out and he goes back to jail. We probably go with him."

"I don't suppose you want to pay me before you talk to the police do you?" the driver asked. "I can even recommend a good attorney."

"I am a good attorney."

We got out of the car and awaited our fate. The driver stood off to the side, hands in his pocket enjoying the show.

He should, I paid for his admission.

When the police drew near, I stepped forward and stopped them.

"Good morning officers. I happen to be an attorney. I would like to first say...," they brushed me aside and slapped cuffs on the driver.

"Thought you could get away with it, didn't you?" The arresting officer asked, elbowing him in the kidneys.

From his front, the other officer exclaimed, "Hey! Attacking my night stick with your nose. That's assault you know. We will just put it on your tab."

"I don't understand officer," Vlad spoke in a daze.

"It's okay son," the one officer said. "A couple weeks ago a very close friend of the District Attorney was murdered. Viciously strangled. We caught the culprit who did it. Regretfully he committed suicide in jail..."

The other cop added, "...stuck a garden hose down his throat and drowned himself."

The first cop nodded. "But before he expired..."

"We resuscitated him three times...," supplied the second.

"…he implicated this man." He held the photo up. It showed a man and a woman engaged in lustful activity.

"But that isn't him in the picture," noted Vlad.

"It isn't?" marveled the first cop. "You know, now that he mentions it, that isn't the same guy. I wonder…"

"It's obvious," chimed the second cop, "this must be the guy who was holding the camera. He isn't in the picture, so he must be the photographer."

"Deductive reasoning." I grabbed the officer's hand and shook it. "It is indeed an honor and I feel safer knowing men of your caliber are out here protecting us."

"Hey, our pleasure. After all, we're here to," he turned and read the lettering on the side of the cruiser. His lips moved silently while he was doing so, then he finished, "to protect and serve. Yes sir, to protect and serve."

"Thank you officers. Now all we have to do is find another taxi."

"Why?" The officer asked. "This one still has the keys in it. Take it. This asshole won't be needing it again."

"But remember," warned the other. "Buckle up and drive safe out there."

ᴄꙅᴂ

Ever see a cat frizz up for no apparent reason, run berserk around the room, knocking over lamps and running into walls?

From the time I hit the main door to the shabby, but depraved building that housed our office, Sarah and Vlad performed a wonderful imitation.

"What in the hell is wrong?" I demanded.

They both spoke at once.

"Nothing…"

"We really don't need to go to the office…"

"I'm sure Vlad would feel more comfortable somewhere…"

"Are you sure you didn't leave the water running at your…"

Their eyes darted every way, it looked like both were in panic attacks and ready to jump out the window.

By the time we had climbed the stairs to the third floor which housed my home away from home they had their arms around each other and were shaking.

"It's a hundred and five in here. You normally can't stand to be in the same room with each other.

Please, just tell me what's wrong." I pleaded.

I was willing to accept the fact that Vlad might be spooked over nothing, but Sarah was a different story. I didn't think much of anything could put the fear into her.

As I reached for the door knob to the office, the hair on my arm stood up and I could...yes...I could smell something.

It was strange.

Nothing that should make my skin crawl. The door knob turned, it was unlocked and this fact didn't bother me that much. Skank would lock the door when he was present, but when he left he often did not bother to secure it.

Everything we had in the office came from the dumpster to start with, so Skank didn't figure anyone would go to extreme measures such as hauling it down three flights of stairs. I was in agreement.

I pushed the door open without entering.

He sat in the open window, his back to the abyss.

Big.

Not just physically, but in presence also. Tight, trim, wearing blue jeans and a polo shirt. Hair close cropped in what we used to call a flat-top. Silvered aviator sunglasses hid his eyes.

He smiled.

Same dental work as Sarah.

"Hello, Sarakasha," he said.

Sarah leaned around the door frame, smiled weakly and said, "Hello, Papa." She turned for a second.

"Don't bother," he said, waving us into the office. "Vlad cut and ran fifteen seconds ago when your...," he looked at me, "...friend reached for the door knob."

He stood and walked – hell he just appeared – in front of me and leaned down. He got a quizzical look on his face and then I swear...he sniffed my hair.

"Oh, Sarakasha, this just keeps getting better and better."

The phone rang and we all jumped. All except for 'him.' He smiled again and said, "It's for me."

He answered it.

"Yes, dear? No, no...they are here...well, the asshole beat feet, but we expected that. No, I'm sorry. Vlad beat feet...is that better? I know...I'm sorry I called the little asshole an asshole." He listened for a while.

He looked impatient and sighed. "No...no...no, I can't do that. Yes...yes...yes, dear I *know* that was what we talked about. No...no I can't explain right now."

He rolled his eyes.

"You remember when you said just sleep on it? Yeah? Right. Well, things got worse. How much worse? Things couldn't get any worse." He listened for more than a minute. "Oh, crap. I was wrong then. I guess they can get worse." He hung up the phone.

Is something wrong, Papa?" asked Sarah in concern.

"You could say that," he answered. "If you would, please, go try and fetch your brother back. I know when last he and I met I promised to draw and quarter him, but, please reassure him that will not happen.

Inform him I have changed my mind. To be precise, your mother changed my mind. I need some time to speak with your...friend here.

I would ask you to step outside, but with your hearing, you'd hear every word anyway."

Sarah meekly walked to the door, looking back once, but not speaking and exited. That left just us men folk left to talk business. The silence grew.

"I'm sorry," he said. "I apologize for barging in like this. Please. Have a chair, we have so much to discuss." He did not look like a man who apologized very often.

I flopped down in my chair while he started pacing, thought better of it, and eased himself down in Skank's chair with only a small expression of distaste.

I was impressed; you couldn't pay me to sit at Skank's desk – I try to avoid biological and toxic waste dumps.

The silence returned. He had offered the first olive branch; I guess I should toss out the second.

"Would you care for a drink?" I offered.

His ears perked up. "You have booze?" he asked.

"Um...yes. I believe I have something here that is essentially drinkable."

"Thank god." He sighed. "If you are going to be hanging around my daughter – as it appears you already are – you might want to consider laying in a good supply."

He removed the sunglasses and I felt a little less like being under a microscope.

Looking in the file cabinet – under "B" for blotto, if you must know – I dug out an almost full bottle of decent Scotch.

It was safe in the files because Skank and Rank would never think of performing paperwork, let alone filing it. Two moderately clean coffee cups resided with the bottle.

"Say when," I told him. When turned out to be on the verge of overflowing. I decided this person could not be all bad and poured myself an equivalent drink.

"It's a common story, you've probably heard it a hundred times," he started. I had my doubts I had ever heard this version, but… "Sarah and Vlad had decided they had enough of living at home.

You know, rules, regulations, code of the pack, that sort of thing. They wanted to be 'on their own.'"

He drained half the cup.

I did likewise.

He coughed. "This is good shit. Where was I? Oh, yes. On their own. I told their mother that it wasn't a good idea. I told her they weren't ready. That they wouldn't fit into NC society quite yet.

Maybe another fifty years and it wouldn't be a problem. But no…she told me I was over-reacting. To just give them a chance."

He drained the rest and I refilled it.

"I gave them a chance. So now…we have Vlad accused of killing the Master of the Undead.

We have Sarah taking you to bed without asking permission from her parents, or that of the pack.

We have the involvement of NC law enforcement." He waved the last off as negligible.

I felt obliged to respond to at least part of it. "Well, the part about Sarah and myself. Yes, that's true. But I love her. I don't know how mixed romances are viewed in the pack, as you call yourselves, or if romantic interludes are frowned upon between NCs and werewolves, but…"

He held up a hand. "One moment." He chugged another half a cup. "I think we are on different pages here." He sat the cup down and stared at me. It was not a comfortable thing.

"Tell me all you know about werewolves."

"Well," I started. "I know you have a real problem with silver - it can do serious damage; I know you are incredibly strong, can hear, smell and see far better than us NCs; and, I have seen Sarah change."

"Oh." He said, shaking his head. "You say 'far better than *us* NCs. Um…yeah."

He looked back at me.

"So, tell me. How is it one becomes a werewolf? In your own words as you understand it."

I smiled. "I suppose the obvious. You could have baby werewolves. Uh, puppies? I hope that isn't a politically incorrect term.

I imagine the traditional method is also possible. To be bitten by a werewolf, but not killed."

He wasn't smiling now; in fact he was quite pale.

"As for sleeping with Sarah, it was mutual. I love her and I am sure she loves me. If she didn't then she wouldn't have even entertained the idea."

He smiled ruefully and slowly regained some color. "No. You are correct there. She is very fond of you. Love? Yes, I suppose so. For her to have done what she did without permission, yes, she must love you and fear for your safety very much.

As I see it, we have two problems. You and Sarah are one. That, I suppose, will resolve itself. You will…some day…um…okay. It will resolve itself.

When it does, you come to me and we get shit faced. We will both need it.

The other problem is this… we have some people who are now posing a threat to Vlad. My idea was that *that* also would resolve itself, but the wifey doesn't like that resolution.

Out there in the darkness of the world there are a group of people called necromancers. They live, love, eat, sleep and drink of the dead. Think of them as politicians and the undead as voters. All of them want to be at the top of the heap.

Many of them, for some asinine reason, believe that Vlad was responsible for Hunt's death. Now, as the voting system isn't quite as refined as your political system, but a lot easier and doesn't tie up public television as much, they view Vlad as the new Master of the Undead."

I laughed. "That's absurd. Sarah pretty much proved to me that it would be impossible for him to have even gotten near Taka Hunt."

He laughed, but it was a grim laugh. "I know. Doesn't matter. They are convinced he did it. They do not like the idea of looking up to Vlad – can you blame them?

No, this is a mix and match from hell. A werewolf as Master of the Undead. Unheard of. Unthinkable. Impossible.

My suggestion was let them bump Vlad off, and unravel their own problems. I loved that idea, but it was voted down at the local level.

The wife, you know.

There lies the crux of the matter. Vlad is a member of the Black Forest Clan. As a member we are sworn to protect him. It's not that all the Clan Black Forest are warmhearted to Vlad, but a lot of them are spoiling for a fight with the undead.

It's been a couple centuries since they have been able to hunt as a global unit.

The kids are back. We'll discuss this more tonight."

CHAPTER SIX
GATHERING OF THE CLAN
PARTY HARDY BOYS
VI

"I don't know. I don't think it's such a bad idea," I said, cramming some Samsonite luggage into the back of the car. Sarah and Vlad looked at me in horror. "We both agreed I would have to meet the family some time."

Vlad smirked. "Oh, this is going to be depressing."

"I don't think so," I countered. "You dad seemed to be a pretty nice guy."

Vlad was dumbfounded. "You liked my father?"

"Yes, he seemed very affable."

Vlad turned to Sarah. "He liked our father."

"I knew he would," said Sarah.

"You did not. You were just as scared as I was. And now, we are all going back to meet up with the Clan.

That doesn't bother you at all?" He addressed the last to me.

"No, it's quite an honor," I said. "I doubt many NCs have ever gotten to attend a meeting such as this."

Sarah cocked her head at me, Vlad just blurted, "No, no NC has ever attended a summit, unless they were invited to dinner as the main course."

He turned to Sarah. "Sister, you had better clarify." He leaned and whispered something in Sarah's ear. She laughed and said, "No, of course he knows. Obviously he isn't going with any possibility of being a hors d'oeuvre. He is new, but he will be welcomed. Papa wouldn't have suggested it if there were any danger."

"We are speaking of the same person aren't we?" asked Vlad. "You know, our father. Papa. The Grim Reaper of the Mountain?"

"No one's called him that for years," Sarah said.

"Of course they haven't. He ate the ones that did."

"There is no proof of that." Sarah scolded. "Besides, it was just an ugly rumor about that village."

"I don't know. If ya added up just the feet that were found, divide by two, it would come out to 60 people. You know father doesn't eat feet. He's afraid of getting athlete's tongue. Mom wouldn't talk to him for a month after the news of the village got out."

"No one could eat that many people."

The ride to the mountains would have been enjoyable, but it had its downside. Vlad and Sarah were lucky. They had their heads stuck out the window. I envied them, because it was obvious that the car's exhaust was in need of repair. The carbon monoxide fumes were atrocious.

By the time we were half-way there – with Vlad asking every ten minutes, *'are we there yet?'* – I was alternating sticking my head out the window, steering with one hand, and then popping back in to gag on the fumes. Sarah leaned back in and licked my cheek in sympathy. It helped.

When I could stand it no longer, I stopped the car and bolted for the outdoors.

After catching my breath, it was wonderful. City life dulls the senses. It becomes such a part of us that we forget there are other realms out there.

The air was astonishing. Crisp and clean, carrying the scents of pine trees, hot asphalt, flowers and more; and its clarity was perfect, a person could see for miles and everything stood out sharp and clear.

Motion in the sky - it was an eagle, soaring in the heavens. It made my heart sing and I could almost imagine the sound of wind whistling past its feathers. Tears of joy came to my eyes.

Sarah leaned against me. "It is beautiful, isn't it?" The sweat from the ride mingled with the smell of the cotton blouse she was wearing. It accented the smell of her hair and all mixed with the aroma of wildflowers growing on the banks of the river of black-top. The feelings made me want to grab her, kiss her and run wild.

"Whoa, dude," said Vlad. "We need to get a move on."

Without realizing it, I was now looking into Sarah's big golden eyes. Somehow, I had grabbed her in a hug, bent her over in my arms and was headed for a massive lip lock; she wasn't near as heavy as I thought she would be.

"I'm sorry," I apologized. "It's just the air. Went to my head. I have to get out more." I set her upright, she wiggled and grinned. Vlad looked ill.

"Get a kennel," was all he said.

It was nightfall by the time we reached Par Fleche Lake and at its entrance two security guards stood with flashlights.

"I'm sorry sir. This is a restricted area reserved for...*hey, Sarah*!" He quickly took the flashlight's intense beam out of our eyes.

"I'm really sorry. Didn't know it was you guys." He leaned his head in the car and took a deep breath and turned to his partner. "It's a go. All good."

He faced Sarah. "Say, if you have some time after the meeting..."

Sarah turned her eyes to me. He looked at me then back to her. He grinned, "That's cool."

For the most part, it was a gigantic family picnic. Over two hundred people of all ages stood, sat – or in some cases curled up on the ground – chatting and catching up on news and gossip. The largest part were friendly, if curious. They looked at me, judged me, but didn't attempt to taste me.

I liked that.

Others were neutral and one or two licked their lips. A quick growl from Sarah and they would wander off, muttering to themselves.

Campfires were starting like small forest fires everywhere I looked. It didn't seem that dark out, but I knew it was getting late and the smell of wood smoke was soothing; it brought forth primal memories.

I sincerely hoped that someone would bar-b-que something pretty soon. I was ravenous, but a small niggle of fear held the fervent hope that whatever was to be eaten wasn't a relative of mine.

A heavy arm dropped over my shoulder while the hand attached to the other arm offered me a beer. Sarah's father. Sarah had disappeared.

"Glad you could make it, Rank," he said with a smile that looked honest.

"I am very glad to be here. Um...you know...I never really caught your name, and I doubt you want me to call you Dad, just yet."

"Jacob," he said. "Jake will do just fine. The only one who calls me dad or father is Vlad. Sarah gets to call me papa, because she is my heart of hearts. Vlad is more like a hemorrhoid."

"I can't help but notice," I admitted, "you don't seem very fond of him.

"Nah, it's not that so much. He's just a pain in the ass." Two more beers magically appeared. He handed me one, then continued. "As a young one, he never learned much in the way of manners or - well, he just never learned much, period.

Momma hired a nanny and a tutor to try to give him a bit of polish. It didn't work."

"Unteachable?" I asked.

"Hungry. He ate them the first day." Jake shook his head. "He's not really vicious, just, as Sarah might have mentioned, the runt of the litter."

It was eerie. I started to wonder if the beer so conveniently offered had been spiked. The campfires were burning brightly now. The woods were lit up and a pulsating glow revealed everything around.

I held the bottle of beer up in front of my eyes. It left faint streamers of light in its wake. Even the lettering, the tiny print, was legible in the dusk.

Its flavor was intense. The bubbles in it felt like tiny explosions in my mouth. I struggled to keep a grasp on the conversation.

Jake was watching me closely now. "It's okay. Probably just the beer going to your head. Fear not, it will stabilize fairly quickly."

He laughed a booming laugh.

"Sarah was so worried about your safety. I don't think she realizes your potential." He clapped me on the shoulder again, "You, Rank, are going to open some eyes."

"Jonathon. John. Please call me John or Jonathon. Nothing formal. My potential? I am a pretty good attorney, and I do learn quickly."

Sarah's father nodded. "Yes, I am sure you are and do, but let's just fly with this. I am a very good judge of people. I have very few…ah…friends if you will. In the clans, it is a pyramid of power.

There are those above you, and those below you. If they are very far in either direction, then you never really get to know one another."

He raised his head and listened. "I have a sneaky feeling I will get to know you very well. Now, my attention is needed elsewhere. Enjoy yourself."

And he was gone. Just vanished.

The world swam before my eyes. My senses were stomped flat, inflated, stomped again, and then twisted.

Somewhere along the line Sarah reappeared.

"It's okay hon. It's fine. Just relax. You will be better in a little bit."

I watched her face turn to fire and the world explode into blackness. Her smell was still there when the world was born again into the red light of the campfire then melted into a kaleidoscope of colors.

I found myself flat on the ground, my head cradled in Sarah's lap. I buried my face in her lap to cut off the visions.

The sounds still echoed and reverberated in my ears and the smells were still there. Strange visions. Dreaming. A nightmare with people coming at me with pliers; of screaming then blackness once more.

I came out of the blackness yet again, my mind and soul a stranger to me, my head still in Sarah's lap, but when I looked up it was another.

She looked like Sarah, but older. She had a kind smile on her face and was stroking my brow. She smelled safe and protective.

Minutes?

Hours?

It must have been hours later. I awoke and was still cradled in a lap. The morning sun was not yet above the horizon. False dawn lit the world with a blue glow.

"Are you feeling better Jonathon?" The strange, yet familiar woman asked.

"I'm not sure," I whispered. "I just feel numb now." I did not trust myself to move. "What was that? Acid?"

The woman laughed gently. "No. Nothing so melodramatic." She placed a finger on my lips to silence me. "I will explain. You see…there has been a bit of a misunderstanding. And, as always happens when my beloved family screws up, it falls to me to make things right again - or at least explain."

She leaned closer. "I am Sarah's mom, in case you haven't guessed."

She moved slowly and adjusted herself into a more comfortable position, yet never seemed to jostle me.

"Do you love Sarah?" She asked.

"Of course I do."

"NCs have marriage vows. Sometimes I think we need to adopt them. Are you familiar with them? In sickness and in health? For better or for worse?"

"Yes," I said, wondering where this was leading.

"Would you accept Sarah in sickness and in health, for better or worse?"

"I do," I said. "I mean of course I would."

She smiled. "That is good. That is important. You see…Sarah thought you understood. We procreate at certain times. If you want to be crass about it, you could say we go into heat.

At other times, sex is fun, diverting, all that, but not normally shared with non-changers.

That is a very, very dynamic decision that is not left up to just one person. That is normally a group decision."

"That doesn't seem right," I said. "Why is it that everyone should get to decide whether I sleep with Sarah?"

"Because, silly," she smiled again. "The size of a clan must be kept manageable. Unlike NCs, we have morals and do not want to overpopulate." She hesitated and stroked my forehead again. "You have to understand. And Sarah thought you did. One doesn't become a werewolf by being bitten. I shudder to compare it, but if you have to have it in a few words, descriptive, if not totally in context, because we do not consider it a disease…werewolf is a sexually transmitted property.

You are a changeling."

She patted me on the head once more. "Don't worry yourself. Nothing can be done about it. You will have these spells for quite some time.

This doesn't all transpire overnight. There is just one thing you must promise me."

I looked upwards at her.

"If this makes you hate Sarah, you must be gentle about it and let her down easy. She feels quite badly as it is.

She never envisioned you didn't know until Jake – Papa – told her."

"I don't hate her. I don't think. She smells nice."

And the sun, that was just starting to come up, decided against it and the world turned black again.

⷗⷗

"Wow, dude. You look trashed." Words of encouragement from Vlad.

"My face feels like someone walked on it wearing golf shoes." I stated from where I lay on the ground.

"It should man. Like, you got into a porcupine. Took eight of us to hold you down and get the quills out."

I felt ill and embarrassed. "Did I change?"

Vlad looked confused. "Change? Like in change clothes…oh, you mean did you go beastie boy on us.

Nope, you just took out of here stark assed naked and went hunting. Human form no less. It will be a while until you can actually change.

Impressed the hell out of my father. You started out small – squirrels and stuff – and started to work your way up. When you decided to go after the black bear, Pops did intervene. He thought you might have bitten off more than you could chew, although Sarah was betting you could take it."

He frowned.

"I got in trouble, cuz I was rooting for the bear."

I sat up, afraid of what I might find. "I have clothes on." I noted. My hands weren't sticky and I could see no sign of blood. My mouth did taste a little bit - well a lot - like fur and feathers.

Vlad rolled his eyes. "Well, duh dude. This is a national park. It was reserved for yesterday, but we have John Q. Non-changer coming in by the car full this morning. Lying naked on the ground might have attracted some attention. Sarah and mom dressed you."

"Oh, that's embarrassing."

"Nah, mom was very complimentary about you to Sarah. Said she could see why…" He looked behind me. "Ut, oh."

Vlad's father was slowly walking towards us. I earnestly hoped that I did not look as bad as he did. He was missing his shoes, his pants were torn, his shirt was missing and his eyes were almost swollen shut.

"Morning, John."

"Morning, Jake."

"Rough night?" I asked.

"You could say that. I am getting too old to have this much fun. We did give them something to talk about until the next meeting," he said, scratching the reddish blotches on his chest.

"I don't know how I missed noticing the poison ivy when I was doing my victory roll on the ground."

I felt rather sheepish. "I hope I didn't disgrace myself too badly last night."

Jake laughed a gurgley chuckle. "Nope, not at all. The old ones were envious and the young ones amazed.

It was basically a pre-game show before the meeting of the pack. Shame you crashed out before the main event, but what the hell. You did pretty good holding your own. Town's people might not flee in terror when you walk, but there won't be a damn squirrel come within a mile of you, that I know for a fact."

He grinned.

"And I thought Sarah could climb trees."

"So what happens now?" I asked.

"We go home. I get some aspirin. We go to war. Soon. Not today." His hand went to his throbbing forehead. "But we go to war next week or the one after.

This week is for recuperation. Werewolves regenerate fast, but this is going to take a day or two. Only two things hurt a werewolf where they don't heal quickly. Silver and a damn hangover.

Oh my god, this is going to kill me for sure. I will have to listen to Mama bitch about it all the way home, to boot."

He looked down with blood shot eyes.

"Do you remember the modifications we made to your car last night?"

"I don't remember much of anything."

"Get up, walk with me." He stopped. "But walk slowly and don't stomp your feet."

The trail was dusty and hot. This morning my sense of smell was deadened. My hearing consisted of the sound of my own blood pounding in my temples. As we topped a rise the parking lot came into view.

The newcomers to the lake were parked in the main lot, while the cars of last night's revelers were in a smaller and separate one. Motorcycles outnumbered cars three to one, but the cars that were there all shared one thing in common - they were convertibles. This made obvious sense to me now.

I looked at my car. "Jake...my vision is kinda blurry this morning, but I don't notice anything different about my car."

He motioned with his hand. I followed. Even standing alongside it, I couldn't find a difference. I indicated this to Jake. He sighed and got in the car and waved to me. "See it now?" he asked.

"Nope."

"Well for Christ's sake," he said and climbed out where the front windshield used to be. "You don't remember kicking it out last night? You weren't kidding about not remembering much."

He laid his head down on the hood of the car and his voice was muffled. "A lot better for air flow, but it sucks if it rains."

"What do we do now? This morning, I mean." I asked.

"We wait."

I went to the other side of the car and laid my head on the hood. Waves of nausea swept from my toes to my head, but the sunlight felt good on my back and shoulders.

Time passed until I heard Vlad's voice.

"Is this like some type of ritual they are performing? Praying to the Carburetor God, or something?"

"Mother warned me about this," Sarah said quietly. "She said they will be cranky and ill tempered. Occasionally they might vomit for no apparent reason. If they do, it is best not to mention it, or they will become crankier. I think it's kind of like distemper, but with some of the symptoms of rabies."

"Anything we can do about it?" asked Vlad.

"Momma said it would be nice if we could have them put to sleep, but that if we did there wouldn't be anyone left but the female of the species. It's some sort of bonding thingy."

Vlad looked again. "I think I prefer to stay un-bonded."

CHAPTER SEVEN
MEET THE CANDIDATES
BAD DOG
VII

We dropped Vlad off at home with instructions to sit, stay, and not venture outside. If I had been feeling better, I would have thrown in roll over and play dead.

Sarah often offered to teach him the latter. I had not vomited, but I will admit to being a bit edgy on the trip from the house to the office.

Neither of us spoke, each waiting for the other to start the dance of words, and neither willing to begin the music with words that might be wrong.

Our first uneasy silence.

I would have spoken (and wanted to) but I wasn't sure what I thought about the situation as a whole. It still had not sunk in.

A parody of something I once read kept popping into my mind. "Two weeks ago, I didn't believe in werewolves...now I is one."

Really?

Truly?

I didn't feel that much different today. Yesterday's senses and happenings were mixed into memories that could have been dreams. What was it they called me? A changeling.

As we turned from the five flights of stairs and started for the office, Sarah asked, "Do you feel it?"

"Feel what?"

"Do you smell it?"

"Smell what?"

"Don't open the...." I swung the door open as she finished... "door."

Once more the office of Crank, Rank and Skank had uninvited visitors. Sarah turned to flee, but from both ends of the hallway others were approaching.

"Oh my god," Sarah whispered. "They're wearing silver. These are contenders for new Master of the Undead."

By their advance, they herded Sarah into the office and she in turn herded me.

In my chair (which pissed me off to no end) sat a man in tailored clothing similar to that I had seen on the late Taka Hunt. On each side of him swayed an undead.

The two silver-sprinkled gentlemen from the hallway entered and stood on either side of the doorway, forcing Sarah to move to the corner where she stood panting - from what I could feel the room was unnaturally hot, but not unbearable - to her it was the gates of hell.

"Please. Please Mr. Rank. Come in. It *is* your office after all." He said regally, and then nodded towards Sarah. "The bitch can stay in the corner. We do not need her for this discussion."

Oh, hell yes. This joker was pushing all my buttons. I couldn't think of one he had missed.

He smiled a greasy smile. "It is unfortunate you are mixed up in this unseemly business, but there is an alternative. A very profitable alternative, I might add."

"What the fuck do you want?" I asked.

"Ah, straight to the point. Crude, but straight to the point. I should have expected that, for you are an attorney after all."

He adjusted his silk ascot with manicured fingertips. "Your client is gone. For some reason the court system is curious about your involvement with his disappearance." He shrugged. "As a token of our good will, that little problem has been taken care of.

He is not missing now in the court's eyes or ours for that matter. Fifteen minutes ago, a few of my business colleges escorted him from your home to...well, another place.

The legal paperwork concerning the case is now confetti. It shall stay that way. As long as *we* have control of dog boy. Interference, and I am sure records might surface again."

He nodded to himself. "Amazing. In this civilized world if the event doesn't exist on paper, then it never really happened. When one learns that truth, society can be manipulated in a broad variety of ways."

He stood smiling broadly. "Now you should not worry about this turn of events. You have become involved with the most loathsome of creatures.

We understand you did this because...ah, how to word it...because you are financially in a bit of a depression. It is understandable."

He waved his hands in a depreciatory manner.

"That we can settle also. Whatever your standard fee is in a matter such as this, we shall triple.

Additionally, we shall remove this unsavory bitch from your life also. A fresh start, no loose ends…"

My memory - or lack of it - is starting to bother me. I do not remember stepping forward and grabbing him. I know it was akin to walking up to the door of a blast furnace; hot, burning and I knew it was going to hurt tomorrow.

I intended to grab him and pull him over the top of the desk – but he came over so easily. I kept pulling and my body seemed to crunch down into itself, my shirt sleeves split on my arm. He did travel the length of the room without touching the floor until he landed in the hallway. A shame about the closed door.

I looked around. No one had moved. How strange.

Well, I thought, *if I have to replace one door, I might as well add a window.*

The undead fit nicely through the window, following the broken glass in its five story descent. If the drop to the street below didn't incapacitate them, it would sure slow them down climbing the stairs back up to the office. By now the two at the sides of the door were starting to move. Their faces had a look of astonishment on them and they were slowly reaching into their jackets. Sarah had the same look on her face.

I tried growling, but they kept reaching. No problem.

It felt like running through molasses, but they were moving slower than I. I found myself next to them before their hands had emerged with whatever bits of nastiness they were groping for.

The heat felt twice as hot in my face, but I grabbed their shirt fronts and bumped them together; their heads took on unusual shapes and they quit reaching.

I stopped and the world around me speeded up.

"Holy shit…" said Sarah.

"Well, that was fun." I had to admit to myself, it had been. "We need to get our asses out of here. I am sure this is going to attract some attention."

"I can't leave." Sarah said simply.

"Why the hell not?" I asked.

She put her hands on her hips and nodded at the bodies scattered in the hallway.

"Oh, yeah. The silver." I raised my hands. "Okay. Okay. I'll take the garbage out." This time the heat I felt when I approached them was less.

That was good, but they were harder than hell to drag now.

"Are you okay?" She asked.

"Well, yeah, I guess. Skin feels a bit tight. Kinda like a bad sunburn."

"It's more like crawling inside a microwave and turning it on." She ripped my shirt open and nuzzled my chest, sniffing and licking. It tickled.

"Luckily all you got was the defrost setting, for some reason. You'll be okay," she finished.

"Thank you. That was fantastic. Papa was right; when you turn you will most definitely be a FON."

"What's a faun?" I asked as we loped down the stairs, trying to look innocent and inconspicuous.

"Not faun, F-O-N. Force of nature. Some werewolves have it. An innate strength. Very powerful. Very dangerous. Papa has it, I have it...I can think of about four others in the clan that have it."

I laughed. "Your mom have it?"

"Oh, no." Sarah answered seriously. "She has something far more dangerous. She has maternal instinct.

That might not sound like much, but the closest thing you can compare it to is a berserker rage. She doesn't fight for fun. If she fights, it is to the death. No king's axe, no time out."

We had reached street level.

"That is why Momma was watching over you the other night when you were out of it. I didn't even have to ask her to. She said she didn't care so much if you got eaten, but she was protecting her future grand children."

Sarah blushed.

"She was fibbing. She does care about you."

The fire trucks were just pulling away as we arrived at the house. Two charred walls remained standing and the lone stack of the fireplace. The gate and a goodly portion of the white picket fenced were lying on the ground where the firefighters kicked them down to get hoses onto the property. Colorful shards from the stained glass lay like crippled jewels on the lawn.

Sarah's father sat cross-legged on the walkway, spinning his sunglasses by one earpiece, staring at the wilted and scorched flowers. He looked up as we approached.

"Morning, John…I mean afternoon." He pointed to the still smoldering ruins. "I don't think the other side is going to let us wait until next week."

"No," I agreed, and filled him in on the morning's events. "No sign of Vlad?" I asked when I had finished.

"Yes and no. I don't know where he is or where they took him, but we can follow the scent easily enough."

He turned to Sarah. "Sarah, you are excellent at tracking. We'll get started here in a bit, when the help arrives. But first, the one thing we don't do in a case like this?"

Sarah sighed. "We don't tell mom."

Jake smiled. "Ah…yes. That is a given. I was thinking in a larger scale, however."

"Small incidents are overlooked by the public, but we can't do house to house warfare in major cities?" suggested Sarah.

Sarah's father clapped his hands. "Straight from the text book."

He frowned.

"This is why we *don't* tell your mom. Sometimes she gets hooked on little rules and regulations. Today we are going to, ah, bend them a little bit."

Two flat-black RVs pulled up in front of the house, tires splashing water that stood in the street from the fire crew's efforts.

"Problem?" I asked.

"Yes, but not for us."

From each vehicle a half-dozen men emerged. Young. Hard. Each dressed in black combat uniforms, tactical vests festooned with extra magazines for the assault rifles they carried. The few, the proud, the fanged.

"Um…they are carrying guns," I noted, feeling dumb for pointing out the obvious.

"Yes," Jake said. "When you can't get close because of silver, a chunk of lead traveling at 2,850 feet per second is a very good substitute for fangs and claws. Sarah," he said, "time to play hood ornament."

CHAPTER EIGHT
S.W.A.T.
SPECIAL WEAPONS AND TEETH
VIII

"You had to take your damn clothes off," said an exasperated man, trying to control his impatience.

"If you interrogated him, while you wore them, all you would be doing is asking questions of a crispy critter. You know damn well it would kill him. The fact you had to be in your skivvies for a half hour isn't the end of the world."

"So? What's the down side with crispy critter? We're gunna do that anyway."

"Yes. Yes we are. However, aren't there a few little loose ends...a few small questions that you would like answered?" He wanted to reach out and strangle the man, but that wasn't acceptable. The mentally challenged individual *was* a Cell Lord. As such he *did* have his own little following of undead.

"Like what?" The guy asked.

"You, my friend, have been hanging with the undead too much. You need to get out, take in a movie, go to the library and look at the pictures in the National Geographic - it's okay, the words you can work on at a later date." He sighed. "So, what have you learned, if anything, from the fur ball so far?"

The guy shrugged. "Not much."

"Define not much."

"Well, we asked him and he said he didn't do it. He also said he didn't know who done it. So we got water guns and shot him with silver nitrate solution a couple times.

He still said he didn't do it. He just kept saying he didn't know who did. Oh, yeah, and he howled a lot and smoked."

The guy's nose crinkled. "Smelled like burning wool."

"Any contact with the guys who went to the shyster's office?"

"Nope. Not a peep."

"That concerns me."

ᨠᨢ

"Sarah, hanging through the windshield is attracting a bit of attention," I noted.

Jake glanced at the pedestrians on the sidewalk. "Yeah, a little bit, but it's Tucson. They notice, but they don't really care. Besides," he slowed for a stop light, "this saves a lot of time. Sarah can follow the scent as long as we keep the speed down to about thirty. Just pray."

"Pray that we're in time?" I asked.

"Nah. Pray that someone's cat doesn't dart across the street. I don't want to have to chase her down and try to get her back on the hood again.

When she was young, we used to have to chain her in her car seat. People do notice things like small children flying from moving vehicles and sinking their teeth into cats sleeping on sunlit porches.

Used to be embarrassing as hell. I don't remember how many times I had to bribe animal control."

He looked at Sarah clinging to the hood. "I think she has more self control now that she's older." He looked over at me. "Sarah told me what happened at the office."

He hesitated, "How are you handling it?"

"Uh, I'm not sure what you mean."

"Well, you just killed three men and had an encounter with undead. Most people would be having a screaming tizzy right now. How do you feel about it?"

I thought for a second. "I'm not sure. I know I should be feeling something. You know, bad...guilty...scared. I'm not. I don't know why and that does bother me some. It's not like it doesn't seem real. I know it was real."

Jake spoke softly. "Is it because you enjoyed it? Is that what is bothering you?"

I was startled. "No. No, I didn't enjoy it. It is just something I did. Something I had to do.

Jake relaxed. "That is good. And it is the truth.

You will find that you can tell when people are lying. They smell different."

He looked in the mirror and shook his head at the man who was riding in the back seat. The passenger relaxed.

"That is very good indeed. You see, sometimes when people start to change, things go wrong. They have a killing instinct that overwhelms them. They can't control the urge at all. They become a danger to the clan. They love to kill and do so regardless of the consequences."

I considered this. "How do you teach them differently?" I asked.

Jake grinned at me. "You can't. You just have to put a silver bullet through their head and get on with life."

He patted me on the arm. "I'm glad that didn't happen with you." He pointed to Sarah. "I'm not sure how she would have taken it, but it would have been traumatic."

"Yes, well I'm happy we didn't have an incident, but I have to ask...I have heard, well, rumors that some people might have taken out whole villages. That doesn't qualify as a 'bloodlust' type of thing?"

He laughed. "Ah, the old Grim Reaper of the Mountain story. A wonderful story it is, as a matter of fact."

I laughed with him. "But just a story?"

"Oh, hell no. I did 'take them all out.'"

"But..."

"I'll have to explain the finer points later. It was not only justified, but required. We're here."

If you've ever watched a SWAT team, well at least watched one on television, you know basically how it functions.

With the body of troops being made up of werewolves, it adds a whole new twist.

When they left the vehicles, they left fast. Not just on the run, but in a blur I was starting to get used to. No battering ram needed. The first man in line launched himself into the air towards the door. Midway there he changed and upon contact with the door; it became toothpicks.

The men behind him never broke step, they went through in the same blur. Every other man raised a weapon and the ones in between them morphed.

Jake lit a cigarette and leaned against the car, eyes narrowed and his lips instinctively pulled up on the sides in a snarl.

"You, ah, don't take an active part in the operation?" I asked.

He flinched. "Nah. The young kids get to have all the fun anymore."

A line of dark holes appeared on the wall about where the second story floor would have been. Small puffs of masonite and siding blew out from them and hung in the air for a moment. Muffled staccato gunshots matched the appearance of each perforation as it materialized.

I sniffed the air. "Is that what they refer to as the smell of cordite?"

Jake sniffed. "You read too many pulps. Cordite hasn't been used for decades. It was a long, string-like powder. They use nitrocellulose based propellant now. Probably Hodgen BLC-2."

"But that's gunpowder, right?"

"Yes. It smells more pungent and noticeable to you now. Part of the change."

A window on the third floor exploded outward and an undead, minus arms, plummeted to the ground. We looked at each other.

"Sarah," we said together. A face appeared at the window, smiled and waved. It disappeared and then reappeared, along with her arm and hand; holding Vlad by the ankle and dangling him in the air like a trophy.

"Do not...," Jake yelled.

Sarah released him.

"...drop him..." Jake said softly.

Vlad hit the ground with a solid thud and Jake waved with his cigarette, "You will note that werewolves do not land on their feet like a cat.

Keep that in mind."

"Is he okay?"

"He's never been okay, but if you mean will he live, yes." His eyes were sad. "This is why we never took the kids to places like the Empire State building or rides at Disneyland. After our trip to the La Brea Tar Pit we figured out that they just are not capable of behaving."

"The Tar Pit?" I asked.

"Yes. It was Sarah that time. Vlad tripped her. We ended up steam cleaning her at a local car wash for an hour." He smiled. "She did enjoy the hot air dry and wax. We let her walk through the automated wash at the end. Used up Vlad's entire allowance buying quarters."

Soft cracks sounded and the windows blew out of the third and fourth floor. White smoke billowed and were soon followed by flames.

"White Phosphorous grenades," he grunted. "That means it's done and they are mopping up the evidence."

He walked towards Vlad who was rolling on the ground and moaning. "Let's get the asshole back in the rig."

CHAPTER NINE
HISTORY & BACKGROUND
YA GOTTA HAVE HEART
IX

Sarah's parent's house was befitting a well-to-do businessman; or even the Alpha male and female of a large and far-flung pack.

Sarah ran for the kitchen to find her mother, Vlad to his bedroom to hide, and Jake and myself made a bee-line for the wet bar.

"You have a preference in booze?" asked Jake.

"I believe in quantity instead of quality," I replied.

"It's even better when you have quantity and quality." Jake grabbed two glasses. They were big enough to make my heart sing. He did warn me, however, "Just make sure you never let Sarah near liquor. She has no real concept of the ancient and fine art of bartending."

"Yes, well she did mix me one a while back. It had teeth in it I have to admit."

Jake looked up. "Whose teeth? She's been known to come up with some strange concoctions, but so far she hasn't added any body parts." He stopped and thought for a second. "That I know of."

"No, not actual teeth. I meant it had a helluva bite to it. Very strong."

He handed me one glass and took the other. "Cheers," he said.

We lifted them and drained them, setting them back down where he promptly refilled them.

Sipping the next one, I decided it was time to ask a few pertinent questions.

"Jake, if you don't mind me asking, exactly what is it I have to look forward to during this change or changeling period. I know I should ask specific questions, hell, that's what an attorney is supposed to do; but I don't even know where to start."

Flopping down in an overstuffed chair, he stared at his drink. "Wow. Where to start? You have to bear with me. It's been a long time since I went through it. Crap, we're looking at almost a hundred and ten years.

Give or take."

I had the feeling that he wasn't really pulling my leg. "You only look about forty or fifty," I offered.

"Yes, well I was, um, turned...when I was thirty. If I remember right. It's kind of a reverse dog years type of thing.

What you really want to know is not the future, but what is in store for you in the next year or so. Assuming of course you live through it. A lot of things can happen you know."

He looked at me.

"Well, I guess you don't know. That's why you are asking."

He definitely had my attention.

"Okay," he started, "here goes. Let me top off you glass, you might need it."

"While it is politically incorrect to compare it to a disease, it has some of the same qualities and characteristics. It might become dormant for a while. Maybe a month. Maybe a year. It might metastasize, hit your lymph system and run rampant. The change can happen in the course of six months or so. That is the dangerous scenario."

He motioned calmingly to me. "Not to worry you, but I have some fear that may be what is happening to you. You displayed signs that should not have happened for a long, long time. This is normally attributed to stress. Have you been under any abnormal stress lately?"

I looked at him dumbfounded. "Uh, yep. I think you could safely say that."

"Damn," he said softly. "Sorry to hear that." I refilled my own glass this time. He nodded approvingly. "Alcohol does have a tenancy to repress and suppress the change. Stay drunk if you can."

"I'll work on that," I promised.

"Adrenaline is your enemy at this stage. Later, it is your friend and can help in a multitude of situations. But try to avoid it for the time being."

"Why?" I asked simply.

"Well, it is difficult to kill you right now. Not so hard as when the full change is upon you, but difficult. If your heart explodes, then you probably will die."

He shook his head.

"No, not probably. You will die. Guaranteed."

"Oh, this is sweet," I was thankful for the hard buzz that I already had.

"Well if you are pushed hard enough, kinda like what happened at the office, one of two things will probably happen." He thought hard and waved with his glass. "Maybe both. Hell, I don't know. Do I look like a veterinarian?"

"Just give me the basics. I will fill the nightmares in for myself later," I pleaded.

"Most likely you would get an adrenaline rush and your heart would just split. It doesn't really explode. Just the sidewalls rip out like a cheap tire.

If that doesn't happen, then you go balls to the wall and into a full change. That's good news unless you do the full change and your heart explodes anyway.

You see, the change works kinda from the exterior in. The heart is about the last thing that makes the change. It takes about five to ten minutes for it to completely adjust. It's not a well know fact, or one that we want to get out, but a werewolf can be killed for the first couple minutes by putting a bullet or, god forbid a stake through its heart."

This didn't totally jive with what I had seen. "I have watched werewolves in their human form take beatings that would kill a normal human."

He laughed grimly. "You are thinking about Vlad. No, its not the same. He was never 'turned.' He was born a werewolf and so was Sarah. You will be the same given time. Just as I was, but it takes time. I was 'turned.' Sarah and Vlad weren't, nor was their mother."

"Then you mean you and Sarah's mother, um..."

"No." He said. "This is complicated. I was turned by another. It's a long story and not one that I mention when there is a chance my wonderful mate might hear."

"Oh, I see. Still a little bit of latent jealousy lingering about the one that you, um, did the deed with?"

He nodded in agreement. "Not so much now. After she killed and ate the one that turned me, she became a lot more docile."

"Say what?" I asked.

At that time Sarah's mom walked through the door, smiling a rather frightening smile. "What are you boys talking about? Everything okay, my dear?"

We both coughed and sputtered on our drinks and profusely assured her that all was good in our lives, the world, and hey, how about that Colorado Avalanche hockey team?

"Right," she said, the smile never leaving her lips, but not reflected in her eyes. "Tell me, I can't remember exactly. Who exactly is their star goalie?"

"Patrick Roy?" ventured Jake.

"He retired a couple years ago," she responded, the smile getting larger. I had the feeling the term domestic violence was about to be redefined.

"Mom!" Sarah called from the kitchen. "Are you two squabbling in front of him?"

"No dear. We were just talking sports. Come on you two. Dinner's ready."

"Excellent, my dear," said Jake. "What treat do we have in store for us tonight?"

I held my breath. This might be grim.

"Well," Sarah answered for her mother. "We have pot roast, baked potatoes, salad with vinaigrette, and for desert we have apple pie."

She appeared at the door also, and her smile was much more fetching than her mother's at the moment.

"Wonderful," Jake and I said together. The two women turned on their heels and disappeared back in the direction from which they came.

Planting myself at the huge table it was strange, but I felt comfortable and a part of the family.

"So," Sarah's mom continued, "what were you men folk really talking about?"

I felt truth to be the best policy, so I said, "I was just curious what was going to befall me in the near future. You know... with my changing and everything.

Jake was explaining the possibility that my heart might just explode and I could drop over dead." I expected that to cause some agitation, but no one even batted an eye.

"Well," she said, "that could happen, and it does make excellent dinner conversation, but Sarah and I have talked about it."

Sarah's head bobbed in agreement. "Mom was close to you one time, and I was the other. No, you didn't really 'change,' but you....Mom, what did you call it?"

"Internal morph, dear."

"Yeah, you did an internal morph. You changed, but only partially and ass backward. We could hear your heart beat. It stayed strong and steady through out."

"Meaning?" I asked.

"Well," Sarah said quietly, "that is both good and bad. The good news is you will be next to impossible to kill. The bad news..."

"...is" Vlad continued, "when you change it will be from the inside out, and that..."

"...will hurt like a son of a bitch," finished Jake. "Pass the potatoes please. Salt too."

Sarah's mom spoke up, "Can't we think of something pleasant and fun to talk about?"

"Yes," Sarah said enthusiastically. "Let's decide how to punish Vlad for causing all this trouble in the first place."

"That's a wonderful idea," Jake caught the glare from his wife and lamely finished, "for after dinner."

He stopped and pointed with his fork at Vlad. "You will, however, explain to me in twenty-five words or less; why people are after you and what happened to Taka Hunt."

"That's not fair. The question was twenty-five words long," said Vlad.

"The question is more than reasonable; and only twenty-three words long. Now don't talk with your mouth full, dear," said Sarah's mom.

"Fine!" said Vlad.

"Twenty-four now," said Sarah.

"Mom, make her stop."

"Sarah, let you brother speak."

"Speak, Vlad, speak," commanded Sarah, who then made barking sounds.

The two of them met in the middle of the large table, hissing and biting.

Jake turned to me. "If you can at all avoid it, do not have children."

When the they had been separated and the spilled food tidied up, Vlad sat quietly, thinking and counting.

"Okay," he began. "I'll try to make this simple...so even Sarah can understand."

She raised her fist and Vlad flinched involuntarily.

"Let your brother talk, Sarah," I told her.

"Sorry, dear," she said.

Jake looked in my direction, eyebrows raised in respect.

"Hunt was at the mortuary. He turned Sam. Emma blew his ass away. I was seen with undead and people think I am Master."

"Well, you hit twenty five on the head, but don't bother getting up. I have a few questions and, zowie, we won't bother keeping the answers short and truthful, we will concentrate on truthful," said Jake.

"Suppose you give me the full story, just don't wander in doing so." He finished.

"Dad," Sarah said, "remember, you are talking to Vlad."

Jake sighed. "Vlad just do your best. Hold on a minute and let me get set." He looked at me and I got to my feet, saying, "I'll do it. Wait one second."

I returned with our glasses from the other room.

"You didn't think to..." he started.

"Of course," I said, setting the bottle down.

Vlad started out. "Taka was at the mortuary looking for any potential recruits for his army. You know that every once and a while undead slip by the medical examiners and masters are only as great as their armies of undead.

Well while looking around, Hunt got to talking with Sam, Emma's husband. Somehow, and Taka maintained it was accidental, one of the undead took a bite out of Sam's arm. Naturally he 'turned' a few minutes later.

Emma was real upset and Taka learned that silver lined shirts won't protect you if a pissed off grandmother type shoots your ass with a 40 mm grenade launcher.

Emma felt bad about it," he thought about it for a moment. "Nah, maybe she didn't. She loaded him in the back of their old pickup and dumped the body along the road so the cops would find it."

Sarah's mom piped in, "That explains a lot, but not why people are looking on you as the new master of the undead."

CHAPTER TEN
೮THE NEW MASTERೞ
೮SLAY IT AGAIN, SAMೞ
೮Xೞ

"Oh, Sammy. I didn't intend for all this to happen." Emma bowed her head, letting the tears fall down her wrinkled cheeks. At her side an undead swayed and slowly reached a decaying hand out, laying it on her shoulder.

To those in the know, he was freshly undead; as in two months ago he was alive and standing in the same spot.

Unfortunately, at the time he had been alive and vibrant, he had been the husband of forty years to Emma.

That changed during Taka Hunt's last visit. Sammy's mind was deteriorating to where the memory was vague and unimportant.

To Emma the memory was burned on her soul.

A Saturday morning...a lifetime ago. A life ago, anyway, for Sammy...

"Taka, you are just plain mean and evil," said Emma, those months earlier.

"Thank you," Hunt said with a grin.

"I suppose you are in looking for any recruits? You know that I separate them out for you."

"And a fine job you do of it Emma. I'll just look around," he said, dropping a hundred dollar bill in the 'sponsor' jar.

It bothered Emma. Not being around the undead, but the way this high falutin' Hunt fella treated them.

The undead were people too; at least they had been, and for all Emma knew they still were. She had always gone out of her way to be, well, nice to the undead.

It amazed her just how far a little kindness went. The undead responded to it the way little children would.

Often they wandered away from their Masters, when unobserved, and gathered around the morgue. Not once had the undead ever given an indication that they intended attacking her.

On that fateful morning, two months ago, life had been...normal. Samuel was helping Emma in the morgue. Nothing on television, so it was an opportunity to indulge in some quality time; helping fill the formaldehyde bottles that would replace the coagulating blood in the corpses. Helping carry the recently deceased, in the gray body bags they were delivered in, and gently lay them on the stainless steel tables where they would receive the last 'hands on' attention from the living.

Sam was in the back when Taka Hunt came in. Emma didn't think much of Taka's arrival. He showed up almost every week.

She did think it strange he stayed in back so long. They had only gotten in three new bodies that week and, let's get real, how long did it take to figure out if someone was undead or not. An hour seemed a bit much.

Sadly, the answer to the question, 'how long did it take to figure out if someone was undead?,' was forth coming.

Sam wandered in and stood silently, looking at a picture of their grandkids, his back to Emma. Emma carried on a standard conversation for almost five minutes before it dawned on her that Samuel was being a lot quieter than normal.

"Sam? Are you okay?" No answer to her questions. "Did you take your pills this morning?"

Sam once more declined to speak, just standing and rocking from foot to foot. Emma reached out and touched him on the shoulder, then noticed the blood on his right forearm.

She pulled on his shoulder.

He turned and stared at her as only the undead can. Eyes rolled up in his head, mouth agape with saliva running out the left side, down his chin and onto his chest.

She screamed.

Emma went instantly into shock. Sam, having been turned but minutes before, tried to comfort and consol her as best the ghost of his mind could.

At some time - be it minutes or a half hour - Taka Hunt reappeared. He took the time to consol her himself.

"Bloody sorry Emma. Terrible bit of an accident, don't you know?" He looked Sam up and down. "I promise I will take better care of Sam than the 'others.'" He paused.

"You do realize this has a bit of a perk to it? Of course I will compensate you for the accident. I will also show you how to file the paperwork for benefits.

You can visit with Sam anytime, and you are eligible to collect his pension, insurance and file social security on him."

Taka smiled and led Sam from the building with a smile on his face. Emma could move, but it was as if in a dream.

She opened the file cabinet and pulled a short M-40 grenade launcher from its bottom drawer. Pushing the top lever to the side she broke it open like a shotgun and removed the tear gas grenade. She replaced it with HE, high explosive.

At the front door she looked to Hunt's car, beside which he was standing. With numb fingers she set the rear sight for 75 yards; the distance she guessed between them.

When he turned, she pulled the trigger and it fired with a dull 'thump.'

She sat down on the front stoop.

After a while Sam wandered back and stood before her; rocking back and forth.

When Vlad found her, he was surprised to find a couple dozen undead standing around her.

Many times when death befalls those who dabble with the occult, police have a habit, policy or procedure to where if the problem - that means body - disappears, then so does the case.

Vlad knew that wouldn't happen. Taka Hunt was too well connected. He also knew he couldn't bear to see the cry of 'murder' leveled at Emma.

The lady was always nice to him, more grandmother than friend.

With Emma's help - he still couldn't approach the silver clad body - and that of a dozen undead; they ingloriously tossed Hunt's body into the pickup, hauled him a reasonable distance from the morgue and tossed him in the ditch.

He then rode back to the mortuary in silence with Emma. She bore her grief stoically.

Two hours later, Vlad left the mortuary to perform a cursory inspection of a new café. These were always the best. None of the equipment had been used yet, so all remained sparkling and shiny.

Have a cup of coffee, bullshit for ten minutes and sign off on the form. All while on the clock.

Call it morbid curiosity, guilt, accident or what ever would ease your mind, but Vlad found himself on the road past the location they had performed the grisly dump.

Vlad chose accident, although there were six roads that led to where he wanted to go.

What amazed him was not the lack of police and crime scene units, but the gathering of over one hundred undead standing around the body. This went far in explaining the lack of cars and civilian onlookers as well. A few cars were parked in the general area, but their occupants had probably been bitten and turned by now.

While curiosity killed the cat, although not in the sheer numbers as his sister, Vlad pulled over. He was not worried about the undead.

He had always treated them with respect, and even as a pup, they would hunt him out and play with him.

Vlad made his way to the center of their gathering, and sure enough, Hunt was still there.

As he started to walk off, the entourage of undead moved with him. At the same time two patrol cars pulled up.

As it turned out all the law enforcement officers were curious also.

Why was he standing here with a dead body? Why was there a flock of undead following him around? It scared Vlad and put him on the defensive.

"Now son, here's how we see it," said one burly cop as he placed Vlad in cuffs. 'For his own safety.' "This is part of some cult ritual killing. You decided that you wanted to be leader, sorry, what did you call it?"

"Master," Vlad said.

"Right. Master. You decided you wanted to be 'Master,' and you figured it would be easier to kill the guy, than wait for the election, or whatever you do."

Vlad shook his head. "They don't have elections, they have eliminations."

"So you admit it? You killed him to be leader."

"No," Vlad shouted. "I didn't kill him. I'm a werewolf for God's sake. Werewolves are the natural enemies of Masters of the Undead."

The conversation went downhill from there, until Vlad spoke the words he should have said in the first place. "I want an attorney."

A cop who had been scribbling furiously handed him a paper and pen saying, "Sign this release that you want one."

Vlad grabbed it and signed with a flourish. The cop slapped the other on the shoulder and shouted, "Another one solved. Ya gotta love a signed confession."

And Vlad joined the ranks of perp, villain, assassin and bad dog.

CHAPTER ELEVEN
THE BEST LAID PLANS
VLAD & DUMBER
XI

Everyone sat for a moment in silence. The story wasn't exactly what we expected.

"Is it possible…I mean would the police stoop to…," Jake directed at me.

"What you are really asking is if Vlad is dumb enough to sign something like that and if there are any cops smart enough to write something like that." I said.

Jake thought, "Vlad, do you remember when Sarah stabbed you in the hand with fork at the restaurant?"

"Of course I remember. It was just two months ago, and she did it three times."

Jake explained, "Sarah asked him to put his hand on the table. He did and she stabbed him."

I must be missing something, so I remained silent.

"She kept asking and he kept laying his hand down. After being stabbed three times, he picked up on it. So, yes. It is very believable he signed it without reading it. Just because someone told him to."

Sarah's mom broke the problem down to its basics.

"Our problems are double. We have to get Vlad cleared of charges. They have miraculously reappeared. We have to convince the undead crowd that Vlad isn't Master."

"We could just let them execute Vlad," offered Sarah.

"We go to war and erase every wanna be master from the face of the earth," Jake suggested.

"I think everyone is…over reacting to a small degree," I said.

"I agree," Sarah's mom said, returning to the table with a cup of coffee.

"Is that decaf?" Sarah asked.

"No, dear."

Jake, Sarah and Vlad scooted their chairs farther away from her.

I looked questioningly at Sarah, but she just responded with the slightest shake of her head.

"Rank, dear. You are an attorney. What are the odds you can get Vlad off?"

This was the question that every attorney hates. No matter what the evidence, it's a crapshoot. The proud look in Sarah's eyes told me there was only one acceptable answer.

"Come hell or high water, I will get Vlad off. Even if I have eat the damn judge myself," I said.

"Hell yes!" said Jake, toasting me with his glass.

"And I," Sarah's mom said, "will attempt to reason with those people." She turned to her husband, "Jake, if I fail, it will be up to you to convince them."

"Any restrictions?" he asked.

"None," she said, looking deep into his eyes. Those eyes turned shiny, black and cold. His smile was chiseled on his face. I knew I was looking into the face of the reaper.

Jake turned to me.

"I am taking a trip to talk to Emma. Is there anyone you need to talk to?"

"I can't use Crank, because he's not only in hiding, he's probably hiding with headhunters in Borneo. I would like to team up with Skank, but she's in hiding too. Best bet would be to get rid of her as a partner. Get her out of the line of fire."

"Is she out of the country or just hiding in town?" Jake asked.

"Just in town somewhere. Also I should talk to the District Attorney to see exactly what we're up against."

Jake nodded, "Give me her address. I'll have some one sniff her out if she's still in town. How about I drop you off at your office and deliver her there. I can have the DA delivered also, if you would like."

"Sounds good with Skank," I said, "but, we'd probably better not with the...," I thought about it. "You could really grab the DA and deliver him to my office?"

"Just say the word," Jake said.

"Let's do it."

CHAPTER TWELVE
MEETINGS
RANK THE RIGHTEOUS
XII

The door and window going into my office were still broken, but no yellow tape barred entry. It seems no one was worried about the bodies that had been chucked out the window.

I pulled the door off its hinges and set it in the corner. Five minutes with a broom and dust pan and the office could have been in Better Homes and Gardens. Then again, maybe not.

A hot flash hit me again. They were getting more common and becoming exasperating. I poured a glass of scotch and sat down to wait.

It was amazing, I could taste every nuance of the single malt. The smell was over powering. I could almost see the peat moss fires involved in its production. With all that it still went down like ginger ale. My body metabolism was on turbo. Six ounces and I wasn't even sure I felt a buzz. Even more incredible, I wasn't stressed out or bored. It was relaxing to just sit and watch dust motes floating in the air. Then I heard it.

Ground floor. Door opened, door closed. Three people, six feet coming up the stairs, one pair clomping around and the other two pair padding so softly I could barely hear them.

It was the smell of stale sweat mixed with cigar that told me it was Skank. Escorted by two young gentlemen I had never seen, they both nodded and gave Skank a push through the door.

"Jesus, I'm glad to see you," Skank said, stumbling to her chair and flopping into it. "They kidnapped my ass and never said a word. I thought they were mob. I've gotten a little behind playing the horses...."

I waved her to silence.

"I took the case on the werewolf," I told her. "I need to know. You got any leverage, markers or favors floating around out there? I need some court muscle."

"Nope. I'm tapped out. Did you get any money up front?" She asked.

"Money?" I was surprised. "No. You know, I haven't even thought about it that way. How strange."

"So we are doing this….," her tongue tripped over the words and I saw her shudder slightly, "pro bono?"

"Skank, I'll tell you what. My life has changed in the past week. I think I've been fooling myself that it would be life as normal." I looked at her.

"I know *you* don't have the money to buy *me* out, so what would it take to buy you out? Don't worry about Crank, he's already been taken care of," I said.

"Whoa, fella," I could feel the greed radiating off of her, "since when did our company become so valuable?" She asked.

"It hasn't. I want to fight this one last case, then dissolve the partnership and the company."

She eyed me with distrust. "I figure after this last case the cops will be standing in line to bump us off," I finished.

"God, I don't know. Make me an offer," She said.

"Twenty-five thousand," I said.

"Sounds a bit low. How about thirty?" She said.

"Twenty thousand," I said.

"You are going the wrong way," she said, panic stricken.

"I don't know. It's the way I negotiate these days," I said with a smile.

"Deal," she said.

I picked up the phone and made a quick call. "Jake? Rank here. Sorry to bother you, but I'm tying up some loose ends here and need to borrow twenty grand to get rid of my partner."

"Oh, hell boy," he said jovially, "you're almost family now. I'll get rid of him for nothing, if you'd like."

"It's a her, not a him, and the thought is tempting, but I meant more along the line of buying her out so my business can disappear."

"No problemo, son," he said something to someone on his end I couldn't catch then, "Just send the yahoo home and it will be delivered to her this evening."

I relayed all this to Skank. I now had a head ache and a bad taste in my mouth.

"What would happen if I decided to keep the office open?" She asked innocently.

Without thinking I reached out, picked up the folding metal chair next to the file cabinet, wadded it up like a piece of aluminum foil and tossed the crumpled little ball into her lap.

"It's been a pleasure doing business with you," she shouted from halfway down the hall.

I laid my head down on the desk and waited for the pain to subside.

୦ଓ୧୬

The search for a common gathering point for Cell Lords and hence potential Masters of the Undead, was not as difficult as she had first thought. In fact, Vlad, of all people, came up with the solution.

"Geeze, mom. Type it in Google and hit enter. If ya still can't figure it out, type the address it gives into MapQuest and it will print you driving instructions."

Anastar didn't know whether to hug him or smack him.

Sarah solved the dilemma as she walked past by slapping him on the back of the head and saying, "don't be a smart ass."

What came up on the monitor was the name of an obscure gentleman's club; nice area of town, couple of photos, everything screamed old money.

In the driveway was her transportation. Kickin' it old style. Anastar didn't like the new cruisers, nor was she all that inspired by the new crotch rockets. Her old 750 cc Ducati was twenty years young and in perfect condition. A blend of shear power and...dare it be said...classic styling.

One might even say a mechanical version of Anastar herself.

The ride to the "club" took less than fifteen minutes.

Being a werewolf did have an advantage when it came to motorcycles; one didn't need a helmet.

The disadvantage of the bike was that when she pulled up, valet parking had no idea what to do with the motorcycle in the first place, and to top it off, a woman was seeking access to a strictly male club.

Anastar tossed him the key to her bike and he caught it. This was a good thing. Then he stepped in front of her, to bar her way. It could be said that was a bad thing, but amazingly the car that she threw him in front of only ran over his legs, and clean breaks heal quickly.

Entering the aged brick and stone building she entered a dank, dark and luxurious atmosphere.

It didn't take long for a crowd to gather around her. It seemed to be equally divided between angry and curious.

"Gentleman, we need to talk. I am Vlad's mother. You may call me Anastar." She shook her head, hair flying, as she pulled out a chair and sat down. "Things are getting too far out of hand."

A well dressed, ramrod straight waiter walked up to her.

"Madam, if you please…" as he thought of some way to politely request her to leave.

"Yes, thank you. If you would be so kind as to bring me a gin and tonic. Bombay Sapphire if available."

Wisely, he nodded and left to fill the request.

Anastar looked around the crowd. The crowd looked at each other; finally they parted and a distinguished looking man (other than he was only five foot tall) pulled another stuffed chair over and sat facing Anastar.

"Madam. My name is Carter. Please realize we are surrounded by idiots and anything we say will be twisted, misinterpreted and in general be used to discredit us."

"Excuse me?" Anastar asked, amazed.

"Madam, Anastar if I may, I realize you are here to intervene on behalf of Vlad, your son. I also know, and acknowledge the size and power of the clan you represent."

He took both drinks from the servant and handed one to Anastar. "I have a very difficult time believing that Mr. Vlad Lupes has anything to do with killing Mr. Hunt. You have to realize, however, my credibility with these people has been sorely strained. I admonished against moving against Vlad, but stated that your clan wouldn't mobilize against us if they detained him. I also told them that the attorney representing Vlad was strictly human, no changer as you call them. I was proven wrong on both accounts, evidently."

"Well, Mr. Carter. That certainly was refreshing. I will attempt to meet your honesty with my own."

He laughed. "Of course you can smell if I am lying and I have not that capability." He raised his glass, "Not to imply any dishonesty on your part, my dear."

"Of course not," Anastar laughed. "Let me tell you a story.

It seems that a human acquaintance of Vlad's killed Mr. Hunt. With good reason I might add.

Vlad was in the wrong place at the wrong time and doesn't pay any attention to things he puts his name on.

The…human…to whom you refer is now my daughter's mate and a changeling. He *is* Vlad's attorney. If something happened to him, my husband and I would be upset. While that would be bad, my daughter would be devastated. You may interpret devastated to mean an incredibly high body count.

As to my clan mobilizing against you, that was not a mobilization. That was a handful of people on an unauthorized training mission recovering Vlad."

Carter nodded. "All very much as I envisioned. By any chance would you be willing to part with the identity of the human who killed Taka?"

"No," Anastar said, "I think not."

"A shame. That might simplify things greatly, but let us brainstorm."

ßßøø

Jake was surprised by the large amount of undead lounging around the mortuary. Yes, he knew all that Sarah and Rank - sheesh, going to have to start thinking of him as John, or son - had said; and he knew that Emma was reigning Master, but damn, watching over a hundred undead stand in concentric circles around the mortuary, rocking from foot to foot disturbed him.

At least the sidewalk was clear, with no ensuing incident as he walked into the place.

Emma was sitting at the desk, she looked up and gave a half-hearted smile, turned and went back to looking out the window.

"Well," she said softly, "from the look on your face I guess you know the story."

"Yeah," Jake said, "and I am sorry. So sorry."

"I am lost. I don't know what to do. I don't want to be the Master of the Undead. I just want my Sammy back, and neither of those things are going to happen."

"Isn't there some way you can, you know, just step down from the position?"

"That's what I thought at first, but it seems in a large part, the decision isn't up to the living." Emma stood up. "The existing Master is killed by his replacement. The undead acknowledge the passage of human life, in particular the passage of a Master.

I could 'step down,' but the undead might not accept it."

Jake smiled a cold smile, "So unless someone kills you, it's not really official?" Jake laughed. "Why, oh why, does that make sense? Here I thought only werewolves had mindless and ridiculous rules and policies."

Emma gave him a strange look. "Are you here to negotiate some kind of a truce with the Master of the Undead or express your sympathy about

Sam?"

Jake ducked his head, "Negotiate more than anything. I feel bad and all about Sam, but I have a son being hunted, a daughter sleeping with a non-changer, and a wife breathing down my neck. I'm out to save my own ass here. Sorry."

Emma grinned. "I knew I could at least count on *you* to be honest and keep things in perspective." She dumped some papers off a chair and offered it to him.

"So…what can the Master of the Undead do for the Grim Reaper of the Mountain?" she asked.

CHAPTER THIRTEEN
DISTRICT ATTORNEY
VAMPYRE MASTER
XIII

While my office was - comfortable, I found that I no longer wanted to wait around for things to happen. I wanted to make them happen.

Which was probably why I wasn't too upset when the young werewolves that had brought my partner walked through the door alone and approached me apologetically.

"Mr. Rank?" said one. "Jonathon, sir? It seems we have a bit of a problem."

"Life seems to be a bit of a problem, could you be more specific?" I asked.

"Well, we brought information, but not the District Attorney."

"How am I supposed to be sure it's accurate?" I asked.

"Cuz we beat it…I mean we interrogated the *assistant* District Attorney and it smelled like he was telling the truth."

"That makes sense," I admitted. "Why exactly didn't you bring the DA?"

"Sir, it seems he isn't a day person, he was still sleeping."

"Maybe you'd better run this by me from the beginning."

"Max and I, I'm Zach by the way, went to the Courthouse. No problem getting there.

We took the elevator up to the chambers and offices; then we asked to see the District Attorney."

"Demanded, actually," said Max.

"They took us in to see the assistant District Attorney," said Zach. "Naturally we weren't happy with that. We roughed up the assistant a touch, just to make our feelings known.

He informed us that the DA wasn't there. I could smell he was lying so I bit his pinky." He raised his hand in protest. "I didn't eat that one…the first pinky, I swear. The second one I swallowed by accident."

"Enlighten me," I instructed, "I'm just a tad confused. How can you swallow a finger by accident, and why did you bite the second one off in the first place?"

Max spoke up. "That would be my fault. You see, while Zach was playing with the assistant, I kicked the door down to the District Attorney's office and then got my ass kicked."

"That's right," Zach said. "Max's screaming startled me so much I just…well…bit down. It's a lot like biting your tongue, but I happened to have his hand in my mouth."

"Why did you let yourself get your ass kicked Max? Why didn't you change?"

"Oh, I did. In the nick of time," Max said. "I kicked the door down and the room was empty, except for this coffin on the desk.

"A coffin?" I asked.

"Yeah, I thought it was weird too. Maybe someone had bumped off the DA, hell, I didn't know. I pushed the lid open and sure enough," he spread his hands, "the DA was in there. Looked dead as a door nail."

They both looked at me like that explained everything.

"So…how exactly did you get your ass kicked?" I asked.

"Geeze, well, that's what happens when you smack a Master Vampyre in the nuts to see if he's really asleep," Max said.

"Oh, my God," I cried, "Vampyres are real too?"

"Well that one convinced me he was real, and I don't give a shit what Jake says, there has *got* to be a better way to tell if they are asleep."

He composed himself and continued. "I morphed just as fast as I could, and that is fast because I had initiative to do so.

He came after me. He was faster and stronger. I put my hand through him and he never missed a beat."

"And the assistant was volunteering information as you fought?" I asked.

"No," Zach said, "but with the screaming and yelling, and havin' ate part of him for real, the assistant was just a fountain of information, interspersed between prayers."

I looked at Zach. "You didn't go help your partner?"

"Fuck that, he was the one sayin' the prayers. If him and God couldn't do it, I figured I wouldn't be much help."

"Okay, so what did you learn? That is useful, and I don't mean words of wisdom from Jake when he's been drinking."

Zach thought. "The DA's girlfriend was killed. And the guy that took the fall for it didn't do it."

He looked at Max, then back to me. "The DA killed her himself, but that isn't the interesting part."

He quit talking and looked at me expectantly.

"You are going to make me ask, aren't you?" I said.

"No," he looked disappointed, however, "but it's going to surprise you."

"So surprise me," I said, talking a swig straight from the bottle of single malt.

"He killed her because she was having an affair. With Vlad."

A terrible waste of scotch to spit it all over the desk.

"Hold it," I said. "Can the do that? Physically I mean? He's neutered. Would she turn? Would he turn? Why would he do that?"

Max answered. "Yes. Absolutely. No. Nope. Love or he is one sick puppy."

"Wow." It was all I could think of to say.

"So," Zach went on, "the DA didn't want to link Vlad anywhere close to this crime, so he is just letting the Taka Hunt killing be pinned on Vlad because the Cell Lords are dumb enough to believe it. Now Vampyres hate the undead, because they are undead themselves, but consider themselves far better. The undead like Vampyres anyway," he thought. "Probably because they are stupid. They like Vlad because he has always been nice to them, *and* has got it on with an undead." He looked troubled. "Hopefully just the Vampyre. A lot of this is conjecture and what I figured out."

"I still think the assistant was lying," said his partner. "He was plenty weird all on his own."

"Wow." That still seemed as good as anything to say did.

છ⃝ઓ

"Mr. Carter," Anastar said, "I can see where these people might not trust me, but why would they try to discredit you?"

"Ah, you cut to the heart of the matter. You see Cell Lords, or even just humans who deal with the undead, have different viewpoints. Different political parties if you will. I understand both viewpoints and need adopt neither. Therefore, I make an admirable spokesperson. Right up until the time I say something true, that they disagree with." He set his glass down, reached out, and took both her hands in his. His right hand was bandaged.

"Tell me, Anastar, what do you see when you look upon me?"

She studied him for a moment. "I see a man. Elderly. Someone who has spent much time outdoors. Desert perhaps, as indicated by leathery, wrinkled face and brow. Well educated. Personable. Polite."

"Oh, dear lady," he said, "you honor me much yet you surprise me. What do you *hear* when you listen to me?"

Anastar's eyes opened in alarm. "You have no heartbeat."

"Precisely, my dear." He stood and paced. "Here," he sighed, "is where I fear I will lose what trust we have between us.

I am, you see, undead. I know I do not fit what is generally considered the stereotype, but the truth."

He stopped pacing. "If you need a 'tag' or designation, then think of me as a mummy. We, or a very small amount of us, were the original undead." He frowned. "I fear the whole mess has gone downhill rather badly since my time."

He picked up his glass and studied its emptiness. "I believe I could use another. Yourself?"

"Please," she asked.

"Lest you think later I am flying under false colors, I am...let us say...in the field of public relations. I take no *real* interest or joy with outcomes. I am, after all, dead. Cheers, my dear," he said taking a drink of his fresh one and pointing out the new he had set before Anastar also.

"In addition to working with the Master of the Undead, I also am liaison for the Vampyre Master of the region."

"Vampyres exist?" she asked.

"A werewolf has trouble accepting their existence?"

He resumed his pacing. "Forgive me. Long ago, I taught in the country now known as Egypt. The floors were stone and the only way to preserve one's feet was to keep moving," he laughed. "Now my feet are well enough preserved, but the habit remains.

I will also mention, in passing, that the Vampyre Master is also the District Attorney, but the full information on this - and your son's involvement with the undead - is already circulating at your home. Of this, I am sure. Try to remember that much of what you hear is both second hand, and if not false, then much distorted.

I am not ignorant; I understand the part that Emma play's in this game also. The question was more to test your integrity. It is refreshing to find one who will not sell out their friends on a whim. Your husband will fill in the gaps, but suffice to say, she doesn't belong to either party, and one cannot do public relations with someone of neither, and whom both would hate.

The parties. Yes.

There are, of course, the Ramparts. The previous Master was of this party, as all have been. That is due to their election policy.

Next, we have the Sledmen. They believe in elections where both living and undead vote for Master. The Ramparts just believe in assassination. That is always hard to argue with.

The Sledmen also believe that every ruling member should register his or her undead. For voting purposes, contact and closure of loved ones, and to prevent their theft.

Now you, and your clan, must decide which side you are on and to what extent."

He smiled wistfully. "Of course there is always Emma's party. I have no idea what it is and I doubt she does either." He smiled again. "But then you would be initiating something new. I cannot recommend that. I was executed for it."

"Do you regret your choice?" Anastar asked.

"No, dear lady. Never for an instant."

CR80

"Jacob, how long have we known each other?" Emma asked.

"Hell, Emma, I can't even remember back that long."

"You brought me from the village, an infant, just a babe. You even found me foster parents."

Jacob shook his head in disgust. "Yeah. Right. I saved you. After I slaughtered all your people, including your parents." He slapped his knee. "You should hate me, but you don't. You know more of the truths behind werewolves, the Grim Reaper of the Mountain and our history than most young werewolves."

"I was too young to remember my parents, and you had to. You could smell the plague, you kept it from spreading. You took only those infected."

"Yes," he said softly, "and that was all, but you."

"Why did you let everyone believe you were a berserk killer?" she asked.

"I knew it would save me a lot of trouble later in my life. People think that you are the baddest thing to walk the face of the earth, and you don't have to harm or kill as often." He thought of his future son in law. "All I am is a Werewolf. And now, John Rank - the guy you saw with Sarah - seems he is going to be one also."

"He seemed like a nice boy," said Emma.

"Yeah, he is."

"What do you think I should do?" she asked.

"Take names and kick ass."

"I'm not a fighter," she said.

"You will either be a fighter or dead."

"What do I do?"

Jake thought. "You gather all the undead you can. It will either be enough to incite the others to attack, surrender, or ignore you. The clan will stand by you. At least those that follow me. I honestly don't know how many are loyal to me and how many are just paying lip service.

There hasn't been a true war for 500 years."

"About time then, I suppose." she said.

CHAPTER FOURTEEN
꧁REGROUP & FIGHT꧂
꧁CHANGE IS GOOD꧂
꧁XIV꧂

I hadn't had much time with Sarah, and it was taking a toll on my good humor. A quick kiss here, a hug there, a touch most tender…but, there was *always* someone around.

Sarah left a standing invitation, but for some reason I had never felt comfortable sneaking into her room at home. I knew for a fact everyone in that house could hear a mouse run across thick shag carpet. I had caught Vlad eating several of them, he had offered to share.

I had rapidly come to the understanding that when it was said werewolves ate humans, that's like non-changers saying they eat beef.

Sure, people eat cows - hamburgers, steaks, whatever, but they eat a helluva lot of other things in conjunction. Potatoes, chicken, veggies, bread… and so do werewolves. Like Anastar (I was starting to like her more every day) said, "You have to have a balanced diet," she shook her finger at Sarah, "and a steady diet of cats is not balanced either. You need to toss in grains and dairy." The jury was out as to which food group mice fell into. Junk food was the general consensus.

I sat on the front porch, trying to sort out my options. I didn't like any of them and most flat assed terrified me.

Jacob came along, slapped me on the shoulder and asked, "What heavy thoughts are pulling you down?"

I just shook my head. "I've gone over it a hundred times and there is no alternative."

"What's that?"

"You have to take the clan against the main body of undead." I looked at him and he nodded. "Anastar will team up with Emma. Problem is, that leaves a loose end that needs tied up at the same time. Could cause a major problem if it's left until after the undead is sorted out. The Master Vampyre. Seems like he is my own personal problem."

"You could read it as being Vlad's problem, or mine as he's my son; may haps one that can wait till last." Jake said. "It all seems here say so far."

"I wish I could. I am the one that said I would take Vlad's case and get him off the hook," I said, "besides, you have your hands full with the rest of the world. Vlad? I just don't see that happening."

Jake spoke softly. "Do you know anything about a Master Vampyre?"

"I was told how to see if they are asleep," I said.

Jake choked. "I can't believe he took me serious. In reality, however, they are one of the meanest and most dangerous opponents in existence. I wasn't positive they were real, I thought they might be just legend." He looked serious, "Otherwise I wouldn't have joked about them." He thought a moment. "No I probably would have anyway."

"Your point is?" I asked.

"You are not ready. You haven't even turned yet. No way you could even fight him to a draw. What makes you think you can?"

"I don't think I can. I just figure he will come after Vlad and Sarah some day…or they will go after him. I know his secret now. He knows it too. It makes sense he would come after me during the confusion of the battle."

Jake was expressionless, "You know you can die, don't you?"

"Yes."

❦❧

I don't know why I had bothered to worry about it. It was all taken out of my hands that very night.

Talk at the house was subdued. No one was saying much, nothing on television, the mortuary was closed. People tried planning, but either turned up indecisive or in arguments. I gave Sarah a peck on the cheek and laid down on the couch.

Sleep did not come, so I wandered out onto the back yard which was where we had parked the extra cars. It was quiet there. Anastar kept the yard immaculate, and I understood where Sarah got her gardening from. I plucked a single blossom from a rose bush and sat down with it.

The fragrance was cloying.

"Your sense of smell is heightened? You are changing quite rapidly. You are aware of the danger in that?" he asked.

"Yes." I hadn't heard him approach. I hadn't smelled him. I hadn't seen him. Yet here he was, sitting at my side.

He was dressed in dark clothing. Its quality and cut superb, the type that was ageless and bespoke taste and elegance.

"It is a shame. We are both in the business of law and justice, but our lives over shadow it all. I would give much to drop back into obscurity," his shoulders slumped. "I do not wish this to happen between us. Your word. Give me your word that past deeds will not be spoken of and we will part company never to meet again."

It would have been so easy. One word.

"I wish I could, but I gave an oath," I said.

"And it is worth dying for?"

I am not sure how it started. Did my frantic dive out of the way precipitate his blow, or did his lightening fast strike cause me to duck? I know I never answered his question.

His overhand swipe missed, although it was fast; his hand impacted the ground with a solid 'thud.'

I had managed to roll out of the way of his fist, but he swung his leg around like some kind of crazed break-dancer and caught me in the side. It lifted me and sent me flying six feet backwards.

I heard ribs break, but the pain took a moment.

His body continued its spin; still crouched on the ground, moving him next to me again. His hand flashed out and struck me in the face, knocking me back only a foot, but shattering my jaw.

He was moving fast, so fast he blurred. Like watching an old-fashioned film. I was getting the shit kicked out of me so I did the only thing I could think of and kept rolling until I was under my car. I lost some skin, but that didn't seem to matter a helluva lot.

It came flooding in on me.

Ever come in on a hot, hot day; dry and tired, and take a drink of cool water? Where you can feel it go down and seems to spread out through your body?

That was the pain. It just kept spreading and spreading. My heart was racing and every beat was a slam of pain in itself.

I couldn't see, nor breathe; the pain was extruding into every cell of my body and hammering out of every pore. All I could think was this is what it felt like to have your heart explode.

I thought I was going out. My vision faded briefly then came back. In color. I mean a person always sees in color, but there were…more colors. Colors I could not name.

I saw his hands reach down and grab the bottom edge of my car. Long slender hands with long, black fingernails. He pulled as hard as he could.

I reached out - my hands were hairy, gnarled, and had *big* black claws - and pushed as hard as I could.

The car went away, onto its side. Lights were coming on in the house.

He looked moderately surprised. I, on the other hand was not surprised, just pissed. Still lying on my back, I grabbed his ankles, picked him up, and smashed him into the ground. Several times.

I was surprised when I started biting and clawing, but we both had fangs and were using them. I knew I was inflicting damage, but it didn't phase him. The people coming out of the house did.

He disappeared into the dark and I screamed at him. When I tried, no words came out, just a vicious and drawn out howl.

℃℘

Everyone seemed a tad nervous about approaching me.

I knew I had changed, but it didn't bother me. Yeah, the pain had bothered me, but that memory was fading. All emotions seemed different. More distilled and pure. Mentally I was here, but even that was different. My thought process no longer went from 'a' to 'b' to 'c' to 'd.' Now they seemed to occasionally jump straight from 'a' to 'd,' bypassing the middle. I could see (but it didn't bother me) where that might lead to impulsive and erroneous behavior.

Jake was the first to come up to me. He was acting very strange and I wasn't sure why.

He held his hand out and slowly put it under my nose. Very strange indeed. When I inhaled, his scent was immediately familiar and I noticed the hair all over my body laid down. Even that on my neck.

"Good boy," he said. "Sorry, I'm not trying to be patronizing I am just glad to see you alive." He looked relieved.

"Well, that makes a couple things I have never seen. A real live Master Vampyre, a person change in less than a month of being turned - and live through it, and a knock down, drag out dog fight."

He tossed his arm around my shoulder, "You have absolutely no fighting technique whatsoever, but you gave it hell."

I tried to tell him about my jaw and chest; about how they didn't hurt and were better, but all that came out were some yips and growls.

"Don't worry about it. Sarah will work with you. There is a rudimentary sign language using body language and hand signs.

Lets go inside. I need a drink," he said.

CHAPTER FIFTEEN
WHAT'S DONE IS UNDONE
THE NEWBIE
XV

Jake downed a fast drink before turning to me. "You want one? Might be a good idea."

I shook my head.

"Do you remember how much it hurt when you changed?"

I nodded. Thinking about it for a moment, I nodded vigorously and reached for the glass. All I managed to do was pour it down my chest.

How the hell do you drink, when your mouth and nose are sticking way out there? I thought. I was frustrated and howled again.

Jake seemed to understand my plight. "Sorry, old boy, I forgot. You have to learn to lap it. Honestly it even tastes better that way." He thought for a moment then snapped his fingers. "Okay, John. Hang on a second." He disappeared then returned carrying something. He held it up. "Straw," he said. "We'll try it again."

This time I managed to get most of it down, before chewing so many holes in the straw it was unusable.

"As I was saying," he continued, "you know how much it hurt when you changed, it is going to hurt just as bad when you change back."

I shook my head vigorously.

He nodded yes. "You have to change back. Fairly quickly also. You kind of just mentally say change and you will." He looked concerned.

I shook my head.

"Yes, he said. "You are an internal morph. You begin the transformation internally both ways. Well your brain is on the inside. Internals run the risk of forgetting how to change, if you remain in wolf form very long the first couple times. You are going on half an hour. It's time."

Somewhere deep down, I knew the truth of his words, and seeing as how no one was offering another straw, I figured I would give it a shot.

I couldn't.

The closest I can explain it is, ever tried to go to the bathroom while someone is watching or can hear?

I am a quick learner and already appreciated howling. It is useful in expressing so many emotions. The only thing that would come close, or possibly be more satisfying would be to bite someone. Trouble was, everyone here would bite back.

Mentally I made a note to make a list of people to eat. At least bite the hell out of, if they tasted bad.

That thought made me mentally smile, relax, and the change was upon me.

The last time, I had been adrenaline rushed, what with the Count trying to waste me, changes in my life and tax time. During that pitiful stretch of my existence the mad rush had... soothed... if that could possibly be the word, the pain of transformation.

This time I felt both embarrassed and bad for tearing so much tile up off the kitchen floor and scoring the linoleum in the hall.

Laying there naked and human, the release from the pain brought with it a relief that nullified any possible humiliation.

A pair of pants would have been nice, but the tall glass offered by Sarah was just as good. It was another of her creations, this time it went down smooth.

Jake shook his head in disbelief. "I watched her mix it," he said. "I firmly believe that if you can survive her bartending, the Master Vamp has no way of harming you."

Half-way through the pick-me-up, Vlad brought me a clean pair of fruit of the looms. I was beginning to feel human. Literally and figuratively.

Anastar came back, took one look at Jake and myself and scolded, "The two of you need to get something in your stomachs other than the booze. Otherwise you both will be outside, eating grass, and puking your guts out.

I'll fix you a sandwich."

"So," I asked between bites of the sandwich, "how does this change plans?"

"Not much," said Jake.

"Quite a bit," said Sarah.

They looked at each other in annoyance. It was time to sort this out. "Sarah, you first, Explain please."

"Simple," she said and wiggled. "You changed. You survived. We can hunt together…you can even have the first cat. I don't have to be so darn gentle with you. Vlad knows you can kick his ass right now," she smiled, her dimples showing, "and there is nothing you need be embarrassed about. So now you don't even have to sneak into my bedroom." She turned red. "Just don't howl afterwards."

Jake looked at me and asked solemnly, "Please tell me that you already know my answer has absolutely nothing to do with any thoughts floating around I Sarah's mind."

"Jake, I understand. Sarah is just on a different page."

"Page hell, she's in a different book. So please, feel free to howl all you like, before, during or after, and here's my take on the situation in general.

The Master Vamp is still a problem, but you gave him food for thought. You weren't as easy to take out as he thought, and now he knows you have a clan behind you." Jake studied his fingernails. "I might add we are one of the biggest and strongest. We are in North America, South America and Europe, along with Russia, but more on that in a bit, plus, got an idea with some of my buddies to run past you. Particularly now.

So the MV will undoubtedly put himself on the back burner, hoping the undead will do his dirty work."

Anastar was staring at Jake and licking her lips nervously. "Jake, dear…are you working around mentioning this idea in front of me?"

"Maybe."

"And," Anastar continued with a frown, "are these *buddies* of yours your *howling' buddies*?"

"Well, I *might* have mentioned something to them."

"Oh, for Christ's sake," and Anastar stomped off.

Jake looked to Sarah.

Sarah looked to Jake and said, "Father, dear father, you have most assuredly stepped in it." She pointed in the direction her mother had traveled. "Mend your fences, dear father."

"She doesn't scare me," he said, but I noticed he scurried after her anyway. I mentioned that to Sarah.

She wrinkled her nose and giggled. "I think you would call that slinking, rather than scurry." She took me into her bedroom and pulled me towards the bed.

"Hold it," I said. "You must have some idea what your father was talking about."

Her eyes clouded. "I was attempting to divert your curiosity with wild wanton sex, but I guess I don't excite you anymore." Her eyes got shiny.

"It's not that," I protested. "I'm just very curious about what…"

She started crying. Why me.

""I'm sorry," I said contritely. "I'll make it up to you. I'll catch you a cat, personally."

She brightened up immediately, but warned, "Deal. I'll talk, but you don't get any happy time until I get a Siamese."

ଔଞ

I had to admit, this was nice. Laying on the bed, listening to both our hearts beating, just smelling so many things. Fresh linen, lingering odors of the evening meal, Sarah, and a hundred other aromas. My vision and smelling was less than when changed, but more than standard, or non-changer.

Sarah snuggled up, her head on my arm. I hadn't dressed beyond the skimpy briefs, but a strategically placed pillow seemed effective enough to avert a rampant sex drive.

She began.

"In every clan there is a 'pecking' order. Please don't think it weird. It is more like your military than anything. Officers and chain of command. If you challenge it, you don't get shot, but you will end up in a fight were you either win or get your ass kicked. Normally it's nonfatal, but it all depends on the mood of the victor, time, if the looser rolled for the winner. God, a zillion things.

Yes, you can be killed in battle. You heal like a son of a bitch, but if you get taken apart enough… well…each part will not heal into a new you.

Which brings us to the fact, and you might have guessed this, father is the alpha male and mom is the alpha female of the local clan."

I looked at her. "What does that make them?" I asked.

"Meaner and tougher than shit," Sarah said. "But don't interrupt.

Being an alpha is socially inhibiting. One just doesn't go out and mess around with other werewolves. It always seems to end badly, and with teeth marks."

She reached out and laid her hand on the pillow. "That is why we were all so surprised that father took a liking to you. Having seen you in your first fight, I understand a little more.

I think he's grooming you for his position."

"Yeah, right," I said.

"Most pack members, alone, wouldn't have faced a Master Vamp, or charged into those silver wearing dudes at your office. No," she patted my pillow, "That's why father is cutting you so much slack. He doesn't criticize your actions." She giggled rather sharply. "Do you honestly think my father would let somebody bed his daughter, in his own house with a smile, unless he truly believed the person was his equal and respected him?

Trust me. We are not as strict as non-changers when it comes to sex, but I will tell you if you promise not to get mad or jealous, when I was younger one other person was brave enough to sneak into my bedroom. Father caught us."

"What did he do?"

"Like I said, enough small pieces and they don't heal. Particularly the first piece he tore off. I wouldn't even do that to Vlad."

I hit the door, headed for my room and never dropped the pillow. No sense taking chances.

CHAPTER SIXTEEN
ႇRUNNING WITH THE BIG DOGSଜ
ႇTHE KENNEL KLUBଜ
ႇXVIଜ

The morning sun hurt my eyes. I now appreciated why Jake always sported those aviator sunglasses. I got in the passenger side of his convertible as he was getting behind the wheel.

"If you get a chance, stop at the nearest store and I will get some shades," I begged.

He grunted positive, drove one block, pulled into the dollar store, parked and leaned his seat back.

I approached the clerk.

"Glasses," I croaked.

"Dinner, wine or beer?" She asked.

"Sun."

"Isle two, half-way down, past the tampons."

The selection was not great, but what could I expect for a buck? They all seemed to be neon colors and perverted shapes.

I almost believed they were for children, but kids have better taste than that.

When I got to the car, I was mollified. The glasses helped immensely.

"You know your glasses are shaped like starfish and have a little yellow sponge type character on the nose piece?" He asked.

I was going to explain it was better than the purple ones with little dancing ponies on them, or that I couldn't see them while wearing them but it was easier to just say, "Yes."

I decided to throw the bulk of the conversation back his way.

"Did you get things resolved with Anastar?" I asked, using ninety percent of my strength.

He slumped in his seat as he pulled out.

"Yeah. Sorta. Around the edges." He turned to me. "No jokes about 'being in the dog house.' I've heard a million of them and haven't appreciated any. Remember that when we get to the bar."

"Look out," I yelled as he drifted into the wrong lane.

"Sorry," he said. "I patched things up enough we got out of the house with our skins intact.

We are going to meet my buddies. I have mentioned clans before, but I don't know if I mentioned how many or where. Are you familiar with motorcycle clubs and what not?"

I shook my head no.

"Pity. Would have saved some time. We are like the biggest club there is, with a lot of … chapters. There are a lot more clubs out there, each having chapters.

Thing is, seeing as how we are the biggest and most powerful, they exist because we have granted them permission.

Each of them have an alpha male and female. We conduct business often. It came to be that I, and many other alpha males, liked getting together and hanging out.

Sarah says it's the big dog club. Evidently that references something, but I'll be damned if I know what.

I got to thinking, rather than endanger the entire clan; what would happen if a couple dozen of the big dogs, the alpha males, went to war instead?

They all have a vested interest. It would attract less attention."

He pulled into the parking lot of a nondescript bar. There were a lot of motorcycles there and a few pickups.

"Plus," he said. "It would be a lot of fun." He waved to the bar. "Welcome to the Kennel, as we call it. If you are an NC, then it's the Greyhound Bar and Grill. Named after the racetrack down the street. The name Kennel comes from the fact we don't keep dogs as pets," he grimaced, "too much like some warped slavery.

Seeing as how we never have dogs, we never have doghouses. So the wives and girlfriends joke we never end up in the dog house when we get in trouble, but we spend a lot of time at the Kennel."

He held the door open for me. "I know you do not have need of its refuge right now, but some day, when you least expect it, you will need sanctuary from your sweet Sarah."

Jake waved me in ahead of him. "Here it be, in all its glory. Keep both feet on the floor when shooting pool. No credit. Don't piss on the bar stool to mark it as yours. Other than that...anything goes."

He stopped me. "Do me a favor. The Kennel allows undead zombies and such, but don't tell the guys you are an attorney." He looked embarrassed. "This place has class."

The interior was dark. Normally I would have to let my eyes adjust, but this time it was...pleasant. I could see fine and the smell of spirits, food and patrons blended into a warm, inhaled world of its own.

Plus, the testosterone level was through the roof. I don't know why I didn't expect that, with a gathering of alpha males. Everybody seemed engaged in competition; pool, foos ball, darts and biting empty beer cans in half. Even those relaxing appeared trying to out-relax their buddies.

There wasn't two dozen alphas, but there was half that. I don't know why I did it, but it just seemed to be the thing to do. The hairs on the back of my neck stood up; and my body started a deep, dull ache. I stepped to the middle of the floor.

"My name is John. I am an attorney. Anyone got a fucking problem with that?"

"Crap," Jake said.

A dozen faces turned to me. The faces became agitated and surrounded me. Each face brought a big, muscular body with it. I had an urge to piss on the floor, and not to mark my territory.

One face spoke to me.

"Young sir, before you perish, would you mind explaining a few things. What did you mean by that statement? Do you think you can take us all? Do you want to start with me?"

The face was adorning a head with no hair. It was bald. I don't know why, but I laughed; thinking of a hairless werewolf.

I couldn't help but grin at that mental vision. There was no neck under the head either. Just a herd of colossal muscles each with its own set of muscles.

The face stuck a flattened nose, obviously broken and healed many times, in my face and sniffed. He got a funny expression and took a step back. All the other faces looked at him and followed suit.

I raised my hands slowly before speaking. "Gentlemen, I am proud of my profession, even if not other practitioners of it. I doubt if I can take all of you at once, but if you go in groups of three, we'll give it a shot."

I turned to giganto. "And yes, you can be first, but I'd really like to have at least one shot and beer first."

He looked me up and down. "Blast the bones. You have no smell of fear around you. A drink does sound good, even - and seeing how you are with Jake it means I will - I have to buy the first round." He shook his head. "Plus, I figure any bloke that would wear sun glasses like that has to be one tough son of a bitch."

He stopped and scowled. "Just don't think I'm rollin' fer you."

"Never," I said, "But I gotta ask something about your hair."

ଓଃ৪০

I never got around to talking business with the boys, but that was Jake's job anyway.

I spent my time drinking, talking, playing pool, drinking, throwing darts, drinking, took a ride on no-neck's Harley drinking, playing the juke box, drinking and generally shooting the bull.

I opened up to them and was comfortable about it. They introduced me to all that came through the door as 'our shaggy shyster."

There wasn't that many more Lupes that came in. Most of the clients were NCs. The crew wasn't bashful about saying they were werewolves, and most of the NCs weren't bashful about telling them they were full of shit.

That was where and when I learned to hide. It's easy. Hide in plain sight and be honest. No one will believe it.

It was also where and when I learned no-neck's secret and made my first new friend.

No-neck's name was Izzy. The secret was that he wasn't a muscle bound thug, he was a muscle bound intellectual.

"Yeah," he said. "I studied and trained to be a teacher." The hick accent disappeared. "Originally, my good man, I was a college professor...physics." He smiled. "Couldn't do it. All those smart assed kids. Most of them too dumb to sniff a turd. I gave serious thought to taking a hundred of them out on a field trip, and only coming back with five."

He clinked his glass against mine. "Here's to common sense."

"So common sense prevailed and no field trip?" I asked.

"No," Izzy said. "Field trip went like clockwork. I brought back ninety-five." He took a swallow.

"Amazing thing about the whole adventure...no one even missed the five that didn't. Now I work with Kindergarten kids. They are almost as intelligent, plus they are trainable."

"What made you go to the young ones?" I asked.

"I tried explaining Quantum physics to university students. I explained that things are made of particles; they store all the information about what they make up.

They never are destroyed; if you could access the particles of say - a solar system and star that went super nova; you could rebuild it exactly, down to all creatures and their history.

University students just drooled and said, 'what?'

I tried it on pre-schoolers. Sure, they slobbered, but they had enough imagination they could grasp the concept."

"So, ya don't have anything good to say about college students?" I asked.

"No sir, I didn't say that." he replied. Izzy gave it a moments thought. "They don't taste all bad."

CHAPTER SEVENTEEN
EXPLANATION
STANHENCEN
XVII

We had a good time and still made it home early. Early the next day.

Things had gotten a little out of hand late at night. It was then the bar officially closed and it became a private party.

Somewhere along the line, I changed. I think it was when I was playing foos ball with One Eared Elvis. Strange character. Got an ear bitten off and it didn't grow back. I was loosing badly and changed. The pain was intense. They charged me for two pool cues I bit in half and a foos ball that I, evidently, swallowed when I was loosing.

God, I hoped it came out okay. I was getting used to pain, but come on.

Jake was far too messed up to drive, so I took care of it. We took the bus. The bastard driving charged me full rate for Jake, even though I carried him over my shoulder, had a luggage tag put on his ear, and he fit in the overhead compartment.

Sarah and Anastar met us at the door. They seemed unusually upset. It was difficult to understand them with their yelling, but I did pick up two questions that kept repeating.

Where had we been?

Why were we so late?

CC38O

I awoke that evening to a moderate hangover and Sarah shaking my shoulder.

"John, you need to wake up. You need to get up. Right now."

I dressed and staggered downstairs. I will be the first to admit I wasn't up to my normal sharp and observant self. It took me a few moments to notice the small, brown man sitting at the kitchen table.

That wasn't so bad, but when I recognized the guy standing at the window, I damn near shit.

The change was involuntary, painful, and almost instantaneous. So was

Jake's, but his didn't hurt him.

He body checked me in mid-air, as I leapt for the man at the window. The impact was bone crushing. At the time I was not sure what was happening, just a very scary thing had hold of me. As we hit the ground, I struck out catching the creature, Jake, square in the chest with a clenched fist. Interestingly two things happened.

Jake was knocked back, and I managed to drive me own claws deep into my hand. Mental note: werewolves should never box. When you make a fist you are gouging the hell out of yourself to start with.

Sarah stepped in front of me without changing. I recognized her immediately.

"Bad John," she said, slapping the shit out of my nose with a newspaper. "Stop it and change back."

The slap was not earth shaking painful, but it stung so bad it brought tears to my eyes. I remember seeing Vlad's blurred image shake his head in sympathy.

The change back was incredibly painful also. It sounded like it was going to be every time. At least my shorts had stretched and came through intact. My t-shirt was shredded.

My hand still seeped blood, but was healing as I watched. Anastar was picking Jake up off the floor.

"Christ," he muttered as he stumbled to a chair. "He is stronger than hell and I sure wasn't expecting a punch. I'll have to remember that."

The man at the window had not turned around. Credit given, the Master Vampyre was one cool cucumber.

Sarah planted me in a chair next to Jake.

I started to apologize to Jake, but he waved it off.

"No biggy. You reacted about the same as I did."

"No," said Carter. "I am very certain you did not envision us arriving on your door step, unannounced." He smiled. "It would be difficult for you to react in any other fashion.

Anastar, when last we spoke I told you a portion of the truth about myself and the Master…"

"Portious."

"Excuse me?" said Anastar.

"Portious," said the man at the window. "The name is Portious. Port will do. I can't see everyone calling me Master This or Master That all night long.

Anastar nodded.

"I should have done it this way the other night. Sometimes a person gets so used to issuing orders or threats; he forgets that others are equal. I apologize, it was wrong of me."

It took me a minute to digest all this.

"Well Porty," I said. "Does that mean we aren't going to do the snarl and growl thing tonight?"

Carter flinched.

"I don't think...I hope..." he laughed, "...that will not be required tonight." He turned from the window. "However I have yet to feed tonight. I fear I might grow...peckish." He waved to Carter. "Thus, my esteemed associate will enlighten and entertain questions."

He turned back to the thin pane of glass.

Carter bobbed his head, and then began.

"Mankind's cry for law, order and justice has rang out, sounding down through the ages.

In this day and age, it is sad to admit, we are lacking in all of those things. Why? Too many laws, requiring too many enforcers. Everyone trying to do everything, which means no one does anything.

Portious and myself have been in...'law enforcement' for centuries." He looked at us. "Have you never wondered where and more importantly *why* Vampyres, werewolves and the undead exist?"

He shook his head. "No. Probably not. No more than a non-changer, as you call them, human wonders about the cradle of humanity; the Tigris and the Euphrates.

Would you be surprised to know that genetic engineering was being performed about 8,000 BC? Maybe not totally true. Let us call it selective breeding. Optimistic. Not a failure but it took them longer than they thought. About 4,800 years longer.

Think of it. Imagine the frustration of those people wronged and denied justice.

There was no communication at that time. If someone say...killed another; all they had to do was walk off. They did not exist once they had traveled two or three villages away. You could write a letter, but to whom would you deliver it?

How could you even identify the villain to another? No cameras. If you could not draw a perfect image all was lost.

Therefore, it was set about to 'breed' effective law enforcement.

Trouble was, the time it took. People figured it might take two, three lifetimes.

Not so. By the time it was becoming effective, 3,000 had passed. The humans controlling the breeding lost interest or at the least, focus.

The last thousand years, plus, the experiment ran itself, so to speak.

A small bit of evidence has survived. Guesses as to its meaning has enticed man for ages. Not surprising. At the time it was created, it was a mystery to all but those involved.

In 8,000 BC the main *base* if you will, consisted of four large posts and one big-assed tree.

By 3,100 BC, the experiment was at the height of its success. Bones from the site, and this era have been dug up and attributed to animals and people. Technically correct. They were from the dead lawgivers and criminals. Fifty-six pits in a circle, to be exact.

The beings created were two fold. The judges, the decision makers, were blood drinkers. Vampyres. Fast, impervious to most things that can cause death.

A vampyre can do two things of import. Their bite can kill and turn others into Vampyres; if they so choose. Their bite can kill and turn others into undead; if they so choose.

Those undead can then toil under the auspice of a Master of the Undead, to pay amends for their crimes.

Around 2600 BC, the Vampyres continued the building of the court with stone. That amazes people, but four Vampyres can carry massive stones.

Construction continued until 1600 BC. We continued using it until the seventh century.

Nothing stays the same. People no longer needed us so much…at least that was their feeling.

Vampyres cannot go out during the day, so we had the equivalent of police officers. Only they were far superior to man and could hunt night and day. They could smell when people were lying."

Carter nodded at us.

"Yes, werewolves. You were a prime part of it. Born and bred as partners to the vampyre. Part of the Stanhencen. Stone Henge.

Stan means stone. Hencen means gallows, or instrument of torture. The early medieval gallows consisted of two uprights with a lintel joining them. Modeled after Stanhencen's trilithons.

In the eyes and minds of man, our usefulness vanished. Worse we became monsters and then myth.

With no requirement of performance, the werewolves wandered off; to forest and mountain.

Vampyres, with no requirement of performance, faded into the night and the crypts of the world.

All would have been good, well not good per se, except…what about all the undead and Masters thereof?

They continued. Over time, they degraded. It happened because the undead were producing undead, not Vampyres creating them. Every new undead was slightly 'off,' from the previous.

The Masters of the Undead were no longer chosen by the Stanhencen, but by themselves. Soon it degraded even from even that.

At one point, the werewolves came forth in an attempt to resolve some of their problems, but the makeshift Masters of the Undead wanted no challenge to their power.

That was the origination of the hate between groups.

Which brings us to this," Carter said, pointing to the Master Vampyre.

CHAPTER EIGHTEEN
♋PORTIOUS AND DARLA♌
♋SCISSORS - ROCK - PAPER♌
♋XVIII♌

Portious turned from the window. "Any additional questions come to mind?"

A person should know better than ask that in the presence of an attorney.

"Did you kill your girl friend?" I asked.

"Yes, absolutely." He said. "But not because she was playing around with Vlad."

"Oh," I said eloquently. "Um...don't you think the dead lady deserves justice?" Not my best effort, but I hadn't expected honesty. Go figure.

"I don't know. Why don't you ask her?"

A cold wind blew on me briefly, and I felt two hands on my shoulders. I turned my head and two mischievous, but blood shot eyes peered into mine.

"What the hell," I yelled and jumped. She jumped also, but somehow stayed attached to the ceiling.

"John, where are your manners?" Chided Anastar, while Sarah tried to coax her down.

"I'm really sorry," I said and I meant it.

"It's okay," Port said. "New Vampyres are very jumpy.

Thank god they can't turn people for years." He thought. "Small consolation if they suck you dry, I suppose."

He watched as she slowly floated back to the ground.

"John, meet Darla; Darla meet John."

For the life of me, I didn't know what etiquette was required. The only thing I could think of was when I had just changed and Jake had approached me and let me sniff him.

"That was really fucking stupid," noted Vlad as he stared at my hand in Darla's mouth, a small smile revealing her fangs were sunk as deep as possible.

"And that, ladies and gentlemen, is why we were the judges and you guys hunted them down," said Portious.

"But he's an attorney," Carter said in explanation.

"Yes. I forgot. Point taken."

"Darla dear?" He said.

Her eyes turned to him, but her teeth never left me.

"Let go of the nice man's hand."

She shook her head, and my hand.

"Yes dear, you have to. He wasn't offering you a bite."

She looked at me. I smiled and shook my head.

"Sorry," she said after she had let go of my hand.

Portious looked at my hand. "Sloppy," he told Darla. "You broke the skin with all your teeth. As I explained, no massive wound is needed. Our saliva contains a powerful anticoagulant. That way you only need use the fangs." He patted her head affectionately. "Keep practicing."

I put my hands behind my back.

"I didn't feel it was a good idea for everyone and his dog - no offense - to know about this. It was unfortunate she was found before she rose again. The maid dialed 911."

He shrugged. "I had a scarf around her neck to hide the fang marks. Somehow the story got out she was strangled. It all snowballed."

"Fine," I said. "What about Vlad? Don't you think that was a farce? He got blamed wrongly. Well, except for messing around with your girl friend, which I can understand would piss you off..."

"Bullshit," Portious said. "He signed a confession. I had a deal with a judge. When he appeared in court it was going to be dismissed on technicality.

His being friends with Darla had nothing to do with anything. I never inquired, but it was my understanding that nothing could happen, even if they wanted. If something did happen, then that is between them. People have the right to make their own decisions.

Unfortunately he got out of jail. Question exists as to whether it was a bail bond or jail break. Doesn't matter, it screwed up my plans."

"Why didn't you explain this before?" I asked.

"What? You mean when your men snuck in, roughed Carter up and kicked me in the nuts while I was asleep? That they got their story wrong? I don't know. For some reason I was a touch put out. Forgive me," he said sarcastically.

"Mistakes made all around," Jake said soothingly.

Anastar, Sarah and Darla had departed for the living room, all enthusiastically talking girl talk. More precisely they were compiling a verbal list of all the inconsiderate things the men in their life did.

It appeared they would be occupied for hours.

"So where does that leave us," I asked.

"Finally," Carter sighed. "We get to the gist of the matter.

It shouldn't matter who the Master of the Undead is. They perform no useful service - by they I mean the undead themselves - and have degraded to the point all they really do is rock back and forth and moan.

On occasion they catch someone slow enough and dumb enough, eating their brains or turning them.

This time, however, the Master is a woman who shows some promise. Not totally self serving. Moderately intelligent. A welcome step backwards.

It would seem unjust if she were killed for doing good."

Portious took over. "To be honest with you, it would have been interesting to see a Werewolf in the position.

We are *not* attempting to go back to the old ways. That would be ludicrous. Can you imagine trying to enforce the stupid assed laws? They change from town to town, let alone country to country.

And face it," he said sheepishly. "We both have fed on an occasional innocent bystander. Not something I'm proud of, but you can't justify draining a person of blood; or in your case eating them, for say…jay walking."

We quickly checked in on the women.

"I didn't know Vampyres drank coffee and ate popcorn," I said.

"Me either," Portious said. "Coffee maybe, but the popcorn hulls could get caught in the fangs."

"Not as big a problem as you would think," Jake said, displaying his. "Floss, or chew on a good solid bone and problem resolved."

"I'll keep that in mind," Portious said.

"Which brings us to summation," Carter said.

"Its screwed up, but functional. There is an acceptable Master of the Undead. Acceptable to Werewolf and Vampyre, if not the Cell Lords.

Not a well known fact, but there are only about fifty of them any more.

What might not be acceptable is full scale war. I will have to research that some."

"Why are there so few," Vlad asked. "And why are they so frickin' stupid?"

"Vlad," Jake warned.

"No," Portious said. "That is a totally valid question, Vlad.

There just aren't a lot of people standing in line anymore to be Cell Masters. That is a new term, by the way. It used to just be Masters. Varying degrees in status, but all Masters.

Face it, how many kids say 'When I grow up, I want to be a Master of the Undead?'

Most opt out for doctors or nurses. Police or firemen."

"Makes sense," Jake admitted. "So - forgive me if I'm dense - what's happening? Whatzup?"

Carter raised his hand. "Long story short. Fifty Cell Lords with about 5,000 undead versus Emma who can field about 500. We want her to win."

"And you can't handle it?" Jake asked.

Carter looked at the Master Vampyre who said in disgust, "Tell them. They will find out about it sooner or later." He turned. "This is part of what I have researched so far."

"Very well," Carter said. "It's all about checks and balances. A judge has the power of life and death over almost everything.

But not the Undead.

That way, power cannot corrupt."

"So who rides herd over the Undead?" I asked.

"The Werewolves."

"And over the Vampyres?"

"I thought I made it clear. Masters of the Undead."

"Okay then who is over the Werewolf?"

"That's obvious; Vampyres."

"Look," Portious shouted, "It's like a game of scissors - rock - paper, it runs full circle. So if we follow the old ways at all, you have to go out there and fix this crap."

"Why didn't you just say so. That's what we were planning on doing. We have a group of Alphas together, we were just trying to figure out how to get the opposing team all at one spot." Jake was beaming. "And no out-and-out war."

Carter pondered, then brightened. "She picks up the phone, makes a call and says, 'I am going to be at such and such a place on this day and time.

Anyone have a problem with me be there.

If you aren't there, you are accepting me as official Master."

"Would that work?" I asked.

"It's a plan," said the Master Vampyre. "I am not totally comfortable. Might does not always make right. Plus," he added, "it sounds too easy. Nothing is ever easy."

CHAPTER NINETEEN
CARTER THE UNDEAD
VAMPIRE SECRETS
GRIM REAPER TRUTH
XIX

Emma seemed to grasp all the concept and explanation without problem. She didn't even have a problem with the lateness of the hour.

So easily did she seem to understand that Izzy (all the Kennel crew was present) asked, "Emma, do you know about Quantum physics?"

"Oh, Lordy. I think so, but when it comes to a black hole, and someone falling into it, I have a problem.

They are ripped to shreds, or particles, and smeared on the event horizon. Therefore they are killed, but they themselves would notice nothing out of the ordinary. I wrote to that Hawking fellow about this but never got a response."

Izzy wiggled.

"Emma," the Master Vampyre asked. "Did you make your phone call?"

"Yes, Dearie. I told them October 30th, midnight, to meet at the site of Maryhill, in Washington State."

"Ah, how appropriate," said Portious.

"Sorry, but I never heard of it," I said.

"Not so strange," Emma said. "The town of Maryhill burned to the ground at the turn of the century. In the center of it was...is still...a perfect replica of Stanhencen. A gentleman named Sam Hill built it above the Columbia River Gorge."

Portious continued, "Mr. Hill mistakenly believed the original was a sacrificial site. He constructed the replica in homage of the World War One dead.

It was to remind viewers that humanity was still being sacrificed to the god of war."

He shook his head.

"Regardless of his inaccuracy of reason, it is spot on for detail of the original Court. It is a fine place for battle. Its seclusion ensures all will play out beyond prying eyes."

"Hold it," Vlad said. "Would that be the morning midnight leading into the 30th, or the night midnight at the end of the day? People might get confused."

The phone rang and Emma answered.

"Yes.

Yes, this is her, how can I help you dear?

No. No, that would be Halloween Eve.

No that's okay. I understand you want to take your Undead out trick or treating first. I am doing the same.

No, we will wait for you before starting. You have my word on it.

Be sure and give them all flashlights and tell them to watch out for traffic and to stick together.

I will. You too, be sure everyone knows the exact time we start the battle. God bless, dearie."

She hung up the phone and smiled a gentle smile.

"You're right. That was one of the Cell Lords."

ᆫᆯ

I was antsy. Two weeks to kill and it seemed I really had no purpose, except a warm body at the battle.

The only good news was Sarah and I were getting a lot more time together. I had Darla to thank for that.

During their evening's discussion of the evils brought on by the men in their lives, she had innocently told Sarah that she thought I was cute, polite, and tasted good.

From that point on it was rare that Sarah wasn't by my side after dark. I was concerned, and Sarah told me it was my imagination, that the after shave Sarah bought me smelled suspiciously like garlic.

My freedom came in the daytime. Sarah bounced off with her mother shopping. I was welcome with Jake, but felt I was in the way.

I could have hung out with Vlad, but decided I would chase parked cars before I stooped to that.

Instead I cornered Carter one day.

"Carter, you are supposed to be Undead, but you are unlike any today. If you are from the past - at least that far in the past - you must have committed some crime to get where you are," I stated.

"You are looking for my life story?" he asked.

"I guess I am."

He shrugged. "Boring, but you are welcome to it.

Carter is not the name I was born to, rather it is a translation - loose I might add - of my initial profession.

I carried things. I literally carted them.

Of the people using my service were some erudite personas. You have to understand, education was not as cut and dried as it is today.

Our recreational drugs were nowhere refined as today either. Initially you had wine. Mead if extremely fortunate and swill otherwise.

Think of dipping a horn of unaged wine from a bucket sitting on the floor." He looked wistful.

"If we had access to weed then I would have been a flower child. And substantially richer.

Where was I? Yes. Teachers, as they were, would gather around fountains wells and such; people would just congregate and gravitate to them. Myself included.

After years of speaking with them, I suddenly noticed that I drew my own crowds. Not big at first, but enough to buoy my ego.

One evening I was approached by a woman who revealed many mysteries. I had been chosen by a group, but approached by a different group. For that reason I can emphasize with people when they are confused by the pecking order of the court.

It was explained to me and I was offered the position as *one* of the Masters of the Undead. I accepted."

"But you are Undead," I said, stating the obvious.

"And you are correct," Carter said, without missing a beat. "But I wasn't then," he looked at me peevishly. "Who's fucking this chicken anyway?"

"Sorry," I said, "your chicken. Go ahead."

"I accepted the position. It wasn't all that hard, nor time consuming. We did a lot of work for the local government.

That's what got me in trouble. If I had been below their radar, it would not have been a problem.

I was still gathering crowds. One day, solely in idle conjecture, I mused about the evils of government and possible alternatives.

After that I could have crawled on my belly and not been below their radar.

Politicians are fickle, paranoid, petty, and take everything as a personal affront.

Come to think of it, that is pretty much what I told the crowd.

I was scheduled to be publicly hung.

During the night a Master Vampyre came to visit. He explained that he wasn't supposed to interfere. He also said it wasn't right what was to befall me. He offered me an out.

Although being turned Undead was normally a punishment, he could turn me if I so desired. Then they could hang me like a damned salami if they wanted.

He said I couldn't remain a Master of the Undead, but could work at his side and learn of the world, life, and death.

He did. I did. To this day I travel and work with Portious."

"Speaking of Portious, what's his story?" I asked. "I know him and I have a truce, so to speak, but he still scares the crap out of me."

Carter smiled gently. "That is a hard question to answer.

He is old. Older than I am, and I have centuries weighing on my shoulders. There is a reason for their longevity.

It is very true that wisdom comes with age, and stability. Mentally you have to be exceptionally stable to live that long. That is one reason they perform at night and sleep during the day."

He waved me closer. "They can get up and move during the day. Sunlight doesn't hurt them. Well, the sunlight hurts their eyes because they are not used to it.

They stay as close to nocturnal existence as possible to prevent sensory overload. You put up with the world all day. After five days you are ready for a weekend to decompress.

They are the judges. They have no weekends."

"Okay," I said. "I can sorta understand that. What's with sleeping in a coffin? That is fucking creepy. And does garlic really stop them?"

He laughed. "I can understand that. A police officer has a badge. A regular judge has a gavel. More than anything those are symbols of their power and identity. What better symbol of a man who hands out death or undeath than a coffin?

Garlic? Surprisingly enough, yes. Exceptionally allergic. The very smell will drop them."

"Carter, I am surprised. Giving out all my secrets." The Master Vampyre stood in the doorway. "Did you tell him about peanuts and shellfish?"

I jumped. This was embarrassing, I felt like I was caught scheming.

Portious walked into the room. "Yes. A wooden stake is bad, but for true lethalness…a peanut butter sandwich." He smiled that toothy smile. "We have many food allergies. A primary reason we stick to blood.

Interesting to note, and proven by Darla, we don't handle popcorn well either. It didn't kill her, but she vomited clots for an hour."

He thought hard. "I suppose it might have been the extra butter and salt, but I'm not going to try proving it one way or another."

He removed his jacket and hung it over a chair. "I've never heard of an allergy to werewolf, and she didn't get more than an ounce or two from you."

He looked directly at me. "I apologize for that. I also thank you."

"For what?" I asked.

"She bit you without warning or provocation. I know from personal experience how fast and strong you are. You showed great restraint and control not striking back in reflex."

I contemplated telling him the truth; it startled me so bad I never thought about retaliation, plus, I had damn near put a bite me sign on my hand by shoving it in her face. "No problem," is all I said on the subject, but there was one question I had to ask.

"That night in the yard. Were you trying to kill me? No hard feelings if you were."

He folded his hands and stared at the floor. "I am not sure. I was hoping not to have to and I don't know if I could have. After years of striving not to execute innocent men, I am not sure I could make an intentional exception.

Morally I would have been guilty of the same crime I used to punish. That might have been the straw that pushed me over the edge."

He looked up. "You really want to know what the most dangerous thing is to a Vampyre? It's other Vampyres. We watch each other closely and police our own. When one of us go off the deep end, he is taken out and given peace."

"Then how is it that Werewolves can eat people and you condone it?" I asked.

"Same reason I don't hunt down man eating tigers or lions. Its in the blood. It had to be kept. That's what good hunters do. You are a predator.

We kill also, but we take the dregs of society and the ill. Have you never wondered about the Grim Reaper of the Mountain? It is commonly believed to be mass murder. Far from it."

Portious sat at the table and I joined him.

"I am going to tell you a tale that I shouldn't. I do so to spare Sarah the guilt of breaking an unspoken oath and telling you herself.

The year was 1911. A man named Jacob Turnley had been turned the year before by Sturtgen of the Black Forest clan. A bewitching bitch with a passing fondness for Jacob.

He was a man with good qualities. Not always the best judgment, but a good heart, as NCs say.

The influenza plague was sweeping the globe. It killed more people than the Black Plague. Wiped out entire communities.

One such community, in Canada, happened to be the birth place of Jacob Turnley. He had left it for education, prestige and work in the States. He had much success. Go ahead and ask what he was?"

"What was he?" I asked.

"An attorney," Portious said. "Retained by the Pinkerton Agency." He smiled while I choked on my coffee.

"He was barely more advanced than you, but he had trained with the claymore. A large two-handed sword werewolves used to carry."

He looked at Carter, "At one time that was their 'symbol.'

As a werewolf can smell disease, if severe enough, he went to the village to attempt to curb its spread. Diagnosis was followed by decapitation. All too soon he found the entire village was infected.

He was half-way through, not saving anyone, and causing them to die in more terror than if left to the fever.

He went a bit mad. All in all he killed sixty people, dismembered them, and attempted to bury them.

Even a werewolf cannot dig that large a hole in frozen ground.

Crazed, he threw body parts in a mineshaft and collapsed it in upon itself.

Except the feet. He missed them. They were found later and became part of the myth.

The only good that came out of this was the finding of a three year old girl. Healthy.

He carried her home and she was given to the NCs
to raise. Her name was Emma.

Sturtgen basically discarded Jacob. He was broken of spirit and mind. He was to be eliminated, but her sister saw promise in the man. The old saying, 'that which does not kill you makes you stronger.'

Sturtgen would not hear of sparing him and she was alpha female. It was solved in the old way. Sturtgen and Anastar fought to the death and Anastar became the new alpha female. Jacob, after twenty years, came back from the veil, and indeed incredibly strong of mind and body. Intelligently his opponent rolled and Jacob became alpha male and the Grim Reaper of the Mountain."

"Wow," I said, and that seemed to cover it all, except, "How the hell do you know all this?"

"The system has fallen apart, but it's still...a hobby of mine. A death here and there is not worth playing judge. Sixty is mass murder and could attract attention. I investigated it and assured myself of the truth."

"Did Jake ever find out about your investigation," I asked.

"No, I was only found out by one werewolf," he shrugged. "Different clan even."

He frowned. "Was a helluva fight though. He managed to get a stake into me but missed my heart. I bit his ear off. You might remember I said our saliva has an anticoagulant? Under heavy adrenaline rushes, we don't get the adrenaline. The saliva, however, gets superbly powerful. If we bite something off in a fight, it won't regenerate."

"Ever been to the Kennel Klub," I asked. "I think an old friend of yours hangs out there.

CHAPTER TWENTY
PUPPY CHOW
THE TOME OF STONES
XX

There was a surprise when I returned to my office. I felt sad, thinking about closing shop and pulling the shingle. I wasn't sure what I would do now that I was a fledgling werewolf, but I knew I would need a job of some kind.

The surprise was that Sarah was there. More than that, she wasn't alone.

Scampering around on the floor were two dogs. They appeared to be pedigreed, and well groomed. I noted that everything in my office, lower than four feet, had been knocked over, broken, or chewed on.

They weren't all that big, maybe twenty-five or thirty pounds each, but when they jump up on you they pack some momentum.

Together they managed to knock me on my ass. I found myself rolling on the ground with them licking my face. God help me, I almost succumbed to an urge to lick back. The way they wagged their tails made it impossible to be angry, or at least to stay angry.

"What gives with Kibbles and Bits?" I asked Sarah.

"Ohhh...don't be mad. I promised I would take care of them for the day." She smiled, but it was a forced smile. "It's kind of my penance for...well, for being a bad girl."

It struck me as strange. "Sarah, I thought...ah, nothing."

"No, what dear?"

"Well I thought it was considered wrong for werewolves to keep canines as pets." I rolled one over with my foot and rubbed its tummy with my shoe. "I admit though, they are cuter than a button." I gasped as the other sank its teeth in my ankle.

"Okay, kids," Sarah yelled. "Get ready. Aunt Sarah and Uncle John are going to take you out for ice cream."

The one let go of my foot and the both beat feet into the bathroom.

"You mean?" I asked.

"Yep," Sarah said. "Get used to it. Someday you and I might have one. Papa is making me take care of them as an object lesson. Not to have any." She sniffled. "It's working."

Voices came from the bathroom and a young boy and girl exited, pulling their clothes on as they ran for Sarah.

"What's ice cream?" The boy asked.

"Aunt Sarah says you know lots of neat places and things to eat...and you don't have to chase them," the girl chimed in, to me.

"Your mother fixes and sets a fine dinner. I know you don't have a steady diet of people. Is your mom the only one that knows how to cook?"

Sarah looked uncomfortable. "That was a uh, special occasion. Have you seen any other meals? We eat on the fly most the time. A raw carrot tastes better than a cooked one. A raw steak better than well done."

She clapped her hands and both came to a stop in front of me.

"Honey, meet Barney and Carmen." She put a hand on top of each head. "They may look like they are five or six, but they are about twice that." She saw my expression and explained. "Born werewolf, they 'appearance wise' age about half of human. Then at puberty, for us about fifteen, we go to dog years.

Five years temporal ages us one year, after that. I am around forty some."

She giggled. "We don't keep track. If a person doesn't know the date of their death, why should they worry about the day of their birth?"

"My god, you are ten years older than me? You look twenty."

"Don't worry dear. Now that you are turned, you are on the same calendar."

She smiled, and her dimples showed again. "Normally we are not allowed 'out' among people until we are about thirty eight.

It would attract too much attention. It would look like kids running around without parents, truancy ...and the self restraint isn't there. That's why we are, for the most part, under the radar.

"Then why," I asked, "are we taking these two out?"

"They are driving me fucking crazy," she said. Tears forming in her eyes.

"Works for me," I said. The two just grinned at me. "Whose your parents?" I asked.

The boy piped up. "Izzy is paternal." "And Isabel is maternal."

Finished the girl. She looked at me with serious eyes and said, "Father told us we shouldn't use the words 'sire' and 'bitch,' around non-changers."

"But Sarah called Vlad a ..." The boy got that much out before Sarah clapped her hand over his mouth. "That means getting poked by something. I misused it, so forget it," she admonished.

Sarah turned to me. "And lest *I* forget, there has been a change in the up coming battle. Carter will meet us at Barkin' Robin's and fill us in."

"Any idea what the change is?" I asked.

"All I know is that mother blew screws when papa told her. She spent the day crying." Sarah looked frightened. "I have never seen or heard of her doing that."

CB80

After watching all the classic zombie movies it was hard to watch a mummy/zombie/undead pack away a three scoop cone.

"If I had access to this when alive I could have ruled the known world," Carter said. "You know the best part?" He asked.

"I give up."

"Undead never get brain freeze if we eat it too fast."

"Makes me want to run right out and join the ranks," I said.

"Sarcasm ill becomes you."

There was a slight commotion at the counter. The kid behind was explaining to Carmen, "Nope. I'm sorry. We don't have that one. Not too many requests for raw liver flavored ice cream."

"The flavors are all fruits and nuts," Barney pouted. "Haven't you ever heard you are what you eat?"

"You could always load it down with gummy worms on top," the soda jerk suggested.

"Yeah! Cool..." The kids both started dancing around with such enthusiasm I was afraid they would change.

"Worms, worms, worms, worms, worms," they began what sounded like a cabalistic chant as they danced.

"Are most like this?" I asked.

"No," Sarah said, "most are ill mannered and evil." She grabbed me by the front of my shirt. "Never. Never will I subject myself to children. I believe in pro-choice."

"Pro-choice?"

"Every mother should have the option to eat their children for the first five years."

Sarah went for the children who were backing the soda jerk into a corner. I turned back to Carter.

"So, what's new?" I asked. "It sounds like something has stirred the pot."

"Yes, well I am afraid I was the chef on that." He looked up at me and, so help me, he looked his age. Old. Old and tired.

I sat down. "Talk to me."

"The Tome of the Stones. I have packed a copy of it for centuries. A rather large work, compiled over 2,000 years."

I thought about it. "Is that kinda like the bible?" I asked.

"No, the bible is a recent work. Actually it is a cut and edited compilation of a lot of works.

The Tome of the Stones, or Tots, was created for the purpose of giving a backbone to the Triad. The Vampyres as judges; the Werewolves as enforcers; the Masters of the Undead as wardens; that is the triad. Tots is the guidelines for its functioning. The rules. The Constitution."

"Then why is it so...upsetting?"

"Hmmm," Carter said. "I told Anastar that I worked with both the Undead and the Vampyre. I was turned by Portious, so I have allegiance to him. As being Undead, I naturally work with them.

Most definitely a conflict of interest.

However, as the only holder of Tots, I couldn't ignore what I'd read.

You see," he leaned closer, "it is banned, verboten, aced out and shut down to wage a full scale war between the factions. Period.

And the idea of using Undead to fight for the Masters ... well ... impossible. Make them fight and kill? That is what got them turned in the first place, possibly."

"Hold it," I said. "I thought this whole thing - your precious Triad - had fallen apart. Why should anyone be bound by a set of rules that they probably never heard of?"

"Logic. For the most part. If you have something all agree to, the fight won't stretch out for decades, with sniping here and random killing there.

There won't be massive battles with hundreds of people attracting the attention of non-changers."

"So what's the problem?"

"Well, according to tradition and scripture, Emma and the second in command of the Masters should square off."

"Then that is going to be a short fight," I said.

"Yes, but Werewolves ride herd over Undead, so one of them can champion for Emma or the Second. Jake stepped forward for Emma."

"That doesn't sound all bad," I said.

"It's not, but a Mr. Tomatura, of the Fuji Clan, stepped forward for the Second."

"I'm starting to understand," I said. "Now we have two werewolves going head to head."

"Yes, and there is a caveat to the combat. They are not allowed to change. They also fight with the traditional weapon - the sword." Carter frowned. "It all comes down to a problem that Mr. Tomatura works for the Yakuza. Japanese mafia. He is a trained killer and definitely no stranger to swords."

He wiped the last of the ice cream from his lips with a napkin out of the dispenser. "People think I am playing both ends against the middle, but I'm not.

Everyone gets to know the rules and who they are playing against."

CHAPTER TWENTY ONE
◌RETURN TO THE KENNEL◌
◌BATTLE◌
◌XXI◌

"I'm going back to the bar to talk to your father," I told Sarah. "You can come with me or stay with Carter."

"You aren't getting rid of me that easy," Sarah said. "Besides, maybe Izzy will be there and I can dump the kids off."

"Can't you get Vlad to watch them?" I asked.

"Oh my god. No. I tried that one time. He watched three kids. They said they wanted to go to Disney Land. He thought it was a great idea.

It took us three days to catch up to them. They were hiding in the Castle. Tinkerbell had disappeared and the dumb bastards had attacked the animatronics.

Vlad still has nightmares about Mickey. That's why he hunts down and kills those poor little mice at night. He thinks they are going to grow giant and come after him."

"Its okay to take them to the bar?"

"Sure, but you still have to keep an eye on them. They got away from Izzy once and ended up at the track.

They were no where near as fast as the greyhounds, but the were smarter. Barney cut across the field to catch the rabbit.

Played hell with the odds and betting. Intimidated the dogs too."

◌◌

"Hey Shaggy," I was greeted as I entered. It was still dark, dank, and friendly.

"Izzy here?" Sarah asked, a kid in each hand

"Out back tossin shoes," the bartender told her. That was his favorite pastime. He liked to bet five dollars he could throw a ringer, then bend the horse shoe in half. I paid ten, because I wanted to see it twice. It was worth the money.

I found Jake, sitting in the corner, cup of coffee ignored in front of him and a canvas wrapped object laying there.

"Morning Jake," I said.

"You just said morning didn't you? Not *good* morning?"

"Right. Thought I would get a feel for the day before I got too bubbly."

"Good idea," He said.

"So what the hell is happening?" I asked.

"Well," he started, "being the big bad hero and the Grim Reaper of the mountain, I stepped forward and said, 'bring it on, give it your best shot.'

And the bastards did. Tomatura. Crap, they don't come any colder than that one."

"I don't understand. Exactly what the hell is going on?"

"John," he said. "The playing field has been leveled and I am knee deep in a damn hole.

It's a one-on-one fight. No morphing. We fight it out in human form using traditional weapons. Traditional weapons being swords."

I thought back. "I seem to remember you mentioning swords before. I got the impression you were trained with them."

"Perhaps that was a bit of an exaggeration. I certainly used one, but it was all hack and slash against unarmed non-changers. And I was in full change, so I had the speed and the strength." I won't have it to a large degree. At least no more so than Tomatura. He *is* trained. Years and years of training."

"All of which means?" I asked.

"I'm screwed."

Jake reached out and unwrapped the bundle before him.

It was beautiful. Massive. A Claymore. I didn't want to admit too much knowledge about these things, but I realized the problem. This thing weighed a ton. It could inflict incredible damage, but in a sword fight it would be like a bus against a sports car. It couldn't be wielded fast enough to parry the strikes of a lighter sword.

"Get somebody else to play." I suggested.

"Crap, I wish I could, but there's no one good enough or dumb enough to do it."

"Then call the whole thing off," I said.

"No way I can do that. How would it look? I was willing to send clans into battle to face death, but I won't, cuz I don't like the odds?

I don't have to win to keep the clan's honor, I just have to fight."

"And die." I said.

"Yes, there is always that,"

"When Sarah comes back in, tell her I had to go somewhere." I hesitated. "When and where is all this supposed to go down?"

Jake took a drink of his cold coffee. "Halloween is shot down. Turns out that we are considered the challenger. They get to choose. Sunrise tomorrow. Front lawn of the Mortuary."

C33O

I wasn't always the suave and debonair attorney I am today. After I had passed the bar I found that people weren't beating my door down begging for help.

Come to think of it they still weren't and I now had to split it three ways. More reason to close it down.

When I had started, however, I had been fortunate enough to have a lengthy case that kept me in food and entertainment. Such as it were.

Miru Tofuni ran an import business/museum. He was a great guy, but he didn't understand the finer points of what could and could not be imported.

The ancient and the modern clothing was fine. The ornate vases were beautiful and welcome. The detailed opium jars were a problem, particularly when they still had opium in them. I spent a lot of time 'on retainer,' explaining to the judge that those fully automatic, AK-47s were for display at the museum as a counter piece for the Folsom point spears. I won some, I lost some, but it was never more than hefty fines. No jail time involved.

That seemed to be all Tofuni cared about.

For my dedicated work I got a stipend of two hundred dollars a week, all the oriental food I could eat, and full access to his gym.

He called it a Dojo, but anything with mats and weights is a gym, to me.

I remembered the bamboo sticks. They were split into long splinters for most of their length. The front was bound, the handle solid, and people would come in and beat the hell out of each other with them.

They yelled and screamed and chased each other back and forth on the mats. I asked what it was about and was informed Kendo. Formalized fighting with the sword we call a Samurai sword, the Katana.

When I expressed an interest in learning, they cheerfully chased me back and forth on the mats, screaming and beating the hell out of me.

His students did not speak English and I didn't speak Japanese so the only way to get them to stop knocking the shit out of me was to get good with that piece of dried bamboo.

I found that a lot of it was muscle memory. If you repeat the same action over and over, about seven hundred times, it becomes reflex. You do not have to think about doing it, it just happens.

The other part I learned was to relax and not think. It gets in the way. Ever been sitting, talking, or just doing something mindless? Something rolls off the table, or you drop it. Before you even realize anything is going on, its in your hand. You reached out and snagged it. If you had been waiting to do it, you never would have came close.

They had a name for it, but like I said, I don't speak the lingo. Tofuni said, 'mind like water, you fix parking ticket,' when I asked him.

The man hadn't changed too much - physically. He was sitting at his desk, going through invoices. He didn't look up, so I gently reintroduced myself, taking care to address his slight grasp of the English language.

"Mr. Tofuni. I'm John Rank. I hope you remember me…I used to…"

"Run errands and do your best to keep me out of trouble," he said without trace of accent. He tossed his pen down and folded the laptop computer closed.

"It is good to see you again, but I confess I am a bit stymied." He waved to a man - servant perhaps - who left the room, giving us privacy. "I sense you are no longer the innocent and naive young attorney you were those years ago. As such, it probably won't take long for you to realize I am not exactly the meek little museum curator I act out."

I wasn't surprised, in fact this made me quite hopeful.

"I seek your help," I said. "In order for you to agree, I will have to be totally honest, and therein lies the problem. My story is borderline unbelievable."

"Because a person does not believe something does not make that thing false," he said. "Myself, I do not believe color TV is real, but daily I see many of them. So sit," he said indicating a chair in front of his desk. "Tell me your story so unbelievable."

It took the better part of an hour. Tofuni stopped me only once, to have hot tea delivered. At the end he made one request, a couple observations and asked a few pertinent questions.

"Could you change for me?" He asked.

I complied. It hurt like a son of a bitch, but it was the fastest and easiest method of proving my words. He responded with an increased heart beat, and I could smell the fear, but no outward sign.

The change back hurt just as bad and I laid on the floor regrouping. He sent for spare clothing to replace that of mine which had torn.

"Tomatura. I know him; how is not important. When you were here you studied the sword. For less than a year. You weren't bad, but you weren't that great.

Tomatura is that great. What makes you think you can even come close to matching him?"

I explained my plan and he just grinned. "Spoken like a true attorney. It might just work, but don't get your hopes up."

When I was redressed, he bid me to follow. "The least we can do is make you look the part. You know I have the museum. What I offer is real. That fact will not be missed by Tomatura. We are going to play a mind game on him.

Mental victory is a large portion of physical victory."

The car ride took less than fifteen minutes, which was good because he didn't want me hanging out the window.

We entered (without paying admission, I might add) and went to a small room in the back. He wrote a list and handed it to a woman.

She read it and said, "Some of this is on display."

"Pull it," he instructed.

When the material had been gathered he started his final lesson for me.

He held up a sword, but left it sheathed.

"At one time all swords were straight. A master sword maker was approached with what we would call a 'rush job.

The sword he made was flawed. It had a slight curve to it. Flawed swords are destroyed, but the person took it anyway for he was riding out to battle. At the end of the battle he returned singing praise for the curved sword.

It seems the curve made it stronger and improved its cutting ability. The straight swords he had ran across shattered when they met his."

He slowly unsheathed the blade. "This was made by that same sword maker, centuries ago. Two bars of metal were hammered together, folded and rehammered. Two layers became four, four became eight, eight became sixteen, sixteen formed thirty two; when done, this blade had more than four hundred layers."

He resheathed it religiously.

"That must have cost you a fortune," I said.

"No," he replied. "I killed three people to obtain it. When you are done, and if you still live, return it. Its legend will be enhanced by this battle."

I didn't question his words. The sleeves on his white dress suit were rolled up and I could see the tattoos covering him like a second shirt. One shouldn't make a habit of questioning Yakuza.

He lifted the bamboo armor. "On a lonely mountain top, a respected diyamo, or royalty was assassinated. Politically it was for the best, and his death was assured and accredited to around fifty Samurai.

Five men remained loyal to the slain leader. They created this armor. Yes, the stains on it are blood. The calligraphy is done in blood. It says 'Justice knows not death.' Three of the men were killed supplying vengeance. When each died, the body was stripped and another would wear it. I pieced this legend together over the years.

The popular belief was that it was the same man, when killed he returned because his cause was just. This is a universal legend among swordsmen.

To this day warriors are warned that if they forget their honor, the ghost wearing this armor will pay a visit to remind them."

He hesitated. "To be honest, I am not sure which story is true. We took it off display because once it disappeared, only to return days later with the blood words on it much fresher and clear."

He patted it gently. "It should at least give Tomatura pause for thought."

"And the helmet?" I asked. "What is the legend or mystic symbolism behind it?"

He shrugged. "None. It's just a copy of the one worn by Tom Cruise in the movie Last Samurai. I thought it looked neat."

꿈꿈

I spent the rest of the time thinking. Well, that's not totally true.

Under no circumstances did I want to be around anyone. It would take too much explanation. And it would be far too easy for someone to talk me out of the whole mess.

I sat in the cemetery with two large duffle bags. I sat at the base of a large marble angel, in its moon shadow. I tried to draw what comfort and solace I could from the stone saints around me.

The comfort was small.

As false dawn was starting to break in the East I heard the footsteps about the same time I identified the smell.

"Good morning Mr. Tofuni. I didn't expect to see you here."

I think he smiled in the darkness. "Nor did I expect to be here." He sat next to me. "I owe Tomatura a bit of a debt. I was ah, exiled, because of him." Yes, he definitely smiled. "While it hasn't been a total hardship, long have I been separated from my family and loved ones."

"You seek revenge?" I asked.

"No. No, that would lack honor and mean I did not take responsibility for my actions so many years ago." He ran his fingers through his hair. "Still, I would not be overcome with remorse if I were to witness his defeat." He laughed. "To see his head removed from his body. Yes, that might supply me with a measure of amusement."

"What happened to the guy that couldn't speak English, imported mostly legal stuff and taught bamboo bashing?" I asked.

"Oh, hell. He's still around, but he's getting pretty jaded. I just don't give a damn these days."

He held out a roll of white linen. "Strip down, we'll get you started."

I was intrigued. "What's that for?"

"It's wrapped tightly around your torso. That way when you are cut, your insides don't fall out."

"You mean if I'm cut."

He sighed deeply. "No, I said when. Think of it as putting the band aide on before the owie."

CHAPTER TWENTY TWO
HAPPILY EVER AFTER
XXII

"Tell me," Tofuni asked, "Are you really any good at all, or should I start composing a eulogy now?"

"If you want an exact accounting, I am pretty good for 'the man on the street,' and piss poor for a real warrior. Two kyu[1]."

Tofuni nodded. "And you believe that will be good enough?"

I would have laughed, had it not been so serious. "Of course not. What I do believe is that when I turn...*inside*...I will have the reflexes, the speed and concentration for *Kikentai-itchi*[2]."

"Spirit, sword, body as one," Tofuni said. "That is the goal. When that stage is reached, the win or loss means nothing. Life means nothing, nor does death. There is no thinking, there is only action."

"Do, or do not. There is no try," I said.

"Exceptionally wise. Who did you learn that from?" He asked.

"Yoda," I said. "He is a sensei for the Jedi."

"I would like to meet this Yoda," he said, and frowned. "But Jedi? That is the Japanese slang for the old martial arts movies."

Tomatura could be seen sitting on the lawn, not fifty yards off. He did not appear fearful or anxious. As a matter of fact, he did not appear angry or happy either.

"Mokuso[3]," Tofuni grunted.

"I am not quite calm enough to contemplate the what of the why," I said.

Tofuni just grunted again.

"I have to go to the bathroom," I said.

Tofuni laughed. "You should have gone before we left." He studied his

---

[1] *A medium Kendo ranking.*

[2] *Spirit, sword, body as one. Where the person acts before consciously deciding to, or realizing the need to.*

[3] *A brief moment for meditation.*

handiwork. "I am not taking this shit off you and putting it back on."

"That's okay," came a voice. "This is my fight anyway."

"Jake, as much as I would give my left nut to just say *fine*, I can't do it. You are hell on wheels when it comes to furry fighting, but you know this isn't your forte."

Jake was not happy. "You are an expert at it?" He asked.

Tofuni answered for me. "No, he isn't. He is a talented amateur, however. He has a chance at it."

Jake looked confused. "A good chance?"

"Oh, hell no," Tofuni said. "I give him about a ten percent chance of coming through alive, and a three percent chance of winning."

Someone was walking towards us.

"Sensei ni rei[4]," Tomatura whispered. Instinctively I bowed, as did Tomatura towards the approaching man.

"I am neither teacher or master," Carter stated. "I am here to verify the outcome."

"Jake, who all is here for this incredible display of stupidity?" I asked.

He looked around. "Well, so far we have you, me, Carter, Emma, the guy dressing you..."

"Tofuni," I said.

"Whatever the fuck," Jake said. "Tomatura and the stooge from the undead..."

"Timkins," Carter said.

"Whatever the fuck," I said. "This crap is getting out of control." I turned to Tomatura. "Might I have a moment of your time?"

He didn't answer, but simply nodded.

I pulled him aside so we could talk. "Look. I have a confession to make."

He frowned and held up his hands. "Hey! If you want, contact a minister of your choice." He looked very uncomfortable. "I haven't led the purest life around, so I am probably not the best choice to air all your sins to. Although," he paused, "by the same token, unless it involved small children or hamsters, I will forgive you almost anything. Had I listed the sins I would have used the back of a matchbook rather than two tablets."

---

[4] *Sensei ni rei is where opponents both bow to the teacher or sensei.*

"That's good to know, but this is more basic and between you and me."

"I'm sorry," he said. "I didn't know she was your sister."

"I don't have a sister," I assured him.

"You slept with my sister?" He asked.

"No, I didn't."

"So what did you do that was so foul?" He asked.

"It was more what I was going to do," I admitted. "You see, Emma is the one who is, was, whatever…challenged. Taka turned her husband undead and she blasted him for it."

"Good for her," he said earnestly.

"Yeah, that's what I thought, but she's too old to fight like this."

"That sucks."

"Yes…but Jake said he would stand in for her." I said.

"Problem solved."

"Naw," I said. "He is the father of my girlfriend. He knows he can't beat you but still feels he has to try."

"That is very honorable," Tomatura said.

"Yes, but I can't let him do so, because his clan - which is now mine - and his family need him. I can fight for him and probably win."

Tomatura smiled. "Confidence is strong. Shall I wish for the force to be with you? Or is the sin that of pride?"

"No," I said, "in order for me to win, I would have to cheat."

"You have my attention," he said.

I quickly gave him the condensed, reader's digest version of life in general, my evil plot, and the demise of my hamster - in case it might, on the off-chance, buy me some pity points.

"Let me see if I have this correct. There has been this plan and that plan, thoughts of deception, they all fell to shit and you are caught with your hand in the cookie jar?" He asked.

"Yeah, that pretty much covers it."

"Yet you felt it required to tell me you were going to cheat," he said; not a question, but a statement. "This Tome of the Stones … the rules that we are apparently obliged to play by … have you ever seen them? Of more importance, exactly when did you agree to be bound by it?"

"Well I didn't, but everyone else is following them."

He sighed. "And if all your friends jumped off … never mind." He thought for a moment. "Tofuni should have known the answer to this, but then again maybe not. He is not a warrior, as you and I are. He is a businessman." He spit on the ground in contempt.

"I am not a warrior either," I felt embarrassed. "Just another attorney."

"Really?" He said. "Kamae!"[5]

I brought the sword up in front of me. The classical position and felt time slow as my body instinctively morphed inside. I noted that he did not take a stance, but merely stood there smiling at me.

Then he disarmed me.

Literally.

Between the elbows and wrists of both arms.

More so, his sword was back in its scabbard before my hands - still holding my sword with proper form - hit the ground.

He was still smiling. I was not.

He leaned close. "Fast and sharp does not hurt at first. I suggest you change. It will stop the flow of blood quicker." He patted me on the shoulder. "This fight is over. I declare myself the winner and as such I am going to resolve these little problems."

It hurt to finish morphing, but the arterial spray stopped almost immediately. It was with morbid curiosity I noted that my severed hands did not change.

The people had not even noticed the non-fight until I morphed. They all, then, flocked down on us. Tomatura stopped them.

"It is done," he stated flatly.

The man known as Timkins surveyed the battle ground and declared, "I win! The fight is to the death, however. You have to finish it."

Standing back, I saw it happen and understood what had happened to me. Generically it is called Battojutsu. It is the method of drawing the sword and cutting, all in one motion. The closest analogy would be a old west quick draw. Tomatura was good. Better than good. In his 'normal' shape, he was faster than I was when morphed.

His sword was once again back in its sheath before Timkins head hit the ground.

"Does everyone *now* agree it is finished?" He asked.

Those that still had their heads wisely nodded.

---

[5] *"On guard position. There are 5 in Kendo. Chudan-no-kamae = Middle-level guard, Jodan-no-kamae = High guard (sword overhead), Gedan-no-kamae = Low guard, Hasso-no-kamae (sword to side of head), Wakigamae (sword hidden by body).*

Tomatura smiled once more, remonstrant of a shark. "Excellent," he said. "With that in mind I want to set a few matters straight.

I won the fight. Period. I did so for the *Master of the Undead*. Then I killed him which, it is my understanding, is a totally acceptable method of ah … ascending to the throne … so to speak."

Tomatura singled Carter out.

"By your own words, you are neither sensei, or master. That is sad. You see, I care nothing for your Tome of the Stones. I follow the code of bushido.

The code of bushido has seven precepts. They are all that matter and more than enough to guide one's life.

Rectitude. That is the first. Strong moral character in thought and deed. I see that in this man," he said pointing to me.

The second is courage. The act of facing that which one is uncomfortable with and even afraid of. I believe we all agree this man has it.

Third is benevolence. The trait of being kind, generous and caring. Sort of like going to bat for a person unjustly accused, or an elderly lady in peril." He bowed slightly to me.

Respect. The fourth code of bushido. To respect those older, those deserving of it … and even those beliefs one did not agree too." He frowned. "Even silly assed rules from twenty centuries ago that have very little validity today.

Honesty and honor. The next two, and they intertwine. The act of going to your enemy and telling the truth, even though you know it means you death.

Loyalty. To place your family, your loved one, your clan before yourself. Yes," he said. His sword was out and poised, "yes, I see all these things in this man."

He pointed to the gathering. "I do not see any of those in the rest of you. You cheerfully would have sacrificed a diamond to save a piece of dirty glass."

Tomatura paced for a while, without speaking.

He motioned Emma forward. "Dear lady, much thought have I given this. You are good hearted, but too invested in this. You would also be far too easy for assassination down the path."

He raised his hands in denial. "As for myself, I honestly have no desire to stay as Master of the Undead. I find it both laughable and contemptible. The only satisfaction I derive is that I am in a position to change it.

The Tome of Stones is no longer the guiding *rules* of the undead. It may be used as a guide, but will hold no sway over common sense."

He pointed at Carter. "You have long lived ... if that may be said ... as an undead. This man," he pointed to me, "mentioned you were once in line for Master.

I see no reason that being undead should be a breaker in being Master of the Undead. Would a vampire accept a master who was not a vampire? Would a werewolf accept a pack leader other than a werewolf who was exceptional?

I think not. In your case you are 'old school' undead. You think and reason well. *When you do so for yourself and do not let ritual and dogma think for you.* Therefore, by the powers I grant myself, I am declaring and demanding that you be, are, and shall act as, Master of the Undead."

Carter made a half bow to Tomatura. "I thank you, but you realize that will not be accepted by the other cell lords?"

Tomatura nodded. "Yes. They are free to declare themselves or another as Master. Likewise, I am free to remove the head of any that do. I believe that after a half dozen die it will not be so highly sought after as a position."

"And if I should not change?" Carter asked.

"Your head is not attached any differently than anyone else's." He smiled once more. "Think of it as an elected position and you have to keep the voters happy. In this case there is only one voter. Me."

"So," Carter asked, "you will be keeping an eye on me?"

"No, I have better things to do with my time. There is one, however, in whom I trust to perform this chore. Plus, he will be very handy," he looked at me and shrugged. "Sorry about the choice of words. You will be in a month or two when they grow back. You will serve myself and the new Master as um...an attorney on retainer. Because I did kick your ass and didn't kill you, I believe you owe me. Therefore I expect a reasonable reduction in your rates."

I couldn't talk, but I did manage to yip a bit in agreement.

Tomatura faced Tofuni. "You did not turn your back on this man. You helped him. What's more, you were willing to part with both prized and valuable personal possessions. You displayed honor. As that person is now in my service, I find I must retract some of my previous opinion."

His lips turned down in distaste. "Not all, however. You are not a warrior, but you display you are not totally ignorant of the path. The sword I will keep, but I noted he wore some armor once worn by my ancestors.

I would be pleased if you personally returned it to Japan. Should you so desire, you may feel free to live there, or come and go as you please."

My turn. I morphed back. The pain was intense, even after the change, but the wounds were scabbed over and no blood fell to the ground now. Tomatura looked at my wounds.

"My apology," he said. "I would shake your hand and tell you it was an honor to stand in battle with you," he laughed, "but I don't want to walk over and get one."

"I find it difficult to thank you for cutting my hands off, but…"

"No," he said. "It's okay. My pleasure. I wish you great joy with your love, I do expect a report from you now and then, and not just a bill."

I was going to answer, but he had already turned and was walking off. Jake wandered over and looked at my stumps.

"Damn. That has to hurt."

"Yes," I agreed. "It does. What the hell do we do now?" I asked.

"Simple," he said. "We buy lots of straws. You won't have opposable thumbs for a month and I am not holding your drink for you."

TINY TALES OF TERROR

THREE SHORT STORIES

BY
W.G.
MARSH

First Rose Notes -

First Rose - why is it different, short, and picked for this book? I am glad you asked. Oh, hell. You didn't ask, I typed that. Its okay I talk to myself, but don't worry. I seldom listen to all the voices in my head. What do they know anyway.

The story was written for a speculative fiction contest in an e-zine called, Anotherealm. Its theme was "making people better." It could be no more than 1,000 words.

I was playing around with dialog. You are supposed to *show people* in stories and not *tell people*. Something that is impossible to completely do. I felt that dialog was a good way to do so. This story was written as practice.

What? Yes, it won first place.

Dark Lessons Notes -

This is one of those stories that a writer does to punish himself for living. An author always wonders if he should write in a different style. This one was. It honestly went through about eight rewrites, all trying to stay in a dark, formal and old voice. It is my homage to H.P. Lovecraft.

- WGM
 Tucson, Arizona

Never Volunteer Notes -

Say what? Okay, I will explain it one *last* time. I *know* it's weird. It's *supposed* to be weird. I was asked to write a short story for an e-zine and it had to have a story line that has not been done.

I did so.

- WGM
 Tucson, Arizona

FIRST ROSE

"A flower…a beautiful spring bloom. The first rose to explode after the snow, blossoming in all its glory." The young man grinned joyfully, pointing to the Rorschach card held tightly by the doctor, like a shield between them. Smiling thinly, the physician placed another on top of the first, doubling his armor.

"Yes…" Cradling chin in hand, the intense green eyes stared once more. "I think…of course! It is a mother, suckling her newborn."

Sighing, the doctor pressed the stop button on the VCR and swiveled his chair to face the detective. "This was the last tape. You can observe for yourself the remarkable change in both personality and perception that four years of intense one-on-one therapy brought about."

Nodding, the detective flipped idly through a stained spiral notebook, flopped it shut and asked, "The other gentleman - the doctor in the video - that would be Doctor Solano?"

"Yes, although at the time he was an intern working under my guidance. He implemented the therapy procedure, the progressive purging if you will, that I developed over the last two decades. He was quite enthusiastic about serving his internship at our facility. The patient was Peter Wolberg, as you know."

Tapping his forehead with the folded notebook's edge, the detective gazed at the blank television screen. "Forgive me doctor, but it didn't appear - my opinion only - that Solano was all that enthusiastic in that last tape." He raised his hand, "I am not a doctor, but I have learned through my work to judge people's mannerisms and expressions." Lowering his hand, he waved in the general direction of the video equipment. "That doctor did not seem to be a happy camper."

Lowering his eyes, the psychiatrist cupped his hands around a mug of coffee long cold. "You are astute, detective, and everyone is allowed opinions. An opinion is not a diagnosis, so have no fear of treading on sensitive toes here."

Sighing once more, he continued. "Dr. Solano was not, as you so quaintly put it, a happy camper. His performance of therapy was impeccable, focused and he took quite seriously our credo at Nordstrom Hospital. *Fabricatio multitudo meliuscule.* Making people better. His disgruntled expression was vectored from a diagnostic schism between attending physicians." The detective's eyes narrowed. "Excuse me?"

"We disagreed on the progress of the patient."

"Ah, then sit-rep the therapy M.O. if you please," replied the detective.

The psychiatrist's eyes narrowed. "What?"

"Tell me about the therapy and the disagreement."

"Touché," chuckled the psychiatrist. "We will restrict ourselves to the universal language known as layman. Might I get you to prescribe another cup of this caffeine alkaloid?"

"Your stomach." Turning the detective dumped the stale coffee into a wastebasket and refilled it from an antique Mr. Coffee machine. "Precinct coffee isn't renowned as gourmet quality."

"Nor is hospital coffee, but to your question. A man's life-style is the very core of his being. His mannerisms are all learned and unconsciously decided upon, based on what he perceives in the world around him.

While one person might see a homeless man, dressed in rags wandering the street as an object of pity, another will view the same chap as a skulking threat. A dangerous and dark stranger who instills fear. Perception is everything," he emphasized.

"Our therapy teaches the patient to observe and interpret things - people, events, actions if you will - around them in a positive and pleasant fashion." He sipped his coffee and warmed to the explanation.

"It was explicitly put to me by a former patient who told me after treatment, 'I realized that the crowds of people gathered around me were not there to harm me. They were there to help me."

"And the disagreement?" Prodded the detective.

"Ah, yes. Solano and I were not at total odds. Both of us agreed that the patient now viewed the world in a positive manner. We were united in our belief that the anger and fear were gone from Peter.

We butted heads because Solano maintained that there was a flaw in the therapy. He felt," the psychiatrist shrugged, "that there was something missing. Yet he could not identify the missing factor. He acknowledged the success in previous clients, but with Peter...well, he believed that the patient was - in Solano's own words - 'out to get him.' Sound familiar?" The psychiatrist smiled. "Solano's beliefs bordered on paranoia, and I never use that term lightly. Indeed, if pressed, I would sign that as a diagnosis. Solano freely admitted that the new perception by Peter was not faked. He simply refused to believe that the patient had inherently changed."

The detective shook his head. "If you would please, doctor, accompany me. There is something you should witness."

Their footsteps echoed down the deserted nighttime corridors until they entered an unmarked door. Inside the lights were off allowing a darkened view through a one-way mirror. The voice they heard was clear, if tinny, coming from the cheap speakers built into the wall.

Gesturing, the detective stated in a flat voice. "By half-assed reassembling what body parts we could find, we know the blood is probably from Solano, but that's my opinion. DNA and dental will give us our final diagnosis."

Before them sat Peter Wolberg, shirt stained and covered with gore. Slowly and with careful movements, he pointed to each bloodstain and spoke to himself.

When his attention was drawn to the blood caking his arm, he touched it gently and said, "A flower...a beautiful spring bloom. The first Rose to explode after the snow, blossoming in all its glory."

Dark Lessons

"You have summoned me," whispered the voice from the stygian darkness, a voice deep with silken promise.

Barely seen hands moved swiftly, flicking the enfolding darkness aside to reveal his countenance. He sat there before me, gloriously perched atop a jagged boulder that towered over me.

He was as I had dreamed he would be.

As I knew he would be.

As I feared he would be.

In the ashen wash falling from the full moon his form cast no shadow. Through my fear I noted he wore the darkness of evening as a gentleman of yore might wear a cape; his being was the embodiment of night itself.

Slowly, to better gaze upon the one who had summoned, his dreadful head turned towards me. His ever-changing face displayed a flash of inconceivable bewilderment, then a glimmer of false smile, followed by genuine amusement; only to be snatched away and a cold stare set in its place for my viewing.

"You," he snarled, pointing at me with ebon tipped finger, "should be honored. I am summoned by many. I cull and chose those beggars and kings to whom I unveil myself," he laughed, "and they are few."

"Thou were different" he chuckled again while his dead eyes searched the darkness before returning their frozen gaze to my own, "and this audience I felt should not be denied. I find so little amusement in…life."

He hesitated. "Of all the requests that have been made of me over the eons, of all the cabalistic prayers and offerings, yours was by far the most singular in its nature and concept," he said, the faintest trace of respect in his voice.

"Of all the conceivable Elders that were possible, you directed your pleas towards me." Shaking his head in disbelief, he shrugged with a tenderness that frightened me far more than the strangeness of his appearance. He turned his eyes to the moon, savoring its cold beauty with a rueful smile.

"At first I believed it to be madness on your part, but insanity is the child of my loins and I did not observe its savage stain upon your soul."

Without warning, as a black torrent, he flowed from the top of the stone to the ground, silently and with oily grace. His shape crouched hesitantly at the bottom only to spin towards me suddenly, forcing me an involuntary pace backward.

Hot winds swept the nightscape, bringing the smell of death and decay.

"Perhaps 'tis a trick you plan?" he whispered through clenched teeth.

He stood before me, frozen hands caressing my face, stroking my throat, icy fingers brushing graying hair from my brow, and all the while his dead eyes searching my soul for treachery.

In the glassy universes of those orbs I saw my own reflection; my image displayed a look of horror unknown to it before.

For an eternity he stood in contemplation. "Would you desire that the last act of your miserable existence be a prank on the father of tricks?" he queried, pulling me closer.

I shuddered violently.

In disgust he released me and my trembling legs were unable to support me. I sat down hard in the dirt. My hands flew to my face only to find it unmarked. Turning, he raised his arms to the midnight sky and the stars flared into points of sullen red fire.

"Such abominable innocence you have! Such thirst for truth!" he declared to the dark realm above us. "I should slay you as you stand, simply for the fact that death can be the only suitable answer for your questions," he screamed. "And perhaps the only suitable reward," he finished in a whisper.

While his behavior was ominous, surrounding him was an aura that, while not comforting, led me to believe that my fate was not to be sealed in the next few moments. Feeling nothing to be won by my timidity, I steeled myself, deciding to press onward with my quest.

I stood and moved slowly across the dew-moistened grass to where I leaned indifferently against a tree; in hope this support would still the shaking brought on by the fear gripping my mind and body. All the while, above me, leaves rustled, churned in their sleep by fetid night winds moving aimlessly through the evening.

"I had little choice," I said, speaking in tones low and measured to keep my voice from faltering and breaking. My thoughts were fragmented and

I needed to purchase a minute in which to gather them. "I am an old man," I explained, "and short time is left to me. Should you take my life I would be loosing little and you would be gaining even less."

"Sit," he sighed. "Your legs still shake and your posture cannot be comfortable. You need not attempt to impress me," he motioned carelessly in my direction. "Your mere presence is diversion enough for me."

Unbidden by conscious thought my legs folded, body sliding down the tree trunk as rough bark scored my back, until I came to rest a boneless heap atop the exposed roots. Sitting in this fashion I gathered my thoughts into the tidiest bundle I could manage. I felt the fool for my slowness of thought and speech and by his next words I could tell that my embarrassment was not lost upon him.

"Take the time needed," he soothed. "The hour-glass means nothing to me and I can stomach the passage of its sand far better than the babbling that spews forth when most converse with me."

We sat in silence, although it was a tainted silence; things seemed to move in the darkness around us. The slight noise made by their passage betrayed them and brought to mind claws and teeth gnashing. He took no heed of these creatures, though I knew he did observe their effect on me. Raising a hand he extended one fingernail, drawing a symbol in the air that glowed briefly then faded. True silence settled around us.

"While you are unique in your method," he continued, "you are far from the first that has sat before me." He laughed and reassured me. "Not to set you as one of those who have groveled at my feet. I realize you confront not only me, but also your fears. Indeed the fears of your ancestral memory."

I felt his clammy touch once more upon my shoulder in what I was presumptive enough to believe as a gesture of encouragement. "At lease you have the manners and dignity not to fall dead upon confronting me," he smiled. "You must understand…your perception of me is distorted by lifetimes of myth and legend. It is not my intent, nor berth, to correct those fallacies, rather permit me a slight narrative explaining what it is you have requested of me."

I interrupted without thinking. "But I know what I am asking and how we came to be in this glade."

"You know nothing," he snarled. "You have only the vaguest concept of what you wish to know. You possess only the slightest wisp of knowledge that brought this meeting to pass."

Pacing a predatory circle around me, his eyes did not waiver from mine, but gradually, with the tense passage of time, a calm demeanor returned to him.

"First," he sighed, "you think me a demon. You believe me to be a devil. The devil and evil incarnate if you will. Thus, it has been for such as you and thus it shall always be in the minds of humanity. You and your brethren have passed judgment upon me through eternity even though you have not the knowledge or experience to validate such accusation." He paused his circling to kneel beside me. I was struck by the lack of noise generated by his activity. No twigs crackled beneath his weight, and from his apparel, if indeed clothing he wore, came no noise of cloth upon cloth.

He studied me before speaking again. "You are a man of age 78 by your species reckoning," he said in a monotone. "You say you have little time left and in this you are correct." Staring deeply into my eyes, the passion returned to his voice. "Do you wish to know the time and place of your demise? I have observed it and have it in my power to tell you when and how." His voice lowered to a conspiratorial whisper, "I can describe it for you. I can describe it down to the last shuddering breath." Rising to his feet, his voice returned to normal. "Your answer if you please, and do consider the gravity and generosity of my offer."

Temptation tore at me. "No. Please no, I do not wish to know, but if you will – is it in the immediate future?"

He laughed coldly, "Your choice in many ways, but we will embrace a simplistic 'no' as an answer. One does not solicit the truth by asking for hopeful portions of it. Truth must be consumed in its entirety, or it will consume you."

"I digress," he continued. "You have lived a full, but common life," he raised a hand precluding comment or interruption and with the same gesture bid me to rise. "Perhaps not domestic to you, but in the cartography of mankind it does not spring to light as more than a flickering candle. A spark spiraling upward from the fire to disappear into the darkness."

"You have regained your spirits enough to take more than slight offense at my imputation of a common life. If this be the case then you have regained your capacity to walk. Come," he prodded, "walk with me now."

I rose to my feet with difficulty. "You speak somewhat differently to me now."

"Mankind has spoken a thousand languages through a thousand ages. From where and when I came before our meeting you need not know," he replied. "Let it suffice to say that I bend my mannerisms, by my own choosing, to accommodate you. Let us journey in this direction," he said, indicating the pathway leading upwards towards my home with a nod of his head.

"No, another pathway if you please," I said. In my heart I had no desire for him to cross my doorstep.

Amusement brightened his voice, "I do not so please. You take liberties that are refreshing, but could easily become tiresome. Be warned."

Around us a luminous fog appeared, held at bay approximately fifty paces in any direction, in its boiling clouds strange figures appeared only to vanish within the glowing mists. As we walked the damp soil of the footpath he resumed his lecture.

"Your childhood was as most of your kind, no worse – no better. You learned, you erred, and death brushed your face many times unnoticed by yourself," his hands made gentle bird-like motions in the air before me. "You aged to...ah, what word do you use now? Oh, yes...manhood." He paused, and then continued, "You aged to manhood surrounded by primitive ceremony and tradition."

I was startled. "Ceremony and tradition?" I asked.

He grimaced and addressed me as one would a child. "You were surrounded by it and yet did not take note of it. You filled your late teens with drink and fornication. I applaud you for that. Thus do many judge their coming of age. It falls well within the boundaries of describing both ceremony and tradition in many cultures."

"Then, slightly before your second decade ended, you involved yourself in that squabble. The one humanity has the audacity to refer to as a 'World War.' How typical." He shook his hands in the air, shooing the concept away. "A handful of tribes decide to kill each other and you proclaim it to be worldly. Not the first World War, mind you, but the second. It was then – right then – that you made the first, tentative step onto the pathway we travel on this night."

By this time, our journey progressed to a small bridge spanning the creek next to my home. Standing on the rough planking, I peered across the distance into the swirling fog and was stunned to find no trace of my home. Where it and the other structures surrounding it should have been was only an undulating plain of mist, glowing scarlet as if clouds reflecting the fires of Hell.

"It is gone," I said woodenly to myself.

"It has not been built yet," he replied. "Nor has most of the world, except for the small area I deem necessary for your sanity and thus constructed." He patted my arm gently. "Do not be overly concerned. It is but a small matter."

"You have the power to create?" I asked. "Not only destroy?"

The question startled him, "One power cannot exist without the other. Indeed I have both, though not to the degree of some of the other Elders." He sighed once more. "Nor do I employ destruction to the extent attributed to me by your religious leaders. I really have no need to. It is so much easier for mortals to point their fingers to deeds performed of and by them and attempt to blame them on another," he said. "Namely myself," he said placing his hand on his chest.

He stopped, placing both hands on his hips and made a comical face, saying, "The devil made me do it!" With this, he laughed hysterically until tears glistened on his cheeks, sparkling in the light from the horrific fog.

Ignoring the splinters, I leaned upon the rail watching the water flow by beneath our feet. It steamed and rolled beneath me, possessing the color and smell of blood. Cold swelled in my chest once more and my fear (only recently forgotten) stabbed down my spine to pool in dampness at its base.

"Before you inquire," he said, "it appears thus to you because this is what you...expected." He raised his hand once more, "Nay, not what you laid foremost upon your thoughts, but what your mind deems proper." He smiled sarcastically. "I felt it my duty not to disappoint you by interference." He gave a nonchalant wave. "If it troubles you then change it."

"I cannot change it," I stammered. "That is not in my power."

"You have the power to change yourself and your fears. You are so determined to make it more complex than it is." He put both hands upon my shoulders and stared intently into my eyes. "Did you hear what I just told you?"

"Of course," I said, unable to meet his eyes.

"Hmmmm...I wonder," he mused, looking away then releasing me.

Returning my sight to the gory stream below me, I became entranced; my mind caught up and carried away by the crimson ripples and waves.

Looking up I found my companion gone, walking relentlessly down the path, already some distance away. The fog began to close between us, pushing ever closer around me. Hurrying as much as possible I followed, and after less than a minute, I came near enough to make out his voice again. He was lecturing heedless of my absence.

"…questions began. You saw things that to this day horrify you. At the onset, you fought for 'your way of life,' and 'freedom.' Later you questioned the truth of this and whether your ideals were lofty enough to support the deeds of slaughter going on around you. After a while your mind sought absolution in rationalizations, your body performed for the sole purpose of self-preservation."

The darkness had abated somewhat and my ears detected the sound of waves crashing somewhere in the unseen distance. A part of the mist surrounding us sank into the ground, or perhaps it became the ground. I could not tell which. What I did know was that the firmness I had grown accustomed to give way underfoot to softness that grabbed at my searching feet. The smell of salt hung heavy in the air and it brought back deep and forgotten feelings. Not good feelings, but powerful ones I could not identify.

"Look around you for a bit. It could be enlightening," he said.

Stopping, I looked and listened carefully, staring until my eyes started to water, until the landscape became clearer. More sounds came to my ears. They were indistinct, yet familiar noises. Looking down I saw at my feet small cylindrical objects gleaming like gold. Bending with stiff joints, I plucked one from its place of rest. My fingers felt hardness. Metal. Fleeing between my fingers was sand. Before I had brought the object closer to my eyes, I knew what I held. Cradled in my hand was the spent casing of a Garand rifle. It hovered between hot and warm. Rising from it fumes of burnt gunpowder reached my nostrils.

The sounds pounding my ears were hideously clear now. Screams and explosions crashed in from all around, along with sharp cracklings as if a hundred whips were flicking past my head. The dull, flat booms of high explosives blossomed around me and could be felt as well as heard. Terror long forgotten claimed me and I fell to the ground digging deeply into the sand for safety. Dignity was a coin not to be found in my small pauper's bag of bravery.

"Take peace into your heart," he said generously. "Where we are Normandy does not truly exist. That which is around you has been delivered by yourself." He scooped a handful of sand and threw it scattering towards the darkness. "If reassurance you need, then take heart in the knowledge that harm shall not befall you tonight."

My voice failed me twice, "There is nothing here that can hurt me?"

"No, that I did not say. There are things here that could slay you without effort. I simply told you that you would not be harmed," he said. "Should you care to interpret both as being the same you may do so, but you would not be accepting the truth, however."

Springing to his feet, he performed a graceful dance across the damp sand. His arms swirled and legs kicked majestically to the music of battle echoing around us. "I cannot convince you," he shouted. "Therefore you must convince yourself. It was here it all started. Amongst death you questioned the meaning of life." Pirouetting he bowed to the dying, who watched with glazing eyes. "Did you think that I was going to inscribe on a piece of parchment the answers to your questions?" He shook his head. "No, that would not be proper. Nor would you understand it or appreciate."

Leaping high into the air, he lit next to me, drawing me into his grim dance. "Repeatedly you have raised your voice to the heavens and beseeched your 'God' for an answer. You pouted, became angry, depressed and resentful when you believed you did not receive an answer. I apologize, but this dance is taken, perhaps the next."

Releasing me, he seized a dying soldier from the ground, they waltzed smoothly, blood spraying from the gaping chest of the wounded man who looked vaguely familiar. Sixty years ago perhaps I could have place a name to the shocked and unbelieving face.

"Your only thought was that you were denied," my sinister mentor informed me. "Never did you wonder if you had asked the right question. Never did you wonder if you had been presented with an answer that you might be shunning because of its obviousness."

Laughing he flung his dance partner back to the ground where the corpse sank gratefully into its foggy grave. In an instant, gone were the ocean, the beach, the gunfire and the death.

Sitting in the mist next to me, he patted my knee and spoke. "Let us review a few basic facts." He pulled me to the ground, which was no longer sand. "You have spent your life asking certain questions. Questions you repeatedly asked, but seldom listened for answers to. What is the meaning of life? Why is life so hard? Why do all the bad things happen? Why do we have war and famine? Oh..." he smiled. "The list goes on and on."

Clasping his hands behind his head, he stretched out on the ground. The mist swallowed him and only his voice could be heard.

"So, in desperation, you asked these queries of me. Do you think that the answers will change?" he asked.

He sighed once more, unseen, and yawned. "While most of your religious teachings are drivel and drudgery, there are a few kernels of truth amidst the garbage. As you created this battlefield tonight, thus were you created. You were given gifts that you choose to ignore. One of your books – I forget which, as you have so many tomes and religions – says you were created in the likeness of god."

He rose on an elbow and stared at me, his head and torso perched atop the mist. "Do you interpret that to mean that you only received the looks or appearance of God?" He stopped and said in a strangely child-like voice, "I got mommy's hair and daddy's eyes."

He sank from sight again. "You are even referred to as 'children' of God. Are you so simple of mind not to know into what children grow?" he asked in a mocking voice. Silence grew between us.

After a time he stood, turning his back to me. "You were given a most glorious gift of all – which you treat as a curse, if you observe it at all – free will. You have an unlimited power to do what you wish, regardless of the consequences. At the bottom rung, you have the power to start and end wars. You have the power to grow food and distribute it, or not, as you will. You have the power to accept responsibility for your actions or to blame them on the giver of the power." He stopped for a moment and stared at me. "It does not have a top limit unless you choose to give it one."

Turning he stabbed a finger at me in accusation. "When you peered into the creek of blood you created you saw only evil. You saw death. Never once did your thoughts turn to a river of life, although your kind constantly talks of 'life-blood' and even the 'blood of Christ.'" He shuddered, looking around him as if in fear. "I wonder what has possessed me to even bother with the repugnance of attempting to enlighten you."

I rose to my feet, mind whirling with possibilities. "Yes, if you find it so repugnant, why do you bother to mentor one such as myself?"

He now seemed less a god and more a supplicant. "That kernel was planted also," he said. "Repeatedly you have been told that I have no power over you unless you grant it." He laughed, but there was sadness in the laughter. "Yet, once more, the only thing you indulge yourself in is the ability to summon me."

He beckoned me towards him, not so much an order as a request. "In the past I have asked for things as payment from those who requested my audience. You so quaintly refer to some of my chattel as souls, although never have I demanded a soul. I merely request. A simple request and – lo and behold – usually my request is cheerfully granted. Do I have the power to wrench anything that is yours from you or anyone else? Only if that power is given to me."

"Then what," I asked with a dawning seed growing in my head, "makes my summons so different from all the others?"

"You did not ask. You demanded. You did not offer anything of yourself, nor expect to give anything. The difference is oh so subtle, but also so very rare. Call it egotism. Call it innocence."

"I begin to understand," I hazarded. "Your appearance was demanded and you complied. In a way you had no choice, but somehow your doing so must benefit you in some way. Why would you attempt to instruct with no possible gain? The fact that I can command you is in doubt in my mind. Granted I accept the fact that you have no power over me unless I so choose, but to command you? I think not. What reward could lie in the dark lessons of this meeting? As your view points, I could demand of you your own soul if I had the whim to do so."

His eyes brightened to fire. "So close. You fly so close to an astounding answer. Alas, I have no soul to give to you. Even if I allowed you that power over me. Which I do not." He continued in a voice attempting to minimize the moment. "My desires are slight and trivial, but ones that have plagued my being for eternity. I do indeed wish for a soul. My own. Not a cast-off item as a coat found by a beggar in the street. The ones that have been 'given' to me in the past are as worthless as those that gave them up. There is much truth in the statement that quantity is not quality. If one values their soul so little that they would part with it, then it becomes an item of little value."

His shoulders shrugged slyly and his voice became a whine. "The right person, however – with the right understanding – could create a new, virgin soul and present it to me." He finished with a spark of hope in his voice.

What was being asked washed over me in a wave of understanding. "I understand more now than I desire to know. You attempt a barter worthy of all that I have ever heard of you." I said with disdain.

I looked around with clarity for the first time. "I see now that you have given me nothing I have not had. Do not be mistaken, I am grateful to your awakening in me the realization of the true extent of my knowledge," I said. "Earlier you referred to yourself as the father of tricks." He nodded. "You know also you are referred to as the father of lies," said I.

I walked to face him without fear. "If indeed you have no soul, there is a reason. It is not in my knowledge if that reason is right or wrong, let alone present you with a gift of which I can only vaguely fathom the value."

Rage was growing in his face, but I confronted it unshaken. "I believe that the time of our parting is at hand. I also believe there is a possibility. Those that gave you their souls – they valued them only slightly. However, what if...what if one valued their soul not at all. What if they were so consumed by the power that they did not feel a soul was of any use whatsoever. In the 'drivel and drudgery' of 'our kinds' religious tomes – as you call them – there is another saying." I turned my back to him. "The lord giveth and the lord taketh away. Perhaps it is more than a saying."

"Fool," he hissed. "The decision to part shall be mine. I do not grant you that. Our business is not yet done."

"No," I said, "you need grant me nothing. I cannot order you to go, but then, you cannot order me to stay." With that, I turned my back and closed my eyes to reflect on the simple lesson that had been placed before me ages ago. I would still have to bestow a meaning on Life. Now I realized I could make that meaning as trivial, or as important as I wished. Nor did the meaning have to remain the same forever. It could change with each sunrise and sunset.

I opened my eyes and I stood on the bridge near my home. The water gurgled and sang sweetly in the morning light of the new day's sun. With only a slight thought, I looked again on the water. Its color was subtly different now. Walking down to the bank of the stream, I dipped my hand and cautiously tasted. Even with my new knowledge, I was disappointed to realize that I was still not a good judge of wine.

Turning to home, my bones and joints felt the ache of age and night air.

Some things should not be changed. I have earned my years and pain and shall keep them.
  For today.

NEVER VOLUNTEER

A lone ray of sunshine fell through the cracks between the planks and warmed his back. Without thought the muscles in his body relaxed and a rumble escaped from deep within his throat. *Oh, for god's sake, what was that? A purr again? Marine Corps sergeants do not purr.* He tensed once more.

Lying under the decking of the barracks, watching enemy troops strut past with weapons slung, he offered a small prayer. *God, please don't let them have guard dogs. Anything but guard dogs.*

ᛒ

The techie had explained. "Here's the deal. You get two weeks medical leave, during which we induce an artificial coma - just like being asleep, suppress your dreams, copy your mind, and put it in a cat. What could be more simple?

Anticipated side effects are temporary muscle weakness, constipation, and massive hangover from dream deprivation.

In compensation you get a promotion to Second Lieutenant, and two weeks leave." He hesitated. "To recover from the hangover or build it to greater heights."

Sgt. Ralston contemplated for thirty seconds.

"Hoo-rah!"

One side effect known by the techie, but not mentioned, exhibited itself on the last day of transition.

From his viewpoint seven inches above the floor ,inside a cage, he watched himself shake hands with the general, salute, and walk out the door. His ears flattened. Being a copy didn't feel any different from being the original. Looking to his furry shoulder, he halfway expected to see three up and two down sewn on. Nope. He might have paws, and claws, but inside he was John Ralston, Gunnery Sergeant, U.S.M.C.

The techie leaned close to the cage and whispered. "You forgot the first rule, Gunny." He smirked. "Never volunteer."

☙❧

"Yes, General, the mission is going according to plan." The white coated technician pointed to the array of monitors. "The images coming back from the collar-cam are crisp. Far beyond what we hoped. We have troop counts, vehicle identification, and position of weapon emplacements."

"Good," barked the three-star. "How's my soldier doing? I heard there were some problems in processing. Is he handling the transition smoothly?"

The tech studied a clipboard. "I think so, but anytime you clone a cat, genetically alter its brain to function at total capacity, and imprint it with the mind of a human. Well, communication can become a bit fuzzy. The only hard data we could derive is that Sergeant Ralston doesn't like to chase mice or drink milk. He does enjoy lapping coffee from a bowl, nestling in the secretary's lap, and being petted."

He fingered the sutures on his arm. "At least he liked being petted by the secretary. If agitated by hair balls, an ounce or two of beer mixed with his kibbles has a pronounced calming effect."

He rubbed the Band Aid over his eye. "I would suggest a post note that if more beverage is administered the subject becomes belligerent, aggressive, and vomits in his cage."

He closed the clipboard. "Sir, we *are* going to put that creature down when it gets back aren't we?"

"That's the plan, son." The General turned. "It was created disposable."

☙❧

The mission was over, but Ralston was not over the mission. His tail twitched. The escape from the compound was anticlimactic. He waited until night fell and walked out - no big thing - just another stray cat on the prowl. Now that he was safe, his heart pounded worse than when he'd been in enemy territory.

If ordered to charge a machinegun post, there is a chance of survival. If sunk at sea you might not drown. If I follow orders to the end, they gas my ass. What's wrong with this picture?

He slunk through the night on silent feet. Ralston had felt hunger for two days now. He remembered lying hidden between fender and tire on a jeep in camp, when some moron fired up an electric can opener. Ralston was halfway to the man before he realized his error.

So strange. I couldn't help myself.

A scurrying sound came from beside him and his twisting body was in mid-air with claws extended. No thought, no plan, just action.

Hmmm...crunchy. Flavor isn't bad.

He ripped another mouthful and swallowed.

I draw the line at eating the beady little eyes or tail.

He licked his paws, smoothing the fur. Curling up in a tight ball, he laid his tail over his nose and sleep came instantly.

ᥱᥲ

In the dawn's warm sunlight, Ralston awoke with a stretch that would have broken every bone in his 'other' body. Instinctively he knew the direction of the extraction LZ. It was probably 0600 - although time did not seem to matter as much now - and his ETA would be 0700.

ᥱᥲ

"What the hell was that?" The General demanded.

The techie stared at the monitor. The picture twirled and tumbled, vivid yellow wings filled the screen for a moment.

"Sir. I think...it looks like. Sir, he's chasing butterflies."

As he pounced along his march, another thought came to Ralston.

"And that?" The General sputtered, pointing to the display.

The image of a rock came closer on the screen until it filled the glass. The image retreated and came closer again, slamming to a stop. This repeated until the display showed only static and snow.

I never liked people looking over my shoulder.

ᥱᥲ

Ralston watched the rotors of the chopper slice the air and listened to the "whup-whup-whup" sound he knew so well.

I have never disobeyed an order in my life. He stood and took one step forward.

Then again, cats really don't come when you call. His paw stopped in mid-air and his eyes turned to slits.

Dogs roll over and play dead, not cats. Or Marines.

In a blur, he bounded away from the helicopter.

END NOTE

Well, the deed is done. Dastardly, nobel, painful or soothing; descriptions to be supplied by the reader.

However it seems that an author is expected to reveal - after all is said and done - some great *truth* or *revelation* about his work. Failing that, he must supply an insight.

I have no great truth or revelation to generate awe, or such. Sorry. I once had a great revelation, but that was in the late 60's and I no longer remember it. Or even remember the late 60's themselves. Plus, as I get older, I find that truth itself depends greatly on which side of the fence one is standing.

So I will have to attempt to appease you with an insight.

The title. Yes, the title. It went through many variations until *Six After Midnight* was mentioned. I chose it in a heartbeat, but not for the reasons most would assume.

Most would probably rationalize: Midnight, a scary hour; Six After, six stories to be read after midnight…to cause insomnia. No. Not even close.

On November 24, 2006 I had a stroke. It was going on when midnight rolled around. Kinda the stroke of midnight. Sorry, crappy pun, but anyhow that was the midnight of my life when things were the darkest. These stories were finished - or at the *very* least revamped - while sitting with my left side paralyzed in the spring. Most were long short stories, or in the case of the included short stories, mothballed for one reason or another.

Ergo, they are six stories resurrected after my midnight.

- W.G.M.
Tucson, Arizona
June 30, 2007
1:17 A.M.